M000303371

FIRST VICTIM

BOOKS BY L.A. LARKIN

L.A. LARKIN

FIRST VICTIM

bookouture

Published by Bookouture in 2023

An imprint of Storyfire Ltd.
Carmelite House
50 Victoria Embankment
London EC4Y 0DZ

www.bookouture.com

Copyright © L.A. Larkin, 2023

L.A. Larkin has asserted her right to be identified
as the author of this work.

All rights reserved. No part of this publication may be reproduced, stored in
any retrieval system, or transmitted, in any form or by any means, electronic,
mechanical, photocopying, recording or otherwise, without the prior written
permission of the publishers.

ISBN: 978-1-80314-884-7
eBook ISBN: 978-1-80314-883-0

This book is a work of fiction. Names, characters, businesses, organizations,
places and events other than those clearly in the public domain, are either the
product of the author's imagination or are used fictitiously. Any resemblance
to actual persons, living or dead, events or locales is entirely coincidental.

To Jonica Newby. You make me laugh, keep me on track, and console me with wine. What more could I ask of a friend?

ONE

FRANKLIN

July 26, 2016

Fiona Austin was getting too old for two flights of stairs to the bedroom. It was all very well for her husband to feel smug that they lived in the best house on the street in a sought-after Franklin suburb, but he didn't suffer from arthritis in the hips and knees as she did.

Fiona still marveled at their Tudor-style, four-bedroom house with steeply pitched roofs resembling steeples, a double garage, and three thousand square feet of lush garden—her pride and joy. She was so lucky to live in such a wonderful home, she reminded herself. But as she took one painful step after another, clinging to the handrail for support, she couldn't help but feel sad that the three unoccupied bedrooms had never been filled with the children she had hoped for. No laughter or squabbles. No bedtime storytelling. No rushing the kids to get ready for school. How she would have loved children. Sometimes she imagined she heard running thuds as her children played chase up the stairs and she heard herself telling them to slow down. Or she would stare out of the living room window at the swing hanging from the giant oak and imagine one child pushing the other on the swing.

Pausing on the first landing, she waited until the aching pain in her knees and hips subsided. Gripping the wooden rail, she looked down through the rectangular void to the ground-floor hall table and the vase of purple chrysanthemums she had arranged earlier that day.

"Joseph!" she called down. "I forgot my glasses. Can you bring them with you?"

"Sure, honey," her husband called from his study where he liked to hide away at the end of the evening. "Won't be a minute."

Earlier, Fiona had fallen asleep in front of the TV and woken with a start to discover it was almost midnight. Not that it really mattered what time they went to bed. They had no reason to rush out of bed in the morning, except tomorrow the gardener came at 7 a.m. and Fiona liked to be dressed and ready to brief him on what she wanted doing. And she enjoyed his company. He was such a lovely boy.

Walking stiffly to the base of the next set of stairs, she peered up. They looked so steep. It was time they vacated the top floor with their connected bathroom and uninterrupted view of Lake Crow. The level she was on now had three lovely bedrooms, with views almost as fine as the top floor, plus two bathrooms. She was tired of the pain she experienced each night and if she forgot to take something downstairs with her during the day, she would have to retrace her steps all the way up to the top floor. They'd talked about installing an elevator, but Joseph was careful with money, always reminding her that they only had their savings to live on and they couldn't squander it on luxuries. Fiona sighed and began the next climb, the pain now sharp, causing her to wince. By the time she reached the top stair she had just enough energy to collapse into the armchair she had asked Joseph to place there. She panted from the exertion. Through the open bedroom door, Fiona could see the wall-mounted photo of their wedding day forty-two years ago. She smiled. It was still the best day of her life. She just wished he had told her before they were married that he couldn't father a child.

The doorbell chimed like a church bell. Who would come calling at this hour of the night?

"I'll get it," Joseph called, a hint of annoyance in his voice.

Fiona shuffled forward in her seat so she might overhear the conversation. Perhaps a neighbor was in trouble?

She heard the slap of Joseph's leather slippers on the tiled hall floor. He must have opened the house door because she heard him speak angrily.

"What are you doing here?" he shouted.

If the visitor replied, Fiona didn't hear it. Her hearing wasn't as good as it used to be, and the person must have spoken quietly.

"This is an imposition," her husband said, but he continued with, "I can give you five minutes. Come in."

The house door slammed shut. The slap of shoes on tile, then the familiar click as Joseph's study door shut.

Muffled voices. Was their neighbor yet again complaining about the branches of their tree that overhung the shared fence? Surely not this late? Fiona considered heading downstairs and offering the guest some tea or hot chocolate. But her hips throbbed and she wanted to sleep. She was about to stand, her butt hovering above the seat, when she heard a smashing sound. Glass. A cry, like the sound Joseph made many years ago when his leg broke.

Then silence.

Fiona turned her head and listened as a cold sense of dread ran up her spine. The silence scared her.

A scream, like an animal in pain.

If Joseph was hurt, why didn't he call out to her? Her skin

prickled as she dragged herself up, using the banister for support.

"Joseph? Are you all right?" Fiona's voice wobbled as it carried down the stairs.

"Help!" It was Joseph, high-pitched and desperate.

"Joseph!" she screamed.

He didn't call back.

A rush of panic took a vice-like grip on her throat and she couldn't catch enough breath. She staggered and had to use the banister to stay upright. She must reach a phone. Call the police. Whoever was in their house, they had heard her cries and knew that she was upstairs. The landline was next to the bed. Her mind fought with her body. *Get help,* she told herself, but her slippered feet were frozen to the spot. *Joseph needs you.*

Willing her aching limbs to move, she shuffled as if she wore lead boots. A door clicked open downstairs, then she heard hurried footsteps on tiles. The stranger was coming.

Her heart was racing, but her legs weren't. She glanced into the void and saw someone in a hoodie at the bottom of the stairs, dark clothing, a hammer in his hand.

Fiona shrieked, then set her sights on the bedroom, moving her old bones as fast as she could. There was a sharp pain in her chest. *Don't let me down,* she said silently to her heart. She heard boots stomping on the stairs. *Thud, thud, thud.* She shuffled faster. *Thud, thud, thud.* How could he climb the stairs so fast? She passed through the bedroom doorway and cursed the fact there was no lock on the door. She had to get to the phone on the nightstand, just six feet away. *Thud, thud, thud.* A floorboard on the landing creaked. He was behind her, his breathing ragged. She reached out a trembling hand toward the phone.

"Don't!" the intruder said.

In that moment she knew who it was.

"Leave me alone. Please."

Shrieking, she lunged two steps closer to the phone, the

pain in her heart more intense. Just a few more steps. The phone.

The blow to the back of her head caused her head to jerk to the left. She fell sideways, just missing the bed. Her hand knocked a framed photo to the floor. The carpet failed to cushion her fall. Crack. A burning pain in her shoulder. Barely conscious, she reached for the photo. Then blackness.

TWO

CHICAGO

July 26, 2016

At ten-thirty at night, Harper Fairburn's son should have been tucked up in his bed, dreaming of whatever toddlers dream of. Safe, fed, and loved. But it was Harper's love for her child that finally gave her the push that she needed to run away. If her husband caught her, he'd kill her. He had warned her often enough to be a good girl and do what he said. It was her fault she got pregnant, he'd said. She should be grateful he'd married her, that he paid the rent and Eli's medical bills. She was a stupid, stupid girl.

Maybe he was right about that. She had been sixteen. Flirty. Plenty of attitude. She had thought that losing her virginity to a good-looking older guy would impress her friends. They had all been with boys their age and boasted they were now women, and she was still a girl. They taunted her over and over. So, she'd gotten into his car while her friends were watching. They waved and whistled as the car drove away, and then her life changed forever.

Now, beneath Chicago's King's Way viaduct was a tent city

of the homeless that stretched two blocks. The makeshift shelters lined the concrete median strip beneath six lanes of traffic that rumbled overhead. In winter, this area stayed relatively dry when it rained but the winds were bitter as they blew snow at the homeless who shivered beneath whatever clothing and bedding they could find. It was a warm summer night and the occupants sat outside their tents or roamed around, some yelling, some muttering, some wide-eyed and silent. Some lay against walls, the drugs in their bodies taking them far away from their miserable reality. An old guy with two missing front teeth yelled at a Black guy seated on a plastic milk crate, both men in heavy coats despite the hot night. Down here, in Chicago's underworld, if you turned your back for a second, these people would steal your tent and rip the coat off your back. The guy yelling lunged at the bottle of spirits in the other man's hand and tried to wrestle it from him. There was a smash as it shattered on the concrete ground and a fight broke out.

The young mother watched the scene from behind a rectangular concrete pillar, one of many that supported the viaduct, where the stench of old urine made her retch. Her skin was clammy beneath the leather jacket that she dared not remove. All she had were the clothes and toys she'd crammed into her backpack and $217 she'd saved from the grocery allowance he gave her each week. The cash was sewn into the lining of her jacket.

Her back muscles and shoulders ached. Eli was asleep in the sling toddler carrier, which she wore on her front with her son facing her chest. She hadn't dared to use the stroller—Eli was less likely to cry if he was held close to her body. The combined weight of the pack and her child, however, caused a shooting pain up her neck and her head throbbed. She looked down at her son's angelic face, half expecting the bottle smashing to have woken him. His delicate eyelids stayed closed, but for how long? If he woke and had one of his tantrums, all eyes would be on her and she needed to stay unnoticed at all costs.

She glanced behind her. Was her husband watching from behind one of the dark concrete columns? She turned her head and stared down the length of the tent city, past the shopping carts and cardboard boxes and tarpaulins to the twinkling lights of the city's skyscrapers and the indigo sky. She had chosen tonight because he was at work and he wouldn't know that she had run away until he got home at seven in the morning. He'd taken their car to work so she was on foot. She hadn't dared call a cab or take the bus because he would find her that way. She had no friends here. No family. It was just her and Eli.

Yesterday, she'd stopped by the library, ostensibly to pick up some books she could read to her boy. She had also used the library's computer to search for women's shelters that took kids. Then, on the inside back cover of a kids' picture book she'd written the addresses and phone numbers of two shelters. Her plan was to go to the one in Haberfield and hide there until she could work out how to reach her hometown. She didn't dare switch on her phone. She didn't want him tracking her through it.

The shelter she was heading for was about a mile away in the Little Saigon neighborhood, known for cheap eats and cheap thrills. A car sped down the road bordering the tent city and her heart rate surged. She pulled into the shadow of the concrete pillar, her mouth dry with fear. She pulled her son close to her and whispered, "Stay quiet. Please stay quiet."

The car slowed, the tires sounding gritty as they crushed the trash accumulated at the curb side. A window lowered. A woman stepped into the glare of a streetlight, sexy black boots, tight shorts, a cut-off T-shirt, long brown hair. She was about the same age as the young mom. The girl leaned through the window, spoke briefly and got in. The car drove away. Harper hadn't realized she had been holding her breath. It was time to get moving. *Don't look at the homeless people, just walk.*

Eli wriggled, then was still.

She set off again. A drunk heckled her. A group, gathered in a circle, watched her. Her step quickened. The farther she walked, the fewer people she saw. The tents were mostly zipped up, the inhabitants asleep. Another car slowed, and she dared to look at the driver, because if it was her husband she had to run. The driver, a man in his fifties, saw the bundle she carried and drove on. He was looking for a prostitute.

The next road on the left took her over the Howe Bridge and on the other side of the bridge was Little Saigon: her destination. This would be the most dangerous moment. If he found her on the bridge she would have to outrun him and she couldn't do it, not when she was carrying her child and the backpack and when he'd made sure she was physically weak.

She'd always been slim and long-limbed like a foal but since Eli's birth, she'd been dieting. He'd told her that her flabby stomach was gross, and he shamed her when she dared to eat carbs. It had gotten so bad that when he gave her cash for the weekly food shop, she would buy a chocolate bar or a muffin or a bag of chips and devour her purchase before she left the grocery store. She would stare at herself in the mirror and see how sharp her elbows appeared and how her hips stuck out through her nightie like little pyramids. But he told her to lose more weight. Sometimes it had been so bad that she shared Eli's mushy food, because her husband wanted him to grow big and strong like his dad.

She darted across the road bordering the tent city and increased her pace as she stepped onto the sidewalk of the bridge, an ugly concrete slab spanning the dark waters below. Between her and the river was a four-feet-high concrete barricade. Two lanes of traffic were heading downtown. Two headed uptown. The bridge's streetlights turned the gray concrete and the water below a sickly yellow. A man stumbled toward her, clearly inebriated, using the solid wall to keep him upright. She gave him a wide berth. Sweat trickled down her back. Her long blonde hair was tucked under a baseball cap, which she hoped would make it harder to identify who she was but the toddler was a dead giveaway. Soon she was halfway across, inhaling more than just gas fumes. A hint of Vietnamese food carried on the warm breeze as did the sound of excited voices from the revelers in Little Saigon. The women's shelter was above a restaurant and the entrance was down an alley.

Her leg, back, and shoulder muscles burned. But she was almost there. Every time she heard the rev of a car engine her stomach churned, fearing it was him. Music and laughter greeted her at the other end of the bridge. She waited at the street crossing for a green man to appear on the traffic light to indicate that it was safe to walk. Across the street, the sidewalks were busy and the café and bars were full.

She crossed the road and searched for the restaurant called Pho Gia Hoi, with its orange plastic sign and the backlit pictures of the dishes it sold. She followed the scent of roasted duck, but the whole street was full of eating places, karaoke bars, and Vietnamese grocers. Then she saw the brightly lit orange sign. The alley was just a few yards beyond. She had called the shelter earlier that evening from a public pay phone. Begged them for a bed. Told them who she feared. Why the police couldn't be involved.

Eli began to wriggle. He opened his eyes. *Please don't scream*, she thought.

His brown eyes, the color of his father's, looked up at her, then they roamed to the bright lights of the restaurant awnings. The sidewalk was busy and noisy. His forehead creased.

"Hello, sweetie, you're okay. Just go to sleep. Mommy's got you."

But his inquisitiveness was piqued. He reached out and gripped her jacket lapel.

"Pwitty," he said, reaching out to the multicolored lights.

There was a sudden movement ahead. A man running toward her, dodging the revelers who walked at a relaxed speed. He was in his uniform, the darkness of it in stark contrast to the cheerful reds and golds around her. Her breath caught. She stopped walking.

How had he found her?

Eli must have sensed that something was wrong. His arms bounced and his legs kicked. Any moment he would cry.

The mother pulled him to her chest and mustered her last reserves of energy and ran. She had to get to the door before her husband did. She dodged pedestrians. Her shoulder was knocked by a passer-by. Eli cried out at the jolt, although the person hadn't banged him. She turned into the alley. The doorway was illuminated by one overhead lightbulb. There was an intercom. Any moment her husband would run down the alley and grab her. She kept her finger on the buzzer.

"Come on! Answer!"

"Yes, may I help you?" a woman said through the intercom.

She gave her name. "Let me in. Now! My husband's chasing me."

There was a buzz. She used one arm and shoulder to shove open the heavy metal door. Inside was a small, boxy hallway and stairs. A woman came running down the stairs and pushed her hand against the door to shut it. There was a satisfying clunk. A bolt was then drawn across the top of the door.

The intercom buzzed again, and the young mother backed away from the door, terrified.

His voice boomed through. "I know you're in there. Open the door!"

The woman from the shelter raised a finger and gestured for her to stay silent, then she beckoned for Harper to follow her.

She was shaking so much she had to cling to the handrail as she climbed the steps.

"Open the door, you stupid bitch!" her husband shouted.

His fists thumped the door, but he wasn't getting in.

"You'll be safe here," the woman said.

"He's a cop," the young mom said, tears blurring her vision.

"He needs a warrant. By the time he gets one, you'll be long gone."

Her husband's voice followed her up the stairs. "I'll kill you. You can't escape me, you hear!"

THREE

July 27, 2016

Harper's heart was racing.

The women's shelter had organized a delivery van to take her to a country town where they hoped her husband wouldn't find her. She'd been told to stay in the back with Eli, so she wouldn't be seen. When the van pulled over across the street, she froze, too afraid to set foot outside.

"It's the only way," the shelter manager said. "We have to get you far away from him, then you can speak to a lawyer."

The woman took her arm and steered her out of the shelter's reinforced door and along the alley to the main road, which at 4:40 a.m. was empty. The noisy, vibrant Vietnamese restaurants were closed and all that remained was the stench of rotting garbage coming from the industrial-sized trash cans.

The van was black. The driver, a woman about Harper's age, held the sliding side door open for them. All Harper had to do was cross the street and get in. It was the gentle tug of the shelter manager's hand holding hers that kept her moving, her little boy sleeping in the sling against her chest.

I can do this, Harper thought. *Then I'll be free.*

How she crossed the street she wasn't sure. It felt as if she were on a conveyor belt but she made it and the driver urged her to get in.

A flash of movement. The driver was the first to notice. She grabbed Harper's arm, pulling Harper into the van's dark interior.

"Get in!" she said with an urgency that caused Harper to flinch.

"He's coming!" the shelter manager screamed.

Then the man she was running from was upon her, shoving the manager out of his way so forcefully that the middle-age woman fell back on her rump. Harper's husband was still in his pale blue and navy Chicago PD uniform, his gun on his hip, a reminder of his authority—he must have waited in the street all night.

"What are you doing with my wife? I could arrest you for kidnapping."

The manager struggled to get up off the greasy asphalt. "She's leaving of her own free will."

"Like hell she is!" he said.

The driver, a young woman in dungarees, stepped between Harper and her husband. "She's coming with me. You leave her alone."

"Out of my way, whore." He ripped his Taser from its clip. "You want me to use this?"

He was going to hurt the girl. Harper had to do something. Perhaps that's what drove her to run. She didn't get far, just to the street corner, when he caught up with her and grabbed her arm forcefully. She screamed.

He picked her up, her legs dangling above the sidewalk, his arms around her waist and carried her to the patrol car. By now, Eli was wailing into her chest, frightened by the shouting.

"Get in," he said through clenched teeth.

All her strength was gone. She climbed into the back, where she sat behind a grille, like the caged animal that she was. He locked the doors and drove away. Harper heard the women shouting at him to stop, but it was too late and, as he always did, he had gotten what he wanted.

The look he gave her in the rearview mirror as he drove across town had her convinced that she was a dead woman. Pure hatred in his narrowed eyes. Fury too. The raised vein pulsing in his neck. The white knuckles as he gripped the steering wheel.

"Shut him up!" he yelled, spittle flying.

Eli lay against her chest in a sling, close to her heart, which was racing. The toddler picked up on her agitation. He smelled it in her sweat.

"It's okay, little one," she soothed. She tried bouncing him a little, but her emaciated body was all out of energy, drained like an empty gas tank.

The view outside the police car was a blur to her. Streets shrouded in shadow. How could she ever escape this hell? He was the spider, and she was the bee struggling to be free of his web. What chance did she stand against a cop? Not just a cop, but a cop who used his badge for his own means, who was using a patrol car to drive his wife back to her prison. Because that was what her life was. He'd got her hooked on antidepressants. He'd ostracized her from her friends. Only when he was at work did she dare invite them 'round. How could her life have turned out so badly at just nineteen?

"Look what you made me do!" he yelled. "Now I gotta explain to Louie why I left him behind." Louie was his patrol partner, a lazy cop who ate and drank too much. "If I'm seen driving you home, what am I going to say, huh?" he shouted. "That my ungrateful bitch of a wife ran out on me? You know how that makes me feel? Huh?"

She knew, only too well. He'd lock her in the bathroom with Eli and not feed her until she begged for his forgiveness.

"Answer me!" he yelled.

"I'm, I'm sorry, I... I want to see my mom."

"You're my wife and you do what I say!" He shook his head. "Fuck! What is wrong with you women?"

Harper's thoughts turned to his first wife. Had he abused Sally Fairburn in the way he abused her? Scott had made out Sally was a total bitch, just as he was making out that Harper was now.

Lucky woman, Harper thought. *You're free. Now he has me to torment.*

FOUR

FRANKLIN

September 6, 2016

Sally Fairburn's jaw dropped. She had always told her kids not to gawp, which was exactly what she was doing now, but she couldn't help it. Detective Fred Clarke, who headed up Franklin PD's homicide team, wasn't a prankster or known for cracking jokes. But he had to be pulling Sally's leg, surely?

"Can you say that again?" Sally asked.

When Clarke had called her at the bookstore where she worked and asked her to come and see him on her way home, she had readily agreed. She knew him well enough to know that it must be important and Olivia Wiesner, the bookstore owner, had agreed to let her leave work early, given it was a Tuesday and the store had been quiet all day. Clarke and Sally had history, of the crime-solving kind. As a civilian, she had been sucked into two murder cases and by luck, more than judgment, had helped Clarke to crack them.

Clarke, as usual, sat bolt upright, his shirt pressed to within an inch of its life—if, of course, a shirt had a life. His crinkly Shar-Pei-like face was set in his usual serious position.

"I want to bring you in as a consultant detective on a cold case. Three months should do it."

Sally still couldn't believe he was suggesting this. Only a few weeks ago Sally had almost died trying to track down her neighbor's killer. Clarke had been unhappy about the risks she took and irritated that she hadn't had time to give him a heads-up on the killer's location.

"I don't understand," Sally said. "I left the police force twenty-three years ago. I'm hardly qualified."

"I disagree. You've helped my team solve two murder cases in the past year. Your problem-solving skills are exceptional. And your victim advocate experience will be useful. You make people feel comfortable. They talk to you, sensing your empathy. I figured you could bond with the surviving witness, the wife, when she comes out of her coma. The doctors are hopeful that she'll recover. The question is when."

Had she heard right? At the time, Clarke had found her involvement in the two cases irritating, and he'd warned her off on several occasions. She never thought she'd hear him admit that her input was helpful, let alone ask her to consult.

Sally used the fingers of her right hand like a comb through her feathered gray hair, buying herself a few seconds to think. At forty-six she was too old be a cop again, wasn't she? And she enjoyed her job at Olivia's Bookstore. Zero stress and flexible hours. Although the pay wasn't much and now that her son was fifteen, she needed to think about a college fund. She was hoping that he'd win a scholarship through his football skills, although, even if that came off, he'd still need money for his studies. A consulting fee sounded good, though.

"How can I be a consulting detective when I've never been a detective?" she asked.

"Your resignation from the PD in 1993 was never formally processed. Your boss clearly hoped you'd change your mind. This means that technically you're still a cop. And second, in this state, police certification doesn't end when you leave the police force, unless you've been found guilty of a crime. Sally, you are and always have been a certified police officer. It's my decision to promote you to consulting detective. You'll need to take a firearms test but that'll be a walk in the park for you."

Clarke knew that she went to the shooting range once a week.

"I... I don't know what to say. I'm excited, of course. But I think you've overestimated my abilities."

Clarke leaned back in his chair and stared at Sally across his scrupulously clean and tidy desk. How he managed to keep it that way was anyone's guess. Apart from his computer, there was a neat row of manila folders, stacked vertically in a wire rack. No matter his workload, Clarke always managed to keep himself and his desk tidy. Outside Clarke's office, there was a whole department of detectives with desks cluttered, paper files piled high, take-out coffee cups, pens, notebooks, and food cartons.

"You won't be doing this alone. You'll report to me each day and I'll assign you a cop to work with."

"A homicide cop?" she said, hopefully.

"No, patrol. Every cop who's worked a homicide is moving to the Megan Chou case."

"Ah, the assassinated politician?" Sally said.

"The police chief and the mayor want all hands on deck on that one. Which means the murder of Joseph Austin is all yours."

He drew a manila file out of the metal rack and pushed it across his desk.

Sally leaned forward and picked up the folder. Opening it, the first thing she saw was a photo, probably given to the police by the family, of a balding old man with a chubby face and a bulbous nose. He was the victim. Behind it, another photo was paperclipped to the top, an elderly woman, her wispy hair in a bun, with a kindly smile. She was Fiona Austin, the wife. Sally saw the address: 59 Willow Way, Peakhurst—an exclusive neighborhood of large houses.

A quick flick through the file revealed an autopsy report for Joseph Austin, crime scene photos, statements from neighbors, phone call records, and bank statements. The folder trembled in her shaking hands. She shook her head. She was out of her depth. Her heart went out to the victims' family, but more than anything, she felt a rising panic take hold of her. The back of her neck prickled as a trickle of sweat ran down her spine. She must be out of her mind to even consider it.

"This is beyond my capabilities." She closed the folder. "I'm sorry."

"Sally, I need a fresh pair of eyes. Your lack of experience might actually work in your favor. I need you to think outside the box. Come at it from a different angle."

Clarke was deadly serious about this. She should at least listen to him.

"Okay. Can you summarize the case for me?" Sally noticed the date of the incident. July 26, 2016. That was six weeks ago.

"Sure. Between eleven p.m. on July twenty-sixth and one a.m. on July twenty-seventh an intruder broke into the home of Joseph and Fiona Austin through the study window. The intention, we believe, was burglary. The robber was confronted by seventy-one-year-old Joseph Austin who was tortured, then hit three times on the head with what we believe to be a hammer. The killer then ran up the stairs and hit Fiona on the head once, rendering her unconscious. We assume he thought she was dead. She's in a coma at St. Alfred's Hospital. The robber then took the entire contents of the safe, the details of which we do not know. Joseph's iPad was taken—we found a receipt for its purchase but no iPad."

"Why do you think the offender is male?"

"It was a violent, close-contact attack, plus the boot mark at the point of entry is a male shoe size ten."

"You think it was a random burglary that went wrong?" she asked.

"We believe so, although for a while we had our eye on a neighbor, who lives opposite. Criminal record, known to be in a dispute with the deceased. Name is Salvador Sobral."

"So it could have been a targeted attack? Personal?" Sally asked.

Clarke rolled his lips together, which he did when he was thinking. "Yes, but there's been a spate of violent robberies in that neighborhood in the past year. The victims tend to be elderly and the perpetrator ties them up and tortures them, as happened in this case. All the suspect interviews are in the file."

"Who found them?"

"Gardener, the next morning. Saw Joseph lying on the floor through the window. He called nine-one-one."

Sally did her best to absorb the information.

"Neighbors see anything?" Sally asked, hoping that she was asking the right questions.

Clarke pursed his lips, "The only one who claims he saw the intruder is a suspect—that's Salvador Sobral—and he says he saw a man in a hoodie being invited into the house."

"Did the victims have surveillance cameras?"

"Unfortunately not."

Sally placed the manila folder on the desk. "I'm flattered, Detective, but I have no training. The cases I've helped solve were because I became a killer's target or because a neighbor asked for help."

"You're more than capable, Sally, and you can walk away whenever you like. And if you do a good job, I might consider offering a permanent position, if you want to stay on." He put his elbows on the desk. "The old lady deserves to know who killed her husband. She deserves justice. And I have nobody else available to look into it. So what do you say?"

At least Sally understood now. Clarke was scraping the bottom of the barrel by asking her to work the case, and this made her feel strangely better about taking it. Clarke's expectations were low. Good.

Excitement fluttered in her belly. She'd be crazy to turn down his offer.

Clarke opened a drawer and placed her police badge on the desk. "Take it, it's yours. I've booked you in for a firearms test this afternoon. If you pass it, as I'm sure you will, I'll complete the necessary paperwork."

She craned her neck to get a better look at the badge. Her heart swelled with pride. She reached out, then quickly retracted her hand.

"I have to talk to my son first."

"About what?"

"This is a big commitment. I want to know if he's okay with it. And I'll need to clear it with my employer."

Olivia Wiesner, owner of Olivia's Bookstore, would no doubt encourage Sally to take the temporary role and be happy to find someone to cover for Sally while she was gone. Olivia had always believed that Sally's investigative talents were wasted in a bookstore.

Clarke considered her for a moment, then put her badge back in the drawer. "Sure, go ahead, but take the firearms test anyway. What have you got to lose?" He gave her a knowing smile. "I expect to see you in my office tomorrow at eight-thirty, sharp."

FIVE

Sally's son, Paul Fairburn, was in his bedroom playing a video game with his best buddy, Reilly Doyle. They didn't even hear Sally shout a hello when she entered the house, still flushed with pride at having passed the firearms test with top marks.

Placing her bag of groceries on the kitchen counter, she then put the meat and vegetables in the refrigerator. From the whoops of delight coming from Paul's room she guessed that they were enjoying the action-adventure game *ReCore,* which Sally had bought Paul on the day it was released, despite her misgivings about the impact the fight scenes could have on Paul —especially after he was involved in a knife attack only two months ago. Paul hadn't been wounded, but Sally was acutely aware of the psychological trauma, and she had taken Paul to see Dr. Janine Kaur, a child psychiatrist who Paul had seen before. The sessions revealed that Paul still carried a lot of anger toward his father, Scott Fairburn, who walked out on them six years ago. Paul also blamed his father for his sister's suicide.

That broiling anger had gotten Paul into trouble in and out of school, starting fights and lashing out at people who teased him. Paul was a tall, wide-shouldered and muscular boy and Dr.

Kaur had worked with Paul to help him manage his anger before he seriously hurt someone. She had suggested that he play football. It had proved to be the best advice. Playing linebacker for the Pioneer Panthers, the school team, enabled Paul to expend some of his pent-up energy and to find a friendship group where he felt he belonged.

Paul was on an even keel these days, but would Sally's consulting role on a homicide set Paul back? The role might involve long hours and might land her in danger. That's why she had to talk to her son before she accepted or rejected the role.

Sally left her purse on the kitchen counter, took the stairs, and knocked on Paul's bedroom door. Neither boy answered, so she opened the door. Paul and Reilly were glued to the screen, their thumbs on their Xbox One controllers.

"Hi there," Sally said, stepping into the fuggy room with its teenage boy smell.

There was a bag of chips and a box of opened cookies next to the screen, crumbs over the desk where Paul was meant to be doing his homework.

Paul glanced behind him, "Hey, Mom."

"Hey, Reilly," she said.

"Hello, Mrs. Fairburn."

Reilly's mom was coming around any moment to take Reilly home and Sally knew she was facing a losing battle if she tried to extricate Paul from the game. She'd wait until they had dinner to broach the topic of her taking a temporary job at the Franklin Police Department, better known as the FPD.

"Dinner's in half an hour, Paul. And don't forget to do your homework."

Her words fell on deaf ears.

In the kitchen she took the lid off the slow cooker and stirred its contents. Steam rose up, carrying the delicious aroma of chicken and pumpkin curry, which she'd prepared that morning and left to cook during the day. All she had to do was boil rice and fry the poppadoms. Grace Doyle arrived and they had a brief chat before Reilly left with his mom. Paul and Sally sat down to eat the curry, which was a new dish for Sally.

Paul eagerly ate the meal.

"Do you like it?" she asked.

"It's real good, Mom. Maybe make it more spicy next time."

"I can add more." She bit into a crispy popadam. "How was school?"

"Okay."

"Anything new?"

"New girl in class. Really tall. Word is she played in basketball state finals when she lived in New Jersey. Seen her play. She's, like, amazing."

Paul was six feet tall and still growing so this new girl had to be at least as tall as him.

"I didn't know you were into basketball."

"Nah, not much. But everyone's talking about her. She's real fast."

This was the first time she had heard Paul talk about a girl at school. She wondered if he might be sweet on her, although he hadn't shown interest in girls before.

"Invite her 'round, if you like. It's hard being new to a school."

"Maybe I will." Paul stared at his plate and shoveled big forkfuls of the curry and rice into his mouth.

"My day was kind of different," Sally said. "Detective Clarke offered me a job. Well, for three months." She waited for a response.

Paul looked up, his fork positioned above his plate. "As a cop?"

"Not exactly. A consulting detective. It's temporary. There's a cold case they've had trouble solving and they've had to move the homicide team to the Megan Chou murder." Paul looked at her blankly. "The murdered politician." Paul shrugged. He wasn't interested. "Okay, so how do you feel about me taking the job?"

He leaned back in the kitchen chair and looked her in the eye. "Go for it, Mom. Why not?"

"Well, it means I may not be around so much, even on the weekends. I know you're independent and you get around, but for three months I'll be working long hours."

He shrugged. "That's okay. I've got plenty of friends. Do you get a badge and a gun?"

"Yes. I had to do a firearms test today and I passed."

"And handcuffs? A Taser?"

Paul was fixating on the tools that were exciting to a teenage boy. Sally wanted to prepare him for the downside of the role.

She used her fork to chase a chunk of chicken around her plate. "I guess I'm concerned that this might set you back, you know, if the case gets dangerous."

He tilted his head to one side and grinned. "Mom, you took out a serial killer and found our neighbor's killer, so I think I'm used to you chasing the bad guys."

"It also means I can't work for Olivia for a while. I haven't spoken to her because I wanted to speak to you first. The thing is, you could maybe take my place on the weekends, if you like? Earn some money. She's busiest on the weekends so that's when she needs an extra pair of hands."

Paul creased up his nose. "Me and books? I'm not really a book lover, you know what I mean?"

"I imagine you'd work the cash register and stack shelves. Olivia can offer advice to the customers on book choice. Is it worth me asking her about you?"

"Okay, I guess it's easy work and Olivia's nice."

"So you're okay with me taking the detective role?" Sally said.

"Yeah." He gave her an approving nod. "Not everyone has a mom who's working a homicide case."

Sally left her seat and gave her son a hug. He tried to push her away because he thought he was too old for hugs from his mom, but she didn't care. "I love you so much," she said.

Then she picked up her phone to break the news to Olivia.

"OMG! That's so amazing! A detective!" Olivia screamed. "When do you start?"

"Ah, Clarke wants me to start tomorrow." Sally cringed. She was being unfair to Olivia. "I could ask him to wait a week or two."

"You can't do that. There's a murder to solve," Olivia said. "How long will this be for?"

"It's a three-month contract."

"What do you think, Pajamas? Can we manage on our own?" Olivia was addressing her cat who almost always lay on the countertop next to the cash register. "Pajamas says we can cope, except on the weekend."

"Paul can help out on a Sunday."

"Hmm. Is he interested in books?"

"I wouldn't say he's a big reader but he's personable and can stack shelves, work the cash register."

"Maybe he'll draw in a younger crowd. Sure, why don't I give it a try? Ask him if he'd like to do a trial on Sunday. Come in at, say, ten? Oh, and lunch is included."

"That should do it," Sally said. "He loves his food."

SIX

September 7, 2016

It was Wednesday and Sally and Margie were doing their morning run as they always did before work. Although today was not going to be an average day for Sally. Her empty stomach churned at the thought of walking into the FPD building in a few hours. Was she really capable of solving the case?

"So you think I'm doing the right thing?" she asked Margie, whom she'd known since elementary school.

The forest leaves were just beginning to turn yellow, but the running trail wasn't too slippery underfoot because they'd only this week started to fall. Give it another month and she and her friend, Margie Clay, would be ankle-deep in soggy leaves.

Margie gave her a big smile. "Yeah, I think it's the right thing. It's what you've always wanted, right? To be a detective?"

They burst out of the tree cover and onto the trail that looped right around Angel Lake. They varied their route each day. Sometimes it was just forest trail. Sometimes along the four-mile lake trail. Sometimes, like today, a mix of both. One of

the many reasons Sally loved living in Franklin was the prox-
imity to mountains and national parks. The sun had come up
only twenty minutes ago and the flat surface of Angel Lake
reflected the still pink sky and the snowcapped mountains in
the distance.

Sally nodded a hello at a jogger she knew, then answered
Margie. "Yes, but am I up to the job?"

"You were born to be a detective, my friend. I mean, look at
the way you solved the Poster Killer case. You're a natural. It
was that pig of a husband of yours who held you back."

"He sure did. When I think back to all the times he dissed
me, how he persuaded me to leave the PD, I could kick myself
for being so easily manipulated."

"You were gaslighted, hon. Happens to lots of people, and
like Scott, the gaslighters get away with it." Margie glanced at
her friend. "How's Paul taking it?"

"He's more excited than I am, if that's possible. We talked
last night. It'll mean long hours. And I'll have to be super organized. He has football practice and matches to attend, and I'm
worried that if I'm not there to nag him, he won't do his
homework."

"Can I help? If you're ever stuck at work, call me." Margie
was director of a mental wellness charity. Her hours were flexible and she could choose to work from home or at the office.

"Thanks. I might take you up on that."

They followed the shoreline toward Pioneer Park where
they would end their run and part company.

"How did Olivia take the news?" Margie asked.

"She was so nice about it. She's happy to keep my job open
for me but she'll need part-time help while I'm gone. Paul's
interested in working there on Sundays. The yacht club doesn't
have enough work for him, now that the kids are back in school
and the learn-to-sail classes have finished." Over the summer,
Paul taught kids to sail and cleaned the boats.

Margie glanced at her friend. "We'll support you, Sally. Me, Paul, Olivia. You do what makes you happy."

"What would I do without you?" They ran in companiable silence for a while. Sally felt more reassured after their talk, although there was a knot of worry still. "How will the other detectives react to me?" she said aloud. "Some of them were Scott's buddies. They still believe that I'm the evil one and he's the saint."

"Well, they're stupid to believe that. And don't worry yourself about them. Just focus on the task."

Five years had passed since Scott left Franklin to join the Chicago Police. But his poisonous legacy lived on. Sally just had to hope she could prove him wrong and demonstrate that she deserved her title of consulting detective.

Sally arrived at the FPD at 8:20 a.m. and was beckoned into Clarke's office. Standing to one side of the cramped space was a young Black cop, fresh-faced and fidgety. He fiddled with his heavily laden belt from which his gun, Taser, radio receiver, handcuffs, and other police operational tools hung.

"Sally, this is Officer Clarence Pew. You'll be working together on the Austin home invasion murder."

Pew stepped forward and offered his hand, which she shook. "Ma'am. Looking forward to working with you." His palms were warm and clammy.

She guessed he was no more than twenty-five years old, and he had the aura of a rookie—keen, nervy, optimistic.

"Sally Fairburn. Good to meet you," Sally said. "How long have you been on the beat?"

"Two years, ma'am."

"Oh, please don't call me ma'am. Sally will do."

Without any ceremony, Clarke handed Sally her badge and

a Glock 19, which came with a hip holster and ammunition. The badge felt familiar. To Sally, it was like shaking hands with an old friend. She attached the holster to her belt and the solidity of the gun against her hip felt good.

"I'll show you to your incident room," Clarke said.

They left his office and followed, Sally first, Clarence second. The floor was already buzzing with twenty or so detectives and uniforms milling around the room. A large whiteboard had been set up for the Megan Chou case. Sally glanced at the photos and recognized a few faces, including a rival politician. Sally didn't envy Clarke the political tightrope he would need to walk and how much pressure he must be under to find the assassin quickly. Recognizing Detective Esme Lin, Sally waved. Esme's petite frame and slim figure stood out among a predominantly male team. Lin smiled at Sally, then was distracted by an incoming phone call. One or two other detectives were familiar from the Poster Killer case last year, but when she acknowledged them with a nod and a smile, they returned the nod with a questioning frown. Did they wonder, as she did, if she was up to the job.

Clarke opened a meeting room door to a small and airless room. Inside was a whiteboard, two rectangular tables facing each other, two chairs, one landline phone, no computers, and a grubby window facing the next-door building's wall. Clarke put the case file on one of the tables.

"IT will be up shortly to set up your computers. They'll help you with logins, et cetera. The case evidence boxes are stored at the Herring warehouse. You'll have to sign them out. I've assigned you an unmarked Ford Interceptor."

He threw Sally the keys to a Ford, which she thankfully caught. She would have looked an idiot if she'd dropped them. Sally's reflexes were good. She was also fit, running ten miles, five days a week. But did she know how to work a homicide case?

Clarke continued, "Sally, I want you to report to me at the end of each day." He made to leave.

"Sir," Sally said, "where can I find the suspects' recorded interviews?"

"IT will show you." He looked at his watch. "I have to brief my team."

He walked away and left the door open.

Sally followed him. "Sir!"

Clarke turned. "Yes?"

Sally shut the room door behind her. "Why Officer Pew? Does he have investigation experience?"

"He asked to work with you. He's ambitious. Wants to be a detective. You can show him the ropes."

More like the blind leading the blind, Sally thought.

"Is the Austin house locked?" she called out.

"The house key is in the desk drawer. No one is home. Oh, one more thing you should know. The killer took a shower. In the victims' bathroom. What kind of person has the nerve to do that?"

She watched Clarke stride away, leaving Sally with a sinking feeling in her stomach. Was she going to end up making a fool of herself? Taking a few deep breaths, she repeated to herself, *One step at a time. Just read the case file and see where it takes you.*

Then she went back into their incident room to find Clarence seated and reading the case file. He looked like a boy reading an exam paper. At that moment, a young woman arrived with a cart full of computer equipment. Sally introduced herself.

"How long will it take to set up the computers?" Sally asked the young woman.

"Maybe an hour."

"Okay," Sally said. "Do you mind if we leave you to it?"

"No problem. I'll set up a password for you. You should then change it."

Sally nodded then looked at Clarence. "Let's go." She picked up the car keys and the case file.

"Where are we going?" Clarence asked.

"To the crime scene."

SEVEN

Seated on the sagging bed, Harper watched Scott admire himself in the wardrobe mirror, turning from one side to the other so he could view from different angles his new Franklin PD uniform. To think that Harper once found him sexy in a cop's uniform. Now it filled her with a cold dread.

"Lookin' good," Scott said to himself. He turned sharply and stared at Harper. "Right?" he demanded.

"You look very handsome," Harper said.

She would say whatever it took to keep him on an even keel. Her life was like walking on eggshells.

Opening his wallet, he took out a fifty-dollar bill and held it above her head, but out of reach. "For groceries. Nothing else. I want to see the receipt when I get home. You got me?"

"Sure." Harper tried to keep her expression loving, when in reality the hatred she felt was eating her up. Scott dropped the money on the bed. "I can take Eli to the park, right? You promised."

Their son was on the floor, smashing an empty plastic bottle onto the bare boards, grinning at the sound it made. Harper was secretly relieved that the old lady who lived downstairs was hard of hearing. It was a shitty rental apartment that smelled of cheesy feet and cigarettes. The previous tenant had left his furniture behind and because Scott was low on cash, they had kept it.

"You take Eli to the park, you buy groceries, and you come home, you hear? Do anything else and I'll lock you in here for another week."

If he did that to her again, she would kill herself. She couldn't bear it.

She rose from the bed, and a wave of dizziness took her. She waited a second or two for it to clear. "I made you lunch."

She went to the kitchen and handed him a brown paper bag containing turkey and ham sandwiches, two protein bars, and a bag of chips. She wasn't allowed to touch the chips or protein bars. They were for Scott only. He snatched the bag from her.

"I want steak for dinner."

He shut the apartment door behind him. Harper stared at it until she could no longer hear the thud of his boots on the stairs. Then she sat on the sofa and listened for the roar of his macho Jeep Wrangler Rubicon's engine. Scott liked to rev the engine and make the tires squeal.

How could she ever have imagined that Scott was attractive?

She'd been young and stupid, that's how. And he'd faked being a nice guy. Scott did a talk at her high school on women's safety. He was handsome, if a little too old. But he seemed to really care about keeping women safe at night. So, when he flirted with her, she reciprocated. The first time they had sex, he was gentle. He wore a condom. Then, each time after that he was rougher and more selfish. No condom. When she said she didn't want to, he did it anyway. It only occurred to her afterward that he had raped her. She grew afraid of him and his temper, and she was going to end it when she found out she was pregnant. She didn't want Scott in her life but her mom told her that she had no choice except to marry him.

Three years later, her every move was controlled by him. She was in a new city. She had no friends. He kept her cell phone in his Jeep and the apartment didn't have a landline. Her only money was the fifty-dollar bill in her purse for groceries.

He kept telling her that their move to Franklin was because of her. Because she ran away and the women's shelter recorded him on the security camera threatening her. Despite that, he'd *persuaded* the women's shelter to withdraw their allegation. Why, oh why, would they do that? This question had haunted her day and night until she came to the conclusion that he must have threatened to hurt her and Eli if they didn't back off. Scott was never charged, but his career at the Chicago PD was over. There had been other complaints made against him and even though the complainants had miraculously withdrawn their allegations, it was surely only a matter of time before Scott would be dismissed.

Harper's situation was hopeless. She was too depressed to move. Then Eli called out for Mommy and Harper tried to stay focused on the trip to the park. It would make her feel more positive, she was sure of it. A few minutes later, she and Eli were on their way to the park. Just feeling the sun on her face and hands and hearing people chatter and receiving the occasional smile from passers-by lifted her spirits.

Fairlight Park had a kids' play area with swings, a slide, a climbing castle with a short wooden walkway between the two turrets, a sandpit, and two wooden horses on springs that bounced back and forth. Eli headed straight for the baby swing and she lifted him into it.

"Hang on, I'm going to push you."

He giggled. She removed her jacket. Beneath it she wore a blouse with short sleeves. The air was cool but she didn't care. She felt like she was coming alive.

"Mommy!"

"Sorry, sweetie." Harper gave the swing a push and Eli squealed with delight.

She tried to be in the moment. But whenever she thought about her miserable life, a despair came over her. She had to get away from Scott. But how? She couldn't do it alone. Would her mom and dad help her if they knew how cruel Scott was? Harper had no way of contacting them. What if she saved some dollars from the grocery store and used a pay phone? But would they listen? Her pregnancy had brought disgrace on her family and they hadn't forgiven her.

Eli tried to scramble out of the swing, "Play." He stared at the castle.

"Okay, Eli." She lifted him and held him while he found his feet on the ground. Jeez, he was getting heavy, or was she just getting weaker? "Give Mommy your hand."

Eli let her take his little hand and they walked to the castle. She wasn't sure if it was okay for a three-year-old to climb. But Eli was stocky and strong like his dad, and with a little help he had taken the four steps up to the turret's platform where he poked his head out of a circular window and waved at her. She felt a surge of undying love for her boy. He was the sole light in her life and if she could find a way to escape Scott, she'd only use it if Eli could come with her.

Harper hadn't noticed the mom approach with a little girl of similar age to Eli. The mother, fair-haired like her kid, said hello to Harper. It had been so long since anyone other than Scott had spoken to her that she momentarily lost her tongue.

"Hi," Harper said after a pause and then she smiled at the girl who was frowning at her. "Hello, my name's Harper. What's your name?"

The girl confidently said, "Emmie!"

The mother said, "It's really Emily but we love Emmie just as much. I'm Sara. And who's this cute little guy?" She nodded at Eli, watching them through the circular hole in the castle wall.

Harper introduced Eli and soon Eli and Emmie were playing together on the castle, watched by their mothers.

"I haven't seen you here before," Sara said.

"We're new to the area. Moved here from Chicago. My husband got a job here."

"How are you finding making friends? It can be tough in a big city like this."

"I, er, I haven't been out much."

"It's hard moving interstate," Sara said. "We moved here from San Francisco. I hated it at first, then I met this group of moms and now we meet for coffee and take our kids to the pool together. We have fun. You should come along."

Could Harper do that? Could she use the money Scott gave her to buy a coffee?

"That would be nice," Harper said. "When do you meet up?"

"On Mondays, at the library. In the big meeting room. We take turns at reading a story to the kids. Tomorrow, we're meeting at a coffee shop. Give me your cell number and I'll text you the details."

This woman was Harper's lifeline. She longed to keep in touch with her, but how? She went over to the stroller. In the tray under the stroller she had a purse and a grocery list. She rummaged in the bag, found the list and pen and handed both to Sara. "If you write down your cell, I'll call you. My old phone's died on me."

Sara jotted down her number and also the name of the café where the moms' group would meet tomorrow. Harper put the piece of paper inside her purse, determined to keep it secret from Scott. Was it possible that she had a new friend?

The toddlers went on the seesaw and then dug holes in the sandpit. When Sara said that she had to leave, Harper almost begged her not to. It was on the tip of Harper's tongue to ask her new friend for help. But it was too early in their relationship for that.

"Sara, could I use your phone before you go? I want to tell my mom that she can't reach me on my cell." Her request was partly true.

"Sure. I'll watch the kids."

Harper thanked her and walked away from the play area so that Sara couldn't hear her. She called her mom, hoping that she'd pick up. Her mom had this thing about not answering her cell if she didn't know the caller's number.

"Hello?" Harper's mom sounded suspicious.

"Mom! It's me."

"Harper? What's going on? Why haven't you returned our calls?"

Harper glanced back at the playground to check on her son. Eli and Emmie were throwing sand everywhere, squealing excitedly. "Scott wouldn't let me. He took my cell."

"Why would he do that?"

"I tried to run away, Mom. He's cruel. I'm so unhappy."

"But I don't understand. He's such a nice man. You're lucky to have him, both you and Eli."

"Mom, he locked us in the bathroom for days. Barely gave us enough food." Tears welled in Harper's eyes. She turned her back on Sara so her new friend wouldn't see her distress.

"This is crazy talk, Harper. I'm sorry, but I don't believe you. He married you. Did the right thing by you. You should be grateful."

"I have to get away!" Harper said, louder than she had meant to. "Please. Help me, Mom."

Her mom sighed. Harper imagined the fierce line of her mom's lips. "You got yourself into this mess. And I'm not having you shame us again. It was bad enough when you got pregnant and the whole town knew."

Harper had been sixteen and pregnant and her parents were so ashamed they wanted to send her to stay with Auntie Barbara in Eacham, where she was to stay until her baby was born and adopted.

"But—" Harper began.

"I won't have it, you hear? A divorced daughter, a young kid to bring up alone. Dad's not well. You know he isn't. He can't deal with that."

Mom always used Dad as an excuse if she didn't want to do something. Her father had celiac disease. Having Harper and Eli stay with them wouldn't have impacted his health, even though her mom suggested otherwise.

"I have no money, no phone. Please help me. I just need some money to fly home. You want to see Eli, don't you?"

"Fly home? Where are you?"

"Franklin."

"Dear Lord. We don't have that kind of money. Why don't you and Scott come visit us at Christmas? One big happy family."

Her mother was hearing only what she wanted to hear, and she didn't want to hear that her daughter needed rescuing. Harper would cast a shadow over her mom's standing in the church community, which she valued so highly. The truth was clear: her mom didn't want her back. The despair Harper felt made her unsteady. She had to put out a hand and lean on a tree trunk. If her mom wouldn't help her escape Scott, who would?

Harper pressed the end button, then wiped away the tears. Would Sara notice her red-rimmed eyes? She had shades somewhere in the bag under the stroller. She put them on before handing the phone back to Sara.

"Everything okay?" Sara asked.

"You know what parents are like," Harper said as nonchalantly as she could. "It's been so good meeting you. I'll try to make it for coffee tomorrow."

She'd have to do the grocery shopping carefully today to save the money she would need tomorrow to buy a cup of coffee, then she'd tell Scott that she had lost the receipt, but she was determined to do it. Sara was her only hope.

EIGHT

Sally pulled up outside 59 Willow Way, Peakhurst, the scene of the home invasion murder. She peered through the windshield, up the steep slope of the front yard, at the imposing house with a large balcony extending from a top-floor bedroom, which must have stunning views across the city to the mountains. The crime scene tape was gone—nothing to suggest that a violent murder had taken place here. Six weeks had passed since Dr. Anna Mani and her forensics team had gathered all the evidence they could. To Sally, it felt wrong that the house looked so normal. It was as if the neighborhood had forgotten about Joseph's murder and Fiona's assault and moved on.

The house loomed over Sally. For a second she was overwhelmed with the task. She must have been out of her mind taking this on. It was all very well for Clarke to ask for a new perspective on the case, but what if Sally couldn't come up with one?

She imagined her friend, Margie, telling her to *fake it until you make it*.

In the passenger seat, Clarence, in his cop's uniform, whistled through his teeth.

"Man! They had money," Clarence said.

"Still do. At least Fiona does, if she recovers."

"Guess a place like this was always going to be robbed one day."

"I don't want to assume anything," Sally said. "We start this with an open mind, okay?"

"Okay. But the boss thinks it's linked to a stream of robberies in the area."

"I want to pretend we don't know that. Fresh pair of eyes."

On the way there, as Sally drove, Clarence had read out the crime scene and the autopsy reports. Joseph died from blunt force trauma to the skull. Fiona was hit once, a less heavy blow, but enough damage to cause some bleeding on the brain. She was in the top-floor bedroom, having collapsed next to the bed.

"I hope the carpet hasn't been cleaned," Sally said. "I want to see it as the killer left it."

Clarence looked at her as if she were crazy.

Sally left the Ford Interceptor. The gun on her hip felt heavy. She'd get used to it but at the moment it felt weird. Sally was a good shot and had her own Glock. Once a week she went to the rifle range to maintain her accuracy, then it was stored in her gun safe. It had been a long time since she carried a gun all day.

Clarence left the printed case file on the car seat.

"Bring it with us," Sally said, nodding in the direction of the file. "If it's stolen, we'd be in a whole heap of trouble. And besides, we need it. We're going to walk in his shoes."

"You mean the killer's shoes?"

"Yes." She squinted into the sunshine at him. He was tall and broad like her son. She wouldn't want to arm wrestle Clarence, that was for sure. He was, however, as green as they came to detective work, which made two of them. "We could be here a while. I hope you don't get bored easily?"

"No, ma'am. I mean, Sally."

The street was lined with maples, the leaves of which had turned gold, but their canopy didn't block the view of the house.

"Easy to watch the house from the street," she commented.

The driveway was at a steep angle. The footpath through the front yard meandered like a road through the Italian Alps, with hairpin bends and a metal handrail, and then there were steps up to a brick porch. Sally took the driveway. It was quicker and doubled as a good workout for her leg muscles. They paused at the top.

"Are we looking for a male suspect?" Clarence asked.

"Clarke thinks so and the size ten boot prints suggest a male intruder."

The keys Clarke had given her included front and back door, side gate, and the double garage's remote control. She headed for the side gate, which had nothing at the top to prevent someone from climbing over. She pulled on some latex gloves and then handed Clarence a pair.

"Why this way?" Clarence asked.

"Because the forensic team think the perp entered through the study window at the back and footprints indicate that he used the side yard." She put the key in the gate's lock.

Sally paused. "Clarence, I need to be honest with you. I was a cop for three years, then I worked for the District Attorney's Office in victim advocacy. My only real experience of detective work is more recent and thoroughly amateur, but I guess you know about the Poster Killer and the Carolyn Tate murder. She was my neighbor."

"I know. Clarke told me. I did some research too. You won a bravery medal. That's a big deal. All I've done is patrol streets and broken up bar brawls or dealt with domestics. That's when I'm not dealing with paranoid old ladies or domestic disputes. The way I see it, I can learn heaps from you. This is what I've always wanted to do, since I was a kid. I want to be a detective."

"Okay then. Let's do this together."

The key turned stiffly, and the gate needed a shove to open. The rusty hinges squeaked.

"We should check if there was music playing, or the TV was on when the first responder arrived. This gate is noisy. Did Joseph hear it?" Sally walked through as Clarence jotted a note in his notebook, then hurried to catch up with her.

It had rained in the night and the side yard was wet, so any footprints were long since washed away. On the other side of the fence was a property owned by Roisin and Carlos McGettigan. When they reached the rear garden, Sally stopped. The lawn gently sloped upward. On two sides was a thick camellia hedge. Sally couldn't see to the end of the backyard through the shrubs and established trees. But if she looked up, she saw the house that backed onto this one because it was higher than the Austins' house.

"Maybe the people at the back saw something? We can check when the computers are up and running. Can I have the floor plan?" Sally asked and Clarence handed it to her.

Level one was the living, dining, kitchen, and study, where the murder took place. To its left was a double garage. Level two included three bedrooms and two bathrooms. The top floor was the primary bedroom with a connected bathroom and balcony.

She hurried to the boarded-up window. "And this must be the study," she said.

Lining this part of the wall was a flowerbed. Goldenrods grew there although some had been trampled on. "This must be where they found footprints," Sally said, peering at the lumpy soil. She then looked up at the window. The sill was at her shoulder height. "Not the easiest means of access."

Clarence had been glancing at the crime scene report. "Says here that the glass fragments and frame had no prints."

Sally headed for the French doors, which led into the main living area. "Much easier to break this glass," Sally commented.

"Just step inside. No need to climb up and through the study window. Why didn't he enter this way?"

"Maybe he chose the first window he found?" Clarence suggested.

Once inside the house, they found the living room trashed. Pictures taken off the walls and smashed. Drawers were pulled out and their contents tipped out. A display cabinet of blown glass animals and figurines lay in pieces on the polished wood floor.

"Why destroy the figurines?" Clarence asked.

"Good question," Sally said. "I imagine that if you enter a house to rob it, you take what you want and leave as fast as possible. Why would you make so much noise smashing glass?"

"They hate rich people?" Clarence suggested. He screwed up his nose. "What is that stink?"

A smell of rotting food was coming from the kitchen. Again, drawers had been pulled out and emptied.

"Jeez! What a mess!" Clarence said, trying to tiptoe through it.

Sally checked the trash: the can was empty, even the plastic bag was gone. Forensic investigators would have gone through the trash with a fine-tooth comb. She suspected some food somewhere had gone off. She found the refrigerator door was ajar with a pool of water beneath it. The fridge made churning sounds as it tried to maintain a cold temperature. She opened the door wider and found a pack of chicken thighs five weeks past their sell-by date and some soggy, rotten vegetables in the crisper. She reared back at the stench.

Finding a trash bag under the sink, she filled it with the fridge's contents, tied a knot, then put it in the trash can outside. Then they headed for the study.

Sally and Clarence stopped in their tracks. Sally had never seen so much blood. The light gray carpet had a large brownish-red stain circling the desk chair. The back of the chair, walls, desk, and windows were speckled with dried blood. There were bloody footprints everywhere—the killer's. Was he careless or just plain cocky?

Joseph had been bound to his chair with the cord to his bathrobe, tortured with cigarette burns to his chest, then killed.

"Dr. Lilia believes the killer used a hammer. Three blows to the back of the skull. He died sometime between eleven p.m. and one a.m."

She took the relevant photos from Clarence and held them up, trying to imagine she was the first police officer on the scene. She glanced at Clarence, who was looking ashen.

"Are you okay? There's no shame in stepping outside for a breath of fresh air."

"I'm good," he said croakily, putting a hand out to touch the doorframe, then quickly retracting it, aware that his prints would then be part of the crime scene.

The desk was a simple wooden table with no drawers, and it faced the window. On it were a computer monitor, a reading lamp, an ashtray, pens, and a notebook. But an iPad, for which there was a paper receipt, was missing.

The room smelled a little of cigarettes but the rusty, slightly sour smell of blood dominated the space, like the smell of a beef steak beginning to go bad. In one corner was a walk-in wardrobe, partly hidden behind a wall. Plastic file storage boxes had been rifled through, the files opened. The crime scene photos showed documents all over the floor, but they had been gathered up and checked by detectives seeking a reason for Joseph's murder other than a burglary gone wrong. On the other side of the room, a painting of a mountain scene lay on the floor and a wall safe, inset into the brick, was open. White dust lay over the safe door, the picture frame, and every conceivable item the thief-killer might have touched.

"Poor old guy," Clarence said. "It makes me sick when these

criminals pick on the elderly. I mean what kind of person tortures old people?"

"Good question. And here's another one. What was in the safe?"

"Cash?" Clarence suggested. "Old people like to keep cash in the house."

Sally glanced at Clarence, wondering how he came to this conclusion. Did his grandparents do this?

"If we run with that idea, then the next question is how did the home invader know there was cash in the safe?"

"Big houses like this always have a safe and the burglar assumed there was something valuable in there."

Sally's phone rang. It was the IT manager. Their computers were now set up with temporary passwords and they had full access to the case details. But Sally wasn't ready to return to the station.

She imagined the offender sliding an arm through the smashed windowpane and lifting the metal latch. The area around the shattered glass was dusted with white powder, as was the L-shaped latch. She switched on her phone's flashlight and pointed it at the remaining shards still attached to the frame.

"Does something seem odd to you?" Sally asked.

Clarence stepped forward and took his time to study the window. "How do you mean?"

"Some of these glass pieces are bent outward, as if the window was broken from within."

"There's nothing about that in the report," Clarence said.

Sally faced the chair where the bound man's head was smashed in with a hammer. The chair was covered in the poor man's blood.

"Let's say that Joseph heard the window shatter, entered this room, and the intruder tackled him, tied him up, and forced the old man to reveal the safe's code, then he cleared out the safe and killed Joseph."

Clarence nodded.

Sally continued, "Why kill Joseph? The burglar has what he wanted—the contents of the safe."

"Because Joseph saw his face?" Clarence suggested.

"This intruder was confident. He's evaded arrest. He'd have the sense to wear a balaclava so he couldn't be recognized. Three blows says to me that this is personal. Fury. Hatred, maybe. It doesn't feel like a random burglary."

"You're thinking he knew his killer."

"It's possible. This whole scene looks to me like the killer worked hard to make it look like a robbery gone wrong."

Clarence frowned at Sally from where he stood near Joseph's desk. "Clarke won't like that."

"He wants us to find the killer. That's all that matters." She quietly hoped that Clarke's ego would take the hit if she was right about it being personal. His homicide team had spent six weeks on a different track.

"Just go with me on this one," Sally said. She stared at the chair, imagining Joseph's torture. "I'm the intruder. I have a backpack with me. I put everything from the safe into the pack. Then I kill Joseph. I'm now slick with blood. Why do I go upstairs and attack Fiona, who hasn't seen me?"

Sally left the study and followed the bloody footprints up two flights of stairs to the bedroom at the top of the house. There was an armchair in faded ink-blue velvet and a cushion on the floor.

"Fiona is sixty-eight and suffers from arthritis. That's a lot of stairs to climb. I wonder if she used this armchair to catch her breath before heading for the bedroom. Anyway, she wasn't assaulted here." More bloody footprints led into the bedroom. Police tape stuck to the cream carpet marked the position of Fiona's body when the first responder found her, a cop called

Vivek Mishra. "Her head was pointing toward the bedside table where there was a landline phone. I think it's fair to assume she wanted to call for help and didn't get to the phone in time."

There was a small patch of blood where her head had lain and additional spatter on the bedspread, the carpet, and the door of the nightstand. "Why didn't he finish her off?" she pondered aloud.

"Maybe he just wanted to stop her from calling the police?" Clarence suggested. "Maybe he didn't like killing women. Or he liked Fiona?"

Sally nodded and headed for the bathroom. "This is the weirdest bit. The intruder took a shower."

"Yeah, that's really freaky," Clarence said. "And stupid."

"Except he was clever enough to take the towel with him and clean away fingerprints." The tiles around the bath and the taps, doorhandle, mirror, bathroom cabinet, and towel bar were dusted for fingerprints, to no avail.

"Although," Clarence said, "he left behind strands of brown, short hair."

Sally looked around the bathroom one more time. "I find it hard to fathom why he risked taking a shower when Fiona lay on the bedroom floor, unconscious but alive."

"He thought she was dead?" Clarence suggested.

"If that's the case, Fiona is in real danger."

NINE

It was after midday by the time Sally and Clarence arrived back at the FPD and left their unmarked car in the police parking lot at the rear of the building. Sally had put in a call to Clarke to check that Fiona had around-the-clock police protection and he reassured her that she did.

They picked up sandwiches from the local deli and chatted about the case on their way to their incident room. Sally was happy that Clarke had paired her with the eager young cop. They might both lack experience, but she found his enthusiasm about the case motivating and he didn't judge her for her lack of experience.

They were a few yards from the building's rear entrance when a patrol car pulled up and Officer Walt Jackson got out of the driver's side. Walt was her former husband's best friend and for two decades they had patrolled Franklin together. Once upon a time, Sally had been close to Walt's wife, Bettina. After Zelda, Sally's daughter, took her own life and Scott walked out on her and Paul to live in Chicago, Walt and Bettina had turned their backs on Sally. They even went so far as to blame Sally for Zelda's suicide.

Walt Jackson had put on a few pounds around the waist and grayed some more at the temples since they last met. Sally didn't know if he kept in touch with Scott but she guessed that he did; they had always been thick as thieves. Sally had dreaded bumping into Walt because it reminded her that Walt and Scott had gotten away with lying, fabricating evidence, and, in Scott's case, sexually assaulting a thirteen-year-old girl, Stacy Green, although this was never proven.

"What's up?" Clarence asked.

Sally barely heard his question. Walt was a patrol officer and she was homicide, so she'd hoped that she would have settled into her new role before they bumped into each other. Sally felt unprepared for this moment. She wished she had thought of something to say. Could she head off in another direction? She dithered for too long.

The rookie with Walt was the first to notice Sally. She didn't hear what the young cop said, but Walt's head snapped around and his relaxed expression hardened upon seeing her. Then he kept moving toward the front entrance, clearly keen to avoid her. At that moment, Sally's brain stirred. He wasn't surprised to see her. He must have known that she was consulting on a case and he wouldn't like that one little bit.

She had to show Walt she wasn't the timid and easily manipulated women she'd once been when Scott was gaslighting her. She knew her own mind now. She had gained confidence in her abilities.

Walt was almost at the back entrance and if she were going to speak to Walt she must hurry. She released the breath she had been holding and moved her legs jerkily, as if she had been sitting on them for a while and lost the feeling in them. She caught up with him just as the sliding doors sprang apart.

"Walt, can I have a word?" Sally said. He continued walking. The rookie looked over his shoulder. Walt must have heard her too. She tried again, "How is Nikki?" Walt's daughter, who had been one of Zelda's best friends.

Walt stopped and swiveled on the heels of his work boots. "I can't talk, Sally. Running late."

"Aren't you going to congratulate me?" Sally said, unwilling to let him get away so easily.

"Sure. Congratulations. Temporary, right?" Walt sounded as if the words stuck in his throat.

"That depends on a lot of things. Maybe I'll decide to stick around." *Take that!* Sally thought. "How long before you retire, Walt?"

"Two years." He eyed her suspiciously.

"Well, we might be seeing a lot of each other over those two years. We might even work a case together. Now, wouldn't that be something?"

Walt said nothing.

"Hi," Sally said to the rookie. "I'm Sally Fairburn and this is Officer Clarence Pew. I'm working on the Austin case." The rookie introduced himself and shook their hands, despite the supercharged atmosphere. "See you around," Sally said, smiling at both of them, then walking away.

She couldn't maintain the fake bravado for a second longer. Her heart was pounding and her mouth had lost all moisture.

When her back was turned, she heard Walt say, "Stay away from her. She tried to frame a good pal of mine, Scott Fairburn."

Sally bristled at the lie.

"Are they related?" the rookie asked.

"Ex-husband."

"She seemed nice enough."

"She's an evil bitch and she's got a big surprise coming her way," Walt said, disappearing through the door.

Sally felt suddenly freezing, like she'd had an infusion of cold liquid through her veins. Any surprise from Walt was bound to be a nasty one and would have Scott's maliciousness stamped all over it.

TEN

Sally's lunch lay on her desk untouched. No matter how hard she tried, she couldn't focus on the case files. All she could think about was the nasty surprise coming her way. What did Walt mean? Had Walt poisoned his colleagues against her? The homicide detectives too? At least Clarke and Detective Lin were on her side. Or did Walt mean a nasty surprise that was more personal? She left her son a voicemail, checking that everything was okay. Clarence must have noticed her jitters because he looked up from his computer several times with a questioning frown on his face.

Concentrate! Don't allow Walt to mess with your head, Sally thought.

She went through the autopsy and the forensic investigator's reports and began going through the suspects' statements. Taking a break from reading, she phoned the forensic pathologist who carried out the autopsy, Dr. Robert Lilia, and arranged to see him that afternoon. Lilia was a friend.

"Welcome back," Dr. Lilia said. "And congratulations on your consulting role."

When Sally worked in victim advocacy she had helped

Lilia's son through a difficult time and her friendship with Lilia had grown from there.

"Thanks, Robert. It's just for three months. After that, who knows? I guess it depends on how I do with this case."

"I'll do what I can to assist. Come by at three p.m."

Sally then turned her attention to setting up the white-board. She stuck photos onto the slippery surface with Blu Tack putty, then wrote their names beneath them. Top left were photos of Joseph and Fiona Austin, the victims. Top right were the suspects who Clarke's homicide team had identified.

"Clarence?"

He looked up from his monitor, then pushed his wheeled chair back so he could more easily see the whiteboard. Sally pointed at a photo of a man with a thick head of black hair and a goatee, his eyes deep-set.

"Troy Vincent. Has served time for robbery with violence and has a track record of tying up and torturing his victims. Six months ago, he tied up and tortured Bert Gonzales, then stole his valuables. His girlfriend, Angie Williams, is his alibi for the night Joseph was killed."

"Is she reliable?"

"She has a criminal record. Shoplifting. So, no, she's not reliable."

Sally moved her finger to the next photo. "Salvador Sobral, age twenty-nine, served time for identity theft. Lives opposite the Austins with his partner Justin Griess."

"With a criminal record, he's gotta be worth talking to again, right?" Clarence suggested.

"Yes. But computer crime is very different from blud-geoning an old man to death."

Clarence scanned the case notes on his computer screen. "He claimed he was victimized by Joseph because he's gay. The notes say there was even a petition circulating to get Sobral to leave the neighborhood. Joseph started the petition."

"That's a motive." Sally pointed at the next photo. "Dallas Austin, forty-one, nephew on Fiona's side of the family. If Fiona dies, he inherits the house." Dark brown hair and a side part, a cheery smile.

"The house has got to be worth what? Two million? Maybe two and a half? Worth killing for."

"Yes, but he has an alibi. Dallas was working that night. Managing staff at a yacht club event. Didn't leave the venue until two a.m."

"Okay, but he could have slipped out unnoticed," Clarence suggested.

"We should find out."

Sally now pointed at a tanned, blond man in a wide-brimmed hat. "Andy McCarron, twenty-six, gardener. He made the nine-one-one call. He inherits ten thousand dollars if both Joseph and Fiona die."

Clarence again checked the notes on his computer. "Has an alibi and we're only talking ten thousand dollars. Why is he even a suspect?"

"He's more of a witness, I guess. We should talk to him, though. Maybe he'll remember something new."

"Why would they leave money to the gardener?" Clarence asked.

Sally considered his question. "They're a childless couple. Maybe they saw him as a son they never had."

"If Fiona comes out of her coma, we can ask her," Clarence said.

"I hope she does, but we need to work on the assumption that she won't." Sally tapped a photo of a smart, bleach-blonde woman in her forties. "Roisin McGettigan, married to Carlos, has her own real estate business. Lives next door to the deceased at number fifty-seven Willow Way. She signed the petition to get Salvador Sobral to leave the neighborhood." She moved on to a photo of Carlos. Tanned skin, black eyes, curly brownish-gray hair. "They gave each other alibis for the night of the murder."

"Looks to me like we don't have a whole lot of good suspects," Clarence sighed.

"That's why we're reviewing the case," Sally said, doing her best to hide her disappointment at such few real leads.

"I guess Roisin could be lying to protect her husband?"

"Possibly. But what is Carlos's motive?"

Clarence shrugged. "Who do we see first?"

"Bert Gonzales, then Troy Vincent."

"I'm confused. If you think this murder is personal, why go see Troy?"

"To eliminate him once and for all."

"He lives in a bad neighborhood. Maybe we should take backup?" Clarence said.

"No need for that. But first, I'd like to speak with the victim, Bert Gonzales. Troy was the main suspect and there are similarities between the Austin case and what happened to Bert."

The Longford Nursing Home didn't look like much from the outside. It was on a busy main road, a single-story cream brick building, the hard edges of which hadn't been softened by the shrubbery. The entrance was through a security gate and down a side yard, past the windows of some elderly residents. At the end of the pathway was a paved courtyard where a woman in her seventies sat reading her Kindle. The reception area was through double doors that led to a faded blue carpet and cheap prints on the walls. There was a distinctive smell, much like boiled cabbage. A friendly receptionist asked Sally and Clarence to sign the visitors' book and then directed them to the lounge room where they would find Bert Gonzales playing cards.

Most of the residents' room doors were open. They walked past a woman who lay in bed moaning. The bed was at an angle, with the top half raised. Next to her hand was a button on a long cord, no doubt so she could call for a nurse. Sally stopped, concerned that she might be in pain.

"Don't mind her," another woman said from a chair in the corridor where she was knitting. "She moans all the time. Nothing wrong with her. I wish she'd shut up." She turned her gaze to Clarence. "My, aren't you handsome?" She winked, then resumed the knitting of what looked like a baby's cardigan.

The living room and the TV room were next to each other. The TV was blaringly loud. The living room was arranged with chairs in a row facing inward, plus some around tables. Of the three old men in the room, only one was playing cards. He sat in a wheelchair, his back bent like a C. With him were two women.

"I'm sorry to interrupt your game but are you Bert Gonzales?" Sally asked.

The women immediately looked up. Bert continued to stare at his cards.

"He can't hear you," one of the card players said. "He's not wearing his hearing aid." The woman then waved her hand in his face. He looked up.

Sally moved into his line of sight. "I'm Detective Fairburn and this is Officer Pew," she said in a raised voice.

Bert looked up. They both showed their police ID.

"Police, hey? Did you catch the brute?" he yelled.

His wispy white hair and paper-thin skin and his bent posture made him look so vulnerable and fragile.

The old lady seated opposite him shouted, "You're shouting, Bert, where's your hearing aid?"

"Say that again?" He cupped one ear.

The old lady repeated the question, louder.

"I have it somewhere," Bert said, tapping his shirt and then his pants pockets. "Where did I put it?"

"Is it by your bed?" the woman shouted.

"You could be right."

Sally kneeled next to Bert. "I'll wheel you to your room so you can find your hearing aid and we'll have a chat, okay?"

"Is that where I left my hearing aid?"

"It could be," Sally shouted back. "Apologies, ladies, we shouldn't be too long."

Bert was light as a feather to push to his room, which contained a bed, wardrobe, nightstand, and a smattering of personal belongings. There was a singular photo of a young Bert on his wedding day, but Sally wondered why the daughter hadn't put up more of Bert's keepsakes and pictures. There wasn't even a bathroom or a TV. It was obvious that this nursing home was at the cheaper end of the market. As soon as they entered the room, Sally saw the hearing device on the nightstand. She wheeled Bert close to the nightstand and, after some fiddling, the hearing aid was in his ear.

Sally sat on the edge of his bed and Clarence stood, making notes.

"Have you caught the monster who hit me and stole my things?" Bert asked, at a normal volume.

"I'm here about another case similar to yours. Can I ask you some questions?"

"It was a long time ago. Must be, ooh, weeks. My memory's not so good these days."

"That's okay. Just do your best. Can you remember how the intruder got into your house?"

"I didn't hear him break the window. I was watching TV, you see. All of a sudden, there he was, right in front of me. It was... terrifying."

"Can you describe him?"

"Not really. It was night and I was snoozing in my recliner. Only had a table lamp on."

"Can you describe his face?"

"He wore one of those balaclava things. I remember his eyes, though. Too close together. Beady."

"What did he want?"

"He wanted money. Cash. I told him I didn't have any. He got angry. Slapped me. Tied me to my recliner, then used a cigarette on me." Bert whimpered.

"I'm sorry to have to ask you these questions, Bert. Is it okay for me to continue?"

Bert nodded.

"Did he have an accent?"

"I don't remember."

"Did he smell of anything?" Sally asked.

Bert looked puzzled. "Smell? I don't know. Let me see. Nobody asked me about his smell." Sally waited. "Cheap after-shave, and too much of it."

This was new information. "That's good, Bert. Why do you say it was cheap aftershave?"

"Like the stuff teenage boys use when they're trying to impress a girl."

"How did the intruder leave?"

"Same way he came, I guess. He left me tied up."

"Did you hear a car start?"

"Not that I can remember."

"And what did he steal?" Sally had a list of the items stolen but she wanted to hear it from Bert.

"My wife's jewelry. She died many years ago, but I kept it to remember her by. You know, rings, watch, necklaces, that kind of thing. The cash in my wallet, my credit card. Silverware. I had a silver circular tray, passed down by my mother to me. And my hat."

"Hat?"

"Yes, I had a trilby I always wore when I went out." He shook his head. "I was in the hospital after that. Broke my eye socket, he did. I couldn't go home after that. I knew I'd never be happy there again. My daughter put the house on the market and set me up in this place. It broke my heart to leave my home. Lived there forty-one years."

How terrible, Sally thought. *To be frail and vulnerable and afraid to go home.*

"This might seem like a strange question, but did the intruder shower at your house?"

"No, why would he do that?" Bert said. "I sometimes think I see him. But it's someone else, you know, visitors and the like. At night, I have to sleep with a light on. If I don't, I see him in the dark shadows." He turned his rheumy eyes to Sally. "He's walking around, free to do what he likes. Me? I'm always afraid."

Bert hugged himself.

Sally put her arm around him and held him until he stopped trembling.

She and Clarence left the nursing home overcome with sadness. It rankled them that his assailant had never been found and sent to jail.

She glanced at Clarence who was very quiet. "Any thoughts?"

"Yeah, I'd like to beat the shit out of the pig who did this. I mean, I won't. You know that, right? It just makes me so angry."

"I get what you're saying but we play this by the book. There are enough similarities between the two cases to talk to Troy Vincent. Bert was tied to a chair and burned with a cigarette and so was Joseph. We talk to Troy next."

"And if we find Troy didn't kill Joseph, what then? We can't let him get away with what he did to that old man," Clarence said.

Sally's heart swelled. She wanted justice for Joseph and Fiona *and* Bert, but she had to keep Clarence on course. "One step at a time."

ELEVEN

Yarra Bend, where Troy Vincent lived, had the highest crime rate in the city. It was also one of the poorest areas. As Sally and Clarence drove down South Trenton Street searching for number 87, Sally was relieved that their car was an unmarked police car, even if Clarence was in uniform. At least their car wouldn't alert Troy of their arrival.

The street contained mostly low-rise apartment blocks, with some crumbling wooden houses in-between. Walls and street frontages were covered in graffiti. Two men leaned against a wall and watched their car suspiciously. Number 87 was a run-down house with an old sofa in the front yard. Sally pulled up on the opposite side of the street. There was a filthy car in the dirt drive.

"Somebody's home," Sally said and left the car.

Clarence followed. Sally was careful to lock the car. A teenage boy on a stationary bicycle watched their movements. When he saw Clarence in his police uniform, he spat on the ground and then made a call on his cell phone.

"I don't like the feel of this place," Clarence said.

She looked up and down the quiet street, her hand resting

on her Glock on her hip. She hoped she would never have to use
it but feeling it in the holster was reassuring. "We'll be okay.
We're just having a chat."

Clarence gave her a look that implied he wasn't convinced
she was right but nevertheless followed her to the flimsy deck
that bowed as they stepped on it. She pressed the doorbell but it
didn't ring. She listened for a noise inside the house. All was
quiet. The screen door on rusty hinges screeched as she opened
it and thumped on the front door.

"Troy Vincent?" Sally called through the door. "I'm Detective Fairburn. Can we talk?"

Clarence shifted from his right boot to his left. Then he
looked behind him. Sally did the same. A second boy on a
bicycle came hurtling around the corner and skidded to a halt
parallel to the other teenager.

There was a crash at the back of the house.

"He's getting away!" Clarence said.

"Get after him. I'll watch the front."

Clarence ran down the side yard. Sally hammered on the
door once more, in case the noise was a ruse to distract them.
"Troy, open up. I just want to talk."

She heard Clarence shout, "Stop! Police!"

Clarence was right. Troy was trying to run away. Sally
leaped off the front porch and took the side yard, dodging a
trash bag that had split and spewed its contents. As she rounded
the corner, she saw Clarence land on the other side of a chain
link fence. She raised the two-way radio to her mouth to speak
to him, when she heard a screech, just like the screen door at the
front of the house and Sally realized her mistake.

Running like the wind, she headed to the front yard. A car
engine growled to life and just as Sally reached the yard, Troy
reversed onto the street.

"Damn!" Sally muttered, then shouted, "Troy! Stop!"

Without so much as a glance at Sally, Troy sped away, tires squealing.

"He's driven away. Where are you?" Sally said into the radio.

Clarence replied, "On Henry Street. On my way to you." He was breathing heavily.

Sally ran toward her vehicle. "What the hell!"

The Interceptor was raised at the back and leaning to one side. Three heads bobbed on the other side and from the haircuts she recognized the boys.

Sally ran across the road. "Police! Stop that!"

The teenage boy in a hoodie darted out from the far side of the vehicle, rolling a rear wheel down the road, accompanied by his friends on bicycles who laughed and whooped. The lead cyclist gave her the finger.

Sally couldn't believe her eyes; the kids must have jacked up the car.

She used the radio. "Teenage boys stole a wheel. I'm giving chase along George Street."

"Say again?" Clarence responded.

Sally sprinted after the boys. They turned a corner. By the time she got there, the boys and the wheel were in the back of a speeding pickup truck that was too far away for her to catch the number on the plate.

Red in the face, she watched the truck disappear. "How am I going to explain this?" she said aloud.

She would be the laughing stock of the police department.

TWELVE

By the time the roadside assistance service arrived to replace the wheel, Sally and Clarence had an audience of residents who found their predicament highly entertaining. Even the mechanic shook his head at Sally in disbelief. Clarence kept the crowd away from the vehicle while Sally made a phone call to explain to Clarke what had happened.

"Jesus! What were you thinking?! Not so long ago, an officer was shot dead there. You should have had a couple of patrol officers with you," Clarke said.

"It was dumb. It won't happen again, sir." Sally knew now that she should have listened to Clarence when he suggested getting backup.

"I want an update on the case at eighteen hundred hours," he said tersely and ended the call.

Sally hoped that a visit to the Forensic Pathology Unit might spark some inspiration because right now she had nothing positive to report.

They pulled up outside the Pioneer Valley Hospital, a red brick, three-story building. The Forensic Pathology Unit was around the corner. Sally preferred to reach it through the

Japanese Garden where the hospital patients could sit, rather than through the main entrance.

"Have you been here before?" Sally asked.

"No."

"You won't see an autopsy. But the smell can make people nauseated. It's okay to leave the room."

The Japanese Garden consisted of two cherry trees, a miniature maple, a pond, and a small waterfall constructed with boulders. "I should warn you that Dr. Lilia is fond of loud music."

She pushed open the double doors and stepped into a corridor. She pressed the buzzer on the wall and announced that she and Officer Pew were there to see Dr. Lilia. The door buzzed open and they went through. A short corridor, with an office on either side, led to more double doors, which took them to the area where the autopsies were carried out and the bodies kept in cold storage. The doors opened and Lilia appeared, accompanied by a blast of Pearl Jam's "Alive."

"Just finished a particularly distressing autopsy. A child. The music helps."

He used a remote control to switch it off. Dr. Lilia, was a bear of a man with bald head, trimmed white beard, and piercing blue eyes.

Sally introduced Officer Pew.

"You're lucky," Lilia said to the officer. "Sally's the nicest person I've met at the PD. Just don't go taking advantage of her."

"No, sir, I wouldn't dream of it."

He asked them to follow him to his office, a cramped room by the entrance. In a corner was a circular table with four chairs and he invited them to take a seat.

"So, they've handed you the Joseph Austin case. Nasty business," Lilia said. "I take it you've read my report."

"Yes." Sally took a notebook and pen from her blazer. "In it you say the weapon is likely to be a hammer. It was never found. Is there anything distinctive about it?"

"The circular head has a milled face. It left behind distinctive marks because of the pointed pyramid pattern." He glanced from Sally to Clarence and must have seen the confusion on their faces. "Come over here. I'll show you."

He sat on a stool by a computer screen and searched for an image. When he found what he was looking for, he enlarged it. "Joseph was bald on the back of the head, which makes showing you the marks on his skin easier." Sally's stomach churned. The back of his skull was dented. There were circular shapes within which were tiny, pyramid-shaped indentations. "Some hammers have a gripping pattern on the face, which helps the user to catch and sink nails."

Sally looked sideways at Clarence who had turned away.

"And it was the second blow that killed him?" Sally asked.

"I believe so."

"And he was alive when his chest was burned by a lit cigarette?" Sally asked, sensing her mouth was drying up and there was a bitter taste there.

"Most definitely. And the cigarette was one of Joseph's. He smoked Marlboro Gold Pack."

"Once the intruder has the safe code," Sally said, thinking aloud, "he kills Joseph and then opens the safe and clears out everything."

"I don't think so, Sally," said Lilia. "The killer's gloved hands would be covered in blood and that blood would have left streaks on the safe door. But the safe door was clean, which suggests a new pair of latex gloves, or he washed them. Did he shower before he opened the safe?"

"Maybe we have the sequence of events wrong?" Clarence said. "Maybe he tied up Joseph, got the safe code from him, killed him. Then he realized there was a second person in the house. He ran upstairs and attacked her, then showered. Went downstairs. Opened the safe. And left the house in a new set of clothes, with clean hair and face."

"You could be right," Sally said. She then addressed Lilia. "Who organized the burial?" Sally asked.

"The nephew."

"Dallas Austin?"

"That's the one."

"And the killer didn't leave any DNA on the victim's body?"

"I found a hair under Joseph Austin's fingernail. No root, I'm afraid."

"Does the hair tell us anything else?"

"A healthy hair, brown in color, probably from someone under forty. No sign of losing pigment."

Sally had one final question about the weirdest aspect of the home invasion. "The killer took a shower. He then left the house with the towel. He didn't leave any DNA behind, apart from two head hairs in the bathroom. Again, no roots to the hairs and therefore no DNA. How is that possible to leave so little behind?"

"Bleach was used and we assume he wore gloves when he wiped the surfaces clean, then, as you say, he took the towel with him. He must have an eye for detail."

"Or he was a clean freak?" Sally said.

THIRTEEN

It was the end of a long day and Sally hoped there wouldn't be many people left in homicide. She had sent Clarence home, keen to protect him from ridicule, at least for that night anyway. When she exited the elevator and entered the department, her heart sank when she saw that many of the team working the Megan Chou case were at their desks.

Keep it together, she told herself.

Raising her chin, she kept walking, but her legs were unsteady. The detective seated nearest the entrance looked up, saw Sally, and said, "Well, look who it is."

The detectives chatting behind him looked around with a smirk.

"Hear a kid stole your wheel from under your nose."

"Some detective she's turned out to be!" a woman muttered, shaking her head. "Can't even find a missing wheel."

Sally kept her eyes on Clarke's office door and didn't engage with them. What would be the point? They were right. She'd been naïve—too long off the beat. She'd forgotten that in many neighborhoods the cops were the enemy.

After she knocked on Clarke's door, he looked up and beckoned her inside. His eyes returned to his computer screen as he invited her to sit. He continued typing. She waited in silence, her discomfort intensifying.

"Not a good start, Sally. Tell me something positive." His hands fell to his lap and he looked her in the eye.

"We've been through the crime scene. The attack on Joseph feels personal."

"Why do you say that?"

"Smashing someone's skull in with a hammer reeks of anger. Hatred. I think the killer entered the house intending to murder them."

"Why empty the safe if it's not about theft?" Clarke asked.

"I don't know. Was there a document or a video or something the killer had to destroy? Or perhaps he took cash from the safe so that he could then go off-grid and lay low for a while? Also, there's something strange about the study window. Some of the glass poking out of the frame bends outward, rather than inward, which suggests to me the window was broken from the inside."

"The forensic report doesn't mention this. Are you sure?"

"Yes, sir. I wonder if the window was staged to look as if it was how the intruder broke into the house."

"How else did the killer enter the house?" Clarke asked.

"There's a witness who saw a man on their porch shortly before midnight."

"Salvador Sobral. I'd take his statement with a pinch of salt. If the attack was personal, who is your prime suspect?" Clarke asked.

"Too early to say."

"Make talking to Sobral a priority but I want all avenues of inquiry explored and that includes Troy Vincent. Next time you go to his house, have backup."

"Yes, sir. Another thing. The killer showered at the crime scene. Who does that?"

"It's unusual. Instinctively, killers flee the scene. The reason? He had to walk home or take public transport or had someone at home waiting for him?" Clarke suggested.

"Or he is a neat freak, perhaps even OCD about personal cleanliness. And neither fits Troy's psychological profile. One look at his messy house tells me that cleanliness and order are not a priority for him."

"As I said, maybe he had to take the bus home. I want you to locate him and bring him in for questioning."

"If only we knew the contents of the safe," Sally said.

"Lisa La Cava was Joseph's attorney and friend for nine years. I think she knows the safe's contents, but she's refused to comment. You should have a crack at her. She might be happier talking to you."

"Why do you think that?" Sally asked.

"You're approachable. You don't behave like a cop. She may drop her guard."

Sally nodded. "Thank you, sir." Sally stood. Sally was keen to get home and see her son.

"How is Pew doing?" Clarke asked.

"Good. Eager to learn. Asks probing questions."

Clarke interlaced his fingers on the desk. "I wanted to give you the heads-up on—"

There was a knock on the office door and Detective Esme Lin poked her head in. "Boss, there's been a development."

"Can it wait?"

"No, boss."

Clarke unlaced his fingers. "I'll call you later," he said to Sally.

As she left the homicide department, Sally made a call to Margie. She needed to hear a friendly voice.

"Hey, Sally! How did your first day go?" Margie asked.

"Not so good." Sally explained about her disastrous afternoon and how the homicide detectives clearly thought her an idiot.

"Ignore them. Everyone makes errors when they start a new job. Just follow your instincts, my friend."

"Thanks, Margie, you always cheer me up. Are you free for dinner tonight? I'm making my baked tortellini."

"I wish I could, hon. But I have a work function."

Sally left the building feeling more positive after her chat with her friend. On the way home she stopped at the grocery store and as she switched off the ignition, her phone beeped with a text message:

> *Congratulations! Consulting for the FPD. Proud of you. Come and see me sometime.*

Sally's skin prickled. The message was from Richard Foster who was serving life for rape and serial murder. The phone belonged to a prison guard who was under Foster's control. Not so long ago, Foster had kidnapped and planned to kill Sally. It was because of her that he was caught and convicted and yet, not so long ago, she had turned to him for help tracking down her neighbor's killer. Foster had been useful, but he frightened her. He reminded her of a spider luring her into his web.

She deleted his message.

FOURTEEN

Sally had collected Paul from football practice and was in the kitchen putting the final touches to her sliced-sausage baked tortellini. Paul ate from a bag of potato chips as they talked about his trial run on Sunday at the bookstore. He'd warmed to the idea when she told him that Olivia would make him lunch: the bookstore doubled as a café. Paul already knew that Olivia was a good cook. When Sally worked there, she often came home with cakes, pies, and other dishes that hadn't been sold and needed eating. She smiled to herself. The way to Paul's heart was very much through his stomach.

Her phone rang. Her hands were greasy from cutting up sausages, so she asked Paul to take the call. He got up slowly, complaining that he was tired and by the time he picked up her phone, the call had gone to voicemail.

He held it above his shoulder like a trophy. "Clarke left a message."

"Okay, I'll look at it later." She wanted to put the tortellini in the oven first.

"Have I got time for a shower?" Paul called out.

"Yes. It should be ready in thirty-five minutes," she said,

opening the preheated oven door and popping the dish on the metal rack.

As she washed her hands, she heard the familiar thump of Paul heading upstairs. She was drying them on a hand towel when the doorbell rang. Margie had mentioned she might pop in for a glass of wine on her way home, so Sally didn't think twice about opening the front door. She still had the towel in her damp hands and wasn't paying attention to the person who barged past her and was inside her house before she could stop him. Even then, her eyes hadn't sent a message to her brain, warning her that she was in danger. Perhaps it was because she had blocked his memory from her mind for so long. She turned to face him, her lips parted to tell the rude person to leave.

"Hello, Sally."

He was there. In her house. Her worst nightmare.

Still, in the few seconds it took for Scott Fairburn to slam the door shut, her brain was saying that this was impossible. He was in Chicago.

But he wasn't. He was here. Six years after he walked out on them. The day of their daughter's funeral.

Her abuser. The man who drove her daughter to suicide and her son to hatred.

No, this can't be real!

Scott Fairburn was built like a bouncer, his crewcut a little grayer, his eyes just as cold. He held his arms up. "Aren't you going to welcome me back?"

All those years of therapy, little by little moving on from Scott's emotional and psychological abuse, from the utter despair and self-loathing Sally experienced at Zelda's death, blaming herself for failing her daughter. Weeks, months, and years of slow confidence building during which Sally lived for one thing only—for her son. If it wasn't for Paul she might have taken her own life, but Paul was a messed-up kid, tormented with hatred for his father, and she had poured her love into him.

Now her ex-husband stood in her house, so close to her that she could smell the cloying mix of eggs and beer on his breath, using his muscular bulk and his mocking smile to intimidate.

After six years of healing, in that moment Sally forgot everything she had learned from her psychologist. She forgot that she had brought up Paul alone. She forgot that she had a job as a detective. She even forgot that her son was upstairs in the shower, blissfully unaware that his cruel father was downstairs, right in front of her. Sally was right back where she had been when he packed his bag and left the house on the day of Zelda's funeral. She was a broken woman once more.

"What?" he mocked. "Not a word?" He looked around the townhouse—her townhouse—like he owned it. "Nice place. Are you going to get me a drink?"

It was like Scott had replaced all the oxygen in the room with a poisonous menace that radiated off him.

Sally couldn't breathe. Her voice wouldn't activate. She knew she should tell him to leave but he had taken her power away. Like before, she didn't dare to cross him.

She walked in a trance to the refrigerator. It was as if she were back in their house in Memorial Park in 1993. She walked on eggshells back then, trying hard not to upset him. He made all the decisions because, as he drilled into her, she made bad ones.

No, said a voice in her head. *Don't do what he says. This is your house, not his. Say something!*

But it was like her mind had been wiped clean. She couldn't remember what her psychologist had told her to do if she encountered Scott again. Opening the refrigerator door, she stared into the brightly lit void, unseeing, hoping to find the right words to ask him to leave, but her courage failed her.

She flinched when Scott laid a beefy hand on her left shoulder and squeezed, his breath on the back of her neck. "What does a man have to do to get a drink around here?"

She pulled away from his grip and, on autopilot, bent forward, taking a bottle of beer from a compartment in the door. Her fingers felt numb and it almost slipped through her fingers.

Scott grabbed the beer, flicked off the metal cap, and took a swig. He stood too close, way too close. She was cornered. He gave her a cruel smile. "You're looking pale, Sally. You should get out more. Lucky for you, I'm back in town."

Her throat dried up. She made a choking sound. *No, he can't be. Why would he come back?*

He leaned so close that she could see flecks of gray in his chin stubble.

"Why do you hate me, Sally? I was always good to you. Looked after you. Kept you safe."

No you didn't, she thought, shaking her head.

Ah, the lies that dripped off his tongue, as destructive as lighter fluid on fire. He never looked after her or their kids. He used them all and controlled them. Everything was about him. He was a sadistic narcissist with a filthy liking for underage girls. By the time she'd found that out, it was too late and the proof was gone, but every bone in her body knew that it was true.

Was that why he was here? Because she had dared to try to prove that he had sexually assaulted thirteen-year-old Stacy Green?

He gripped her shoulder tighter, digging the tips of his fingers into her skin. "I asked you a question."

Perhaps it was the physical pain, but just then she heard her psychologist's voice. *Take control. Tell him what you want and if he won't do it, call the police.*

"I... want you to leave," she stammered.

"No, you don't. I know what's best for you."

"Get... out!" Sally screamed.

Who is that woman telling Scott what to do? It's you. You're doing it.

Scott took his hand away, a practiced look of hurt crossing his face. He could pretend that he had feelings like empathy, love, kindness, but it was an act only. "That's no way to treat the man who did everything to keep our family together."

"No," she whispered.

"You drove me away, Sally. It was your fault. They told me you were bitter about me leaving, even after all these years." He must mean the Jackson family. Walt, with whom he had patrolled Franklin's streets, and his wife, Bettina. "But you're more than that, aren't you? You always were a vengeful bitch." The hurt look was replaced in a flash by a sneer. "A little bird tells me you've been spreading lies about me. Damaging lies. And I won't allow it, you hear me?"

"It's all true!" she said, like an explosion from her mouth. She was angry and her anger had cut through her terror. "Our daughter killed herself because of you. Because of your disgusting secret! She couldn't bear it. You're a monster!"

Scott laughed.

There was a sudden stomping on the stairs and a shout. "Leave Mom alone!"

Paul, his body wet, a towel wrapped around his waist, jumped the last three steps.

For a second or two, Sally saw fear in Scott's eyes. Paul was nine years old when Scott had last seen him. He clearly had no idea that his little boy was now a man. Paul shoved Scott backward.

"Get out or I'll throw you out!" Paul seethed.

Scott gave Paul a murderous look. Sally couldn't let them come to blows. Paul had Scott's temper—they were both prone to hitting first and thinking later.

Sally used all her strength to push the two apart.

"Go! And don't come back. Ever," she said.

Scott folded his arms and smirked in amusement. "I have a right to see my son."

She stepped away from him, unable to endure his mocking gaze and, in a flash, Scott punched his son in the gut. Sally yelped in shock.

"Oof!" Paul doubled over, gasping for breath, unprepared for the blow.

Scott had abused his family emotionally and mentally. He had never punched his son before. This was an escalation. Suddenly, Sally had her senses back.

She dived for her phone to call 911.

"Don't be stupid," Scott snatched her phone away before she could press the final one. He threw the phone on the couch. "I am the police."

"You have no jurisdiction here." She lunged for the phone, and he blocked her.

"I guess you haven't heard the news," Scott said, sauntering to the door and letting himself out. "I'm back with the FPD, with all my old friends. It's good to be home."

FIFTEEN

September 8, 2016

Sally woke as furious as she had been when she went to bed. Furious with herself for being so weak in Scott's presence and furious with Scott. How dare he walk back into their lives!

Not that she had slept much with the roller coaster of emotions she was grappling with. Fear, despair, anger, hatred, and helplessness vied for supremacy, and it was exhausting. Her head throbbed as if she had a hangover. At 6 a.m., she gave up trying to sleep and went to the bathroom and swallowed two painkillers. Paul's door was shut, as she expected it would be at this hour. She hoped that the punch to his stomach hadn't kept him awake.

Sally wasn't going for her run this morning. She wanted time to talk to Paul about Scott and his violence before he headed off to school. Should they file an official complaint? She sent a text message to Margie, apologizing for pulling out so late and explained her decision in one simple statement:

Scott is back in town. He paid us a visit last night. I need to be with Paul this morning. Call you later.

Sally brewed some coffee and sat at the kitchen table sipping it, hoping that by some miracle she might come up with a plan to rid Scott from their life.

Paul was doing so well at school, and he was headed for a sports scholarship with the University of Franklin. His grades were good. The child psychiatrist had helped enormously, and she liked to think that she also contributed to Paul developing into a well-grounded and happy teenager.

It made her livid to think that Paul's progress might be all for nothing now that Scott had returned. And not just to live in the city. He was determined to invade their lives too. He wanted to control them, as he had done before he walked out and demanded a divorce. It wasn't enough for a narcissist like Scott to have a new wife and child: God help them! He also wanted to inveigle himself into Sally's and Paul's lives so he could manipulate them to his own ends. But Sally wasn't the self-doubting woman Scott had made her during their marriage. She was a survivor. More than that, she was a good parent, a talented sharpshooter, had an instinct for solving crimes, and was empathetic—all the attributes Scott felt threatened by.

"I won't let him win," Sally said aloud. "I won't let him derail Paul. I won't."

Sally went upstairs and woke her son, who after a shower, joined her in the kitchen for breakfast. She'd made egg, bacon, and cheese on English muffins, which she was relieved to see he ate with his normal gusto.

"Can we talk about last night?" she began.

"If he comes near us again," Paul growled, "I'll punch his face in."

Not a good start, Sally thought. "You know what will happen if you do that? He'll accuse you of assault. We have to be cleverer than him, Paul. We could make an official complaint against him."

"No point. He'll deny it," Paul said.

"I won't let him ruin our lives," she said.

Paul was eating with his fingers. He swallowed a mouthful, then put down the remaining piece of muffin. "What if he comes here again? Or comes to my school? I don't want him anywhere near me."

"Nor do I. I wish he wasn't here at all, but he is. That doesn't mean we have to see him. I'll talk to a lawyer. I can refuse him entry to our house, but he could demand the right to see you through a custody arrangement."

"What the...? He ignored me for six years and he thinks he can walk in here and demand to see me? He hit me! No way! I don't care what a stupid lawyer says. I won't see him."

"It's okay. I'll look into it. Just don't let him provoke you. It wouldn't surprise me if he claims I'm a bad mom and you need a father in your life. You know how devious he is. He might try to goad you, make you angry in public. Then he'll claim I'm failing to give you what you need. If you so much as shove him in public, he could say you attacked him and that might ruin your chances of a college scholarship." Sally stretched her hand across the table and took his. "He's a cruel and calculating man but he'll only succeed in messing up our lives if we let him. And we won't let him. Right?"

"Right!" Paul said.

"I'll phone the school. Make it clear they cannot allow Scott to pick you up."

"When has Dad ever allowed anyone to stop him doing what he wants?"

The thought gave Sally gut pain like indigestion. "I'll have a word with Clarke. See if he can help."

"That's not going to happen."

Paul got up and put his plate in the dishwasher. She watched her son leave the kitchen.

Just when their lives were moving up, Scott had risen from hell to drag them down with him. There was no way she was going to let him do that.

The doorbell rang. Was Scott back? Sally stood suddenly, the kitchen chair toppling backward.

"Sally? It's Clarence!"

She was so relieved that it wasn't Scott that it took her a few seconds to wonder why Clarence was on her doorstep so early. She opened the door.

"There's been a murder," Clarence said. "Joseph's neighbor, Roisin McGettigan."

SIXTEEN

Roisin McGettigan looked as if she were asleep in her bed. Her eye mask was still covering her eyes, her arms rested on the slate-gray duvet cover, the same color as the feature wall behind the chunky oak headboard. The bedroom was modern and minimalist and, except for a white bathrobe draped over a chair, free of the usual bedroom clutter. On either side of the feature wall, windows stretched from floor to ceiling to allow views of the mountains in the distance.

Dr. Lilia greeted them as they entered the bedroom. Like him, they were in a head-to-ankle coverall in white, with blue booties over their shoes.

"Perfect timing," Lilia said. He carefully removed Roisin's eye mask, bagged it, and handed it to his assistant for analysis. "See the dots around the eyes. Indicates suffocation. There's bruising around her neck."

Clarence turned away. Lilia clocked it but wasn't the type to tease someone who found the sight of a murder victim distressing, even if the body was relatively undamaged.

Lilia continued, "She fought back." He lifted Roisin's right hand. A fake nail had gone from her middle finger and there was a bruise around her wrist. "There's dirt on her hands. Soil maybe."

"Soil?"

"Give me time, Sally," he said impatiently.

She hardly dare ask the next question, but Clarke, who was in the living room with the husband, would expect her to do so. "Any idea on time of death?"

"I'll know better when I get her back to the lab, but I'd say sometime between midnight and four in the morning."

"Who found her?"

"The husband." Sally's eyes moved to the uncreased side of the bed. Lilia must have read her mind because he added, "Perhaps they sleep in separate rooms."

The spouse was always the first suspect in a murder investigation. But given this murder took place next door to Joseph's house, she suspected that the two deaths were linked.

Clarence had the pallid look of a man who was feeling queasy. Sally steered him out of the bedroom and they paused on the landing. "You okay to take notes while I talk to the husband?"

"Yes, I'm okay. It's just... dead people. They don't look like people anymore."

"How do you mean?"

"They're like waxworks. Their lightness has gone. Their soul, I guess."

"We'll find who did this. It may take time. But we'll do it together. Okay?"

He nodded and followed her downstairs. At that moment, Dr. Liz Mani, the lead forensic investigator, walked through the front door. Sally was struck by how petite she was and yet she had a powerful presence.

"Hello Dr. Mani. The victim's upstairs. Dr. Lilia is with her," Sally said.

"You must be the famous Sally Fairburn. Lovely to meet you." Mani smiled, then shook Sally's hand.

Taken aback by the flattery, Sally missed a beat before she replied, "Lovely to meet you too."

"This isn't a social gathering," Clarke growled, as he stepped out of the living room. "We have a crime to solve. Fairburn and Pew, you're with me."

Carlos sat at the edge of a three-seater sofa and chaise longue, his head of graying curly hair in his hands.

Clarke introduced them both and sat next to Carlos. Sally took the armchair. Clarence chose to stand. Clarke continued with his questioning, "You say you came home at about one-thirty a.m. and you slept in a guest room. Why was that?"

"I didn't want to wake her." He squeezed his eyes shut. "If I'd checked on her, maybe I could have saved her." His voice broke.

"Is this a normal arrangement?" Clarke asked.

"More recently, yes. We were going through a rough patch. It's not easy living and working together."

Clarke nodded. "Did you hear anyone enter or leave the house during the night?"

"No. I'd had a lot to drink. I slept through until the wake-up alarm went off."

"What time was this?"

"Six-thirty."

"What made you enter the room where Roisin was sleeping?"

"She's usually up before me. I thought she'd overslept. And besides, I needed my clothes."

"Then what happened?"

"I went in. Cracked a joke about her being a lazy bones." His voice trailed away. Again he squeezed his eyes shut, trying to stem the flow of tears that were already trickling down his nose.

"Take your time," Clarke said.

Carlos sniffed and opened his eyes. "I sat on the bed. Told her to wake up. She didn't move. I touched her arm. It was cool. Her skin looked... strange. I lifted the eye mask, checked for a pulse, called emergency services. I tried CPR." He hung his head. "I was too late."

"That's all for now, Mr. McGettigan." Clarke got up. He parted his lips to say something when Dr. Lilia entered the room.

"Detective, Sally, Clarence, you need to see this."

The three of them followed Lilia up the stairs to the primary bedroom. The duvet had been pulled back and even from the entrance to the room Sally saw dirt on the underside of Roisin's legs and feet.

"Help me turn her," he said to his assistant. With Lilia at one end and his assistant at the other, they rolled Roisin onto her side. The back of the nightie and her bare legs were streaked with mud and bits of grass.

"I think she was murdered outside and then positioned in her bed to make it look as if she were asleep."

"We should search the grounds for sign of a struggle," Clarke said, heading downstairs to direct the search.

It didn't take long. A patch of lawn near the fence that ran between the two houses was flattened. There were divots and then drag marks.

"If she was killed here, what was she doing in the yard in the small hours of the morning?" Clarence asked.

"Accosting a killer," Sally replied. She nodded at the back of the Austins' house. Some of the plywood nailed to the study's broken window now lay against the wall. "There's a good chance that Joseph and Roisin were murdered by the same person."

Clarke stepped closer to the fence. "That makes sense.

Joseph's killer returned to the scene of his crime and Roisin must have approached him."

"If only she had called nine-one-one instead, she might still be alive," Sally said.

"He must have jumped the fence. A strong person could strangle someone with their hands," Clarke said.

Sally stared at the piece of plywood. "Why did the killer risk coming back?"

"Because you were seen sniffing around the Austins' house yesterday?" Clarke proposed. "Maybe he thought we'd stopped investigating and then you turned up here and he panicked."

"I'll need forensics to examine the plywood," Sally said.

"I'll send them over when they're done here. And I'll send officers to Troy Vincent's house. I want him brought in for questioning. In the meantime, talk to the neighbors. Find out if they saw anything last night and reinterview them about the night Joseph was killed."

"Salvador Sobral has motive for both murders," Sally said.

"Start with him," said Clarke. "If anyone asks about Roisin, say it's a suspicious death but we can't say if the two deaths are connected." Clarke paused. "I think this murder was a spur-of-the-moment act to stop Roisin calling for help. The killer may strike again if he believes there are other witnesses."

Oh boy! Sally thought. This cold case had gotten way bigger and the pressure on her to solve it was huge. She looked around the crime scene, at the patrol cars, the crime scene tape, the forensics team in their white coveralls, then turned to face Sobral's house across the street. She swallowed a lump in her throat.

"You ready, Clarence?"

SEVENTEEN

Sally knocked on Salvador Sobral's door at 60 Willow Way. Roisin's murder had upped the stakes of the investigation and the pressure on Sally to solve the two murders was like a lead blanket on her shoulders. Given the murders had taken place in houses next door to each other, they had to be linked and almost certainly had been committed by the same person even though the MO was different. As Roisin's murder wasn't a burglary, Sally believed the investigation should shift toward the people living on Willow Way and that Troy Vincent, who Clarke was keen for her to reinterview, should be put on the back burner for now.

The Sobral house was the worst house on one of the best streets in the area. In dire need of a lick of paint and a new roof, it had been left empty while Sobral was in prison for identity theft. He'd been released four months ago. His partner, Justin Griess, lived with him now. Sally had reread Sobral's statement before she made this visit. Griess was working a night shift at the hospital when Joseph's murder took place. This meant that Sobral was alone that night and had no alibi. Clarke's team had looked into his finances and he was clearly struggling to make ends meet.

A man called out from the other side of the door. "Who is it?"

"Sally Fairburn and Officer Clarence Pew. I'm investigating the murder of Joseph Austin."

The door creaked open and then stopped when the security chain snapped tight. Sobral blinked at her, his brown eyes round and startled. "Show me your badges."

First Sally, then Clarence held their badges close to the gap in the door.

"May we come in?" Sally asked.

"I've told the other detectives everything I know. I've nothing more to say." Sobral shut the door.

Sally called through the door, "Mr. Sobral, I'm a fresh pair of eyes on this unsolved case. I just need a few minutes." She listened through the door. Silence. She guessed he was still standing there, waiting for them to walk away. "You saw someone on the front porch the night Joseph was killed. I'd like to talk some more about that."

"Your pals didn't believe me," Sobral shouted.

"Well, I'd like to know more about what you saw," Sally said.

Silence. "I'll talk to you. Send the uniform away."

Clarence shook his head at her.

"It's okay," she said quietly to Clarence. "Do you mind waiting?"

He hesitated then walked down the porch steps.

"Officer Pew has left," Sally called out.

She waited and almost gave up, when there was a clunk on the other side of the door and it swung open. "Come in. Hurry."

Sobral peeked up and down the street, then shut the door behind her. His black hair and eyes, brown skin, and his surname suggested he had Portuguese ancestry. His build was small and he stooped slightly, which made him look older than his twenty-nine years. His shoulder-length black hair didn't match the short brown hairs found in the Austins' house.

"Is Mr. Griess home?" His partner.

"At work. Come in."

"He's a nurse, right?"

"Yes, why?"

"Just checking the information I have is correct." She would need to come back another time to talk to Griess.

The hallway smelled damp and she noticed some black mold on the wallpaper near a stain mark on the ceiling. The décor was dated. She followed him to an original eighties-style kitchen with scuffed pine furniture and a stove that looked too old to function.

"You inherited this from your parents?" she asked.

"I didn't steal it if that's what you mean," he snapped, leaning his back against the Formica kitchen counter.

"I didn't mean that at all."

He pinched his nose. He had glasses balancing on the top of his head and they'd left red pinch marks on either side of his nose. "I'm a bit jumpy, okay? Everybody hates me around here. They stare at me like I'm an alien. If it wasn't for Justin, I don't think I could cope."

"He likes the neighborhood?"

"They're a bunch of homophobes, so no, he doesn't like it here. But he says we'd be crazy to sell now when interest rates are high and the bottom's fallen out of the real estate market. He wants us to hang on for another year although I don't think I can stand it for that long."

It occurred to Sally that if they were planning on selling up in a year's time, there wasn't so much of a motive to kill Joseph.

"I hear you work as a hospital orderly?"

"Yeah, there are not many options for an ex-con. Justin helped me apply. Without him I don't know what I'd do." He straightened his back and lifted his chin, as if he were trying to pull himself together. "Anyway, what do you want to know?"

"Can I sit?" Sally asked.

"I'd prefer it if you didn't."

He was certainly jumpy, but Sally suspected it had less to do with her arrival and more to do with how hard life after jail could be. Sally stayed standing and got out her notebook.

"Can you cast your mind back to the night of July twenty-sixth? What time did you notice someone on the Austins' front porch?"

"I've already told detectives this." He sighed. "It was about midnight. I suffer from insomnia and was watching TV, which I do most nights. Justin was working a night shift. I heard voices in the street. I don't know why, I thought maybe Justin was home early, maybe something was wrong. So I opened the front door, it was on the chain, and heard raised voices. I couldn't see much through the small gap, so I took off the chain. Across the street, Joseph had his door open and the hall light was on. He was talking to a guy who sounded upset."

"Could you hear anything they said?"

"No... well, maybe. It sounded a bit like *you can't do this,* but I could have misheard."

"Who said that? Joseph or the other guy?"

"I don't know." He scratched his forehead with his fingernails. "I suppose it must be the other guy."

"Okay, then what happened?"

"Joseph stepped aside, and the guy walked in. That's all I know."

Sobral's fingernails had left a red patch on his brow.

"Can you describe the man you saw entering the house?"

"He was just a silhouette."

"What was he wearing?"

"Pants, a hoodie maybe."

"Why do you think it was a man?"

Sobral frowned. "His voice. Definitely male."

"Did you see the intruder leave the house?"

"No, I went back to watching TV. I didn't think about it again until I saw cops the next morning and the gardener spewing into the flowerbed."

"What time did you go to bed?"

"Maybe two. I slept an hour or so, then I got up, at maybe five."

"Did Joseph get many nighttime visitors?"

"Not often."

"Did you wonder who would visit an elderly couple so late?"

"It's none of my business."

"Did you like Joseph?"

"He wasn't the nice old guy everyone makes out."

"How do you mean?" Sally asked.

"He hated us because we were gay."

"You don't think it was because of your criminal record?"

"Maybe that too. He started a campaign to force us out of our house. Got people signing a petition. He made up all this shit about me running an S&M club from our home. Calling us ungodly. Perverts. Someone left dog shit in my mailbox. My tires were slashed, that sort of thing."

"Did you report this?"

He laughed bitterly. "You think the cops are going to do anything about an ex-con complaining that his neighbors don't like him?"

He had a point. "Now Joseph's gone, has the intimidation stopped?"

"You're kidding, aren't you? That bitch kept up the hate campaign."

"Who is that?"

"Roisin. What's going on over there? Has something happened to her?"

"She's dead, that's all I can tell you at this stage."

Sobral crossed his arms. "Good riddance. And just for the record, I didn't do it."

Sobral had motive to kill Joseph and Roisin. But why would he shower in the Austins' bathroom when he could cross the street and shower at home?

"And what about Fiona?" Sally asked, "Was she involved in the campaign against you?"

"Bless her, no. Fiona stayed in the background. She loved her garden and reading books. I had the impression that Joseph managed her life. She never went anywhere without him."

Sally thanked him and left the house. As she joined Clarence in the street, she noticed Sobral furtively watching her from an upstairs window.

EIGHTEEN

Harper hesitated as she stood on the sidewalk outside Marnie's Café. Through the glass frontage she could see a group of six moms seated around a long table, their strollers around them like wagons circling their camp. The women's body language was relaxed, in a way that implied they knew one another well. Harper was the outsider. They looked so smart and lively and beautiful, and Harper was none of these things.

In his stroller, Eli banged his legs up and down. He was bored. What if he made a scene as soon as she walked in? Harper had dressed him in his newest T-shirt, pants, and jacket but her clothes were old and her newest shirt she had put on that morning was now stained with carrot juice. She couldn't meet them when she looked like this. Maybe another time?

She turned the stroller around. The coins she had saved to purchase a coffee jangled in the stroller's cupholder. Harper had risked incurring Scott's wrath when she'd bought a discounted brand at the grocery store to save the four dollars. She glanced through the café window again. Sara looked up, saw Harper outside the window, and beckoned her in.

Harper's heart felt like it swelled with happiness. She

hadn't been welcomed by anyone for a long time. Then her happiness turned to a nervous tremor. What if the other moms didn't like her? Sara left her friends and held open the glass door.

"You made it!" Sara said.

Harper wheeled her stroller over the doorstep and followed Sara to the moms' table, her cheeks flushed with shyness. Sara made the introductions and Harper smiled sweetly, doing her best to remember everyone's names, then Sara pulled over a spare chair so that Harper could sit next to her. She could now see that at the back of the café was a kids' play area and toddlers were enjoying the toys provided, while the moms relaxed.

I'm being normal, Harper thought. *This is what normal moms do.* She smiled.

"Harper is from Chicago," Sara announced. "We met in the park."

"How are you finding Franklin?" asked a woman with tumbling red hair, whose name Harper had already forgotten.

"I haven't seen much of Franklin yet. Busy settling Eli into his new home."

Did that sound reasonable, Harper wondered. She couldn't tell them the truth, that she and Eli were locked in the bathroom for the first week and then confined to the apartment for the rest.

The red-headed mom smiled. "Toddlers are such a handful." She looked at Eli who was squirming in Harper's lap. "Would he like to play with the others? We all keep an eye on them. It's safe."

Harper hesitated. Eli was all she had in the world. He was her only joy.

"I'll order a coffee, then I'll take him over to join the others."

"Sure."

It was warm inside and Harper removed her coat. The blouse rode up one arm to reveal her emaciated limb. Several of the moms seemed to notice how painfully thin she was, which made her wince. Harper carried Eli with her to the café counter, keen to get away from the penetrating stares. Eli was in a tetchy mood and he fought against her grip. He was strong and she feared dropping him. As soon as she'd ordered a small cappuccino, she walked Eli to the play area. Like an angel, Sara joined her there.

"Hey, Eli, this is Emmie. You played in the park together."

The little girl smiled shyly and held up a red brick. She had been creating a wall of different colored bricks. Eli stared at the brick, then grabbed it from her hand.

"Don't grab," Harper said.

He then threw it at the wall that Emmie was creating. There was a moment's quiet. Eli gave Emmie the kind of cruel smile Harper had seen all too often on Scott's face. Then Emmie burst into tears. Sara kneeled and hugged her child.

Harper caught the moms staring. She picked up her son and said, "Bad boy. Very bad." Then she whispered in his ear, "Why?" not expecting an answer, more because she was in shock. Harper's eyes pleaded with Sara. "I'm so sorry. He's never done that before."

This wasn't true. She'd noticed that since Scott tackled them outside the women's shelter and he'd been a seething mass of fury since, Eli had thrown more tantrums and had even tried to hit Harper with his little fists. Was he picking up on his father's aggression? Could toddlers do that?

"It's okay. Nobody's hurt."

"He's not used to sharing toys," Harper explained. "I'll settle him into the stroller." Her cheeks hot with embarrassment, she clipped Eli into his stroller and gave him a banana to eat. She didn't dare lift her eyes for fear the other moms were watching her.

"Be a good boy for me. Please, Eli. I'll take you to the park later if you're good."

Eli ignored her and focused on squishing the ripe banana between his tiny fingers.

Harper took a deep breath and returned to the table. "I don't know what's got into him," she said to nobody in particular.

"It happens," said the red-haired woman. "My Jamie loves throwing stuff. He smashed a vase the other day when he threw his toy car across the room."

Harper smiled at the woman's kindness. Her cappuccino arrived and she concentrated on sipping it. It really was good. She couldn't recall the last time she'd had one of these. Sara rejoined then at the table. Emmie was playing with another little girl, rearranging the furniture in a doll's house. Sara gave Harper a reassuring pat on the arm.

"It's all okay," Sara said.

Harper listened to Sara chat to another mom about finding the right kindergarten and how difficult it was to get kids on the waiting list. Harper hadn't even thought about kindergarten.

Harper sensed the atmosphere in the café shift. The chatter died back. Their group was the last to notice the new arrival. It was the dark uniform that caught her eye. She choked on her coffee as her eyes landed on Scott striding toward her. He had his professional smile glued to his face, but his eyes were cold.

How did Scott know where to find her? He was on duty. He should have been miles away.

"Hey, Harper. Hello, ladies." Scott gave them his most charming smile. "So sorry to take Harper away. It's a family emergency. I'm her husband, Scott." Then he looked down at Harper who had tried to make herself as small as possible. "Honey, we must go."

She looked down at her half-drunk cappuccino, but she couldn't stomach swallowing anything with Scott looming over her. Eli, in the stroller, raised his messy hands at his father, "Dada!"

Scott bent down and taking a napkin from the table, he wiped his son's fingers. The perfect father. Not that he would ever do this when they were alone.

"You never said your husband was so handsome," Sara whispered.

Harper couldn't bear the way he duped everyone. She stood on shaky legs. "Goodbye."

"See you again," Sara said.

But Harper knew that was never going to happen.

NINETEEN

Sally and Clarence spent the rest of the morning interviewing the neighbors regarding Roisin's suspicious death. It also gave them a chance to question them again about the night Joseph was murdered. Just as before, the neighbors saw nothing out of the ordinary last night. Or, if they did, they weren't willing to share it with the police. Frustrated at their lack of progress, they headed back to the Roisin crime scene.

"Forensics will soon be done here," Clarke said, as he peeled off the white coverall in the front yard. "Then they're moving on to the Austins' home, focusing on the plywood the killer pulled off the window and the side yard. I'm heading back to the station."

"Do you think the killer will come back?"

"I've thought about that. Police officers are going to watch the house day and night until we find who did this." Clarke shook his head. "I missed something. And because of that, Roisin is now dead. And who is next? If he suspects someone knows his identity, he could strike again." Clarke swore under his breath. "And on top of that, we've hit a wall with the Megan Chou case."

Without another word, Clarke walked away, got into his unmarked police car, and drove off.

"I guess he's having a bad day," Clarence said.

"Not as bad as Roisin." Sally considered Roisin's fate, how she was suffocated then dragged into the house, up the stairs, and placed in her bed. "You know, the killer must be strong and fit. He dragged or carried Roisin up the stairs."

Dr. Mani, the lead forensic investigator, called out to her, and they followed the petite woman upstairs to the bathroom. One of the forensics team was leaning into the shower cubicle, searching for fingerprints or DNA. "Looks like the killer took a shower," Mani said. "The husband says a towel is missing. The shower cubicle smells of bleach."

"Let me get this clear," Sally said. "The killer showered, even though this time there was no blood spatter?"

"Looks that way. We'll know more later," Mani replied.

Clarence and Sally stared at each other. They both saw a pattern forming.

"I'll leave you to get on with your work," Sally said. "I'm going back to the Austin house. There must be something we've missed."

This time, the Austins' house was brighter. Sally looked behind her and through the open front door she and Clarence had just entered. Early afternoon sun streamed into the house. Dust motes danced in the sunbeams.

"Where to first?" Clarence asked.

"Right here. But close the door first. I want to imagine that Sobral is telling the truth and the killer was known to Joseph."

"But he's got motive."

"Humor me." She waited for Clarence to close the house door. "Let's imagine the killer rings the doorbell. Joseph opens the door and sees somebody he knows, because he allows them into the house when it's close to midnight."

Clarence said, "Or a stranger spun him a story about his car breaking down and he doesn't have his phone so could he make a call. People fall for that line all the time."

"But Joseph's death was violent. Fueled by rage. I think the killer held a grudge against the old man." Sally set off for Joseph's study. "Joseph takes him in here. Closes the door. That's when he lunges at Joseph. There's a struggle. Perhaps that's when the window shatters. The killer overpowers Joseph, ties him up, and tortures him for the safe's passcode, then he kills him and takes everything from the safe. With me so far?"

"If he found what he wanted, why risk coming back here?"

"He left evidence behind?" Sally suggested. "Or there was something in the house that he still wanted?"

Sally took the stairs, still baffled by the bloody footprints, which the killer had seemingly made no attempt to avoid. When she reached the bedroom, she surveyed the blue tape marking where Fiona lay, the victim's head toward the night-stand where a landline phone was almost within her grasp. Then she entered the bathroom.

"The killer must have had a change of clothes with him,' she said. "He undressed, showered, dried himself, put everything he wasn't wearing into a backpack or some kind of bag, then with gloves on, he used bleach to clean as much as he could. It feels to me like he had it all planned meticulously."

"Yeah, but how is it possible to leave no DNA or fingerprints?"

"I don't know. It's highly unlikely that the forensics investigators missed a vital clue, but I guess it's possible." Sally looked around. The shower cubicle was large and had a plastic chair in it, presumably for Fiona to sit on. The bath had grab bars on the wall. The taps and the towel bar were an expensive brand.

Clarence grimaced. "I need to use the bathroom."

"Not here. I'm sorry. Use the one downstairs."

Clarence left Sally to her thoughts.

She looked at the toilet. It had been checked for fingerprints and DNA. Then she remembered how Scott used to put a hand on the wall behind the toilet when he took a piss. She never understood why and never asked but was that a typical behavior?

Behind the toilet tank was a tiled wall. The afternoon sunlight poured in through the window. It hit the porcelain bowl of the toilet and the shiny white tiles behind it. She moved closer, careful not to interrupt the light pouring in. She ran her eyes horizontally across each line of tiles, searching for a smudge. Nothing. The tiles directly above the tank had been dusted for fingerprints. Disappointed that her idea had not borne fruit, her line of sight dropped to the floor.

Then she saw it. It was crescent-shaped and so small, it was easy to miss, hidden by a pipe entering the wall. Kneeling, she inspected it.

Sally called out and waited for Clarence to come back. Sally pointed. "Does that look like a fingernail to you?"

Clarence joined her on the floor. "It's hard to tell. It could be."

With an excited flutter in her chest Sally called Dr. Mani on her cell. "I'm in the Austins' bathroom. I think I found a torn-off fingernail behind the toilet."

"I'll be with you in five. Just packing up next door."

Dr. Mani confirmed it was indeed a torn-off fingernail. "I'm embarrassed my team missed it." Mani bagged the tiny piece of evidence. "Nails are a good source of DNA. I'll make analyzing this a priority. You have my word."

TWENTY

Sally was happy to return to the station. Her feet ached and she took off her shoes and rubbed the soles of her feet. The torn-off fingernail she'd found earlier was on its way to the lab. Sally dared to hope that when they ran it through the fingerprint database, the killer's name would pop up. Of course, that would only happen if the killer's fingerprints were in the system.

Her phone beeped with a message.

A second body! They're dropping like flies. Who will be next? Come and see me if you want to talk it through.

It was from Richard Foster. He was itching to get involved. Boredom, maybe. Or his sick enjoyment of murder. She deleted the message, just as she did his last one. She was not going to speak to him or see him.

Clarence suddenly sprung up from his desk. "I think I've found something in Joseph's emails."

Sally walked around to Clarence's desk so that she could see his screen. He pointed at emails from Lisa La Cava.

Clarence continued, "She was Joseph's attorney. A month ago, he asked La Cava about getting a protection order. As far as I can tell, he hasn't been specific about the person he wanted to be protected from, but he wanted to stop someone from approaching him or his wife."

"He was afraid of someone." Sally knew exactly how that felt. She didn't want Scott coming anywhere near her or Paul. Did she need a protection order too? "What advice did La Cava give?"

"All I have are the details of an appointment he made with her to discuss it."

"I'll ask Clarke if he pursued this. Otherwise, I guess we find out if the paperwork was filed with the court. That should tell us who they wanted to be protected from."

Sally headed for the door. "Good work."

She found Clarke updating twenty or so plainclothes detectives and police officers on the Megan Chou case. There had been a development and it was all-hands-on-deck. She hovered at the back, trying not to feel envious of the huge team. She scanned the backs of their heads, hoping that Scott's would not be among them. He wasn't. She was being paranoid. There was no reason for a patrol cop to be in the homicide department. When Clarke had ended the briefing, Sally caught his eye and he led her to his office. She closed the door behind her.

"I have a question about Lisa La Cava but before that, I haven't had a chance to thank you for the message you left last night about Scott."

"I meant to tell you earlier."

"He said he's working here. Is that true?"

Clarke had been the one and only detective who believed her claim that Scott sexually assaulted Stacy Green and threatened their daughter into keeping his depraved secret. Clarke had risked his reputation and popularity to investigate that claim. Nobody liked a cop who went after another cop. When he failed to secure solid evidence—Stacy and Zelda were dead so they couldn't testify—the case against Scott was dropped and forgotten. His police record was therefore untarnished, which left Scott free to take up any law enforcement role he chose.

Clarke leaned against the edge of the desk nearest to her. "He starts tomorrow. Patrol officer."

It was as if a dark shadow loomed over Sally. He had invaded her home last night. Tomorrow he would intrude on her working life too. Scott knew how to lay on the charm. He could easily poison the other detectives against her, make out she was a jealous ex-wife. She knew how Scott operated and it terrified her how clever he was at manipulating others. Clarke continued, "He won't work homicide cases and he has nothing to do with the Austin murder."

Sally shook her head. "Couldn't you have stopped him?"

"How, Sally? I checked in with the Chicago PD. There were a couple of allegations, one made by a women's shelter, but they withdrew their complaint. The only way to stop him from working here is for you to accuse him of abusing you. You'd have to go to court. It would be your word against his because, as we know, you don't have proof he abused you. Your son would have to testify against his father for you to even stand a chance of winning and imagine the trauma of that on your son. And you too. Do you really want to go through that hell?"

"Hell is wherever Scott is."

Sally knew it was pointless to accuse Scott of abuse, especially when her abuse was emotional and psychological. There were no photos of bruises and his buddies, like Walt Jackson, would testify to his sound character and make out that Sally was the problem.

"My advice, ignore him," Clarke said. "Show everyone you're unaffected by him. Show them you're a good detective."

She nodded. But, every day at work would be like having a

scorpion on her back, poised and ready to sting. "I'll do my best. But you should know I'm getting an attorney. I have to keep Scott out of my son's life."

"Noted. Talking of lawyers, you had a question about Lisa La Cava?" Clarke asked.

"Yes. Clarence came across emails between Joseph and La Cava about a protection order. Do you know who Joseph wanted protection from?"

"No, we asked and La Cava wouldn't disclose that information."

"What about a warrant so we can access her file on Joseph and Fiona?"

"No chance. She has attorney-client privilege."

"But this person might be our killer."

"Be careful with La Cava. She's married to the mayor's brother."

Sally rolled her eyes and said sarcastically, "Well, that's just great."

The law firm La Cava Allison had a flashy reception area on the tenth floor and a list of fifteen lawyers on the wall covering business, environmental, personal, and municipal law. La Cava and Allison were the founders. Sally had phoned ahead because she didn't want to be made to wait and was pleased that Joseph's lawyer had made time for them. Clarence, in his police uniform, received a flirtatious smile from the young receptionist, which had him staring at the floor with embarrassment. For a moment, Sally wondered if Clarence had a girlfriend. He was good-looking and friendly. She imagined he'd have no problem getting a date, although being a cop tended to put off a lot of people.

Their appointment time came and went. Instead of

preparing her questions for La Cava, Sally's mind was on her own need for legal advice. Sally noted they had several lawyers who practiced family law, and child custody and access arrangements came under that banner. She pulled herself up sharply; it was ill-advised to use a law firm that was closely connected to the case. When this interview was done, she planned to find time away from Clarence and make a few calls. The last thing she wanted was to be preempted by Scott, which would put her at a disadvantage.

Five minutes later, Lisa La Cava walked them to her office in heels so high it was as if she were walking on her tiptoes. In her forties, La Cava's dark shoulder-length hair swung side-to-side as she walked, her white skirt-suit and peach top giving her a powerful yet feminine look. She sat at a dark wood desk and invited them to take the two chairs opposite.

"My brother-in-law tells me you received the Citizen Award for Valor and Service. He tells me you're a woman to watch." Sally hoped that La Cava meant it in a good way, as in watch what Sally would do next. "And here you are, a consulting detective! Congratulations!"

Sally noted how smoothly the attorney had made sure they knew that she was sister-in-law to Mayor Xavier McAllister, establishing her powerful connections before Sally had even asked a question.

"Thank you. As I mentioned on the phone, I'm investigating the murder of Joseph Austin and the suspicious death of Roisin McGettigan. I know my colleagues have spoken to you before, but we were appointed as a fresh set of eyes on a complex and terrible crime."

"Joseph's death is devastating. He was a friend, not just a long-standing client. And Fiona in a coma... It's such a tragedy. They are both lovely people. But as you will be aware, I have already told the detectives everything I can. I am also Fiona's attorney, and I cannot breach attorney-client privilege."

"I believe you've managed Joseph's legal affairs since 2007 and your correspondence seems to be entirely with Joseph. In what capacity did you act for Fiona?"

"Her will."

"I understand Fiona's will is the mirror of Joseph's. Is that correct?"

"Not exactly."

"How is it different?"

"I can't tell you."

"Fiona is unconscious. She can't help us, which is why I've come to you."

"I can't reveal the contents of her will."

Sally moved on to the reason she was there. "A month before the murder, Joseph came to you to get an anti-harassment protection order. Who was he afraid of?"

"I can't tell you that."

Sally closed her notebook. She would have to try another tactic. "May I call you Lisa?"

"Of course."

"I'd like to be honest with you and trust that you'll respect that this is a homicide investigation."

Clarence gave her a wary glance but said nothing. La Cava nodded.

"I took this case, not because I want to rejuvenate my policing career. I took it because an old man was beaten to death in his own home and his wife is in a critical condition. My colleague and I abhor cowards who invade the homes of the elderly and torture and kill them. We want justice for Joseph and we hope that if Fiona recovers, she will at least know that her husband's killer was caught. We also want justice for Roisin McGettigan."

"You believe the cases are linked?" La Cava asked.

"It's too early to say but given that Joseph and Roisin were neighbors, it's possible the two cases are connected. Lisa, I need your help. You knew the Austins well. You have access to their legal documents, in among what you know could be a clue that might enable us to solve this case."

La Cava stood up and turned her back on them so she could stare out the window at the city skyline. Finally, she spoke.

"You asked who Joseph was afraid of. I can only *surmise* that this person would upset his wife. He was very protective of her."

Sally took the use of the word "surmise" as La Cava's way of avoiding directly breaching attorney-client confidentiality. Sally opened her notebook again.

"Can you surmise why this person would upset Fiona?"

"I can only *guess* that he was from her past."

Sally noticed La Cava identified the person as male.

Clarence spoke up. "Is it possible that Joseph was afraid of what this person might reveal?"

La Cava looked surprised at Clarence. "You're a perceptive young man. It might have been something like that, but that's all I'm willing to say."

"Can you tell us why Joseph didn't go ahead with the protection order?" Sally asked.

"I believe he found another way to deal with the situation. Now, if you don't mind, I have a client to see."

"Just a few more questions. Please."

La Cava nodded.

"Do you know why they never had children?" Sally asked.

"I don't. I *imagine* one of them was unable to do so."

"How do you *imagine* they were able to purchase a house for more than two million dollars in December 2006? I believe when Joseph retired, he was earning eighty-five thousand per year and Fiona wasn't working. Not many people on that salary can afford to buy and maintain a house worth two-and-a-half million."

"I wasn't their attorney back then."

"Please hazard a guess."

"I can only *guess* that they might have inherited the money. I believe there was talk about a relative on Fiona's side."

Sally hadn't seen any mention of an inheritance in the case notes.

"Who was their attorney in 2006?"

"No idea."

"Do you happen to know if Fiona has a separate bank account?"

"That I do not know. All monetary transactions that passed my desk were done from their join account."

Sally made a note to search for a separate bank account for Fiona. Was the killer somehow linked to Fiona's inheritance?

La Cava stood and showed them back to the reception area and Sally warmly thanked her, before asking, "Can I have a private word?"

Sally asked Clarence if she could meet him in the building's lobby. He hesitated then took the elevator.

"I'm looking for a family lawyer. Can you recommend someone, not from your firm, of course? There might be a conflict of interest."

"That's not an issue. We don't share details of cases here. Anna Elkington is our family law expert." La Cava handed Sally a business card with Elkington's contact details. "I'll tell her to expect your call."

Sally had wanted a recommendation outside the firm, but she took the card anyway. One way or another she needed to know her legal position regarding Scott and Paul.

She joined Clarence in the lobby and together they walked out onto the street.

"She was more cooperative than I thought she'd be," Clarence said.

"Yes, she was. So far the investigation has mainly been

about Joseph and why he was murdered. Maybe it's time we focused on Fiona. And Roisin."

"Back to the station?" Clarence asked.

"Their bank is a block away. I want to drop in on the manager. I'm curious about the inheritance that La Cava hinted at."

TWENTY-ONE

The Peakhurst branch of the Bank of Franklin was on High Street. Peter Bolster, bank manager, confirmed that he was unaware of a large sum of money entering the Austins' joint account and, as far as he knew, Fiona did not have a personal account.

"When there's a sudden influx of large sums," he said, "we contact the client and offer options to maximize the interest on their account. Or, if they wish to purchase a property, such as an investment property, we offer the services of our mortgage manager. There were no such triggers on the Austins' account."

They left the bank with Sally wondering if La Cava had been wrong about the inheritance.

"Fiona must have an account at another bank, right? How do we find it?" Clarence said, as they got into their car.

"That's a good question," Sally said. "I'll find out."

"Where to next?" Clarence asked from the passenger seat.

"Back to the station," Sally said, turning the key in the ignition. Her phone rang. It was Clarke. A patrol car had spotted Troy Vincent at his house. "Get over there now. Officers Dennis and Nunn will accompany you."

"Yes, sir."

———————

Sally and Clarence pulled up behind the patrol car that was parked near enough to watch Troy's house. Sally asked Dennis to stay with the vehicles and watch the front of the house should Troy try to run. Nunn was to accompany her and Clarence. This time, Sally was determined not to be duped. The three of them headed up the street They had almost reached Troy's house when a woman yelled from inside the house.

"You piece of shit!" she said, furious. "Give it back!"

The front door swung open, and Troy, in black T-shirt and jeans and with a chunky gold chain around his neck, stomped out, followed by a woman with straggly hair and piercings in her eyebrow, nose, and lower lip. Sally recognized the woman as Angie Williams, the girlfriend. Troy's step faltered when he saw the two cops in uniform and Sally, with her badge held up.

"Police. Stay where you are."

Angie shouted, "What the hell do you want?"

In Troy's hand was a delicate gold chain with a small blue gem. Sally was too far away to be certain, but a similar necklace had been stolen from Bert Gonzales.

Troy suddenly bolted to his Yukon in the driveway. Sally instinctively ran at him, as did Clarence who was a few seconds behind her. Troy locked the door. The powerful engine roared into life and reversed so fast that Sally, Clarence, and Nunn had to dive out of the way. The wing mirror clipped Sally's shoulder. She spun and fell to the ground.

"Ouch!"

Angie ran diagonally across the front yard to avoid the three officers and dived into an older-model Toyota Camry and set off after Troy. Officer Dennis, who had watched the proceedings from the patrol car screeched to a stop outside the house, where they all piled in.

"Follow them," Sally said, and Dennis set off, the sirens blaring, the lights flashing.

Dennis was clearly an experienced high-speed driver and it didn't take long for him to catch up with Angie.

At the end of South Trenton Street was a set of traffic lights. Angie ran the red light. Dunn slowed but continued across the intersection. Sally gripped the base of the seat. They made it safely to the other side but Angie was nowhere to be seen.

"Where did she go?" Sally asked.

"This road goes to Hunter Valley. Loads of pawn shops there," Dunn said.

"Look!" said Clarence. "That's Troy's Yukon ahead."

Dunn accelerated. In minutes they were in Hunter Valley. Canal Street was lined with cheap burger joints, pawn shops, Middle Eastern food shops, rug sellers, and discount stores.

"There!" Sally said, pointing out Troy's Yukon parked on the side of the road. "Kill the siren and lights, will you?"

Dennis did as he was asked. "And look who's heading up the sidewalk? That's Angie Williams."

"Pull in here," Sally said and they came to a halt.

Angie must have taken a shortcut. She strode in the direction of Patel's Jewelry & Loan, which had bars on the windows and a reinforced steel door. The sign declared that it specialized in jewelry. They watched as Angie pressed a buzzer and the door opened, slamming shut behind her.

"Let's go," Sally said. "Nunn and Dennis, you take the back. Clarence, we'll take the front."

Sally and Clarence jogged across the street and Sally pressed the buzzer of the pawn shop. A surveillance camera was pointed straight at her and she held her badge up high. The door opened with a heavy clank. The shop was musty and cluttered with pawned goods. Sally caught a flash of Troy dashing behind the counter, shoving the shop owner out of the way and disappearing. Angie took a second or two longer to register Sally's and Clarence's arrival and then hurled a mantelpiece clock at them.

The shop owner tried to stop her but he was too late. Sally and Clarence ducked. The clock smashed into a Perspex display case, and then shattered and toppled to the floor. In the chaos, Angie ran past them and out of the front door.

"Oh, no you don't," Sally muttered and gave chase.

Clarence was hot on her heels.

Outside, Angie darted across the road, then ran into an alley.

Sally dodged the traffic, then sprinted down the alley. The sun was in her eyes and she only saw the metal trash can lid swinging at her at the last second. Sally instinctively raised an arm to protect her head. The lid hit the side of her arm, and she lost her footing on the slimy asphalt. Sally fell sideways, her hip connecting with the hard surface first, then a hand, which landed in a greasy puddle. Old cardboard food packaging floated in the filthy water.

She yelped in shock. Angie dropped the lid. It crashed to the ground and rolled. Angie then threw open the rear door to a restaurant and went inside.

Sally hastened to stand up, wiping her filthy hand on her pants. Sally cursed because she hadn't seen the attack coming but despite her throbbing hip and sore arm, she followed Angie through the restaurant door. This time she was more careful. Opening the door slowly, she heard the clank of metal woks and the aroma of Thai spices. Sally stepped into a small kitchen. Two men were cooking over gas burners. One of the cooks looked her way.

"No, you can't come in here." He tried to shoo Sally away.

"I'm police," Sally said. "A woman ran through here. Where did she go?"

The cook pointed to the front of the shop. "That way. Took a right."

Sally dodged tables of inquisitive customers and left the restaurant. She looked up and down the busy sidewalk. There was no sign of Angie but Sally went right as the cook had said. She used her radio to tell Clarence where she was. After a few minutes it became obvious that Sally had lost the trail. Trying to catch her breath, she leaned forward, taking in gulps of air.

"Damn it!" she said.

She could only hope that Dennis and Nunn were having more luck. Heading her way was a dejected-looking Clarence. "You okay?" he asked. "Saw her hit you with the trash can lid."

"A bit sore."

He radioed the other officers.

Dennis answered. "Lost him. And you?"

"The same. Damn, those two are slippery," Clarence said.

Five minutes later, they were back at the pawn shop. Sally bagged a gold necklace with a single sapphire, which would be checked for fingerprints. It matched the necklace stolen from Bert Gonzales. The security camera inside the shop clearly showed Troy Vincent handing it to the pawn shop owner.

"Looks like we've found Bert's thief," Sally said. "And this gives us probable cause for a warrant. With any luck, the search will establish if Troy was responsible for Joseph's death too."

"I'm not holding my breath on that one," Clarence said.

"Me neither. Did you see the mess in their house? They're not the kind of criminals to bother to shower at the crime scene." Sally sniffed. "Do I stink of garbage?"

"Yeah, a little."

TWENTY-TWO

At the FPD office, Sally changed into a spare set of clothes, which she kept in her desk drawer. Her arm already had a green bruise, as did her hip, but it was just bruising, nothing to worry about. Then she made a beeline for Clarke's office, keen to fill him in on the news about Troy Vincent. Clarence was busy preparing the affidavit for a search warrant.

Male voices reached her from the main homicide room. Laughter too. Had there been a breakthrough on the Megan Chou case? The laughter was infectious, and Sally smiled, uplifted by the idea of their success. Clarke's team worked long hours and were constantly criticized by the media for not instantly arresting the killer. They deserved a break in this high-pressure case. Entering the room, she saw that some, but not all, of the detectives were gathered around a desk, their torsos a thick wall. Clarke was in his office at the far end, his door shut, head down. If they'd had a breakthrough surely Clarke would be with his detectives?

Detective Lin saw Sally and got up from her desk quickly, cutting Sally off as she headed straight for Clarke's office. Lin didn't look happy, like the others. She looked worried.

"Sally," Lin said, her voice low. "Scott's here."

Sally froze midstride. Clarke had worked with Lin on the investigation into Scott's possible assault of Stacy Green. Lin knew that Scott's presence there would be distressing for Sally. Sally had an overwhelming sensation that she was sinking, that there was nothing beneath her feet. She instinctively reached out for Lin's shoulder. Despite Lin's biker boots and the masculine way she dressed, she was eight inches shorter than Sally and had a delicate frame. Lin staggered.

"It's okay, Sally. He'll be gone in a second."

Sally turned her head and at that moment the wall of male detectives opened to reveal Scott, smiling as he spoke, his hand gestures big, just as he'd always done when he told a funny story. Scott, the funny man. Scott, everybody's pal. Scott, who'd never hurt a fly.

The detectives guffawed at Scott's punchline.

"Good to have you back," said one, slapping Scott on the back.

"Good to be back, my friend," Scott said, grinning.

The gathering shifted and through the gap Scott saw Sally staring. His smile turned into a smirk of triumph.

Scott said to the detective nearest him, "Look out. The ex is staring daggers."

The four men with Scott swiveled and looked Sally's way. This was how it would be, Sally realized. He had always belittled her when she was a cop. Then he had turned people against her, making out she was a bad mom, that she refused to help Zelda when she was depressed. The point of his dropping into homicide was to show her that there was nowhere she could avoid him. To show her his power to manipulate people. He was the ultimate actor. He could fake almost any emotion. He could win people over. But it was all an act designed to fulfill a purpose and that purpose always revolved around what he wanted.

"Don't let him get to you," Lin whispered.

Only then did Sally realize that she was still holding on to Lin's shoulder. She let go.

Scott lifted a hand and gave her a little wave.

Bile rose up in Sally's throat, filling her mouth with a bitter taste.

Sally couldn't draw her eyes away from him. She should walk away and knock on Clarke's door, as she had planned. She should stay calm. But she wanted to scream across the room that he was a disgrace to the uniform, tell him to leave her and Paul alone. Just his presence clouded her mind. She felt outranked by his charisma, which he turned on and off like a tap, and outwitted by an expert of deception. Sally couldn't even fake indifference to Scott's presence.

"Come on," Lin said. "He'll get his just desserts one day."

Will he? Sally doubted it.

She dragged her gaze away and walked awkwardly the length of the department, with Lin at her side.

"Did you know he remarried?" Lin asked, keeping her voice down.

Sally's gut twisted some more. "I feel sorry for her. Her life must be hell."

Lin knocked on the door and Clarke waved them in. Lin shut the door behind them. Sally sat heavily in the nearest chair.

"I'm sorry, Sally," Clarke said. "I'm powerless to stop this."

"He's a monster. A monster in a cop's uniform. He'll do it again. Hurt another girl." Sally thought about his new wife and if she might be one of his victims.

"And if he does, we'll catch him this time. In the meantime, ignore him."

Clarke needed to know that she could do her job and Sally wanted to stay on the Austin case. "Yes, boss."

Lin said, "If you ever need to get things off your chest, come find me."

"I will, thank you."

Lin left the office.

"Give me an update."

Sally tried to switch off the turmoil of emotions and switch to using her head. She briefed him on what La Cava had hinted at in their conversation. "La Cava suggested that Fiona inherited the money they used to buy their house. I have a feeling this case may not be about Joseph. It's about Fiona."

"Be careful about following feelings, Sally, but it's a good line of inquiry to pursue. Double-check the printed documents the team took from the house. They're at the evidence storage facility."

TWENTY-THREE

The evidence storage facility at Port Mawsby had surveillance cameras and a security guard twenty-four hours a day. Police officers had to show their badge to a camera before an electronic gate opened and then they had to sign in. Anything removed from the evidence storage lockers was noted by the guard. There were two boxes relating to the Austin case. The security guard, a woman with a grumpy disposition, hardly made eye contact and handed Sally a piece of paper with the number 251B on it. She unlocked the door to the evidence storage, then as soon as Sally was through, she slammed it shut, locking it behind her.

The warehouse was huge and the aisles of shelving stretched into the dark recesses of the air conditioned building. The aisle Sally wanted was number 251, then she needed to find slot B. The guard said there were two plastic boxes stored that related to the Austin case. Sally could find only one. Taking the lid off the box, she found it contained the clothes Joseph had worn when he died, tied inside a plastic bag. The collar and shoulders of a cotton bathrobe were covered in blood, as was the cord used to bind his hands. The slippers, she noted, were size eight. The footprints throughout the house were size ten.

Also in a small evidence bag was the single hair found beneath Joseph's fingernail. Separately bagged were the two hairs found on the bathroom floor. The assumption was that the hairs belonged to the killer. A broken and blood-smudged pair of reading glasses were also bagged. She inspected a pack of Marlboro Gold Pack cigarettes. There was a set of car keys. That was all.

The missing box held the evidence relating to Fiona Austin. Why wasn't it there? Sally carried the box to the electronic gate that separated her from the security guard who was watching a video on her phone.

Sally called through the wire mesh, "Ma'am, I could only find one box. Has the other been removed?"

The guard sighed and paused the movie she was watching. She got up and let Sally through the heavy mesh door, which clunked shut behind her. Back at her computer, the guard pulled up a list of contents.

"Nah, definitely two boxes. Oh, hold up a minute. One box was taken away this morning. That was early. Seven-twelve a.m. I don't start my shift until eight a.m. That would have been Fernando. He did the night shift. And looky here. You signed it out."

"Let me see," Sally said.

Sure enough, it was her electronic signature. And yet she hadn't signed out a box. This was her first visit to the warehouse ever.

"I didn't take it. Can you check the CCTV?"

"The cameras cover the entrance. Not in here, okay?"

"That'll do."

At 7:07 a.m. the camera picked up a person in a police uniform. The hat and the fact he or she kept their head down meant there was no clear view of the person.

"That isn't me. I don't have a police officer's uniform."

Sally had a good idea who it was, but she wasn't going to say it out loud. Only Clarke could deal with such a serious issue.

There could be only one reason why Scott would take the evidence and forge her signature. He wanted her to fail to solve the case and in doing this he'd make her look careless. At the very least, she had to make sure that Clarke knew that she wasn't the one who removed it.

"I'd like a copy of the footage."

TWENTY-FOUR

Sally put the evidence box in the trunk of her car. She was shaken by the discovery of Scott's deceit and took a moment to decide what to do next. Scott was out to get her and he wouldn't give a damn that he was interfering with a homicide investigation. He never cared about anyone but himself.

She thought back to her toxic marriage to Scott and how he always got his way. If she was reluctant to sign a document, which Scott was pressuring her to sign, he had no qualms about forging her signature.

"I don't need you, Sally. See?" he'd gloat.

On the rare occasion she had stood up to him, he made her suffer. Sometimes it was a steely silence for a week until she could bear it no longer and begged for forgiveness. She recognized now how weak she had been, but arguing with him was pointless. He made her feel that she was always in the wrong.

Sally came to the decision that the sooner her boss knew about the missing evidence, the better. She left him a message. Even if Clarke believed that she didn't remove it, rumors would spread that she had misplaced crime scene evidence: Scott would see to that.

She then called Clarence. At least he had good news. The judge had signed off on the warrant. Sally asked him to get a search team together and she would meet them at Troy's house.

———

Two hours later, the search team had bagged enough evidence to send Troy Vincent to prison for a long time. Not only were there items from the Bert Gonzales robbery, including Bert's trilby, but there were also goods from three other burglaries. It would take days for the forensics team to go through everything they'd found, but so far there wasn't anything that obviously linked Troy to the murders of Joseph Austin or Roisin McGettigan.

It was getting dark by the time Sally called it a night. Clarke returned her earlier call, and, to her relief, he was happy to be updated on their progress by phone. First up, however, she filled him in on the missing evidence box and how Scott knew how to forge her signature.

"Leave that with me. I'll look into it. I don't want you getting distracted."

"It's Scott, sir. He wants me to fail."

"That may be the truth, but I can't go round accusing him. As I said, I'll look into it."

Sally had to bite her tongue. Taking a big breath, she informed Clarke about the search of Troy Vincent's house and the stolen goods they'd found, which linked him to at least three violent robberies. "And there's an APB out for his arrest."

"Good," said Clarke. "That ticks the boxes on the violent robberies. Congratulations. But anything to link Troy to Joseph and Roisin?"

"Not yet, sir. It'll take days to go through all the items found in his house."

"I don't want you distracted by this, Sally. I'll allocate two of my detectives to the pursuit of Troy Vincent. I only want you involved if evidence is found that Troy killed Joseph and Roisin. You hear me?"

Sally was disappointed. This was her first win, and it was being handed to some other detectives. "Sir, I'd like to interview Troy when he's brought in."

"I can arrange that, but only in relation to Joseph, Fiona, and Roisin." She reluctantly agreed. Clarke continued, "I hear Angie Williams hit your arm and you fell. If you're hurt, go see a doctor."

"I'm good, sir. Just a few bruises." *And I'll be sleeping on my left side, tonight,* she thought, given her bruises were on the right.

"Go home, Sally. Rest. We'll talk more in the morning."

TWENTY-FIVE

September 9, 2016

Sally was too sore to go on her morning run. A hot shower helped to loosen up her stiff limbs, and she used a cream to reduce the pain and inflammation. Maybe she was too old for this gig? The past two days had been intense, not just because of the murders she was trying to solve but also because Scott was doing all he could to destabilize their lives.

As she drove into the city she made an impromptu decision to drop into the hospital where Fiona Austin was in a coma. Fiona was a mystery; her life was extremely private. No kids. No job. A reclusive life in a big house. She might be the key that unlocked the case. Sally wanted to feel a little closer to the victim. And besides, it might help Fiona's recovery to have some company, other than the cop guarding her.

Sally let Clarence know where she was going and urged him to follow up with the forensics lab on the fingernail.

North Franklin Hospital was one of the largest hospitals in the city and had a reputation for offering the best neurosurgeons and neurological care. Fiona Austin had been recently moved out of an intensive care unit and into a room on a ward equipped to deal with head injuries and comas. As Sally had been advised, a police officer sat outside the room and Sally showed him her police badge.

"You can't speak to her. She's in a coma," the male officer said.

"That's no problem. I'm just going to sit with her. Do you want to take a break?"

He looked delighted and ducked off to the cafeteria.

Sally wasn't sure what to expect but when she quietly entered Fiona Austin's room, she felt a rush of anger toward this old woman's attempted killer. Fiona's skinny arms rested on the sheet and her wispy gray hair lay on the pillow. She looked so fragile. How could anyone attack a defenseless old woman? There was a drip keeping her hydrated. From Fiona's nose was a feeding tube and she had a breathing tube in her mouth. She was unnaturally still. No fluttering eyelids, no twitching fingers. She had been like this for six weeks. The doctors were pleased that her fractured clavicle was healing well, but even though the swelling on the brain had subsided, there had been no signs of Fiona coming out of her coma.

Sally had seen the crime scene photos of the back of Fiona's bloody head, her bruised cheekbone and eye socket, as well as the broken clavicle caused by her hitting the floor. Just the thought of what Fiona had been through made her determined to solve the case.

There was a chair in the corner of the room. Sally moved it so that she could sit right next to Fiona.

"Hello, Fiona. I don't know whether you can hear me, but my name's Sally Fairburn and I'm a consultant for the Franklin Police Department. I've been brought in as a fresh pair of eyes on your case. I want to find who did this to you." Sally paused.

She didn't want to mention Joseph. If and when Fiona awoke, she might not know that her husband was dead. How much of what had happened in the study did Fiona overhear? Even if she did know about her husband's murder, what would be the point of reminding her now? Sally took Fiona's hand, holding it gently, fearful that such delicate bones could so easily snap.

"I wish you could talk to me. I'm sure you'd be able to help me find who did this. But it's okay. You need time to sleep and recover, let your body and brain heal." Sally tried to remember the color of Fiona's eyes. A pale green, Sally recalled from the case file. "You have a lovely home, and what an incredible view from your bedroom, across the neighborhood and the harbor. I'm not surprised that you didn't want to give up that lovely view, but those flights of stairs must have been difficult to manage."

Sally studied the old woman's face, her translucent skin, a couple of long hairs on her chin. Did Fiona wear glasses? Did she have a hearing aid? She stood over the woman and looked from side to side: no hearing aid. If she was hard of hearing, she might not be able to hear Sally. Was she wearing one when the home invader struck?

Sally tenderly placed Fiona's hand on the sheet and poked her head out of the door. A nurse was wheeling a machine down the corridor.

"Excuse me, I'm from the PD. Does Fiona Austin usually wear a hearing aid?"

"I'm not sure. I can check for you."

"That would be great. I'll be in here." Sally shut the room door and settled back into her chair. "I have one child, Paul, he's fifteen but if you were to meet him, you'd probably think he was twenty. He's everything to me and I'm so proud of him for coping with the tough times he's been through." Sally felt a lump in her throat. "I had a daughter. Zelda. She passed away when she was thirteen. I miss her every day. I visit her grave every week and we talk. Well, to be honest, I talk and imagine how she would respond."

There was a knock on the door and it opened. The nurse she'd found in the corridor poked her head in. "Yes, she does normally wear a hearing aid. We removed everything that might get in the way of our treatment."

"Can unconscious patients hear what we say?"

"Potentially, but I don't know for sure. Maybe ask the doctor?"

"Can you ask the doctor if she can have her hearing aid back? At the moment she must be in a world of silence. If she could hear people around her, it might help her come back to us."

"I can ask."

The nurse closed the door behind her. Then Sally heard the nurse say, "No, you can't go in there. No visitors."

"I just want to see her," a man said.

"I'm very sorry. She's under police protection."

"I don't see any cops. Please, I just want to see if she's okay."

Sally released her hold on Fiona's hand and threw open the door. A man with pale brown hair and an upright posture stared at Sally in shock.

"I'm Sally Fairburn, Franklin PD. And you are?"

"It doesn't matter."

The man turned and walked quickly away.

"Sir, may I have your name?"

The man kept walking. From the brief glance she got of him, Sally guessed he was early fifties and fit. "Stop right there!"

The man picked up the pace and ran out of the ward. Sally wanted to give chase, but Fiona was not to be left alone.

"Contact security," she told the nurse. "I want him stopped."

The nurse hurried away.

Sally shut the room door and stayed with Fiona. She would not let any harm come to her. When the cop returned from the cafeteria, she learned that he'd been alerted to the intruder and attempted to stop him. But Fiona's mystery visitor had got away.

TWENTY-SIX

Sally walked stiffly into the incident room and found Clarence on the phone, laying on the charm.

"Thank you, Tammy. I owe you." He put down the receiver and beamed a smile at Sally, looking very pleased with himself.

"Why, Clarence, who were you flirting with?" Sally asked, teasing him.

"Tammy works at the courthouse. She's a friend. And she's told me whose name was on the protection order La Cava prepared."

"So, it reached the courts?"

"But was never presented. Joseph changed his mind at the last minute."

Sally winced at her sore hip as she lowered herself into her chair. "Don't keep me in suspense. Who is it?"

"Niall Pickerd. He moved here from Atlanta in July."

Two months ago. "Good work, Clarence. Did Tammy give you an address?"

"Yep. I also did a search on him while chatting to Tammy. He's fifty-two, a personal trainer and teaches boxing."

"Photo?" Clarence turned his laptop screen so that Sally

could see it. "You know, that could be the man who tried to see Fiona earlier this morning."

"He was at the hospital?" Clarence said, sounding concerned.

"Yes." She stood. "Let's find out what Niall Pickerd wants with Fiona Austin."

Niall Pickerd's dingy one-bedroom condo on Lakeside Avenue faced the parking lot and not the lake. It was probably one of the cheaper units. When he opened the door and he saw Clarence in uniform, his expression hardened.

He was muscular and wiry with a crooked nose, and Sally recognized him instantly.

"I'm Detective Fairburn. This is Officer Pew. I saw you at the hospital." *Running from me*, she thought. "I just want to ask some questions."

"You've got the wrong person."

"Mr. Pickerd, you tried to see Fiona Austin. You sounded worried about her. We've been assigned to find the person who put her in a coma and killed Joseph. May we come in?"

"I've got nothing to say without a lawyer."

"We can take you to the station and formally interview you with a lawyer present if you wish. But what will the neighbors think when we escort you from this condo?"

He swore under his breath and opened the door wide. "Make it quick. I gotta go to work."

Pickerd sat heavily on a dining chair and rubbed the top of his scalp with his hand. There was no couch. Just a set of four cheap dining chairs and a table.

"Can I call you Niall?" Sally asked.

"Call me what you like."

"Niall, what is your relationship with Fiona Austin?"

"That's private."

"This is a murder investigation, Niall, and your cooperation would be appreciated. Where were you on the night of July twenty-sixth?" Sally asked.

"I wasn't anywhere near Willow Way, okay?"

"How do you know I'm referring to Willow Way?"

He shook his head. "No comment."

"Okay, where were you the night of July twenty-sixth?"

"I can't remember."

"Try."

Pickerd slid a hand into his jeans pocket. Sally saw Clarence's fingers move to his gun and rest there. Pickerd pulled out his phone and checked his diary. "At a bar."

"Which bar?"

"The Crazy Horse."

"When did you arrive and leave?"

"I don't know."

"Try."

"I don't know. Maybe eight to eleven p.m."

"Where were you after that?"

"In bed. And before you ask, I was alone."

Therefore, Pickerd didn't have an alibi.

"Have you ever been to fifty-nine Willow Way?"

Again, he sighed. He'd already given away that he knew where Fiona and Joseph lived. She could see his eyes darting around as he made up his mind how to respond. "Yes, but I didn't go in."

"When was this?"

"July some time."

"When in July?"

"First week, I think. What does it matter? I didn't go in."

"Why didn't you go in?"

"Joseph didn't want me to."

"How do you know Joseph Austin?"

"That's private."

Sally decided to try a different approach. "Why did you move from Atlanta to Franklin?"

"No comment."

Clarence piped up. "Sir, refusing to answer questions makes you look guilty. Just tell us why you came to Franklin."

Pickerd scratched his scalp, making the skin red through his short hair. "You won't understand."

Sally noticed that one of his ears was frayed at the outer edge. With his crooked nose, it was clear he'd taken a battering in the boxing ring.

"Try me," Sally said.

He shook his head.

"Okay, I'll tell you what I think," Sally said. "You moved here because of Joseph and Fiona. Am I right?"

"No comment."

"They had something you wanted, and they wouldn't give it to you?"

"Next you're going to say that I burglarized their house."

"And did you?" Sally asked.

"I already told you, no! All I wanted to do was see her. Tell her I forgive her." His eyes widened when he realized he'd let the cat out of the bag.

"Forgive her for what?"

He hesitated. "Abandoning me."

Sally thought back to La Cava's comment about the couple not having children and that possibly one of them was infertile. Was that person Joseph? "Is Fiona your mother?"

Pickerd ran a finger across his stubbly upper lip. "Yes."

"You were adopted by a family in Atlanta?" Sally guessed.

"Yes."

"And you confronted Joseph with this news?"

"Yes."

"Where did you confront Joseph?" Sally asked.

"On their front porch."

"What happened then?" Sally asked.

"I shouted her name to get her attention, but she didn't come to the door, then the old coot said he'd call the cops. I couldn't risk him doing that, so I left."

"Did you try again?"

"Hell, yeah! I'd uprooted my whole life to find her. I wrote to her. He must have intercepted the letter because I didn't get a reply. She's my mom! I can't believe she'd ignore it. I phoned the house, but Joseph always answered. When that failed, I waited outside their house, hoping he'd go out without her. But he never did. One time he was reversing the car out of the parking garage and Fiona was with him. Before I could tap on her window, he sped away. The next day I heard from some snarky lawyer who told me never to go near them again or they'd file some kind of protection order against me."

"And?"

"I told the lawyer where to stick it."

"The protection order wasn't filed. Do you know why?"

Pickerd looked down and drew his thin lips together.

Sally tried again. "Did you agree to stay away from Fiona?"

Silence.

A thought popped into Sally's head. "Did Joseph incentivize you to stay away?"

He shut his eyes for a few seconds, then opened them. "I wish I'd never taken the money."

"How much did he pay you?"

"Twenty grand. It was exactly the sum I needed to buy into a boxing club I had my eye on. How he knew that, I don't know."

His lawyer must have done some snooping around to discover which boxing club Pickerd was interested in.

"Joseph isn't your father. Am I right?"

He nodded, his eyes on the floor.

"And you were at the hospital yesterday because you wanted to see Fiona?"

He looked up then. "I just wanted to know she was okay. I tried so many times, but there was always a cop outside her door. I thought that maybe I'd be lucky, and the cop would take a break some time."

"Did you enter their house about midnight on July twenty-sixth?"

"No!"

"Where were you on the night of Wednesday, September seventh?" The night Roisin McGettigan was murdered.

He scrolled though his phone's calendar. "Must have been here, watching TV."

"Can anyone verify that?"

"No."

"I'd like to take your fingerprints and DNA. I have a kit in the car. There's no need to go to the station. Do you consent?"

"No!"

"Did you kill Joseph Austin because he wouldn't let you meet your mom?"

"No! And if I find who hurt her, I'll kill them."

TWENTY-SEVEN

In the homicide department kitchen, Sally made herself a mint tea and then went back to her office. Two of Clarke's detectives watched her walk by and their looks weren't friendly. They were Scott's buddies and it was likely that he'd shared with them the news that Sally had apparently signed out and then lost an evidence box.

Sally gritted her teeth and hurried on. It was a relief to shut the incident room door. First on her list was to call Dr. Lilia.

"Any news on the McGettigan autopsy?"

"She's scheduled for this morning at eleven," said Lilia.

"I'll be there."

Next on her list was Dr. Mani.

"Any news on the fingernail from the Austins' bathroom?" Sally asked.

"Sally, please be patient. Have you any idea how many bagged items and prints were taken from the McGettigan house yesterday? And also from the plywood on the Austins' study window? We're working as fast as we can. I'd say Monday at the earliest."

That wasn't what she wanted to hear but she would have to live with it.

Clarence looked up from his laptop screen. "I'm trying to locate the adoption agency. Niall was born in 1964. Franklin was a small town back then. There can't have been many adoption agencies at that time." He did a search online. "Looks like there were two. I'll give them a call."

While he did that, Sally updated their whiteboard with Roisin McGettigan's murder and added Niall Pickerd as a suspect for both murders. Her eyes wandered to the photo of Troy Vincent, which reminded her to check in with Clarke about him. She hadn't received a call, so she guessed that Troy was still on the run.

Clarence was on the phone with a woman called Valerie Rose and once again he was using his charm to persuade her to reveal if the Catholic Church Adoption Agency of Franklin had placed Fiona Austin's baby with a family in 1964. It was to be expected that such information would be highly confidential.

"Have you been following the Joseph Austin murder case on the news? And his wife, Fiona, in a coma?" Clarence asked Valerie.

Sally listened in. Would Valerie break protocol?

It seemed not. Clarence thanked Valerie and ended the call.

"I tried, but she wouldn't tell me. Suggested we try the state adoption records and search for Niall's birth certificate."

"At least she tried to help," Sally said.

She caught a glimpse of Clarke walking by their room. Sally ducked into the corridor.

"Sir?"

Clarke turned. He looked exhausted. "Yes?"

"We have a new suspect. Niall Pickerd who claims to be Fiona's son and had an altercation with Joseph early in July." Sally filled him in.

His face brightened. "Good. Keep up the good work."

"Any news on Troy Vincent?"

"Ah, I meant to tell you. He's in custody. Been charged with three counts of assault and robbery including Bert Gonzales. He denied Joseph's and Roisin's murders. We're waiting for forensics to come back, but so far it looks as if he's telling the truth about the murders."

Sally blinked rapidly. "Sir, you said I could be present at his interview."

"No point wasting your time on burglaries. If evidence comes to light that puts him anywhere near Joseph or Roisin on the nights they died, I'll tell you."

"But sir, it was my arrest." She knew she sounded whiney, but it was her first one in her new role.

"Yes, and you did good. But I want you a hundred percent focused on this case."

"Are you saying that Troy Vincent is not a suspect anymore?" She tried not to let her voice reveal her annoyance. It was Clarke who had insisted she pursue Troy when Sally had been keen to pursue other suspects.

"For now, focus on the other suspects."

Sally balled her fists and stifled a yell.

Once again, Sally and Clarence were at the Forensic Pathology Unit, but this time they were watching an autopsy. "Fade to Black" by Metallica was blasting through the speakers. They could hardly hear Dr. Lilia speak as he explained what he had found so far.

"Could you turn that down?" Sally asked.

"Not a hard rock fan?" Lilia reduced the volume.

"Just trying to hear what you're saying."

Out of the corner of her eye, Sally saw Roisin's heart lying in a tray on some scales. She tried not to look at it. "You were saying the cause of death was strangulation?"

"Correct. And she was moved from the backyard, up the stairs into the bed, after death. That takes some doing. She wasn't a small woman."

"Any DNA left by the killer?" she asked.

"No. I'd say he wore gloves."

"And the killer showered afterward?"

"Yes, and there are plenty of fingerprints in the bathroom belonging to Roisin and Carlos. There's one unknown print, which isn't in our database, so it could belong to a friend."

"Or the killer."

"Possibly."

"Anything else?"

"Her kidneys and liver were in a bad way and from the contents of her stomach, I'd say she was a heavy drinker. Sorry, I can't give you anything more."

TWENTY-EIGHT

It was an unsatisfying afternoon with little progress solving the case. Clarence contacted the FBI and asked for their help to track down Fiona Austin's bank account. He was warned that it might take weeks to do this and if the account was offshore, it may take months, or longer. Sally and Clarke discussed arresting Niall Pickerd, which would then give them the right to take his fingerprints. But they had no evidence that he committed either murder and Sally suspected that Pickerd would not react well to such a heavy-handed approach.

By the end of the day, Sally was keen to get home. As she picked up her purse to leave the station, Anna Elkington's business card fell out of a purse pocket, reminding her that she hadn't found the time to talk to a lawyer about keeping Scott out of Paul's life. All Sally wanted was some general advice. Where was the harm in that? Didn't lawyers create walls to protect client confidentiality, the kind of confidentiality that Lisa La Cava was trying so hard to protect?

Sally hesitated, then called Elkington's number. The attorney picked up almost immediately and Sally introduced herself.

"Yes, Lisa said you might call. I believe you need legal advice on a family matter?"

"Yes, but before we go any further, I have to know our conversations are confidential and you won't discuss what I tell you with another lawyer in your firm."

"If you wish, although I may have to share information with my clerical staff."

Sally thought that was fair. "What is your fee structure?"

Elkington went through it. "I'm happy to waive a fee for this initial chat. Why don't you fill me in on your situation? I have fifteen minutes."

Sally found it difficult to talk about Scott. "My ex-husband gaslighted me throughout our twenty years of marriage. He got me hooked on Valium and sleeping pills. I no longer trusted my opinions. He made me doubt myself as a mother. Our daughter took her own life and on the day of the funeral he walked out of the house and flew to Chicago where he stayed for six years. It was a godsend that he went. Only then did I begin to recognize how he had controlled and manipulated me." She cleared her throat. "We heard nothing from him for six years, not even a call to wish his son a happy birthday." The words stuck in her throat, and she grabbed her water bottle and took a sip.

"Sally, gaslighting is all too familiar to me. Many of my clients have been gaslighted. Please, go on."

"Now he's back in Franklin and he's working as a patrol officer. Wednesday night he barged into my home. My fear is that he wants to turn Paul against me. It's payback."

"Paul is your and Scott's son?"

"Yes."

"Why would he want revenge?"

A rush of nausea hit her. "He was investigated for the sexual assault of a thirteen-year-old girl. I had circumstantial evidence proving his guilt: a diary written by the victim. It was lost and with it any chance of putting him away." She looked down at the floor and felt her stomach churn.

"And Scott blames you for trying to do that?"

"You got it. I was thinking of getting an anti-harassment protection order, to stop Scott from seeing Paul. What would you advise?"

"I have some questions. Does Paul want to spend time with his father?"

"No."

"Does Scott have visitation rights?"

"No, he moved to Chicago, filed for divorce, and didn't contest my wish for sole custody."

"And during those six years he never once asked for access to Paul?"

"Not once. Never phoned, emailed, anything."

"And Paul is fifteen years old?"

"Correct."

"I'd need to get a lot more information from you but from what you've told me I'd say that Scott would have a difficult time winning some form of custody arrangement given that he hasn't had contact with his son for six years and because your son doesn't want to have contact with him."

"And if Paul changes his mind?"

"That could make things difficult if you want to prevent Scott from seeing Paul. Is Paul likely to change his mind?"

"Scott has a knack of worming his way into people's lives and controlling them, as he did me at one time."

"Sally, it would be best if you were to come and see me. At this stage, filing for a child protection order might stoke a hornet's nest. It could put the idea of claiming custody for Paul into Scott's head. My advice is to wait and see what Scott does and then we can respond. I urge you to record conversations with him. Video if you can. If he's coercing Paul, you need to be able to prove it. If Scott speaks to you, make sure there's a witness. Do you have an audio recording app on your phone?"

"Yes."

"Good. Use it."

Sally's townhouse on Pioneer Drive was small but it came with a roof terrace and views to die for of forests, mountains, and ultimately the sea. Friday night was take-out night and she and Paul would work through the food delivery options online, although they usually ended up with pizza. She locked the car and on opening the front door, announced her arrival.

"Hey, Paul! I'm home!"

Paul called down from his bedroom on the next level. Music pulsed from his room, which was a sign he had a friend over. She was surprised he even heard her. "Is Reilly with you?" His best buddy. "What do you boys want for dinner?"

The music was switched off and Paul appeared at the top of the stairs, followed by a teenage girl Sally hadn't met before. Paul was in jeans and T-shirt and socks and he put one socked foot on top of the other and gave her a sheepish look. The girl stood slightly behind and to the left. She was pale and slim and she half-smiled at Sally from behind bangs, which were so long they almost hid her made-up eyes.

"Hi, there," Sally said after a few awkward seconds in which none of them spoke. "I'm Sally. Nice to meet you."

She hoped this would encourage the girl with tumbling wavy black hair to introduce herself.

"Hi," she said, giving Sally a single wave with a flick of her wrist.

"This is Leah," Paul said.

No surname, but Sally could find that out later. Was Leah the new girl Paul had mentioned a few days ago?

"Hi, Leah, would you like to stay for dinner? Friday night is take-out night so you guys choose what you want and we'll get it delivered. How does that sound?"

Leah tugged at her baggy turtleneck sweater. The sleeves were way too long and concealed her hands.

"Sounds good," Paul said, "You want to see the DoorDash menus?" he asked Leah.

Leah nodded and they went back into Paul's bedroom and shut the door. Sally looked up the now empty stairs. Did her son have a girlfriend? Or was she just a school friend? He was old enough to have one. It was just that Sally hadn't seen it coming.

He's growing up so fast, she thought. A grin spread across her face. *Ah, young love.*

Sally had so many questions, but she bit her lip and told herself to be a cool mom.

When she returned to the kitchen and was certain that she was alone, she scrunched up her eyes and did a little dance. All she wanted was for her son to be happy.

TWENTY-NINE

September 10, 2016

"He did what?!" Margie exclaimed, referring to Scott removing an evidence box with her forged signature.

Sally and Margie ran across a wooden footbridge through a wooded area. Beneath them a narrow stream bubbled along. It was a Saturday, and the running trail was busier than during the week. Sally wasn't sure if she could do the five miles they had planned to do, given that her hip was still painful.

"I'm lucky there was a surveillance camera. Losing an evidence box when the case hasn't been solved could have gotten me removed from the investigation."

"He's such a nasty piece of work," Margie said. "And the audacity! Jeez!"

"I really wanted to see the box's contents too. Most of it belongs to the poor woman who's fighting for her life in the hospital."

Margie shook her head in sympathy. "How are you going with the case?"

She told her friend about the murder of Roisin McGettigan and how it was likely linked to Joseph Austin's murder. "I can tell you, I'm feeling the pressure." They had left the footbridge behind and were running along a gravel path through deciduous woodland. "Although there is one piece of good news. I solved another cold case, almost by accident really. A thief who tortured his victims in their homes until they revealed the location of their valuable items. He's now been charged."

"Good for you!" Margie glanced at Sally. "So why the glum face?"

"I'm worried about what Scott is up to. He's undermining me at work and he expects us to welcome him back into our lives."

"Oh, my gosh!" said Margie. "I meant to call you back. You wanted me to recommend a family lawyer. I'm so sorry."

The path bent to the left. Only four more miles to go. "I found a lawyer happy to give me initial free advice. My take-away was that if I filed a protection order against Scott for harassment, I'd need evidence of his harassment, which I don't have. And she thought my actions might provoke an angry response from Scott. She thought it better to wait and see what he does. If he starts a custody battle for Paul, then it's gloves off."

"Sounds like good advice. How does Paul feel about Scott's return?"

"He doesn't want Scott anywhere near him. That has to count for something, right? He's fifteen and if he doesn't want to see his father then he shouldn't have to."

"I'm not sure about that," Margie said. "And knowing Scott as we do, I can't imagine him staying away. If he wants you and Paul doing his bidding again, he's going to keep coming. I hate to say it, hon, but the only way to stop him taking over your lives is to fight back. If he hassles you or Paul, record it on your phone. Or write a detailed summary in a dairy about what he did and said."

"The lawyer said the same. Did I tell you that he's married again?" Sally said.

Margie came to a halt, her breathing heavy. "Wait up! He's married? Oh my god! You owe it to that poor woman to tell her to get the hell away from him." Margie leaned forward and stretched out her right calf muscle.

Sally took the opportunity to glug down some water from her bottle. "I know you'll think me selfish. But if I go near his new wife, Scott will turn into the Terminator. I can't risk provoking him."

"What's her name?"

"Don't know."

"She might need your help, Sally."

"I just can't do it, Margie. My priority is Paul. I can't take on Scott's new wife's battles as well as my own. And from what I've seen, he's gotten worse. More physically threatening. He punched Paul in the stomach."

"Please tell me you filed a complaint?"

"Paul didn't want me to, and anyway, what would be the point? Scott would say we ganged up against him, that we're lying."

"It's not too late, Sally. You have a right to feel safe in your own home. You should report him."

"Paul said not to. He's embarrassed."

"Have you thought about having spy cameras in your house?" Margie asked. "They're easy to install. I can help you. If Scott forces his way in again, you'll have video proof. Then you'll have a case for a protection order."

"I'll look into that. Look, I know I brought it up, but can we move on to another topic? Even talking about him makes my stomach churn."

"Sure. I'm having my hair done, then my nails. A morning of pampering. Why don't you join me?" Margie said.

"Thanks, but Paul has football practice and I want to reinterview some witnesses I couldn't reach during the week."

"You're really into this case, aren't you?" Margie asked.

"I guess I am."

THIRTY

Paul was about to leave the house for his football practice when he remembered he'd left his water bottle in the refrigerator. Sally stood at the open house door, the car and house keys dangling from her fingers, waiting patiently. They were running late because earlier Paul couldn't find his football boots due to the piles of clothes on his bedroom floor. There was no point wasting her breath telling him to put his clean clothes away or his dirty clothes in the washing machine. Her pleas fell on deaf ears.

It was the sound of a car with a deep, growling engine that alerted her to Scott's arrival. Not many residents had cars with a big engine and those who did tended not to rev them in such an aggressive way. She snapped her head around and there was Scott at the steering wheel of his Jeep Wrangler, a JK Rubicon.

"Oh, no," she muttered, panic shooting through her body like a lightning bolt. Then she screamed into the house, "Paul, we leave now. Scott's outside."

Paul ran down the stairs and out the door, water bottle in hand, his sports bag banging against his hip. Sally slammed the door shut and they both jogged to Sally's car. She couldn't stop herself from checking what Scott was doing. He was out of his vehicle, but he wasn't chasing them—he was too clever to do that. The neighbors might see. He held up a white furry wriggling creature in the air.

"I have a peace offering," Scott called across the street.

"Ignore him," Sally urged, unlocking the car and jumping behind the wheel. "Hurry up!"

Paul threw his bag on the backseat and was about to open the passenger door when he glanced at his father. "Is that a dog?"

Sally leaned across the handbrake. "Paul, ignore him. Please."

Paul jumped into the passenger seat and shut the door. Scott walked straight at them, the blonde puppy held out, its legs wriggling. Sally turned the engine but before she could leave her parking spot, Scott stepped in front of the car. The puppy, possibly a golden retriever, pedaled its back legs and yelped piteously.

"What is he doing?!" Paul said.

"Get out of the way!" Sally called out, but her voice was weak and scratchy and she didn't dare open the window.

"This is for you," Scott shouted so Paul could hear through the closed window. He walked down the side of the car. "Open the door."

Sally accelerated but Paul yelled at her to stop. He opened his window a fraction.

Scott leaned close to the window opening. "I came over a bit strong when we last met. I want to start again. Here." He held the puppy so that its face was squished against the window.

Paul stared at the pup and his expression softened.

Sally was driven by an overwhelming desperation to get out of there. She felt sorry for the puppy, but if Paul accepted the gift, Scott then had an excuse to see Paul again. And again. It was a clever way of bonding them, but surely Paul wouldn't fall for it?

She pressed her foot down on the accelerator and moved forward a few feet.

"We can't just leave the little guy," Paul said. "Dad won't look after him."

"We have to. You accept his gift and you'll never be free of him." She meant his father.

"Don't listen to your mom. You always wanted a dog, right? Sally didn't want one, remember?"

"That's a lie," Sally said, unable to stop herself. "You never wanted one. Even when Zelda was depressed and needed something positive, you denied her a puppy."

"You got that all wrong, Sally."

Her hands were trembling, but she held on to the steering wheel tight. "Step away from the car!" she yelled at Scott.

Scott didn't shift an inch, but Sally had just enough space to keep driving forward. "We're running late," she reminded Paul.

Her son looked behind him. "Oh, shit!"

In the rearview mirror Sally watched as Scott put the puppy on the ground, then walked away, leaving it alone in the middle of the road. The puppy sat there for a moment, confused, and then attempted to run after Scott.

"It'll get run over," Paul said. "We have to pick him up."

"Damn him!"

"Please, Mom, turn around."

Sally was seething, but Paul was right. She couldn't leave the innocent creature to die. She did a U-turn and drove back, stopping in the middle of the road where the puppy had paused to scratch his ear, oblivious to the danger he was in. Paul threw the car door open and picked up the puppy, hugging him to his chest. "Hey, little guy."

Sally watched as Scott strolled over to Paul as if he had done nothing wrong. "I want to start again, son." He gave Paul a penitent look, dropping his chin a little. "I was a bad father. I want to set that right."

Paul shook his head. "You left the dog in the road! For chrissake! You're sick!"

He got back in the car with the puppy in his lap.

"Leave us alone!" Sally shouted and sped away.

Paul was red in the face and sweating. "I hate him!"

Heaven help any player who makes Paul angry today, Sally thought.

Then she looked at the puppy, so small, so fragile. He couldn't be more than six weeks old. Too young to be taken from his mother. "I wonder where he came from. Maybe we could take him back to the breeder?"

"No way, we're keeping him."

"How? I'm working full-time and you're at school. Who's going to look after him?"

"We'll work it out."

Paul turned the puppy to face him and studied the dog's face. "What am I going to call you?"

"I had a dog once called Max," Sally suggested.

"No offense, Mom, but everyone has a dog called Max. What about Lightning, or Ace, or, I know, Blizzard?"

For the next few miles Paul worked through every dog name he could think of. He finally decided on Jax.

When they arrived at Ronald Reagan High ten minutes late for practice, Paul raced on to the field while Sally carried the little puppy to the viewing seats, where he fell asleep in her arms. She stroked his soft fur and smiled at the other parents, but deep down she was frightened. She knew how Scott operated. This was about taking from her the one person who made her life worth living. He was going to try to turn Paul against her.

THIRTY-ONE

On the way home, they stopped at a pet warehouse. Paul carried Jax into the store. The puppy drew lots of attention from other shoppers and even the staff came up to Paul to pat little Jax. Sally left the pet warehouse with a sizeable dent in her bank balance as well as a bag of dry dog food for puppies, food and water bowls, a dog bed—she bought a big one, which he could grow into—a leash, and a collar with an engraved name tag.

Sally was already in love with the furry ball of energy, but she was angry that Scott had used the puppy to win points with Paul. How was Sally going to manage a puppy when she was working long hours? Paul was either at school, football practice, mountain biking, or, as of tomorrow, working at Olivia's Bookstore.

Sally dropped Paul and Jax home and helped carry in the items they had bought. Reilly, his best friend arrived on his bicycle just as Sally was about to close the front door.

"Hello Mrs. Fairburn. Is the puppy inside?" Reilly asked.

"Sure is." Sally turned her head. "Reilly's here! I'll be home in a few hours."

She and Clarence had agreed to interview some more suspects. Saturday was a good day to catch people at home. She headed over to Clarence's home. It was an old brownstone converted into three apartments.

"Sorry I'm late. I was delayed," Sally said, as Clarence got into the passenger seat. "I had to deal with the unexpected arrival of a puppy."

"Puppy?"

"Long story," Sally said, reluctant to explain.

"Who's first on the list?" Clarence asked, putting on his seat belt. He was in police uniform.

"Dallas Austin. The nephew who inherits the house should Fiona die too."

"I thought he had an alibi?"

"He claims he was managing the staff at a celebrity wedding and didn't leave the venue until two a.m. I've been thinking about that. He could have snuck out, killed Joseph, thought he'd also killed Fiona, had a shower to remove the blood, changed into fresh work clothes, and driven back to the venue. The yacht club is a ten-minute drive from the Austins' house and only the yacht club's parking lot has a security camera."

Dallas's office was in a quiet part of town dominated by apartments. Access to Austin Events was via an intercom and a security door. Dallas answered and when Sally explained the reason for her call, she and Clarence were buzzed in and took the stairs to level one. Dallas's business was run from his apartment with the help of an assistant, Patricia Cooper, who was already at the venue for an event they were involved in that night. He greeted them with a welcoming smile and showed them into a large room set up to meet clients. On the wall were images of corporate functions, weddings, and private events for which he had provided the catering staff.

"What can I get you to drink?" Austin asked.

"Nothing for me, thank you," Sally said. Clarence declined as well. They sat at a long table.

"What can I do for you?" Austin asked.

Sally might be reading too much into his joviality, but it grated on her. Only six weeks ago his uncle had been brutally murdered, and his aunt was in a coma.

"Do you know Roisin McGettigan?"

"Only in passing."

"Are you aware that Roisin was murdered?"

Dallas had a puffy face and a belly that rolled over his belt. Despite his strong aftershave, there was a lingering smell of wine on his breath. He blew out his cheeks.

"No, should I be? Oh, I see. You think her murder is related to Joseph's?" So far, he wasn't showing any emotion. It struck Sally as callous.

"We're not drawing any conclusions yet," Sally said, "but it's a possibility. I'd like to talk to you about the night of July twenty-sixth. You were managing a celebrity wedding at the Peak Bay Yacht Club, is that right?"

Dallas scratched the side of his neck. "Why are we going over old ground?"

"Mr. Austin, you benefit substantially if both Joseph and Fiona die. I therefore need to establish your exact movements that night."

"You can't seriously believe I did it? I loved them. They were family. I mean... *are* family."

"Tell me about your movements on the night of July twenty-sixth."

He rolled his eyes. "As I've said, I was at the yacht club until two a.m. the following morning. Ask Patricia, or the waitstaff and bar staff. They will vouch for me."

"We will. Where did you park your vehicle that night?"

"What the hell does that matter?" His temper flared suddenly, his puffy face flushed red.

"Please just answer the question."

"In the parking lot, I guess."

"What vehicle were you driving?"

"A white Ford van."

Sally made a mental note to check the surveillance footage.

"Did you leave the venue at any point?"

"No, of course I bloody didn't. I had sixteen people to manage. I can't believe you're wasting time asking me these questions. Why aren't you out there catching the killer?" His voice was loud and strident.

"Calm down, Mr. Austin," Clarence said.

"I won't calm down," Dallas blustered. "My uncle is dead and my aunt is in a coma and I can't even see her."

"It's for her safety. Mr. Austin, where were you Wednesday night and the small hours of the following morning?"

"You're seriously... oh for chrissake, I was having dinner with a friend, then I went home, alone."

"Who is this friend?"

"It doesn't matter. We went to Tastes of India. Ask the maître d'."

"We need to know who you were with."

"No, you don't, and I'd like you to leave now. I have staff to organize." He stood.

"One more question," Sally said. "Is your business doing well?"

"Providing hospitality staff is a tough business. We're keeping our heads above water. Now if you'll excuse me, I'll show you to the door."

"One second, can you tell me if you've seen this man before?" Sally held out her phone. On screen was a photo of Niall Pickerd.

Dallas frowned at the image. "No. Who is he?"

"He's one of many lines of inquiry. Thank you for your time," Sally said.

When they had left the building, Sally asked Clarence what he thought about Dallas.

"He's defensive, and he got real angry. And why wouldn't he tell us who his dinner date was with?"

"We should call the restaurant to check his alibi. Maybe it has security cameras."

Clarence agreed. "I'd like to see the accounts for his business too. If it's losing money, he has a big motive for murder."

THIRTY-TWO

It turned out that Tastes of India did have security footage from Wednesday night, so Sally dropped Clarence off at the restaurant to go through it, while she drove to Chestnut Close, the street that ran behind Willow Way.

Felicia and Jonathan Suri owned the striking home at number 25, on a sloping block, their rear garden wall adjoining the Austins' backyard. The house exterior was of rounded stones and concrete with stained wooden window frames and doors with glass fencing on the three balconies. It was protected by security alarms and a top-of-the-range doorbell camera. Sally rang the bell and after a brief moment, a strident female voice said, "Yes?"

Sally introduced herself and the reason for her visit.

"Not again!" the woman said through the audio system. She sighed loud enough for Sally to hear. "I'll let you in."

The woman opened the paneled door. She was dark-haired and dressed as if she were about to visit a smart restaurant or garden party. "We've told the other detective all we know."

"Felicia Suri?" Sally asked.

"Yes, come in."

Felicia had to be twenty years younger than her husband—a successful banker who had emigrated from India with his family when he was a child. Sally guessed that Felicia was referring to the initial round of door-to-door inquiries shortly after Joseph's death.

"We appreciate that, Mrs. Suri, but I've been brought in as a fresh pair of eyes on this case. It won't take long. Just a few questions."

Felicia's eyes dropped to Sally's dark blue, wool jumper. "You have fluff all over you."

Sally looked down. It was Jax's fur.

"Ah, that's my son's puppy."

"I see." The woman hesitated. "What breed is he?"

"Golden retriever."

Her sharp features softened. "Pity you didn't bring him with you. Bobo needs a playmate."

At that moment a black-and-tan miniature dachshund ran toward Sally barking, then stopped at Felicia's feet. Sally put her hand down low so the dachshund could sniff it. He wagged his tail.

"Darling! The police are here!" Felicia called out.

Felicia then led Sally to a living room with a large fireplace and artwork on the walls.

A moment later, Jonathan Suri, in an open-necked blue dress shirt and corduroy pants walked in, all smiles. The couple sat next to each other on a curved suede white sofa opposite a semicircular white stone coffee table.

"How can we help?" Jonathan asked.

"I've been through your police statements, but I'd like to ask you a few more questions. On July twenty-sixth, you attended a charity gala at the Crown Hotel. When did you return home?"

"As we said, it was eleven fifty-six p.m. We know this because our alarm system keeps a log of when it is switched on and off," Jonathan replied.

"Did you drive yourselves home?"

"No, we had a driver."

"Did the driver take Spring Avenue and then Willow Way to reach Chestnut Close?"

"I suppose he did, it's the quickest route," Jonathan replied.

"Did either of you notice someone on the Austins' porch or walking away from the house?"

They looked at each other. "No," said Felicia.

"No," said her husband.

"When you got home, did you see anyone in their backyard."

They both answered in the negative once more.

"Although that guy had his house door open, you know who I mean," Felicia said to her husband. "We can see his porch through a gap in the trees."

There was no mention of this in her statement. "Who do you mean?" Sally asked.

"What's his name, darling, you know, they live opposite Joseph and Fiona."

"Salvador or Justin?" Jonathan suggested.

Felicia turned her head to look at Sally. "Salvador."

"Could you make out what he was looking at?"

"No."

Sally held out her phone and showed them a photo of Niall Pickerd. "Have you seen this man?"

Both shook their heads. "Who is he?" Jonathan asked.

"One of several lines of inquiry." She put her phone away. "Did either of you leave your house during the night?"

Felicia glanced at her husband. "We both were in bed all night. I rose at six the following morning and went for a jog." She hesitated.

"Felicia?"

"As my husband said, we were in bed all night." Her eyes flicked to the left.

Sally had a feeling that Felicia was not telling the complete truth.

"As I expect you know, Roisin McGettigan was murdered on Wednesday night. Again, did you see or hear anything unusual that night?"

"Nothing," said Jonathan.

Felicia hesitated. "Perhaps. It could be nothing significant, which is why I haven't mentioned it before."

"Go on."

"I thought I heard Roisin shout, but when I drew back the drapes, I couldn't see her."

"What time was this?"

"I'm not sure. Sometime after midnight. All these murders are terrifying. I find it hard to sleep."

"Can you remember what Roisin shouted?"

She thought for a moment. "'It's two,' or 'it's you.' I'm not sure."

"So you think she knew the person?"

"Maybe."

"Thank you, that's been very helpful."

Jonathan showed Sally to the door. "Call on us any time. We're always happy to help the police. Did you know my bank is a sponsor of the Police Veteran Support Foundation?"

Was this a hint to leave them alone? Well, it wasn't going to work.

THIRTY-THREE

Sally picked up Clarence from Tastes of India. He was grinning from ear to ear as he got in the car.

"From the look on your face, I guess the security footage was revealing?" Sally said.

"I know who Dallas's dinner date was."

"Okay, who?" Sally said.

"Roisin. And it was very touchy-feely. Looked like a date." He held up a flash drive. "And I have a copy."

"I didn't see that one coming. Great work, Clarence. What time did they leave the restaurant?" Sally asked.

"Ten-twenty."

"And she was murdered about midnight." Sally thought about what this might mean. "Dallas lied to us about that night but why would he want to kill her?"

"Maybe she knew he killed Joseph?"

"Maybe. But why take her to dinner beforehand?"

"Or maybe Carlos killed his wife because he discovered the affair?"

"I have one new piece of information. From Felicia Suri. She overheard Roisin talking to someone in the backyard the night she died. She thinks she either said, 'It's two,' or 'It's you.' If it's the latter, then she recognized the man who killed her."

Clarence scratched his head. "So it could be Dallas. I guess we need to ask him what happened after he and Roisin left the restaurant."

"Okay, while I drive, phone Dallas and tell him we need to speak to him again, wherever he is. And no excuses. I don't care if he's managing the hospitality for the president, he's going to see us."

The event was a bar mitzvah in a marquee at a private house. Dallas's team were preparing the catering and providing the hospitality staff. They found Dallas yelling at a server who had placed the dessert forks in the wrong place on the tables. Sally and Clarence meandered between circular tables and when he saw them he raced up to them.

"Outside," he said, and they followed him out of the marquee and into a leafy garden.

"This better be important."

"How about lying to the police and interfering with a homicide investigation?" Sally shot back.

"What do you mean?" Dallas said.

"You should have told us your dinner date was Roisin McGettigan."

"Ah, I see. I don't want Carlos to know. He's a good friend."

"Such a good friend that you have an affair with his wife?" Sally said.

"Look, neither of us meant it to happen. It just did. Besides, their marriage was over a long time ago. They stayed together for the business."

A server walked past them, clutching a pack of cigarettes, and Dallas remained quiet until he was out of earshot.

"Did you take Roisin home after you left the Tastes of India on Wednesday night?"

"Of course not. I didn't want Carlos to see me drop her at home. Besides Roisin had her own car."

"Did you see her get in her car and drive away?"

"Yes, then I walked to where I'd parked mine."

"Do you know any of her movements from that moment onward?"

"No. And I didn't kill her. Why would I? We had fun together."

By the time they were back in Sally's car, both she and Clarence were weary. She could tell he had had enough, and she drove him home and thanked him for working a Saturday.

"We'll get there, Clarence. We just have to keep picking away at it."

He waved her off. "See you Monday."

Sally checked in with Paul. He was having a great time playing with Jax. Leah had joined him and Reilly. Sally wasn't quite ready to stop work yet.

"I'll be home in two hours or so."

She knew from a previously obtained hospital staff roster that Justin Griess, Sobral's partner, wasn't working today and she was keen to speak to him. She drove straight to his house.

Unlike Sobral, who had been reluctant to let Sally in, Griess opened the door wide and stood his ground confidently.

"You must be the cop Salvador talked about?"

"I'm Detective Sally Fairburn. I'd like to ask you a few questions."

He waved away her police badge. "Come in. Would you like something to drink? Coffee?"

"No, thanks."

Griess was tall and slim with sharp features and light brown hair. Sally followed him to the kitchen and they sat at a small table set up for two. The room smelled of freshly brewed coffee and he invited Sally to take a seat. He picked up his mug, decorated with cats, and sipped from it.

"Salvador isn't here, but I'm glad you dropped by. I wanted to speak to you."

This was very different from Sobral's suspicious and defensive attitude on Thursday.

"Can I change my mind about the coffee?" she said. "It smells lovely."

He asked her if she wanted cream and sugar, prepared her coffee, and then sat back down.

"What did you want to talk about?" Sally asked.

"He said you were far nicer than the detectives who interviewed him before. I want to emphasize that our neighbors have made our lives hell and Salvador is suffering from depression. He's on medication. Joseph was the ringleader. Salvador is trying hard to start a new life after jail and these witches are doing everything they can to make him fail. I want you to investigate the harassment we've endured."

Was this request a clever way to deflect Sally from viewing them as murder suspects?

"The first step is to seek legal advice and report it to the police," Sally said. "Have you evidence of the harassment? Salvador mentioned dog poo in your mailbox. Did you take a video or a photo?"

Griess's upright posture slackened. "We should have thought of that, but we were so disgusted, we used a hose to clean out the mailbox. I did record Joseph and Roisin talking about us though, calling us filthy gays and accusing us of shooting porn in our home."

"I have to ask... did they have any reason to think this?"

"Of course not."

"Can I see the recording?"

"Sure."

Griess scrolled through the videos on his phone, then

handed the phone to her. She played the two-minute clip. Both Joseph and Roisin were making understandably upsetting allegations against Salvador and Griess making gay porn movies, and Salvador was also referred to as the "ex-con" who was no doubt trying to "hack" their computers.

"You see!" said Griess. "It's slander, right?"

It probably was slander, but she didn't want to get sidetracked. "Both of the people in this video are dead. That makes Salvador a suspect. You both had reason to want them dead."

"We didn't kill them. I was at work when Joseph died, and Salvador just isn't capable of murder. He's physically and emotionally fragile."

"When did you leave the house for work on July twenty-sixth?"

Griess scrolled through the diary on his phone.

"I started work at nine-thirty p.m. and finished at seven-thirty a.m. the following day. I called Salvador when I took a break at about one-thirty a.m. He was watching TV. He told me he'd heard Joseph having an argument with a man on his front porch."

"Heard or saw?" Sally asked.

"Saw *and* heard. Why don't you lot believe him?"

"Apart from the argument Salvador overheard, how can you be certain that he was at home?"

"Because of Rocky. I heard him purring."

"Rocky is your cat?"

"Yes, and before you ask, Rocky is a house cat. He doesn't like to go outside."

A cat as an alibi, that was different! *Sadly, cats can't talk,* Sally thought.

"Does Salvador wear glasses?"

"No, his vision is perfect and so is his hearing. If he says he saw a man on Joseph's porch that night, he's telling the truth."

"And where were you Wednesday night, when Roisin McGettigan was murdered?"

"Working. Same shift, nine-thirty p.m. to seven-thirty a.m."

"One more thing. What is your shoe size?"

"Eleven, why?"

"And Salvador's?"

"Eight."

Sally thanked him and left the house. Griess had an alibi for both murders. Sobral didn't have an alibi for either murder. He also had motive and means; he just had to sneak across the street.

THIRTY-FOUR

On the way home, Sally put in a call to Officer Vivek Mishra, who had been the first on the Austin murder scene. She had read his statement but she had questions. It was Mishra's day off, but he answered his cell regardless. As Sally introduced herself, she heard a baby crying.

"My son," he said. "He's teething."

Sally recalled the never-ending crying when Zelda was teething. It had worn Sally ragged. "I can call back some other time."

"Can you give me a second?" There were muffled voices, then the screaming baby grew quieter. It sounded as if his wife had taken the boy to another room. "Okay, how can I help?"

"I'd like to go over what happened from the moment you arrived at the Austins' house. I've read your statement, but I want to hear it from you."

"Okay." He paused a few seconds, presumably gathering his thoughts. "I and my partner, Héctor Becerra, found the gardener, Andy... I've forgotten his surname."

"McCarron."

Officer Mishra continued, "That's him. Standing in the

street. He was real upset. He led us to the study window. I saw Joseph Austin bound to a chair and slumped forward. Man, his skull was a mess. Blood on the carpet. I asked McCarron if he had a key. He said he didn't. Officer Becerra kicked the back door open. The study was a mess, papers everywhere, safe was open, we checked for signs of life, but Joseph was dead. Becerra called for backup and paramedics; I searched the house for the intruder. Bloody footprints on the stairs. I found Fiona in the top-floor bedroom, unconscious. We tried not to contaminate the scene, but it just wasn't possible."

This didn't tell Sally anything she didn't already know.

"And this was at seven-thirteen a.m. on July twenty-seventh?"

"Correct. I'll never forget it. He's my first dead body."

When Sally found her first body, she had been a police officer for under a year. A prostitute's body had been concealed under garbage in an industrial trash can. The woman's gray, lifeless face haunted Sally for weeks afterward.

"How are you now?" Sally asked. "Are you getting help to move past what you saw?"

"I'm good. It took a while. A few nightmares but I can deal with that."

"Was Fiona conscious at any time while you were with her?"

"No."

"Did you notice anything unusual in either the study or the bedroom? Anything at all?"

"Like what?"

"A smell, an item in the wrong place, a strange noise, anything."

"Er... the cigarette burns on his chest, I guess that's unusual. And..." He paused. "This may be nothing, but I thought it was weird the killer broke in via the study window."

Sally had thought the same when she viewed the crime scene. "Why do you say that?"

"Because he had to stand in the flower bed, then stretch up to open the window latch through a broken pane. It would have been much easier to break a pane in the French doors. The key was in the lock. All he needed to do was push his hand through the shattered glass, turn the key, and walk in."

"I agree. Do you think the break-in could have been staged?" Sally asked.

"Yeah, I do, but how else did the killer get in?"

"I'm investigating the possibility that Joseph let the killer in. Anything else strike you as out of the ordinary?"

"It's probably nothing, but next to Fiona was a framed photo. It had bloody streaks on it."

"Perhaps it was knocked off the nightstand when she fell?"

"It was right next to her right hand, like she'd grabbed it."

"Tell me why you think it's significant," Sally asked.

"There's a dust mark where the photo sat. The frame was next to the landline. If I heard an intruder downstairs, I wouldn't grab a photo, I'd grab the phone."

"You make a good point, Officer Mishra. Calling for help would be my priority too."

She thanked the officer and ended the call. Did the killer put the photo frame near Fiona? Why would he do that?

THIRTY-FIVE

Sally switched on her laptop while she sat in her car, then searched the Austin case folder, working through the hundreds of crime scene photos. Eventually she found the one she was looking for: a close-up of the framed picture that Officer Mishra referred to. There was blood spatter on the glass. The photo was of four people in their twenties or early thirties in bell-bottom pants, with seventies hairstyles. She enlarged the image on screen. Who were they?

She checked the notes. There was nothing on their identities.

Sally studied the man on the far left first. Short with a long nose, much like Joseph's, but with a full head of black hair and looking fifty years younger. He had his arm resting over the shoulder of a young woman with long, brown hair and a gentle smile. Sally was fairly certain that was Fiona. But who were the other two people with them? The woman had red, shoulder-length hair, styled so that the sides flicked back. With her was a man with wavy brown hair, in a button-down shirt and smart pants.

"Who are you?" Sally wondered, making a note to look into this on Monday.

It was time to go home. Yet again, however, she made a detour to the hospital where Fiona was under twenty-four-hour guard. She felt sorry for the victim who couldn't have visitors. Sally believed it important for Fiona's recovery to have somebody chatting to her. It was the least she could do for the poor woman.

There was a female cop seated outside Fiona's hospital room, slouched in the chair, looking at her phone. Keeping a victim safe involved hours and hours of tedium.

"Any progress?" The cop jumped at her voice then looked up.

Sally held out her police ID.

"No change." The police officer tucked her phone in a pocket and stood, smiling warmly at Sally. "You don't remember me, do you?"

For a second, Sally was flummoxed. Then the cheeky glint in the woman's blue eyes jolted Sally's memory. "Deidre Kelly! Is it really you?"

"Lord! Have I changed that much?" Deidre said.

"It's been twenty years since I saw you, so I guess we've both changed. It happens," Sally said.

In 1990, fresh out of police college, they had joined the FPD on the same day. Back then, Deidre was loud and confident with black curly hair and an eye for the good-looking guys. Her blue eyes still sparkled but her hair was now a pale gray and she'd put on a bit of weight.

Sally continued, "I heard you left to do private security?"

"For a while. So boring, I couldn't stand it. Came back to the PD in 2001."

"It's good to see you, Deidre. We should get together sometime. Catch up on old times."

"I heard about you and Scott divorcing and the investigation into his conduct. You know he's back at the PD?"

"I do." Sally didn't want to say how she felt about it. Deidre had been one of his biggest fans and she'd been really miffed when Sally, a rookie, was teamed with Scott, the good-looking and single cop, when Deidre was teamed with a cop close to retirement whose MO was keeping his head down and doing as little as possible.

"I can't believe I used to think he was superhot." She gave Sally a concerned look. "I heard rumors he's not the nice guy he pretends to be. I guess I was the lucky one getting partnered with that fat git, Esposito. At least we had a laugh and he never tried anything with me."

Sally briefly considered how different her life would have been if Deidre had been teamed with Scott instead of her. She might then have been happily married, with kids and a career, and none of the pain of Zelda's suicide. But if Sally hadn't married Scott, she wouldn't have Paul, her wonderful son.

"You were lucky," Sally said. "Then again, Scott picked me because he sensed my weakness. He knew I lacked confidence. And you were so confident and always had a joke and a story to tell. I think your vibrant personality saved you."

"Jeez, Sally, I didn't realize it was bad until I heard about Zelda's suicide. Scott told everyone that you refused to act, that you refused to get Zelda help for her depression. He made out you were... well, a cold-hearted bitch." Deidre screwed up one side of her face. "Can you ever forgive me? I should have believed you."

"There's nothing to forgive, Deidre. How's life treating you?"

"Four kids driving me nuts, a lazy husband, two cats who only come near me at feeding time. But I love them all. Still a beat cop, but I like the job, so that's okay. And look at you! A detective! Congrats!"

"Just for three months."

Sally made a move to enter the room, but Deidre hadn't finished. "Scott is badmouthing you already," she said in a low voice. "Telling anyone who'll listen that you're out of your depth and you must be sleeping with Clarke for him to give you the case."

It was an insulting lie but so ludicrous that Sally laughed. "Please tell me no one is believing that! Me and Clarke! That's ridiculous."

"You're a woman, Sally. The team who worked the case were all men, except for Esme Lin. Guys still don't like women showing them up. Those detectives want you to fail. I thought you should know."

Deidre stepped aside so Sally could go in. "Thanks for the heads-up, Deidre."

Inside the room, Sally closed the door. The room was quiet, save for the beeping and humming of machines keeping Fiona alive. The woman lay in the exact same position as she had yesterday. The only difference was the color of the hospital gown Fiona wore in bed. On the last visit it had been white and today it was pale blue.

Pulling up a chair, Sally sat as close to Fiona as possible and took her hand. Cool, just like last time. The bones of the fingers were just as fragile. The skinny hand felt heavy, as if there were no life in it.

"Hello, Fiona, it's Sally Fairburn. I came to visit yesterday. I'm investigating what happened to you. I wish you could talk to me." Again, Sally wanted to be careful not to mention Joseph's passing. "You have a police officer outside your door to keep you safe and the nurses keep an eye on you, don't they? They're all hoping you'll come out of your coma."

On her previous visit, Sally had noticed a collection of get-well cards lining the inside windowsill. Now, she decided to take a look. She carefully rested Fiona's hand on the sheet and then crossed the room. The first card she picked up was of a bluebird in white cherry blossom and was signed Robin Kerns. Sally pondered the name. Kerns. She hadn't come across it before. Was Robin male or female? The card next to it had more of a religious theme and was from Dallas Austin, her nephew.

> *You're a fighter, Auntie! You can do it.*
> *Love you, Dallas*

Next to it was an arty card. Reds, blues, and yellows representing an abstract rural scene sent by Lisa La Cava, the lawyer.

> *Wishing you a speedy recovery. We are here to support*
> *you.*
> *Lisa and the team at La Cava Allison*

The last one was from Niall Pickerd. The card was a funny one. A dog with a plastic cone around its neck and the words *At least you don't have to wear a cone*. It was cute and a touch inappropriate, as if he were making light of her coma, which Sally suspected wasn't the intention. He had just signed it with his first name and these words.

> *Please get better soon. I want to spend time with you.*

Sally sat back down next to Fiona and gently held her hand, then described each card.

"You have a get-well card from Niall. I'm guessing you don't know who he is, although he did approach you in your driveway once. He moved from Atlanta to be with you. He believes he's your son. He's a boxer and personal trainer. He'd like to come and see you. Would you like that?"

It was the faintest twitch, but Sally was certain that a finger had moved.

"I felt it. You moved your finger. Can you hear me, Fiona? Move your finger again if you can?"

Sally's heart was racing. Was Fiona coming out of her coma? She stared down at Fiona's fragile fingers until her eyes were watery, but not one finger twitched even a fraction.

"Did you have a child, Fiona? Was this before you married Joseph? Niall believes you put him up for adoption. It would have been devastating to give birth and then watch your baby taken from you." Sally watched Fiona's fingers. They didn't move. "Niall says that he tried to visit you, but Joseph turned him away. Did you know?"

Another flinch of a finger. Just a miniscule movement, but this time Sally was sure she had felt it. Sally leaned closer to Fiona's ear. "You can hear me, can't you? Wake up Fiona, please. We all want you back. And your son wants to see you."

Beneath her paper-thin eyelids, Fiona's eyeballs moved back and forth.

"Fiona, come back to us. Open your eyes. You can see your son, Niall."

Fiona's eyelashes were so white they were almost translucent. They moved and a lid opened just enough to see the white of her eye.

With her free hand, Sally dived for the nurse's call button and pressed it over and over. A nurse rushed in.

"What's happened?" the nurse asked.

"She's waking up!"

THIRTY-SIX

September 11, 2016

It was Sunday morning at Olivia's Bookstore and young love was in the air. Paul was certainly smitten by the tall dark-haired girl who'd just arrived.

How did Olivia know this? Well, first up, Paul dropped a book on the bookstore counter when he noticed Leah walk through the door. Luckily the book only fell a few inches and was undamaged and Paul hurriedly slid the novel into a brown paper bag and handed it to the customer. Olivia had been busy cutting a slice of Chantilly cake when she noticed Paul give Leah an awkward wave, who then approached the counter and asked how Paul was doing.

"Good," Paul replied. "I think. Er, do you want some cake? Olivia's cakes are to die for."

"Okay. Which do you think is the best?" Leah said.

"I, er, don't know. Er..." He pointed at the revolving cake stand, which was encased in glass. "That one's popular. I think it's a Black Forest gâteau."

"Great pick," Olivia said, coming to his rescue. "If you like chocolate and cherry, you'll love it."

Leah nodded shyly and offered a five-dollar bill. "On the house," Olivia said, winking.

"Thank you." Leah took the plate with her slice of gâteau and the cake fork Olivia offered, then she sat at a shared table not far from Paul's counter.

How adorable, Olivia thought, as she bustled through the bookshelves, through her office at the back, and into the kitchen, where she was baking a fresh batch of raspberry and white chocolate muffins. She took them from the oven, switched it off, and laid them on a wire mesh tray where they could cool down, before she added the frosting and sprinkles. She headed back through the shop. She had two coffees to make and a milkshake. The bookshelves were arranged so that customers could meander through them and find little nooks where they could sit and read at their leisure. Therefore, Olivia couldn't see straight to the front of the shop, not until she was level with the six-seater shared table where Leah was tucking into her slice of cake.

Olivia stopped dead.

She knew something was wrong from Paul's expression. He was flushed. He had stepped back from the counter. Even Pajamas, her cat, had left her much-loved position on the counter where she lay most of the day. Pajamas raced past Olivia's red shoes and disappeared behind a bookshelf. Not one to flinch from managing difficult customers, Olivia patted down her green hair and strode over to the small group.

Paul was shaking his head, his lips gripped tightly together.

The man, in his late forties, stood with legs wide, and even though the bookstore was busy, it felt like he dominated the space. With him was a woman young enough to be his daughter and a toddler who was clearly bored and was attempting to drag the young woman toward the cake display.

"Don't be like that, Paul. I want you to meet Harper and your little brother." The man turned his crew-cut head. "Eli, take Daddy's hand."

Did he just say little brother? Olivia thought. Sally hadn't mentioned it. She must have misheard.

Eli shrunk away and clung to the young woman's legs. Olivia saw then that her leg was like a stick.

"Hi," Olivia said, intervening. "I'm the owner. Can I get you guys some coffee and cakes?"

The man introduced himself as Scott. "Paul's my son."

Olivia was normally adept at keeping a fixed smile on her face, even with the most difficult customers. But the wind had been smashed from her sails. This man was Sally's dreadful ex-husband. Olivia knew that Sally had been gaslighted by Scott and it had taken years for her to recover. She also knew that Paul hated his father.

Oh boy! Olivia thought. *This is bad! What do I do?*

Olivia recovered her smile. "Lovely to meet you. Why don't you take a seat and I'll take your order? Follow me." Olivia's intention was to lead them to a table at the back of the store so that she could ask Paul what he wanted to do about the clearly unexpected arrival.

"I'll sit near my boy," Scott said, eyeing the rectangular table for six at which Leah and an old man were seated at opposite ends. "We'll go there." Before Olivia could suggest otherwise, he pulled a chair out, smiled charmingly at Leah, and said, "I hope you don't mind us joining you."

Leah stared at Paul, then nodded, shifting farther along the table to allow them room. While the table could seat six, it was a cozy fit.

"I'll have what she's having," Scott said, nodding at Leah's Black Forest gâteau. "Eli can have some of mine."

"And your wife?" Olivia asked.

Harper followed Scott, her face blank, her walk weary. *She could do with a good meal inside her.*

"No cake for my darling wife. Just some tap water."

If Olivia wasn't mistaken, Harper was severely under-weight, and Scott wasn't helping to change that. Olivia made up her mind that Harper was getting a slice too and to hell with it!

"Coffee?" Olivia asked.

"No, thanks," Scott said. "Come and sit down," he told Paul.

"I'm working, okay?" Paul barked back.

Leah cringed at the exchange, then she got up, gave Paul a "call me" gesture, and left the store. Paul looked heartbroken. Fortunately, a customer arrived at the counter with a book she wanted to purchase. Paul took the customer's money and then Olivia asked him to take two coffees to a table. She delivered the slice of gâteau to Scott with a cake fork and a teaspoon for the toddler, and a slice to Harper. "On the house," she said pointedly to Harper.

Scott glared at her. Then she raced to catch up with Paul. She cornered him in the history section.

"I get the feeling you're not comfortable with this. What can I do to help?"

"He's, like, stalking me. He turns up at our house, then he gives me Jax, and now he's here. It's doing my head in."

"Do you want to go home? I can call your mom."

"No, don't. Mom will make a scene." Paul started to pace. "I wish he would just fu... leave me alone!" Paul managed to stop himself just in time.

"I could send you on an urgent errand. You can leave by the back gate. Then come back when he's gone."

His face lit up. "Thanks." Then his elation faded. "I can't do that. It's like I'm running away. He'll get a real kick out of that."

"Not if I send you on an errand. Mrs. Greenhorne has four

books that need delivering. I usually drop them around after work, but you could take them now. She lives two blocks from here."

Paul nodded. He stood there looking goofy. He was such a big strong boy and yet his father had taken his hutzpah away. "Okay. Follow me back to the counter."

Olivia made a big drama of having forgotten Mrs. Greenhorne's books and asked Paul to deliver them straightaway. Scott tried to intervene, but Paul was out of the shop before he could be stopped. Scott was clearly livid.

"How long will it take?" Scott asked.

"Half an hour, maybe."

"You got some kids' books?"

"Yeah, would you like me to show you?"

"Harper, go and choose some books for Eli."

Olivia bristled at the rude way he spoke to his wife. At least Olivia had the satisfaction of seeing Harper's empty plate. The young woman followed her meekly to the kids' books section. "My books are preloved but in good condition. I've got some great picture books. This one has textures your son can feel."

Harper opened the chunky pages and ran her fingers over the furry cat, then the squishy sea sponge. Up close, Olivia realized how young she was. Possibly still a teen. The poor girl was clearly unhappy.

"Is there anything I can do?" Olivia asked.

Harper looked up and gave her a quizzical look, obviously unsure if Olivia was offering help or not. She looked as if she were going to open up, but then the brightness left her face and she simply said, "Can I read this to Eli while we're here?"

"Sure you can."

Harper took a couple of picture books back to the table where Scott was growing impatient, drumming his fingers on the tabletop.

Now that Paul was gone from the store, Olivia had to cover

everything on her own. The muffins cooling in the kitchen would have to wait to be frosted later. She made coffees and helped customers locate books, and all the time Olivia thought about calling Sally. Even though Paul had asked her not to do so, Sally was Olivia's friend. Sally had a right to know that her no-good ex-husband was stalking her son. When she could grab a moment, Olivia went to her office and called Sally's cell. It went straight to voicemail.

"Sally, Scott's here. His wife and son too. I sent Paul on an errand so he could get away from him, but Scott's determined to wait. I thought you should know."

THIRTY-SEVEN

The house was empty, and Sally was busy doing chores. She put in a load of washing, then tidied and vacuumed Paul's room. Only when she had switched off the vacuum cleaner did she notice that she had a missed call from Olivia. As she listened to the voicemail, her blood pressure skyrocketed.

"What the hell?!"

She called Olivia, who answered after just one ring.

"I didn't mean to bother you," Olivia said. "Paul was upset."

"I bet he was. Is Scott still there?"

"Yes and he's not happy. He's waiting for Paul to come back."

"I'm on my way."

"Sally, I don't think—"

She didn't mean to cut Olivia off, but she was so incensed, she wasn't in the mood to debate what she should and shouldn't do. "I won't make a scene. But Scott can't do this."

Sally ended the call and broke the speed limit all the way to the bookstore, driven by a motherly urge to protect her son. On the way, she called Paul.

"I heard about what happened. Where are you?"

"Walking home. I can't go back there, Mom. He's spoiled everything." He sounded really upset.

"Do you like working there?"

"Yeah. Olivia's great. But I don't want to see him. He's, like, everywhere and I hate it. He frightened Leah too. Now she'll think I'm a freak." He was getting progressively more agitated.

"Paul, I promise I'll deal with it. I want you to come back to the bookstore. He has to know that he can't do what he wants. And you have to show him that you're not going to change your life because of him."

"I don't want to see him."

"You're my brave boy. A hundred times better than Scott. Show him you aren't fazed by him."

A pause.

"I'll wait for you near the store."

"I'll be there in five."

Sally's skin burned with fury. Only on Wednesday, Scott had punched Paul in the gut because he stood up to his father. How dare he now expect Paul to welcome him into his life. Scott had overstepped the mark.

The street was busy and all the parking spaces were full. Sally pulled into a space that was used by delivery trucks for the grocery store. She didn't care if it blocked the entrance. Her tunnel vision had her throwing her car door open and marching in the direction of the bookstore. Farther down the street, Paul leaned against the wall of a sports store, hands in his jeans pockets. She called his name to get his attention.

Just then Scott stepped out of the bookstore. Sally hadn't even thought through how she would confront Scott and his sudden presence in the street had her mind spinning. She increased her pace. Scott stood too close to his son, as he did when he wanted to intimidate. Even though Paul was taller than his father, she saw him take a wary step back, his eyes fearful.

"Anyone would think you're trying to avoid me, son." Scott placed a hand on Paul's shoulder as if he were claiming him.

Sally almost ran into the back of Scott.

"Scott!"

Without bothering to face her, he said, "So you called Mommy! Pathetic!"

Don't be afraid, she told herself.

She positioned herself shoulder-to-shoulder with her son. "He's not pathetic. You are! Don't you understand that we don't want to see you?"

Sally trembled inside but she would defend her son no matter what it took.

Scott laughed. He was mocking her. "You kept my son from me. That stops as of today. Sally, he's *my son* too. I love him."

He sounded so reasonable that if she didn't know better she might question her own motives. It was an outrageous lie.

"Love! You don't know what love is," she screamed, losing control. "You walked out on us. You never contacted Paul once. You're a disgrace!"

There was movement at the shop entrance. An emaciated but pretty young woman watched them timidly from just inside the door. With her was a toddler, cramming a mushy piece of cake into his mouth. Was this girl Scott's new wife and was this boy his son?

Sally's anger died away, overtaken by pity for his new wife and son.

"You're upsetting them," Scott said, gesturing toward the mother and child. "They wanted to meet you. How can you be so selfish? Why can't you share?" Scott said, sounding hurt.

A small crowd of pedestrians had begun to gather near them. "Paul doesn't want to see you." Sally looked at him, her eyes pleading with him to speak up.

"Mom, leave it, will you? Everyone's staring."

"I don't care. Paul, do you want to see your dad or not? Tell him what you want."

He looked at Scott. "I... stop harassing me."

"You're coercing the boy," Scott claimed. "*You're* the problem. You drove me from the house on the day of our daughter's funeral. You wouldn't let me speak to Paul. You drove a wedge between us."

"Liar!" she screamed. "You're a pedophile. You drove Zelda to suicide, and you tormented Paul and me!" She shoved him in the chest. "You should be behind bars! Stay away from us, you hear?"

"That's assault," Scott said. "Everyone saw you hit me."

The crowd around them had grown. Scott's wife had retreated inside the store, a look of terror on her gaunt face. Olivia dashed out of the door, arms waving.

"Mom! This is embarrassing," Paul said, walking away.

Sally followed him blindly, the crowd of onlookers giving her unfriendly stares. Olivia scuttled down the sidewalk after them. "Sally, it's my fault. I never meant to... I shouldn't have told... Sally, he... he was recording you," Olivia said breathlessly.

THIRTY-EIGHT

September 12, 2016

On Monday morning Sally left the puppy with Olivia, who was happy to look after him. She had a courtyard at the back of the store where Jax could play. Olivia's only worry was how her cat would react to the pup. Sally apologized for causing a scene with Scott yesterday, then headed for the boxing club where Niall Pickerd coached, keen to persuade him to give her his DNA and fingerprints. She and Clarence had agreed to split up that morning so they could cover more ground.

But there was more to her desire to be out of the office. She bitterly regretted losing her self-control with Scott yesterday. She had embarrassed her son who wasn't speaking to her. Years of pent-up fury had burst from her mouth, and she simply hadn't been able to stop it. Worse still, it had been in a public place, with witnesses. Even Olivia was upset by the altercation outside her store; it wasn't good for business. Worst of all, Scott had recorded her outburst. She never should have shoved him. She couldn't believe that she had done it. It was not like her to do that. Her greatest fear was that he might use it to claim she was an unfit mother, or demand she be removed from the case. She shouldn't have taken the bait, but his lies had incensed her. They'd been like gas poured on a smoldering bonfire.

Sally toyed with the idea of going to her boss and fessing up. But she couldn't face the humiliation. Nor could she face the sniggers and whispers from other police officers with whom, she guessed, Scott would share the recording.

She planned to avoid the office for as long as she could and throw herself into her work.

The gym was in an alley, an old brick building with a shoebox of a reception area. One side of the gym was the boxing ring, the other was an open space where members could lift weights, hit punchbags, and do other fitness training. The stale smell of sweat hung in the air. The man behind the reception desk had a towel draped around his neck and beads of sweat clung to his face.

"Can I help you?" he asked.

"Looking for Niall Pickerd." Sally didn't show her PD badge because she didn't want to make life difficult for him.

"He's coaching. Should be finished in ten. You can go in and wait."

Sally entered the main gym where the sweat smell was amplified. The ceiling fans hadn't managed to dissipate the smell, nor had the open casement windows. A coach was shouting at two boxers in the ring. Sally saw Pickerd with a young, skinny guy, no more than twenty, who was doing his best to punch the crap out of the punching bag dangling from a thick chain from the ceiling. At the other end of the gym, a big guy lifted free weights. She guessed that Monday morning was a quiet time there.

Pickerd saw her out of the corner of his eye and excused himself, walking over.

"I heard she's out of the coma. How is she doing?"

The boy he was supposed to be coaching eyed Sally resentfully. "Yes, I hear she's doing well. Hasn't said anything. Sleeps a lot." Sally had called the hospital earlier that morning for an update.

Pickerd's resting expression was a frown, his lips pressed together. It was unsettling. "When can I see her?" he asked.

The boy was now staring daggers at Sally. "Finish your session with the young man. We can talk then."

"Okay. Don't leave, will you? I want to know more."

Sally sat on a bench against the wall, hoping it was far enough away from the ring where sweat was flying off the men boxing. She thought about Fiona. She was alive, but would she be lucid? The doctor in charge of her care was adamant that she couldn't ask Fiona questions.

She turned her attention to Pickerd. He was built tough, but small. She eyed his sneakers. Were they a size ten?

When his session with the boy finished, he came over. "Come outside. I need a smoke."

He stepped into the alley and Sally followed. He lit up immediately. "Yeah, I know. Bad habit." He shrugged and his trapezius muscles bulged. "When can I see her?"

He was straight back to asking about Fiona.

"No visitors, doctor's orders. I can't even interview her."

Pickerd blew cigarette smoke out of the corner of his mouth. "She's my mom. I have a right to see her."

"You say that, but do you have proof that you're her son?"

"Yeah, I got proof. What do you think I am? Stupid?"

"If I could see proof that you're her son, then you'd have a better chance of seeing her."

The tension in his shoulders dropped. "I have the papers Fiona signed when she gave me up for adoption. And the papers my adopted mom and dad signed, Anthony and Monika Pickerd."

"Where are these papers?"

"At home."

"You have a copy of your birth certificate?"

"Yeah."

"Shall we go? I can drive you home."

"I'll drive myself." He continued to smoke. "When you see the documents, I can see Fiona, right?"

"Niall, it's not as simple as that. Somebody tried to kill her. We are keeping her isolated for her own protection." *And you're a suspect*, Sally thought. "The shock of meeting you, if you are her son, might set back her recovery."

"No way! I show you the stuff you want, I get to see Mom."

"Niall, I'm trying to help you. Fiona's health is fragile. A shock like this could be too much. All I can promise is that if we have absolute proof that you are her son, I will consult with my boss and the doctor about a visit, okay?"

"No, it's not okay. My adoptive parents are dead. Fiona is all I have."

"I get it. But nothing's going to happen unless I have proof. Shall we go?"

Niall stamped out his cigarette underfoot and then he picked up the stub and threw it in the trash can behind the reception desk. They then walked along the alley together. "What size feet do you have?"

"Ten, why?"

"It's something we're asking everyone. You said that you left your car at the bar on the night of July twenty-sixth. When did you collect it?" Sally would check with the bar regarding any exterior surveillance cameras.

"Maybe seven-thirty or thereabouts, the next morning. Why?" He flicked her a look. "You think I went back for my car and then drove to Fiona's house and killed Joseph?"

They turned onto the busy main street. "Do you have any idea who might want to kill Joseph?" Sally asked.

"Except for me, you mean? I know how you cops think. I

turn up in Franklin and Joseph is murdered. But I didn't do it, and I'd never hurt my mom. Never."

"There's an easy way to eliminate you from our investigation. You give us a DNA swab and fingerprints. I have a kit in my car."

He sighed. He had refused the last time she had asked. "Do I get to see Mom if I do it?"

He was persistent. She had to give him that.

Pickerd had reached his car, a green Honda Accord that had to be a 1990s model. It was possibly all Pickerd could afford.

"If we can eliminate you from our inquiries, it's way more likely you can see her."

"You got me jumping through a whole lot of hoops, Sally." He smiled at her. "But Mom's worth it. Let's do it."

THIRTY-NINE

Clarence returned to the office late morning, having been to the Peak Bay Yacht Club checking surveillance footage for the night of Joseph's murder. Had Dallas Austin been there until 2 a.m. as he claimed?

"How did you get on?" Sally asked.

"I have a guest list and a staff list for that night." He held up a flash drive. "And the club's surveillance footage too."

"That'll keep you busy. Apart from the main door, how many other exits are there?"

"Kitchen and a fire door."

"Ask the kitchen staff if they saw Dallas Austin step outside."

Clarence nodded. "What happened with Niall Pickerd?"

Sally filled him in. "His DNA swab and fingerprints are on the way to the lab. And Dr. Mani called. It's not good news regarding the fingernail from the bathroom. So far, she has no DNA match on the database."

"Maybe it'll turn out to be Pickerd's DNA?" Clarence suggested.

"Maybe. I'm going to have another chat with Carlos. If he knew of his wife's affair, he had motive to kill her."

At McGettigan's Real Estate office in Peakhurst, Carlos showed Sally into a meeting room with glass on three sides. It was like being in a goldfish bowl.

Sally sat at a round table, facing Carlos, and asked, "You're working today?"

"I have to keep busy. I can't sit around at home all day. It's too depressing."

"Of course," Sally said. "We're trying to follow Roisin's movements on the evening of her death. I understand she had dinner with Dallas Austin."

Sally watched Carlos carefully. Would he be surprised?

Carlos leaned into the back of his chair and gave Sally a crooked smile. "And?"

"And you failed to mention it when I spoke to you. Why?"

"I guess I thought you wouldn't understand our... arrangement."

"Arrangement?" Sally asked.

"We have built a successful business together. Our marriage was over a long time ago and we agreed we could have relationships with other people. It worked for both of us."

"So you knew Roisin was having an affair with Dallas Austin?"

"Yes. Look, Roisin was a nightmare to live with, but she was the best real estate agent I've ever met."

"Did Dallas have a reason to kill your wife?"

"You'd have to ask him."

"What was her relationship with Salvador Sobral like?"

His upper lip curled. "I'm sure you know that Roisin and

Joseph started a petition to remove Salvador from the neighborhood."

"What was her objection to him?"

"I'm not homophobic or anything. Some of my best clients are gay. But those two are bad people. He's been to jail, which I'm sure you know. And then there are the wild parties! Music pounding until six in the morning. We called the cops, and they tell them to keep the noise down. Then, when the cops leave, the music gets cranked up again. Then there's the drug dealers who come and go. One night there was a guy who turned up with a video camera and professional lighting. Roisin was convinced they were shooting a porn movie."

"How do you know it was a porn movie?"

"Why turn up with a video camera and lighting?"

"To record the party?" Sally suggested.

"Nonsense."

"Did you see drugs change hands?"

"Well, not exactly."

Okay, so maybe Sobral and Griess were noisy neighbors, but so far there was no proof they'd done anything illegal.

"How did they react to your petition?"

"Sobral was livid. Accused us of being homophobic. He came here, actually. He yelled at me in front of clients. And I caught him snooping around the back of Joseph's house one day."

"When was this?"

"It was a Monday. The Monday before Joseph's murder. It had to be a Monday because that is usually our day off. Today's an exception."

"Tell me what you saw," Sally said.

"Joseph does the grocery shopping on a Monday, regular as clockwork, so Fiona was alone in the house. I was taking out the trash. Our cans are kept in the side yard. I heard someone running on the other side of the fence. I caught Sobral peering in the back windows. It was weird, because he then knocked on the door."

"Then what happened?"

"He tried talking to Fiona through the door. I was worried about her. Knew she'd be frightened. So I shouted at him, demanded to know what he was doing. He ran away, like the devious little rat that he is."

She found Carlos's bigoted view of Sobral disturbing but she couldn't let her dislike for Carlos get in the way of the investigation.

"What did he say to Fiona?"

"He was pleading, like a sniveling baby. Begging Fiona to persuade Joseph to drop the petition. But Salvador was wasting his time. She was more or less a recluse, and she relied on Joseph for everything. She would never open the door to Sobral. Fiona was okay if she was with Joseph, but she wouldn't leave the house on her own. She suffers from agoraphobia."

This was news to Sally.

"What size feet do you have, Mr. McGettigan?" Sally asked.

"Why?"

"Please, it would be helpful to know."

"Ten."

She thanked Carlos for his time and when she had left the office she called Clarke. She updated him on what she had learned from McGettigan about Salvador Sobral, and Clarke suggested they bring in Salvador for a formal interview.

"Let's shake the tree and see what falls from it," Clarke said. "I'll get him picked up."

FORTY

Salvador Sobral arrived at the FPD office with an attorney, Harold Epstein. Even before the interview began, Salvador's face was shiny with sweat and his mannerisms were jerky—he was clearly finding it stressful. Clarke, who wore his suit jacket and tie, which was a sign he meant business, insisted he lead the interview. Sally was happy to take a back seat, given her lack of experience.

They walked together to interview room two.

"What did the lab say about the fingernail?" Clarke asked.

"No DNA match to Sobral or anyone on our databases."

"Damn. He's got motive to murder both victims and no alibi. But without fingerprints or DNA, we need a confession. I'm going in hard."

"He's fragile," Sally said. "Can't we coax a confession from him?"

"You play good cop. I'll do the bad."

They entered the interview room and Clarke set up the recording, introducing each person there.

"I don't want to talk to him," Sobral said to his lawyer. "He didn't believe me last time."

"I'm the lead detective on the case and I'll conduct this interview."

Sobral stared at his lawyer with pleading eyes.

"We can't choose the detective, Salvador, just do as we discussed," the lawyer said.

"You haven't been honest with us, Salvador, have you?" Clarke began.

Sobral blinked like a round-eyed, nocturnal tarsier, which Sally had seen at a zoo. "I have."

"Tell us about Monday, July twenty-fifth, when you snuck around the back of the Austins' house."

Eyes even wider. "I did nothing wrong. She was nicer than Joseph. I wanted her to put an end to the petition."

Clarke asked, "Did you speak to her?"

"No, she wouldn't open the door. Then I left."

The balding attorney leaned closer to him and advised him he didn't have to say anything.

"It's okay," Sobral said. "I have nothing to hide."

Sally hoped for his sake that this was true because Clarke was like a Rottweiler poised to snap Sobral's neck if he didn't confess.

"A witness saw you that night peering into the windows at the back of the house. Were you scoping out the place?"

"No," Sobral said. "I knew Fiona was in there and I wanted to get her attention. She never goes anywhere, you see."

"What I see is a man who hated Joseph Austin, who waited until Fiona's husband had left the house, then you went to the backyard to plan how you would break in."

"I told you. And her." He flicked a look at Sally. "The following night, I saw the killer. On the porch talking to Joseph. Joseph invited him in."

"There was no man on the porch. It's a lie. You entered the house on the night of July twenty-sixth, tortured and killed Joseph, and then attacked Fiona, right?"

"I didn't do it. Why are you picking on me?" A bead of sweat trickled down his temple.

"What was in the safe, Salvador?"

Sobral yelled, "I don't know! I didn't kill Joseph. And I didn't hate him. *He* hated me and Justin. I just wanted him to stop."

Epstein said to his client, "I advise you not to say any more. 'No comment' will suffice."

Clarke kept up his barrage of questions. "You claim you were at home on the night Roisin McGettigan was murdered. Are there any witnesses?"

"No, I was alone, except for our cat."

"What did you do that night?"

"I don't know. Cooked, ate my dinner. Watched TV. Read a book."

"What did you watch on TV?"

"A Netflix movie. Check with Netflix."

Clarke said, "Just because a movie was running, it doesn't mean you were home watching it."

Epstein intervened. "Detective, can you prove my client *wasn't* home that night?" Clarke didn't respond. "I thought not. You're upsetting my client with your unfounded accusations. Salvador suffers from anxiety and insomnia. Unless he is under arrest, we're leaving." The attorney stood.

Sobral, red and sweaty in the face, turned his attention to Sally. "I thought you believed me. You seemed genuine. I told you I saw a man on Joseph's porch that night. *He* is the killer. *Not* me. Why are you tormenting me when you should be searching for the guy with the sneering voice?"

"Salvador, don't say anything more." This time the attorney gently took Sobral's arm. Sobral stumbled when his foot caught behind a chair leg.

"Wait!" Sally said, rising from her seat. "Salvador, you said the man's voice was sneering. Can you tell me more about it?"

Sobral looked over his shoulder as his lawyer opened the door. He said, "He was educated. Like he thought Joseph was beneath him."

Sally watched Sobral and Epstein walk away. Sobral moved like a broken man. Sally felt guilty that she hadn't intervened and stopped the interview. Clarke had gone too far. Sobral was in a fragile mental state. This interview might push him over the edge.

"He's lying through his teeth," Clarke said, getting up from the table.

"I'm inclined to think he's telling the truth. And the educated voice of Joseph's visitor rules out a few suspects, including Niall Pickerd."

"Educated voice? He's making it up! Only he claims there was a visitor. The killer entered through the study window." Clarke shook his head. "Sobral has motive, means, and opportunity. What we don't have is proof. And I need you to find that proof, Sally."

FORTY-ONE

Sally stared at the suspects' whiteboard. Her gut was telling her that Sobral was innocent, but Clarke was determined to prove him guilty. It felt as if Clarke were shoehorning Sobral into the killer's shoes. Who could she turn to for advice? Clarke was her mentor and boss. She toyed with the idea of asking Lin's view on Salvador Sobral. They got on well and Lin was level-headed. However, she was also totally loyal to Clarke.

There was a knock and Lin looked in, as if she had read Sally's mind.

"The boss wants to see you." Lin glanced behind her, then back to Sally. "It's Scott. He's made a formal complaint against you."

"Oh, great! It's about yesterday, right?" Sally asked.

Lin grimaced. "Sorry to be the bearer of bad news."

"Esme, can I ask you a question about the Austin case, maybe after I've seen Clarke?"

"Sure."

Sally brushed down her blouse and skirt, trying to ready herself to face the music. She mustn't allow Scott to get under her skin.

But as she approached Clarke's office, she not only became aware of everyone watching her, but also to make matters worse, Scott, in his PD uniform, was standing in Clarke's office. She'd thought it would be just her and Clarke. With Clarke alone, she could stand her ground and explain the embarrassing video, which Scott had no doubt shown him. But with Scott present, Sally would get tongue-tied. He had a way of undermining her confidence.

The fine hairs on the back of her neck prickled as she knocked on Clarke's door.

"Come!" Clarke called and Sally entered the room.

Scott was standing at attention, appearing every bit the fine cop that he pretended to be. Her emotions became a swirling mass of anger and fear and she told herself to quell her feelings before they took her over.

"Sally, take a seat." Clarke gestured to one of two chairs opposite his desk.

"I'm happy to stand, sir."

"Okay, Office Fairburn has shown me a video of you arguing with him on Sunday. He says he believes that you are mentally unfit for duty and should be removed from your position. I thought it only fair for you to see this video and to comment."

Clarke stood and passed her a phone, which Sally recognized to be Scott's. She took it, already aware of what it would show. She had spent much of last night reliving their very public exchange. She played the video. It began with Sally walking up to Paul on the sidewalk near the bookstore. It ended when Paul scowled at her and walked away. It was impossible not to flush with humiliation. Her behavior was aggressive. Scott's came across as reasonable. Even Paul's embarrassment was captured on the footage and Sally closed her eyes for a moment before handing the phone back to her boss.

"Sir, this happened outside of work hours. Scott is my ex-husband. Whatever goes on between us outside of work hours has nothing to do with how I perform my job."

"I get that," Clarke said. "But your mental health does matter and if it impacts your ability to do your job as a detective, I have to take that into consideration."

Out of the corner of her eye she saw Scott's mouth crease at the edges into a smirk. He was really enjoying her discomfort.

"My mental health has never been better. Have I not conducted the investigation in a sensible way?"

"You have, but an outburst like this in public doesn't look good for a new detective like you. I urge you, Sally, and you, Scott, to deal with whatever disagreements you have in private. Do I make myself clear?"

"Yes, sir," Sally said.

"Sir, Sally called me a pedophile. It's slander."

It's the truth, Sally thought.

She and Clarke exchanged the briefest of looks.

Clarke said, "Scott, I questioned you in relation to Stacy Green's assault. It's no secret that you were implicated. You should think long and hard before you go down the slander route."

Scott glared at Clarke, but he nodded. "I have no need to sue Sally for slander. I just want to see my son."

"Paul doesn't want to see you. Stop stalking him," Sally said before she could stop herself.

"I'm not stalking him. I'm trying to be a father. Be reasonable."

Clarke raised a hand. "Enough already! Scott, Sally, you need to sort out your differences outside of police time. Do you hear me?"

Sally and Scott mumbled yeses.

"Scott, let Sally get on with her job. Drop the slander angle."

"Can't do that, sir. My lawyer says I'd win if I took it to

court. I want joint custody of Paul." Sally gasped. The floor felt as if it shuddered. Scott went on, "And I want Sally removed from police duty."

"Your rows are none of my business. This argument didn't happen when either of you were working. Sally will not be removed from her current role. Scott, you are dismissed." Clarke said.

Scott didn't budge. His jaw was gritted and a vein on his neck protruded.

"I said dismissed."

"Yes, sir." Scott left the room, giving Sally a livid glance.

Clarke shook his head. "What in god's name were you thinking?"

"I was blind with fury. He barges into my home a few days ago. He punches Paul when Paul tells him to leave. That's assault of a minor! On Sunday, he turned up at the bookstore where Paul was working and wouldn't leave, even though Paul made it clear he wanted him to go. Then he tried to make out that I had stopped him from seeing Paul over the past six years. He stood right in my face, telling lie after lie and I pushed him away."

"Don't let him catch you out like this again. I can brush the allegations aside this time but if it happens again I'll have no choice but to relieve you of your duties, pending investigation."

"Thank you, sir."

Sally stood rigidly tall as she left his office and walked back to her incident room.

Clarence was waiting for her, fiddling with a pen, which he dropped on the floor when she walked in. He then stared at his monitor, using it like a shield to avoid an awkward conversation.

"I guess you know that I lost my temper with Scott this past weekend?"

"It's none of my business," Clarence said. "That's between you and him."

She wanted to take him in a hug, so grateful was she that he wasn't making a big problem of it. "I appreciate that. I'm going out for a coffee. Clear my head. I won't be long."

She left the building through the rear door of the foyer, which took her to an alley where the cops who liked to smoke hung out. She kept her eyes fixed straight ahead and only when she was in her car did she let out a deafening scream.

"Get out of my life, you bastard!"

FORTY-TWO

Sally couldn't face going back into the station. And she needed to think of something other than Scott. Fiona was the key to solving the case and Sally was frustrated that the doctor wouldn't allow her to interview her, even though she had been conscious for two days. Sally couldn't wait any longer. Clarke was very close to arresting the wrong man, and she had to know from Fiona if Sobral was or wasn't the man who attacked her.

This time Sally didn't check in with the nurses on Fiona's ward because she didn't want to draw attention to herself. She walked straight past the nurses' station as if she had every right to be there. She chatted briefly with Deidre Kelly, then went into Fiona's room.

Fiona lay propped up in her bed, eyes shut. She was no longer on a breathing tube and Sally watched as the old woman's chest rose and fell in a relaxed rhythm. Fiona had an IV line, which kept her hydrated, and a machine monitored her heart rate. Sally began to doubt that she should be there. What if her presence startled Fiona? Sally almost turned around and left, then she changed her mind and sat next to the bed. As she had done before, she gently took Fiona's bony and fragile hand in hers. The woman didn't stir.

"Hello, Fiona," Sally said in a hushed tone. "I'm Sally Fairburn. A detective working your case." She stopped speaking when Fiona's eyes moved beneath the closed lids. Sally could just make out the movement through the delicate skin. "I've visited you before. Chatted with you. I was holding your hand when you came round." Sally paused. The eyelids were trembling as if Fiona were trying to open them. "We're all so happy you came back to us. The nurses and doctors are delighted at your progress." The white eyelashes parted slowly, and Sally began to see Fiona's green irises, the inner edges of her eyes sticky with sleep.

Still holding Fiona's hand, Sally stood over her so she could be more easily seen. Sally smiled. "Hello there, I'm Sally. It's so good to see your beautiful eyes."

Fiona looked up but not at Sally, like a newborn who couldn't focus on their mother until much later on.

"You're in the hospital," Sally said. "Can I get you anything?"

Fiona's lips, like her eyes, had a sticky layer on them and they initially stuck when Fiona tried to part her lips. "Water," Fiona whispered.

Sally saw a plastic cup with a straw and water in it. Sally released Fiona's hand, picked up the cup, and placed the tip of the straw on Fiona's bottom lip. "Can you take a sip through the straw?"

Fiona slowly parted her lips then closed them around the straw and sipped, just the once, then her lips relaxed and the straw fell away from her mouth.

Sally waited, cup in hand, should Fiona want another sip. The woman's eyes seemed to focus on Sally.

"Who... you?"

"My name's Sally Fairburn. I'm a detective. Do you know why you're in the hospital?"

A look of confusion crossed Fiona's face.

"An intruder broke into your house. Do you remember that person?"

Fiona's eyes moved around. "Joseph? Where is he?"

This was the question Sally had been dreading and she wasn't prepared for it. If she told Fiona that he was dead, might the shock cause her to relapse?

"He's not here," Sally replied. "Do you remember you were in your bedroom and someone hit you on the head?"

"My head. Yes." The machine next to her bed showed her heart rate was increasing. "He came up the stairs and hit me. Have you caught him?"

Sally held Fiona's hand. "Not yet, but I will. You're perfectly safe, I promise. There's a police officer outside your door, day and night. Do you know who hurt you?"

Fiona turned her head a fraction to the left, away from Sally. "He screamed." Her eyes were teary.

"Who screamed? Joseph?"

"Yes."

A tear slipped from her left eye. "He's dead, isn't he?"

"I'm so sorry."

"Oh, what a fool!"

"Who is a fool?"

"He always was. Now it's too late."

"Do you know who killed him?"

A nurse rushed into the room and raced over to the bed. "What are you doing? Her heart rate's too fast. Leave. Now!"

FORTY-THREE

Sally sat outside the hospital for a while. What had she learned? She was no further forward identifying the killer. She also hadn't had time to ask Fiona if she had a personal bank account and if she'd inherited a lot of money, which she and Joseph used to buy their home. But Fiona had made a strange comment about Joseph. Why was he a fool? Was it because he let the killer into the house, just as Sobral claimed?

Sally called Clarence and asked for the address of the real estate agency that sold 59 Willow Way to the Austins. He came up with the details for Redfern Real Estate. The agent was Michelle Skeel, the owner.

"We can't wait for the FBI to locate Fiona's account," Sally explained. "With any luck, Michelle Skeel can save us a lot of time."

Sally drove straight to the real estate office.

A bottle-blonde woman in her early fifties introduced herself as Michelle Skeel and showed Sally into a meeting room. "Is this about that awful murder?"

"It is. You were the real estate agent who managed the sale

of fifty-nine Willow Way to Joseph and Fiona Austin, am I right?"

"That's right. That must be ten years ago."

"Do you still have the documents relating to the sale?"

Michelle tapped her red fingernails on the tabletop. "I should have them. I keep everything in boxes in the basement. I'm a bit of a hoarder."

"Could I take a look?" Sally asked.

"If you tell me what you're looking for, I might save you time."

"I'm interested in the bank account they used to complete the sale."

"Okay, I'll ask John to show you where the boxes of the house sales in 2006 are."

John, who worked for Michelle, was very helpful. He brought the winter 2006 boxes out of the basement and piled them on the floor of the meeting room. "It's chronological order," he said. "Let me know if you need anything else." Then he left her to it.

The lid was dusty with speckles of mildew. Sally used some tissues to wipe away some of the dirt. Inside were drop files—green cardstock with a metal strip running along the top and the address of the property written on a white tab. Sally flicked through the tabs, bending her head over one shoulder so she could read the tiny writing. Each rusty drop file made a little squeak as she pulled it toward her, which set her nerves on edge. If she could find the details of Fiona's mysterious bank account, she might then discover where the millions came from that enabled Fiona and Joseph to buy their house. Could this case be about someone who felt aggrieved because they didn't inherit the money and Fiona did? Was it possible the money was dirty money?

When she had gone through every file in the winter 2006

box and found nothing on 59 Willow Way, her optimism waned. Had it been filed in the wrong place or not filed at all?

Leaving the meeting room, she found John at his desk and asked him for the boxes for the fall of 2006 and the spring of 2007, hoping it had been filed in the wrong place. He obliged. Sally then went through all the files for the fall of 2006. Nothing. An hour passed and she took a break. Her eyes were scratchy from all the dust in the room. She found the restroom and threw water over her face, drying her skin with a paper towel. Seeing her reflection in the mirror, she told herself not to give up.

Back in the meeting room, Sally moved on to the spring of 2007. Four files in, she saw a tab that said 59 Willow Way and her heart leaped with anticipation. She opened the file on the table and flicked through various documents relating to the house sale, including the paperwork Fiona signed at the auction. It had been incorrectly filed.

She skimmed the details. It was a foreclosed property, which meant that the buyers had to have cash or a cashier's check on the day of the auction. It also meant that Joseph and Fiona would have had to prequalify to bid at the auction by showing the real estate agent that they had cash available to complete the purchase. A tingle of excitement ran up Sally's spine.

She flicked through the pages faster and then she found what she was looking for. A letter from the Bank of Detroit, dated December 2, 2006, confirmed that Fiona Marie Austin had $2,509,000 in her account.

"Got you!" Sally said.

Why bank with the Bank of Detroit when Fiona had never left her hometown of Franklin? Perhaps that was the point. It was hard to find it.

FORTY-FOUR

Sally passed on the details of Fiona's Bank of Detroit account to Clarence, then explained that she wasn't returning to the office because she had a family issue to deal with. Now that Scott had declared he wanted joint custody of Paul, Sally needed to appoint a lawyer fast. La Cava Allison wouldn't have been her first choice of law firm, but Elkington was already aware of her situation and it was easier to continue with her services.

On the way there, Sally updated Clarke on the case, starting with the Bank of Detroit account. She concluded, "It's a hunch, but there's something fishy about how they managed to purchase their home. And why didn't they use a local bank? I want to ask Fiona about it."

Clarke said, "You're wasting your time. Sobral is our prime suspect. Focus on getting a confession."

Clarke had fixated on Troy Vincent earlier. Now he was fixated on Sobral. In both instances, Sally believed they were not the killer. She wasn't about to drop other lines of inquiry.

"Can you put pressure on the hospital for me? I want to interview Fiona tomorrow. I saw her briefly today. I was asked to leave before I could get anywhere."

"Will do."

At the law firm, Sally asked Elkington to prepare a case for continued sole custody of her son. The lawyer warned Sally that the video of her yelling at Scott and then shoving him would work against her, but Sally had to believe that her and Paul's testimony would be enough to convince the judge. Sally then drove to Olivia's Bookstore to pick up Jax.

Olivia sat behind the counter on a three-legged stool, with her cat, Pajamas, asleep on the countertop. Olivia's head of green hair was bowed, her attention given to her cell phone. The shop was quiet, but because of the meandering layout of the bookshelves and the little nooks they created where people sat at tables to read and enjoy their coffee and cake, Sally couldn't be sure how many others were in the store.

"Hey, there," Sally said.

Olivia jumped and looked up. Instead of the usual big smile, Olivia gave Sally a shake of the head. "I can't believe he's put it on Facebook." She held her phone up for Sally to see. It was the video of her yelling at Scott outside the bookstore. Bile rose up in her throat.

Olivia put the phone under the counter, then pushed her glasses up her nose. They had thick black frames that made her look like an owl, albeit an owl with green feathers.

"I feel responsible," Olivia said. "If I hadn't told you about Scott coming here, you wouldn't have argued."

"You did the right thing, Olivia. I overreacted and I should know better."

"Has it caused problems at work?"

"A little. I'm more worried about what it's doing to Paul. I embarrassed him in public and he's not happy."

"I don't have kids," said Olivia. "But it seems to me that if he doesn't want contact with his father, then he shouldn't have to. He's old enough to make up his own mind."

"I think the same, which is why I'm going to fight for continued sole custody. It may go to court."

"Call me as a witness. You were provoked."

"Thanks, Olivia. And thanks so much for looking after Jax."

"He's no trouble."

"Is he still out back?"

"Yeah, I tried introducing Pajamas to the little guy, but Pajamas started hissing." Olivia stroked the sleeping cat. "She thinks she rules the store."

Sally made her way to the back of the store and into the backyard. Olivia lived above the shop and had made the small yard an oasis of lawn and vines growing up the walls and across a wooden framework so that it had the feel of a French rural property, albeit a tiny one. Jax looked up from a fluffy toy snake that he'd been chewing with his sharp little teeth and ran over to her, his little tail wagging. Olivia must have bought him the toy snake from the pet store up the road.

She picked up the puppy who wriggled in her arms and tried to lick her face. She pulled her chin back. "What am I going to do with you tomorrow?" Sally said.

She felt bad about imposing on Olivia again. But with her at work and Paul at school, what was she to do? If she left him in her backyard at home, he would whimper and bark.

Sally found his leash hanging on a doorknob and she carried the pup with her through the bookstore to where Olivia had just finished with a customer. "The toy snake was a lovely idea. You are so good to me."

"Aw, it was nothing. Kept the little guy occupied. Can I have him again tomorrow? The customers love to cuddle him."

When Sally and Jax arrived home, Paul's school bag was by the front door and she could see his bicycle in the backyard through the glass of the back door. She guessed that he was in his bedroom.

"Hi, Paul. I picked up Jax!" she called up the stairs.

No response. Sally took Jax into the backyard where there was grass, a water bowl, a small shed, and a paved area with table and chairs, and left the puppy there while she went upstairs and knocked on Paul's door.

Through the door she could hear music, the volume low, which was a change.

"I'm busy," Paul yelled out.

"Can I come in?" Sally said. "I'm so sorry about yesterday. I really am."

"I don't want to talk about it."

"Please, Paul, I was trying to protect you and I overreacted."

Jax was yapping in the backyard, probably wanting to come into the house. He needed feeding too.

There was a squeak as Paul left his desk chair and the door was opened.

"Dad posted it on Facebook. Now everyone's seen it. My friends too. And you know what they're saying? You're a fruit loop. I hate them saying that shit."

Those dark, angry eyes, so like his father's. Except Paul had a kind and loving heart.

"I'm sorry. I let him get to me. It's just that I love you so much and when he tried to make out that I kept him from you, I snapped. He's trying to drive a wedge between us. Jax is just the beginning. Stalking you at the bookstore was his way of pretending to be the proud dad. He's forcing his way into our lives and now he wants joint custody."

"What!"

"I won't let that happen. I've briefed a lawyer."

Paul threw his arms in the air. "Why doesn't he leave me alone? Does he seriously imagine I've forgotten what he did to

Zelda? She killed herself because of him. He's a fricking psychopath!"

"I'm sure your shrink will be happy to testify about the effect he had on you."

He raked his fingers through his hair. "Then everyone will know. Do we have to go to court?"

"Hopefully not. Don't worry about that now. And you won't have to do anything you don't want to."

"What if he wins? What if I have to see him?" Paul paced the small landing. "I won't do it. I don't care what any court says."

Sally wished she hadn't brought up the subject. "Forget about it. I've got it under control."

"But he videoed you freaking out. Don't you see? It looks like I was pissed with you. I didn't tell him to back off. I messed up."

Sally took hold of her son and hugged him. "I messed up. Not you. I swear to you, I won't let him win."

From the backyard, Jax started to whimper, no doubt wanting some company.

"How about we play with Jax? The little guy needs some love."

Paul looked up then and smiled and they went downstairs. "He has a new toy snake. Olivia gave it to him." Sally wanted to change the subject. "And he has a vet appointment at six for his first vaccinations. You want to come with me?"

"Yeah. Wouldn't want the little guy to be afraid."

FORTY-FIVE

The phone call was totally unexpected. Sally was in the kitchen, thinking about what to cook for dinner. She didn't recognize the cell number but, assuming it must be related to the investigation, she took the call.

"It's Harper Fairburn. Please listen."

Scott's new wife!

Still reeling from the fallout of Scott's video, Sally was tempted to terminate the call at once. But Harper was a victim, just as Sally had been, and for her to contact Sally took some guts. Or desperation. She vaguely remembered how skinny and fragile the woman had looked in the bookstore.

"I'm surprised you're calling me."

"Don't tell Scott, please," Harper pleaded. "He told me not to talk to anyone, especially you. I don't even have a phone. Well, I do, but he won't let me have it."

"How did you know my cell number?"

"Scott has it."

"Whose phone are you using?"

"Sara's. We're at the park. She's real nice. She said I could use it to make a call. Scott doesn't know I'm here. You can't tell him."

Sally cringed at the thought of Harper's predicament. Scott had always been a control freak but taking Harper's phone away was extreme, even for him.

"I won't tell Scott, I promise. But why call *me*?"

"I... don't know."

Her voice trailed away. She sounded so lost.

"What's wrong?" Sally asked.

"I don't know who to turn to. I don't have any friends. I pretend to Sara that we're normal. That I'm happy. She has no idea what I go through. I don't know if I can trust her. Her life is so... perfect. How could she understand?"

Sally understood. She had been through the same experience. It brought back painful memories.

"I was gaslighted by Scott and I didn't even realize what he was doing to me. I lost my confidence, my ability to make decisions. I was always the one in the wrong. He alienated me from friends and family. Does this sound familiar?"

"Yes," Harper croaked. "Did he... lock you in the bathroom to punish you?"

Sally gasped. "That's terrible. He didn't do that to me, although he'd punish me with angry silence until I apologized. I had to say that I was wrong and he was right, even though I see now that I had been right."

"Thank god you understand! When we first arrived in Franklin, he locked us in the apartment for five weeks. No phone, no internet." Her words tumbled out. "I ran away, you see. Back home in Chicago. He found me at the women's shelter. I... I can't bear it anymore. Please help me. You... you got away from him. Help me escape. Please. I can't do it alone."

"I, er..."

Sally was being torn in two. Harper needed help. But interfering in Scott's marriage was dangerous. How would a court of law see her actions? Would Scott's lawyer say that she was hell bent on destroying his second marriage because she was jealous? But how could Sally refuse? It sounded like Harper was physically abused as well as mentally and emotionally abused. No wonder the poor young woman was almost anorexic.

"This is difficult for me, Harper. I have to know that Scott hasn't put you up to this."

"No! If he knew, he would never forgive me. I'm frightened, Sally. Please, I'm begging you. Help me."

Sally looked across the kitchen counter to where Paul slouched on the couch, watching TV, with Jax asleep in his lap. Harper's plea for help couldn't have come at a worse time. If Scott ever discovered that Sally helped Harper leave him, he'd make her life an absolute misery and he'd try to take Paul away from her. Sally would have to be very careful.

"Shall we meet?" Sally suggested. She could better judge if Harper could be trusted if they were face-to-face.

"I'm at Fairlight Park with Eli. Can you come now? He doesn't know I'm here."

Sally looked up at the kitchen clock: 6:31 p.m. "Where is Scott?"

"He won't be home until ten."

"Okay, I'll be there in fifteen minutes, depending on traffic. Stay at the playground."

The sun was setting by the time Sally reached the park. Sally found Harper inside the gated playground, watching her toddler make sandcastles in the sandpit with a cheap plastic blue bucket and tiny plastic spade. The air had a chilly edge to it and Harper held the collar of her coat close to her throat. She looked like a bamboo cane bending in the wind.

"Hello, Harper," Sally said.

The young woman jumped, then exhaled with relief when she saw Sally standing nearby.

"You came! I wasn't sure if you would," Harper said.

"Your son is gorgeous," Sally smiled as the boy tapped the top of his upside-down bucket and produced another sandcastle.

"He's the reason I married Scott. I got pregnant, I was sixteen. It was either marry Scott or be a single mom." She stared at her son. "Don't get me wrong. I love Eli. He's the only good thing in my life. But we can't stay with Scott."

Harper still looked like a teenager. Sally imagined that at sixteen she would have appeared younger than her years and young was how Scott liked them.

"My car's over there." Sally pointed at it. "We can walk and talk."

"You'll help me run away?" Harper asked.

"That's what we have to work out. The wind is freezing. Let's get you both in my car and I'll put the heater on."

Eli threw a tantrum when Harper told him it was time to go. He flung his bucket and spade down.

"This nice lady has a nice warm car. Won't that be nice?" Harper soothed.

"Hi, Eli. We're going on an adventure. Do you want to come too?" Sally said to the toddler.

Eli hesitated then nodded and allowed his mom to lead him out of the fenced play area. She then strapped him into his stroller and they followed the trail through the park, which was lit by the park lights.

"Tell me more about the time you tried to leave Scott," Sally said.

Harper told her about the women's shelter in Chicago and how Scott kidnapped her off the street just as the shelter had a van ready to drive her out of the city to safety.

"And he was on duty?" Sally asked, infuriated by what she had heard.

"Yes, he locked us in the patrol car, drove us home, and them imprisoned us in the bathroom."

"He's totally deplorable." Sally felt like strangling him. "If your parents knew how he's treating you, would they take you in?"

"I tried that. They won't. I don't have a car or money or a phone."

"What about Sara? She sounds nice. Would she have you stay with her while I find you a shelter to go to?"

"He met Sara. He'd find me there. I have to go someplace he won't think to look for me."

Sally momentarily thought of her parents who lived in the small rural community of North Bend, but it was unfair to rope them into such a contentious situation. And besides, her father still thought Scott was a lovely man and that she had been a fool to lose him. He therefore couldn't be trusted to keep Harper's location a secret from Scott.

"Is there another relative, someone Scott has never met?"

"I have an aunt in Eacham, although I haven't been in contact with her since we married. She may not want us. Scott knows about her, but they've never met, and I haven't mentioned her for years."

"Eacham? The old mining town. That's maybe ninety minutes' drive." Sally rubbed her forehead, thinking. "That might work. Do you know what shifts Scott is working this week?"

"I can find out."

"Be careful not to sound too interested in his work roster, otherwise he'll guess you're planning something."

"How can I contact you? I can't keep using Sara's phone. She's getting suspicious. She asked today when I was getting my new phone."

Sally checked the time on her watch. Shops at the mall were still open. "I'll get you a burner phone. I know a store that'll be open. Can you hide it somewhere Scott won't think to look?"

"My pack of tampons."

"Good idea." Sally looked down at the sleeping child in the stroller. "Don't tell Eli about this, or anyone for that matter. Not even your aunt. Don't make any contact with her. You understand?"

"What if Auntie Barbara won't take us in?" Harper said.

"We'll have to do our best to persuade her. And don't pack a bag. He's bound to find it."

Harper smiled and Sally caught a glimpse of how beautiful she had once been. "Thank you."

They had reached Sally's car. She unlocked it. "Get in. I'll switch the heater on."

Harper looked at the car's interior longingly. "I can't. Scott has spies everywhere."

"Come with me to the shopping mall. You can stay in the parking lot if you like. At least it will be warm. It won't take me long to buy the phone."

Harper nodded. They loaded the stroller into the trunk then Harper got in the back with Eli on her lap. It was illegal not to have a child seat, but Sally took the risk, arriving at the parking lot safely. Minutes later, she handed Harper a prepaid cell phone, which had two hundred dollars' worth of calls on it.

"You have to promise me that whatever happens, you'll never tell Scott that I helped you. I can't risk losing my son to him."

"Cross my heart and hope to die," Harper said, crossing herself. "There's something I should tell you. Scott wants sole custody of Paul. He's going to accuse you of being an unfit mother. I thought you should know."

Sally's stomach squirmed. *Sole* custody! "Has he appointed a lawyer?"

"Yes."

"Thank you for telling me. Shall I drop you near your apartment?"

"No, we'll get out here and walk home. I'll call you when I know he's doing a night shift."

FORTY-SIX

September 13, 2016

It was after midnight and gusty weather was shaking the maple tree next to Salvador Sobral's house. He lay in bed, unable to sleep, and stared up at the patterns moving across the ceiling. The leaves, like splayed fingers, seemed to wave at him as the moonlight cast shadows on his ceiling. The sleeping pill he'd taken wasn't working—Sobral was tired, but he wasn't sleepy. He was also twitchy. How could he be anything else after that police interview?

Things were just getting worse. His life was out of his control. Six weeks ago, the cops just ignored his comment about Joseph's visitor. It was irritating, but at least they didn't accuse him of murder. Yesterday, Clarke as good as did just that. And Sally sat there and let him do it. Sobral had been wrong about her. She wasn't a nice lady after all.

He wished Justin hadn't gone to work tonight. Salvador was always restless when he was alone, imagining things that weren't there. But Justin had already missed yesterday's shift, asking a friend to take his place. Justin couldn't fail to turn up again, or at least that's what he said.

Sobral sat up. Was Justin getting bored with Sobral's neediness?

He tore at a hangnail. He had often wondered why someone as together as Justin had started a relationship with him in the first place. He wasn't put off by Sobral's criminal record. They'd met through a gay dating website and three weeks later Justin had moved in with him. At the time, Sobral was so in love he didn't stop to question the speed with which their relationship had progressed. Still, Justin had coped with the slander spread by their neighbors. But then came the police investigation. He had been a fool to tell the cops about his attempt to see Fiona and ask for her help. It had made him look guilty of murder.

He groaned at his stupidity.

Switching on the bedside lamp, he stared at the alarm clock with loathing. The clock was a reminder of his insomnia. While other people slumbered, he fretted. No wonder he could barely think straight. He stared at the bottle of temazepam by his bed, but to take another pill wasn't a good idea. He'd already consumed a half bottle of bourbon. Restless, he threw back the duvet and pulled on his bathrobe, a gift from Justin. Sobral stroked the brushed cotton of the two deep pockets, then he went downstairs to the kitchen.

The wind blew under the back door, making a howling sound that set Sobral's nerves further on edge. The kitchen hadn't been updated for twenty or more years, since it had belonged to his parents. He started to make hot milk and honey. His mom had always sworn by it as a cure for any sleeplessness. He'd do it the old-fashioned way—heating the milk in a small saucepan and adding the honey to the mug. Using a microwave, one of the few newer additions to the kitchen, meant several goes at reaching the right temperature and lots of fussing with the microwave door.

The kitchen window rattled, the latch was old and loose. With his meager pay as a hospital orderly and Justin's as a nurse, they didn't have enough to do the repairs to the aging house. Justin wanted them to hang on to the house until interest rates had dropped and the market was booming again so they could sell it and get top dollar for it. But Salvador had had enough. He wanted to sell and move somewhere new, where nobody knew about his past and where two gay men could live without neighbors saying hateful things about them.

He stirred the warming milk over the gas cooktop. It had just started to ripple on the surface. The honey was already in the mug. He waited a few more seconds, then switched off the gas, and started to pour the hot milk into the mug.

Then Sobral felt the solid weight of someone's arms on his shoulders. Someone right behind him. For a fleeting second, he thought it was Justin cuddling up to him. But hands in black gloves came down on either side of his face. He saw the flash of wire gripped between those hands, then the stinging pain as the wire cut into his throat. He dropped the saucepan, which hit the tiled floor with a crash. He tried to pull the wire away, but he couldn't get his fingers beneath it.

He heard his own choking noises, the crunch of the cartilage in his neck crushing. He was dizzy with the searing agony. His chest felt as if it would explode, but he couldn't get air into his lungs. Clawing at the wire, his fingers grew sticky with his own blood.

Desperate, Sobral reached out one hand, trying to find a weapon. The tip of a finger touched the mug. It crashed to the floor and shattered, his hot milk and honey gone. By now, his head was throbbing, his face swollen and red. He gasped for air, but nothing reached his lungs. He felt his power begin to drain. He raised a hand and reached behind him. His bloody fingers touched a head of hair and he tugged at it, grabbing a chunk. A man grunted, but he didn't release the ligature.

Sobral's legs collapsed beneath him. His strength was almost gone and it was only the ligature holding him up. Sobral clawed at the man's head, clawing, blood seeping from his lips. It was the end. He knew it. His hands fell to his side, and he let darkness take him.

FORTY-SEVEN

Sally was dreaming that Paul was moving in with his dad. She chased after her son as he left the house and he got into Scott's Jeep Wrangler. Sally hammered her fists on the window, screaming at Paul not to leave her. Also in the car were Harper and Eli, both laughing insanely. Scott sat in the driver's seat, his arm resting on the frame of the open window. He pointed his fingers at her in the shape of a gun and pretended to shoot her, then drove away. Sally attempted to run after the car but her legs felt as if they were wading through thick mud.

Sally woke murmuring Paul's name. What was that beeping noise? She turned her head on the pillow and saw her phone was lit up. It was dark in the room and therefore nighttime, but someone thought it urgent enough to call her. She reached for the phone, which was recharging on her nightstand, and answered.

"Hello?"

"Sally, it's Clarke. Get your butt to Sobral's house now. He's been murdered."

"What? I..." Sally held the phone far enough away so she could see the time: 5:37 a.m. "On my way."

Clarke ended the call. Sally leaned over to switch on the lamp and, waiting a few seconds for her eyes to adjust to the light, shoved off the bedspread. As she dressed, she called Clarence Pew. He didn't pick up so she left him a message, telling him to get to Sobral's house ASAP.

Her mind was fuzzy with sleep, but she managed to gather up her phone and police ID and to take her police-issue Glock from the bedroom safe where she kept it every night. Creeping down the stairs so not to wake Paul, she heard the puppy whimper, having heard her. Paul had the puppy sleeping in his room, even though Sally expressed a preference that the puppy should learn to stay downstairs.

In the kitchen, she wrote a note for Paul, explaining there was a police emergency and she would come back later to take Jax to Olivia's Bookstore.

Help yourself to breakfast and don't forget to feed Jax.
I love you. Call me if you need anything.

Sally set off for 58 Willow Way, her stomach churning. "Sobral didn't do it," she said to herself. "I should have believed him."

Sobral was murdered because of what he knew about the killer, she was sure of it. In her head, she heard his voice, pleading with her to believe him. Acidic bile rose up her throat and she had to pull to the side of the road and spit it out of the window.

Willow Way was cordoned off. Patrol cars at either end of the street had their lights swirling and kept the neighbors and news crews away. An ambulance was parked inside the cordon, as was Clarke's unmarked black suburban. Sally tried one more time to contact Clarence. This time he picked up and said that he would be there in twenty.

Sally showed her police badge to a uniformed officer,

ducked under the tape, and took the steps up to the porch. The door was wide open, lights were on. She heard Justin sobbing and Clarke's voice, and, looking into the room to her right, she saw Justin had his head in his hands.

"Sir?" Sally said.

Clarke glanced around. "Sally, join us." Then to Justin. "Then what did you see?"

Sally patted her coat pocket and she realized that in the rush to leave the house she had forgotten her notebook. She saw in Clarke's hands a notebook and pen. She stepped forward and decided to simply listen, to take in everything Justin said.

Justin's angular face was wet with tears. "He was there, on the kitchen floor. I just stood there. I couldn't move. His neck was... oh, god, it was open, blood in a circle around his head. I couldn't think. I saw the saucepan on the floor. I kept asking myself what it was doing there."

"Then what did you do?" Clarke asked.

"God forgive me, but I couldn't go near him. I just... couldn't. I mean, I'm a nurse. I've seen blood and bodies before. But this time it was my beautiful Salvador."

Sally kneeled by him and took his hand. "You're in shock."

Justin jerked his hand free. "You could have prevented this! Instead, you hounded him! He was the sweetest, nicest guy."

His accusation was like a slap because it was true.

Clarke spoke. "Detective Fairburn couldn't have prevented this. There was nothing to indicate the killer would murder Salvador. Sally and I will do all we can to find the person who did this. This is difficult, but I need to ask you to keep talking to us. What did you do next?"

"Called nine-one-one. And I sat on the floor and waited."

"Are you sure you didn't touch him?"

"I'm sure."

"Why were you home early? I believe your shift finishes at seven-thirty a.m.?"

"He'd left me messages. He wanted me to come home. He was stressed out. But I couldn't just leave work. In the end, when there was a quiet period, I asked if I could go home because of a family emergency. That's when I found him."

"You entered through the front door?" Clarke asked.

He nodded and then took a tissue from a box on a coffee table. He wiped his runny nose.

"Do you have any idea how the killer got in?"

"Take your pick. Most of the windows are so old they can't be secured."

"Can you think of any reason why Salvador was murdered?" Clarke asked.

Justin glared at Clarke. "Because he saw Joseph's killer and the killer wanted him to shut up. *You* were so busy trying to fit him up for murder, you didn't listen to him! His death is on *your* head!"

FORTY-EIGHT

Dressed in white head-to-toe coveralls, Dr. Robert Lilia was crouched next to Salvador Sobral's body. Special lights on tall stands were set up around the body. Yellow, numbered markers had already been placed on the floor where anything potentially significant had been found. Sally paused in the doorway. She was also in head-to-toe coveralls with blue booties over her shoes. Clarke had his coverall halfway on, the top hanging around his waist, delayed by a phone call.

Sally tried to quash the guilt that was like a screaming voice in her head. *Your fault!*

She should have been brave enough to tell Clarke that she thought Sobral was innocent. She should have realized that if he wasn't the killer, then he was in danger because he alone had seen the killer talking to Joseph on the porch.

Sobral lay on his back and even from where she stood, some ten feet from the man's head, it looked as if his neck had been almost completely severed. The terracotta floor files were awash with blood. There was so much of it, Sally could hardly believe it was real. His bathrobe, T-shirt, and shorts were stained red and Sobral's eyes were open, head tilted back, as if he were staring at her in an accusatory way.

Lilia looked up, saw Sally, and beckoned her into the kitchen.

"Watch where you step," Lilia said. "This is a brutal one. If you're going to spew, do it outside."

The sight of blood and muscle and cartilage was hard to deal with, but Sally was determined to find whoever did this and that meant paying attention to every detail, no matter how gory. She trod carefully between the yellow markers until she was just a few feet from Sobral.

Clarke arrived suitably kitted out and stepped into the room with the confidence of a man who'd been to many crime scenes.

"What can you tell us?" Clarke asked.

"Rigor mortis has only just set in, so I'd say the deceased died between three and five hours ago."

"So he was killed between one a.m. and three a.m.?"

"It's a rough estimate."

"Cause of death?" Clarke asked.

"It looks like he was approached from behind and wire was used to strangle him. He appears to have fought back. Fingernails are broken. The killer used the wire to cut right through his throat to his spinal cord."

"That would take a strong man?" Sally asked.

"I think so."

"Why are his hands clean?" Sally asked.

Sobral was covered in blood, but his hands had been wiped clean.

"His hands have been cleaned with bleach. I suspect there may have been skin or hair or clothing fibers under Sobral's fingernails."

"Any chance there still is?" Clarke asked.

"It's possible."

"Make this one a priority, will you?" Clarke said. "His death has to be connected to Joseph Austin's murder. Probably also Roisin's. He lived across the road and he claimed he saw Joseph's killer."

"Glad I don't live in this neighborhood," Lilia commented.

Sally could smell sour milk. She stepped around Lilia and the body to look inside the saucepan, which lay on its side on the floor.

"He was heating milk on the stove, his back to the kitchen door. He was taken by surprise," she said.

She looked out of the window. The drapes were not drawn. It was still dark and the moon was bright. Sunrise was another half hour away. She could see enough to know the kitchen backed onto a tree-lined backyard.

"Do we know how the killer got in?" she asked.

"Come with me," Clarke said.

She tiptoed out of the murder scene, and followed Clarke to the doorway of a downstairs bathroom where the casement window was open. A forensic scientist was dusting a window for fingerprints that was just big enough for an adult to squeeze through.

"There's a boot print on the toilet seat." The seat was closed and on it was the faint outline of a muddy boot.

"If it's size ten, that suggests it's the same killer," Sally said, already convinced that this was the case.

"Yet again the MO is different," Clarke said. "First it was a hammer. Then he strangled Roisin with his bare hands. Now he used a wire. Why?

Sally thought about the question. "I think the killer intended to murder Joseph and Sobral and arrived prepared. Roisin was a spur-of-the-moment killing, which is why he had to use his bare hands."

"We have three murders, Sally. The media is going to be all over this. We have to make an arrest soon. Maybe this time the killer slipped up and left DNA behind."

"I have a theory about the boot prints at each crime scene. It's like he's deliberately leaving them behind. What if he isn't a size ten?" Sally said.

"You mean he's wearing boots too big for him, to mislead us?"

"Yes. Our killer is clever. Did he have a shower after killing Sobral?"

"Why don't we find out?" Clarke led her back to where Dr. Mani was gathering forensic evidence. Clarke repeated Sally's question.

"Yes," Mani said. "He's fastidious. Almost obsessive. He scrubs everything clean."

"Sir, I must formally interview Fiona Austin," Sally said. "We can't hold off any longer."

"Agreed. I'll clear it with the doctors. We have three murders and lives are at stake. You head over to the hospital as soon as you're done here." Clarke looked around. "Where the hell is Pew?"

"He'll be here any minute."

Clarke walked away, then called over his shoulder. "Sally, this wasn't your fault. Don't take it to heart."

It was a kindness that she hadn't expected from him. And he sounded as if he meant it.

FORTY-NINE

Fiona was sitting up in bed watching TV when Sally arrived. Her thin hair had been brushed and she was free of the breathing and feeding tubes from earlier.

"I know you," Fiona said, tilting her head. Then a look of confusion crossed her delicate features. "Where have I seen you before?"

"I'm Detective Sally Fairburn. I was here when you came out of your coma and also dropped by yesterday," Sally reminded her.

"That's right. How lovely to see you."

Sally pulled up the only chair in the room and sat at an angle so that Fiona could see her without craning her neck.

"How are you feeling today?" Sally asked.

"Much better, thank you. I'm still a little fuzzy on things, but the doctor is very pleased with my progress. Oh and I have such a lovely policewoman outside my door. She's such a sweetheart. She pops her head in every so often to ask if I need anything."

"Deidre and I were at the police academy together. She's a very caring person. And she has a great sense of humor."

"Yes, she has." Fiona reached out an emaciated hand and patted Sally's. "It's okay to ask me questions, my dear. I might not be able to remember, but I'll try."

Sally couldn't help but love Fiona's warmth. The old woman had lost her husband and she had almost lost her life. And yet here she was giving Sally an uplifting smile. Since five this morning, Sally had been running on adrenaline. Now that she had taken a breather, a weariness hit her, but the day was still young and there was so much to do.

"Do you remember we talked yesterday about the man who attacked you?"

Fiona's smile disappeared. "Did we?"

This didn't bode well. "Not a problem, but I need to ask you about the night Joseph died and you were attacked. Okay?"

"I understand. It's just so very painful to think about."

"I understand. Let's see how we go. On the night of the attack, did you see the man who knocked on the door?"

Sally wanted to test the validity of Sobral's story.

"I saw nothing. I took myself to bed, you see. It takes me a long time to get up those stairs."

"Cast your mind back. Did you hear a knock on the door or the doorbell ring?"

"The doorbell, I think. We have a very pretty chime."

A buzz of excitement gave Sally a burst of energy. This information alone was progress. Fiona had just backed up Sobral's account of a person on their porch that night. If Fiona heard the bell, did she also hear the conversation between the killer and Joseph?

Sally continued, "Joseph opened the door and he spoke to the man. What did Joseph say?"

"Oh, I don't know. My hearing isn't what it used to be."

"Was Joseph happy to see him?"

Fiona's green eyes seemed to brighten. "Now you mention

it, he sounded cross. Joseph can be very cutting when he's angry. And loud."

"What did Joseph say to the visitor?"

"I'm sorry, my dear, I wasn't paying attention, although I did hear the front door shut and Joseph told the man to be quick. Yes, that was it, *be quick*. Then his study door shut. I know that door because it makes an annoying creak just before it latches. I asked him so many times to oil the hinges, but he never got around to it."

"You're doing really well, Fiona. What did the visitor say?"

"I... can't remember."

Sally wished Fiona could remember more of their conversation, but she didn't want to push the ill woman too far.

"What did you hear next?"

"I was almost on the top landing by then. My legs were tired and I get out of breath so I sat on the chair. It was the scream that caught my attention. I thought it must be a night animal, you know like a fox. Then he screamed again. Oh it was awful. It was my darling Joseph."

"What did you do when you realized it was Joseph screaming?"

"I should have done something but I couldn't move. I was so frightened. Someone was in my house and hurting my Joseph. I'm old, I couldn't run to his aid. My only recourse was to call the police, which I tried to do. Then..." Fiona squeezed her eyes shut and went quiet. On the bed, her hand shook.

"Then what?" Sally urged.

Fiona opened her eyes. "Can you pass me my water cup, dear?"

The cup was at the far end of the bedtable. Sally passed it to her and waited as Fiona sipped some water.

Fiona put down the cup and stared at it. "Then I was out of the chair and moving as fast as I could to the phone. But I don't move fast. My arthritis, you see."

"Where was the phone?" Sally knew where it had been, but she wanted to test Fiona's recall.

"On the nightstand." She closed her eyes. Her eyelids were as delicate as butterfly wings. "I heard him coming up the stairs. Running. I tried to hurry but my legs wouldn't move quick enough. I heard him behind me." Fiona squeezed her eyelids tight. "I was so frightened, I peed myself."

"It's okay, Fiona, that happens when people are scared. Did the intruder say anything to you?"

"I don't think so."

"Did you see the man's face or his clothes?"

"I was too afraid to turn around."

Sally's disappointment was profound. If only Fiona had seen him!

"Why did you grab the framed photo on your nightstand?"

"Did I?"

"The photo was found on the floor next to your right hand. It looked as if you grabbed it, then when you collapsed, you dropped it."

"Oh, dear me." She drank some more water. "I must have knocked it off the nightstand. My fingers were almost touching the phone, then I was hit from behind."

It was a plausible explanation, but Sally couldn't help but think that the photograph held more significance.

"Can you tell me who the people are in the photo?"

"Dear friends, Betty and Robin Kerns. We first met in the seventies, you know. We were so young, and we thought we could conquer the world. Robin and Joseph were accountants, you see. They met through work. Betty was an amazing sculptor. You'll see some of her sculptures in the park and in grand houses. She's really quite famous. Poor sweet Betty has Alzheimer's now. Robin struggled for many years to look after her at home, but when he slipped a disc and needed surgery, Betty went to a nursing home where she's been ever since."

"And where does Robin live?"

"Chestnut Close. He rattles around that big house on his own now that Betty is in a nursing home. He is terribly lonely. He often pops in and join us for dinner. The evening meal can be a lonely one when you have nobody to share it with."

Sally felt another flutter of excitement. Chestnut Close was the street behind Willow Way.

"What number on Chestnut Close?"

"Now isn't that funny, I should know it off the top of my head. Um, number twenty-two, I think. You'll know it because his son lives three doors down and he has a very nice Mercedes. You know the ones where the roof folds back. Bob is such a lovely boy."

"When you say boy, how old is he?"

"I don't know. He must be thirty, or a bit older, why do you ask?"

"I like to have all the details." Sally made a note. "Had Joseph fallen out with Robin recently?"

"No. They got on like a house on fire."

Sally was of two minds about revealing the murders of Roisin and Sobral. She assumed Fiona didn't know about them, unless one of the police guards had let it slip. Would this tragic news be too much for the fragile woman to cope with?

Sally wrestled with her dilemma for long enough for Fiona to say, "Is everything all right, dear? You look troubled."

"You're right, Fiona. I am troubled. I have some bad news and I think it's better you hear it from me. I'm sorry to tell you that Roisin McGettigan was murdered."

Fiona gasped. "That's dreadful. I... can't believe it. What is happening to our nice safe neighborhood?"

"We believe she was murdered by the same man who killed Joseph." Sally could feel her heart pounding. "I must ask you again if you can recall anything about the night the killer entered your house."

"I wish I could."

"I should tell you that Salvador Sobral has also been murdered."

"Oh, dear." Fiona looked down at the bedding. "What is the world coming to?"

"What was Joseph's relationship like with Sobral?"

"I'm ashamed to say, Joseph took a dislike to Salvador and his partner." She looked at Sally with rheumy eyes. "I expect you know about the petition?" Sally nodded. "I didn't like it. It seemed cruel to me. But Joseph wouldn't drop it."

"I understand Sobral knocked on your back door the day before Joseph died. Did you speak to him?"

"Did he? I don't remember. Could we stop now? I'm a little tired."

Fiona's memory was good on some topics and poor on others, and it was disappointing that she was unable to describe the killer. "You've been so helpful, thank you. I have just one more question. You and Joseph have a joint bank account with the Bank of Franklin. Do you have any other accounts?"

"No. There's no need. We shared everything."

Up until this point, Sally had believed everything Fiona said, but she found it hard to imagine how Fiona could forget her Bank of Detroit account.

Sally probed further. "Forgive me for prying, but I believe that you inherited a large sum of money with which you purchased the house you live in. Is that correct?"

"Oh, my, it was so long ago I can't remember. I left all the money matters to Joseph, you see."

"You and Joseph purchased the house at auction in December 2006. The funds came from a Bank of Detroit account."

Fiona blinked rapidly and pushed the wheeled bedtable away. "I'm sorry, I must use the bathroom. Can you call the nurse?"

Fiona was wily, using the bathroom as an excuse to change the conversation. "I will, but I need your permission to go through the statements from that account."

"I don't know what you're talking about, dear."

Fiona reached out for the call button and pressed it. A nurse arrived swiftly to assist Fiona, which left Sally with no choice but to wait.

From within the toilet cubicle Sally heard Fiona say, "Would you be a dear and ask the detective to leave? I'm rather tired."

Sally left the room, knowing that she'd have to try to get a warrant to see Fiona's bank statements.

Deidre stood and arched her back to give it a stretch.

"She's a sweet old dear," Deidre said.

"Not that sweet. She's been lying to us. She's had no visitors, right?"

"Absolutely not, except you. Oh, and her attorney."

"You mean Lisa La Cava?"

"That's her. La Cava got the all-clear to visit Fiona." Deidre frowned. "Did I do something wrong?"

"Not at all. Can you do me a favor? If you hear them talking about the Bank of Detroit, give me a call?"

"No problem."

―――――――――――

When Fiona was absolutely sure that Sally was no longer outside her room, she used the landline phone to call her attorney. She couldn't remember La Cava's cell number but she could recall the main switchboard number for the attorney's office. Despite her head injury, her memory was still sharp.

"Fiona? Is everything okay?" La Cava asked.

"I'm very flustered. That detective, Sally what's-her-name, has been here, pestering me."

"How do you mean 'pestering' you?"

"She keeps firing questions at me. I'm not well enough. My head is spinning. I need you to keep her away from me, there's a dear."

"That could be difficult, Fiona. She's trying to find Joseph's killer."

"I've already told her everything I know. Please, Lisa. Keep her away." Fiona didn't like the silence down the line. "Hello? Are you there?"

"I'm here," La Cava said. "Do you have a particular example of her *intimidating* you?"

"That's the word I was looking for. I'm an old lady with a head injury and she refused to leave my room unless I answered her questions." *The lie sounds credible*, Fiona thought. "That's intimidation, right?"

"I'll talk to her boss."

"Thank you. You are such a sweetie."

FIFTY

In the hospital café, Sally grabbed a much-needed take-out coffee and a savory muffin and devoured both on the way to her house where she hoped to catch Paul before he left for school. She also had to drop the puppy off at Olivia's Bookstore. When she reached home, Paul had already gone. Jax's food bowl was on the floor, which was a sign that the puppy had been fed. She scooped the dog up in her arms and drove to the bookstore where she left Jax with Olivia in the back office.

"Thank you," Sally said to Olivia, "you're a lifesaver."

The next stop was Robin Kerns. Sally wanted to find out the significance of the photo.

On the way there, Sally called Clarence.

"Are you at the crime scene?" she asked.

"Yes. I guess we were wrong about Sobral."

"We were and I wish we had taken him seriously. The killer's out there somewhere and we have to find him, fast. Did you get a chance to contact the Bank of Detroit?"

"Yes. They refused to cooperate."

"Fiona denies knowing about the account and says Joseph dealt with the banking. I don't believe her. But without her permission, we have to apply for a warrant, and we don't have probable cause that a crime's been committed by her, or that the statements will reveal valuable evidence. It's more of a hunch and that isn't enough."

The elegant white, beaux-arts façade of Robin's house had a regal door framed by two pillars, which reached to the second floor. A man in his seventies wearing glasses answered the door. Sally showed him her police ID and introduced herself.

"Robin Kerns?" Sally asked.

"Yes. Is something wrong?"

"You're friends with Fiona and Joseph Austin?"

"I am. Do come in." Robin walked with a stoop, perhaps because of his back problem.

He showed Sally into a living room of blues, creams, and golds. What caught Sally's eye were the stunning photos of African wildlife as well as the wooden carvings of giraffes and elephants. "Did you take these?" she asked, referring to the photos.

"Yes, I'm an amateur photographer but I enjoy it very much. May I get you a cup of tea or coffee?"

"No, thank you. I believe you and your wife have known Joseph and Fiona Austin a long time?"

"Yes. I tried to see her at the hospital but a police officer turned me away. When can I see her?"

"Not yet, I'm afraid. I'll let you know when you can. Are you aware there have been two other murders: Roisin McGettigan and, last night, Salvador Sobral?"

"Dear god! I knew about Roisin but not Salvador. Are you any closer to finding who did this?"

"We are. How would you describe your relationship with Joseph?"

"My closest friend."

"When did you last see him?"

"I had dinner with them the week it happened, but I can't tell you exactly when unless I look at my diary."

"Please take a look."

Robin disappeared for a while and returned with a hard cover, page-a-day diary. He flicked back through the pages. "July twenty-fourth. Since Betty went into nursing care, they've invited me to dinner regularly. Fiona knows I'm a hopeless cook." He smiled.

Sally estimated he must be early- to mid-seventies but his teeth were perfect. She guessed they were capped. And the expensively decorated house screamed wealth.

"Did you quarrel that night?"

Robin frowned. "What's this about?"

"We're asking everyone known to the deceased the same questions."

"Detective, I had no reason to kill Joseph."

"Where were you the night of July twenty-sixth?"

"Here, of course, and no, I don't have an alibi. I rattle around in this house alone."

"Did Joseph have any enemies?"

"Detective, he could be a difficult man, but he was generally well-liked."

"And Fiona? Does she have enemies?"

"Fiona?" He laughed. "Not only is she the nicest person you could ever meet, but she's also become agoraphobic over the years so she doesn't cross people's paths very often. She has a small but loyal network of friends and I count myself lucky to be one of them, and my wife Betty, of course."

"Were you aware that Fiona had a son she chose to place for adoption?"

A look of sadness crossed his face. "Ah, this was before our time. I worked for a firm of accountants and met Joseph there.

We were in our twenties. He then left to work for the council. A poor career move but he wanted to work closer to home. I stayed there, worked my way up to senior partner. I digress. Joseph met Fiona at a game of tennis. She was seventeen years old. He fell head over heels in love. Then he learned she was pregnant. Back in those days, Detective, most people frowned on a single woman having a child. Her parents were religious. They insisted she have the baby and have it adopted. He supported her throughout the whole grueling process and shortly after they were married. I know that Fiona always pined for that child, always wondered where he had gone. It was so sad that they couldn't have children of their own."

"I'm guessing that Joseph wasn't the father of the adopted child."

"He couldn't have been. He was... how shall I put it... unable to father a child."

"Do you know why they didn't keep the child?"

"Come, come, Detective. There is only so much a man can tolerate and bringing up another man's child was a step too far."

That might explain why Joseph was so determined to ensure that Fiona and her son, Pickerd, never met. "Do you know who the father is?"

"No."

"Are you aware that her son tried to get in contact with Fiona?"

"What! Joseph never mentioned it."

If they were such close friends, it was surprising that Joseph didn't confide in him. "The son is called Niall and Joseph bribed him to go away."

"No, you're wrong. Joseph wouldn't do that."

"The evidence suggests otherwise." Sally had seen the bank statements proving that $20,000 left the Austins' joint account and arrived in Niall Pickerd's account a week before the murder.

Robin looked genuinely shocked. "I don't know what to say. Does Fiona know about this?"

"No, and I have to ask you not to tell her."

"As you wish. But she has a right to know."

Sally held out her phone and on the screen was the photo of the four friends. "What is the significance of this photo?"

Robin smiled at the image. "Happy days. I don't think it's anything more than a lovely photo of us all. A summer picnic. Betty was twelve weeks' pregnant with our first child. We had just told Fiona and Joseph and asked them to be godparents."

"Do you have any idea why Fiona grabbed this photo moments before she was attacked by the intruder?"

"No idea at all." Robin handed back the phone.

Had Fiona been telling the truth? Had she simply knocked the framed photo to the floor when she collapsed?

"How many children do you have?"

"Two. Robert—we call him Bob—lives on this street. He's the eldest. And Anna. She lives in Australia. We don't get to see her much."

"How long have you lived here?"

"We bought the land in the nineties and have been here ever since."

"What a wonderful place for kids to grow up."

"It was. I miss the sound of kids' voices. Never mind. Bob's getting married in October and I'm looking forward to being a grandfather."

"Salvador Sobral lived opposite the Austins' home and Joseph drew up a petition to get him to leave. Did you sign the petition?" Sally said.

Back at the office, they had a copy of the petition but she hadn't had a chance to see if Robin Kerns was on it.

"No, I bore the man no ill will, although they really did make a terrible noise. It was Fiona who insisted on the petition."

Sally tried not to appear surprised. "I understood it was Joseph?"

"I promise you it was Fiona. She hated the man."

"Why did she hate him?"

"She valued peace and quiet, and Sobral was so noisy."

"Any other reason?"

"She was old school, Detective."

Sally clarified, "She was homophobic?"

"As I said, she was old school."

Sally found such homophobia unacceptable, but she was there to gather information, not judge.

"Can I ask if you're aware that Fiona has an account with the Bank of Detroit?"

"Good lord, no. Why would she do that?"

"It was the account the Austins used to pay for their home."

"No, that can't be right. Joseph managed that side of things. Fiona stayed away from anything monetary." He stood suddenly. "My apologies, Detective, I'm running late for an appointment."

"How did they afford to buy such a house?"

"I'm sorry but I have to ask you to leave. I have an appointment."

Why was Robin suddenly so jumpy? She rose from her seat. "I have more questions. When is your appointment over?"

He ushered her to the hall and opened the front door. "I really couldn't say. Good day, Detective."

He closed the door and left her standing outside. He knew something about Fiona that he didn't want Sally to know and she had to discover what it was.

FIFTY-ONE

Sally entered the incident room and found Clarence staring fixedly at his computer screen.

"Um, Clarke was asking for you and he wasn't happy."

Now what? Sally put her purse under her desk. "Know what it's about?"

"Think it has something to do with that lawyer, La Cava. She's in his office."

Okay, that wasn't good. Sally knew that La Cava had been to see Fiona yesterday because Officer Deidre Kelly had told her. But why would she go over Sally's head and meet with Clarke?

Sally left the room, worried but unable to see how she had done anything wrong. In the corridor she passed a detective who was a friend of Scott's. She looked straight ahead so that she avoided making eye contact.

"Leave Scott alone, will you?" the detective said as they brushed past each other.

Her step faltered. She wanted to tell him that *she* wasn't the problem. That Scott was a liar. But what was the point? They'd never believe her.

She knocked on Clarke's door and entered. Lisa La Cava watched Sally with a steady eye. Her bland expression gave nothing away. Clarke told Sally to take a seat, which meant she was seated next to La Cava.

Clarke was equally unreadable. "Ms. La Cava claims that you are harassing Fiona Austin."

Sally stared at him in disbelief. "Fiona spoke to me voluntarily this morning. I took care to be mindful of her recent trauma."

"That's not what my client says," La Cava said, crossing her long legs. "She says that she told you she wasn't well enough to answer questions and you pressured her into doing so. She said you *intimidated* her. She's recovering from a head injury and she finds it difficult to recall the simplest detail. I insist that you cease interviewing her."

Fiona must have asked La Cava to intervene. Was Fiona spooked because Sally had discovered her Bank of Detroit account? Or perhaps the question about the people in the photograph? Did Fiona know the killer?

Sally turned to look at La Cava and said, "I did not intimidate her. I am very fond of her. You may not know, but I sat with her when she was in a coma and held her hand. I was there when she opened her eyes. I've been patient, but you must understand that there is a killer out there who has murdered three people and Fiona is a key witness."

La Cava replied, "Let me be clear, Fiona will not speak to you or any police officer until I say so."

Clarke spoke up. "Lisa, we have a serial killer on our hands. Fiona has been given the all-clear by her doctor to answer our questions. We will, of course, do our best not to upset her."

La Cava's facial muscles visibly tightened.

"I didn't want to have to raise this concern, but you leave me no choice. My client is of the opinion that Sally and Officer Pew are not up to the task of solving this case. Sally shows a lack of professionalism, which isn't surprising given she has never worked a homicide before. I must object to the low priority you're giving Joseph's murder and Fiona's attack, as well as the two other victims, and I insist that you appoint an experienced detective to lead the investigation."

The shame took Sally's breath away. Why this attack on her professionalism? And both she and Pew were working as hard as they could.

"Detective Fairburn and Officer Pew have my full support and I assure you we are taking this case very seriously," Clarke said. "I oversee everything they do."

"I'm not a fool, Detective. Your team's attention is on the Megan Chou case. That isn't good enough. If experienced detectives had kept working this case, Roisin McGettigan and Salvador Sobral might still be alive."

Sally stared at the floor. Perhaps La Cava was right?

"Sally is not responsible for the actions of a killer," Clarke said, his voice steely. "Accusing her of such is unfair. Which detectives work a case is my decision, not yours." Clarke stood, signaling the end of the conversation.

"Detective," La Cava said, not budging. "I haven't finished." Clarke remained standing. *There's more?* Sally thought. The attorney continued, "I have another objection to Sally: her unethical behavior."

It was Clarke's turn to look shocked. Sally couldn't believe her ears. La Cava continued, "On the pretext of interviewing me about Joseph and Fiona, Sally asked me for free legal advice of a personal nature and, feeling unable to refuse, I put her in touch with my colleague, Anna Elkington, who did indeed give her pro bono legal advice."

Sally stared at La Cava like a deer in the headlights. She saw how La Cava was spinning it, and it made her look bad. How could Sally have been so dumb?

"Sally?" Clarke asked, giving her the chance to respond.

"Anna Elkington offered to give me fifteen minutes of advice for free and if I wanted to employ her services, there would be a fee after that."

"And since then, you have asked Anna to prepare a custody case. At no time have you mentioned paying for her services."

"Paying her is a given." Sally couldn't disguise how angry she felt at such ridiculous allegations. "I didn't think I needed to spell it out. Since when have lawyers been afraid to bill their clients?"

Clarke raised a hand to stop her. But Sally was incensed. "And Anna gave me her word that she wouldn't discuss my legal affairs with you. It's clear she lied to me."

La Cava opened her mouth to speak, but Clarke got in first.

"Ms. La Cava, thank you for raising this issue with me. You have your answer."

La Cava hesitated and then rose. "I expect you to take my complaint seriously. I'm sure the mayor will be interested to hear how you handle this. I'll see myself out." La Cava opened the door.

"I'll have one of my team show you out." Clarke couldn't have La Cava wandering into any of the incident rooms. Clarke called out to Detective Lin, and Lin escorted La Cava away.

Clarke closed his office door and watched the attorney leave the floor. "Either she's afraid of something or Fiona is. My money's on Fiona."

"Agreed," Sally said. "Sir, her allegations are untrue. I think it's a sign I'm getting close to the truth and Fiona is trying to stop me."

"I agree but I have to be seen to take her allegations seriously."

Sally felt like her world was crumbling. First Scott, now this. "Don't take me off the case. Please, sir."

"I need a written account of your conversations with La

Cava and Anna Elkington. I also need a written account of your meetings with Fiona Austin."

"But sir, that'll waste valuable time."

"Just do it, Sally. And I want you to stay away from Fiona. For now, anyway."

Sally's head was spinning. "Yes, sir."

Clarke sat and pressed his fingertips together into a steeple, as he often did when he was thinking. "I know you, Sally. I know you are ethical and you're working hard on the case. But take a step back and look at it from an outsider's point of view. First, an evidence box is lost, signed out in your name. Then you are recorded on video shoving your ex-husband—a police officer. Then you supposedly intimidate a fragile witness, and finally you take free legal advice from the law firm representing our key witness. You have to admit this doesn't look good?"

"I see how it appears, but I absolutely did not sign out the evidence box. Yes, I lost my temper with Scott but that was when we were both off duty, and it has nothing to do with how I behave at work. Fiona told me today that it was okay to ask her questions and she didn't ask for her lawyer. And last, it was a stupid mistake taking legal advice from an attorney working with La Cava. I won't make the same mistake again."

Clarke gave her a sympathetic tilt of the head. "We all make mistakes. Keep your head down and stay away from Fiona."

"Yes, sir."

An hour later, Sally had completed her statement about that morning's interview with Fiona and her earlier meetings with La Cava and with Elkington, when Clarke called her back into his office.

"I've had a call from the police chief. La Cava complained to the mayor, who complained to the chief. He wants a more senior detective heading up the case. I don't have any choice, Sally. I'm sorry. I'm asking Esme Lin to be lead detective."

Sally felt unstable on her legs, but she straightened her back and tried to stay calm. "As long as I'm working the case, I don't care who heads it. And I have a lot of respect for Lin."

"Sally, you look beat. Go home. Take the rest of the day off."

"I don't need time off," Sally said.

"That's an order."

Sally left his office crestfallen and returned to the incident room.

"Sally?" Clarence asked. "You don't look too good."

"I'm taking the afternoon off. Detective Lin will be leading the investigation. Can I rely on you to brief her?" She picked up her purse and phone.

"Sure, but I don't understand. Why the change? Did La Cava say something?"

"The boss is bringing in Lin because she's experienced." Sally didn't want to burden the young cop with her problems. "It's for the best."

Clarence clearly didn't buy her explanation. "Can I call you? Keep you in the loop?"

How Sally would love that, but she had to think of him. "No need. I'll see you tomorrow."

Sally took the fire stairs—she really didn't want to be seen leaving the building in disgrace.

Her shoes slapping the concrete stairs echoed in the void like drumbeats. To be sent home, just when she was so close to solving the case, was galling. And humiliating. Scott's accusations that she wasn't up to the task would appear to be true. Tears welled up in her eyes and she blinked them away.

Don't be weak, she told herself.

At the bottom of the stairs was a fire door exit. She burst through it and gulped in some big breaths.

Was she going to step aside and allow people like Scott and La Cava to get away with making her look bad?

All her working career she'd remained in the background, lacking the confidence to take on a bigger role. Until a minute ago, she'd had that big role: a detective leading a serial murder case. Now she was sidelined and her professionalism and ethics called into question. She had always tried to do the right thing, to be fair and empathetic with people. Maybe it was time to fight for what she wanted, and she wanted her job back.

But how?

The answer came to her in a heartbeat. It was risky and dangerous. But she knew just one way to get ahead of the game and it meant breaking all the rules.

FIFTY-TWO

Sally entered the visitor center of Walla Walla State Penitentiary. She was here to see a serial killer. His name was Richard Foster and she had been ignoring his text messages. She had vowed that she'd never go near the monster again. Yet here she was.

She and Foster had history. Foster was known as the surviving Poster Killer—his son and partner-in-crime was dead, shot by Sally. He was serving life imprisonment in a maximum-security wing where pedophiles and child killers like Foster were kept. Oddly, the fact that she had defeated him had earned her Foster's respect, and in one recent instance, he had even helped her find her neighbor's killer.

And she was about to ask for his help again.

The desk guards acknowledged her with a nod and a smile, as she handed in her phone and purse, which were locked away. Then Glenn, a fidgety guard with a moustache, asked her to follow him. Sally suspected that Glenn was one of the guards doing Foster's bidding. Someone supplied Foster with a cell phone and enabled him to communicate with his people on the outside. Glenn had twitchy eyes and an obsequious way about him that set her nerves on edge.

She kept a few paces back from him. He led her into a meeting room that smelled like vomit and filthy mop water.

Glenn saw her screw up her nose. "Visitor spewed. Pregnant. We cleaned it up as best we could." He nodded at the orange plastic chair facing a wall, the top part of which was Perspex with a circle of holes in it through which she could speak to the prisoner who would be seated on the other side. The bottom part was brick, covered in sheets of steel. "He won't be long. Tank's collecting him," Glenn said, leaving her alone.

Tank was pure muscle and six-foot-four tall. He entered the opposite room with Richard Foster and gave Sally a friendly nod, clearly recognizing her from her previous visits.

Richard Foster was handcuffed, both hands and feet, which meant he had to shuffle. When he reached the only chair, he sat stiffly.

"For chrissake! What's that god-awful stink?" His English accent was as clear as day.

"Vomit, on the other side," Tank said. "You hear Sally complain? And she's got it worse than you."

Foster joked, "Can't get the staff these days."

"You play nice, you hear?" Tank said to Foster.

"I always play nice with Sally," Foster said, grinning up at the giant.

The truth was that Foster could fake being nice, even though he couldn't feel it. Foster had at one time been a respected homicide detective and it was this side of his personality she hoped to tap into.

Tank stood at the back of the room and folded his arms.

"I thought you'd abandoned me, Sally," Foster began. "It's been two months."

"This isn't a friendship, Richard. I helped put you in this jail, remember?"

"Ouch! What's happened to the sweet, kind Sally Fairburn I used to know?" he teased.

A cruel husband. A brush with death at the hands of the man seated opposite. A murdered neighbor. There were many reasons why Sally had hardened her outlook on life recently.

"How are you, Richard?"

"All the better for seeing you. Congratulations, by the way. Consulting detective on a homicide that Clarke couldn't solve, hey? If you solve it, you get a permanent role. Am I right?"

He leaned back in the chair, settling in. Sally was his entertainment, she knew that. He craved anything intellectually challenging and Sally was a means of managing the never-ending boredom of prison life.

"Something like that." She wasn't going to share her demotion, now that Lin was lead detective.

"I heard that asshole was back in Franklin. Scott, I mean."

Foster's network on the outside was on the game as usual, constantly feeding Foster information.

"I don't want to talk about Scott. I want to solve a serial murder."

"It must be galling to have him at the PD again." His eyes glinted as he waited for her reaction.

"I'm here about the murders of Joseph Austin, Roisin McGettigan, and Salvador Sobral. I assume you've been following the cases on TV?"

But he wouldn't move the conversation on. "He's married again, has a kid. What do you think of that?"

"I pity them."

"What if I could remove Scott? What would you say to that?"

"I'd say absolutely not. That's not why I'm here." Was he saying what she thought he was? Foster's method of removing people was usually permanent and brutal.

Foster's laugh sent tremors down her spine. "Call me if you

change your mind. I always despised him. Puffed up peacock, fancied himself as a big shot."

Sally had always wondered why Foster loathed Scott so much. As a pedophile, she'd have thought he'd welcome Scott into his brotherhood. She waited for Foster to calm down. Eventually he'd move on to the homicides.

Foster stared at her for a while then said, "Tell me everything you know about the murders."

Sally briefed him on where the investigation was at. She was here now. There was no point holding back.

Foster listened and nodded occasionally. "Yeah, yeah. I've seen the news coverage. Now tell me something the media rats don't know. What do you know about the victims? What are their secrets?"

She glanced at Tank who was fourteen feet or so away from Foster. How much could he hear of their conversation?

"I'm going to talk hypothetically," Sally said, thinking of how La Cava managed to convey information without betraying client-attorney confidentiality. In reality, Sally shouldn't breathe a word about the case to Foster. But from her past interactions with him, she knew that the evil son-of-a-bitch had his own code of conduct and what passed between them remained confidential. "What if Fiona Austin had a child out of marriage, to an unknown man?" she began. "What if the boy, I'll call him Suspect A, was adopted and what if he later arrives in Franklin, desperate to reconnect with his birth mother? And what if Joseph refused to allow him to see his birth mother, without Fiona knowing, and bribed the son to go away?"

She paused.

"With you so far," Foster said, clearly enjoying the story. "I'd say Suspect A has motive. Does he have an alibi for the time of Joseph's murder?"

"No, he was home alone."

"What does Fiona have to say about him, hypothetically, of course?"

"I've been accused of harassment. I can't question her again and so far, I haven't broached the topic of her son."

"Why the hell not? She's your key witness. Don't allow some sappy doctor to stop you."

"It wasn't the doctor. It was Fiona's attorney. And I've been removed from lead investigator."

"Ah, that's why you're here. You want to be reinstated, right?"

"Yes, I mean no. I want to find the killer." In truth, she wanted both.

"And you need to show your loser boss that you're capable?" Foster was referring to Clarke.

"Yes."

"What do you hypothetically know about Fiona that doesn't sit right? Anything at all?" Foster asked.

"She might have hypothetically inherited enough money to buy a $2.5 million house and that money was kept in a Bank of Detroit account, which she denies any knowledge of."

"If I were you, I'd make finding the source of that money a priority. Smells fishy to me."

"I can't believe that Fiona would be involved in anything criminal."

"Don't be so naïve." Sally flushed at Foster's sharp rebuke. "Dig deep. The three victims were killed for a reason and it all revolves around Joseph and Fiona. Who are they really? Their secrets will lead you to the killer."

"Thank you," she said. He was right, of course. She didn't know enough about the elderly couple.

"You have another question. Ask." She blanched. How did he know? "Ask, Sally, I haven't got all day," Foster continued. He smiled, revealing gray teeth.

The irony was that Foster *did* have all day because he had absolutely nothing else to do.

Again, she looked at Tank, staring straight ahead as if Foster and Sally weren't there.

"Don't worry about Tank," Richard said. "He's trustworthy."

Was he also under Foster's control?

Sally took a deep breath and spoke, "An evidence box relating to Fiona Austin went missing from storage. I want it back. I don't want anyone hurt, you understand? Just the box found and returned to me."

"And you think my people can find it for you?"

Sally didn't want to think too much about his people. "Can they?"

"They can if I instruct them to. Now tell me, is the evidence lost, or did someone take it?"

"It was signed out by a cop who forged my signature. I believe it was Scott."

He chuckled. "He's really out to get you. Sly bastard, I'll give him that. If my people find the evidence box, do you want it delivered to you?"

"Back to the storage facility, as if it was never gone."

"You sure I can't break Scott's legs or something? You know, as a warning?"

"No, I'll deal with Scott my own way." She would do that through the legal system, not violence.

"Do you have the box number?"

She told him the number. "It has Fiona Austin's name on it."

Foster ran a pointed tongue over his pale lips. "If my people find it, what do I get in return?"

"You get the satisfaction of thwarting Scott."

"Appealing, but not enough. Perhaps we can help each other. I also want Scott gone from Franklin, for my own reasons.

I get you that evidence box, and one day I may call on you to assist me with something relating to Scott."

"I can't agree to something as vague as that."

"Let me be more specific, then. I will need information on Scott. That's all."

"I can't make that promise, Foster."

"Then we don't have a deal."

"If I can prove that Scott took the evidence, he will lose his job and may even be charged. You'd like that, right?"

"I told you what I want in return. When I ask, you give me information on him."

She silently cursed herself for expecting Foster to do as she asked without wanting too much in return. She should have seen it coming. She stood slowly. "Forget about it, I'll find another way."

Sally walked out of the room feeling dirty, like his disturbed mind had infected hers. It had been a foolish errand and all the way to her car she asked herself if she had revealed too much to him about the case. She had been careful not to mention names other than those already named in the media coverage. Still, she wouldn't go to him again for help. She had danced with the devil and managed to walk away—this time.

FIFTY-THREE

The prison guard named Glenn stood in Richard Foster's cell. He glanced behind him to see if anyone was watching them through the bars. In the cell opposite, Benny lay on his bed groaning, his cock in his hand. Jerking off was what Benny did, day and night. It was his second favorite occupation. His favorite was to kill his wives—he'd had four—then feed them in pieces to his pigs, but his incarceration at Walla Walla State Penitentiary had put a stop to that. Therefore, he was having to make do.

"You're going to land me in the shit," Glenn said to Foster. "Can't you make the call later? From the landline?"

Foster sat on his desk chair. Unlike Benny and the other maximum-security prisoners, Foster had a desk, chair, bookshelf, TV, and access to Glenn's cell phone. In return, Foster paid for Glenn's mom to live out her remaining years at a nursing home that specialized in dementia care.

Foster stretched out his arm and bent his fingers, in a give-it-now way. Glenn took the phone from the inside of his sock and gave it to Foster. Guards were not allowed to carry phones.

"Make it quick, okay?" Glenn left the cell, locked the door, and stood outside.

Foster didn't waste any time. He called his contact on the outside who picked up straightaway.

"Yes, boss?"

"Scott Fairburn is back in town. He has a wife and a kid with him. Find out where he lives and if he has a storage facility or lockup garage. He's stolen evidence from the police evidence warehouse. The box will have Fiona Austin's name on it and this reference number." He said the number slowly. "I want you to find that box and return it anonymously to the PD storage warehouse."

"You want me to break into a police storage facility? Sheesh! That's a first."

"And no one can know."

"Say that number again."

"Are you writing this down?"

"Yes, boss."

"Don't. I want you to remember it."

"My memory's not so good."

"For chrissake. Just burn the notes when you're done."

"Yes, boss. If you want me to search their place, they'll know I've been there. That okay?"

"Make as much mess as you can. That guy has it coming."

"What's Scott done to you?"

"I'm the pedophile boss in this town. I decide what is okay and what isn't. Scott fancies himself as a kiddie fondler. He got one thirteen-year-old to suck his dick. So what? Now he thinks he's in with my people. I don't like that."

"Nah, not buying that. There's something else, right?"

"And there was me thinking you were stupid, when every now and again you reveal you do actually have a brain." Foster chuckled. "Okay, you deserve an answer. Scott contacted my number two here in Franklin to arrange a meeting with my counterpart in Chicago."

"And you don't like it?"

"You bet I don't like it!" Foster roared, then lowered his voice. Glenn, standing outside his cell, turned his head at the noise. Foster continued, "I decide what happens in this town. Any meeting with the guy in Chicago is mine to arrange. How dare Scott Fairburn interfere in *my* business."

"Got it, boss. Anything else?"

"Yes, arrange for Sally Fairburn to be watched. She has my protection. Scott Fairburn is out to destroy her and that can't happen. I want to know when he approaches her, phones her, sees the son, you know the drill. I won't have him messing with my protégé."

"She's a detective, right? So, how's she a protégé?"

"The trick, my friend, is to make them think that they are calling the shots. The more she comes to me for help, the more she becomes part of my world. She's a protégé, she just doesn't know it yet."

Foster was momentarily distracted from his call by shouting. Glenn darted into his cell like a rat running from a rat catcher. "There's a random search. Give me the phone."

"Gotta go," Foster said down the phone, then he handed it to Glenn, who hid it in his sock.

The guard then locked the cell door behind him.

"Heard you talking about Sally," Glenn said, through the bars.

"You shouldn't be listening," Foster growled.

"Is she the lady who received a warning note back in July?"

It had freaked Sally out at the time. Foster had made it his business to find out who sent it.

"Yes," Foster replied. "'I'm watching you,' it said." He grinned. "Well, now I'm watching him."

"Who sent the note?"

"Scott."

"You know for sure?" Glenn asked.

"I said so, didn't I? Now go away."

FIFTY-FOUR

Paul came home from school with Leah, ditching their bicycles in the backyard. Jax ran to meet them so fast his little paws slipped on the polished wood floor, and he slid on his belly most of the way to the back door. Paul picked up the wriggling ball of fur and tickled the puppy's pink tummy. They all headed for the kitchen.

"Hi. How was your day?" Sally asked him.

"Okay." He cradled the puppy who was trying to lick his face.

"Hey, Leah, how was school?" Sally said.

Leah leaned her back against the pantry doors. "Good, thank you, Mrs. Fairburn."

"Call me Sally, please. Would you like to stay for dinner?"

Leah looked at Paul for guidance. "Why not? The project will take all evening," he said.

"Great, what's the project about?" Sally asked, pausing in the peeling of a potato. She was preparing shepherd's pie.

Paul opened the fridge. "It's about how the school could be better."

"And how do you think it could be better?"

Leah answered. "Water tanks and solar panels. We're going to calculate how much power the panels would generate and the payback period. We want to prove that both will save the school money over the long term."

Sally was impressed. She looked at Paul. This wasn't his area of interest. Paul would normally suggest better sports changing rooms or the installation of another playing field.

"What a good idea," Sally said.

"Like something to drink?" Paul asked Leah.

"Do you have green tea?"

"Mom, do we have green tea?"

"Sure. I'll make you some and bring it up to you."

Paul grabbed a can of Coke and headed for the stairs, but Leah stayed put.

"Paul?"

He turned to look at her. "Yeah?"

"You know." Leah flicked a look at Sally.

"Later," Paul said, taking the first stair.

"Paul!" Leah persisted.

Sally was amused by the exchange. This was the first time she'd seen Paul coerced into doing something. Paul must really like her.

Paul plodded back to the kitchen. "I didn't mean to, you know, get mad at you, after, you know, Sunday. It was just, like, everyone was watching."

Sally smiled. This was Paul's way of apologizing. "And I'm sorry I embarrassed you," Sally said. "I know Olivia likes you and would love to have you working with her."

"Can I think about it?"

"Sure."

Paul and Leah went upstairs, and on the landing, she put her hand around his waist and gave him a brief hug. Leah was most definitely more than just a friend. And she seemed, so far, to be a good influence on him.

Sally smiled to herself. As long as Paul was happy, that's all that mattered. She switched on the kettle and took a green tea bag from the pantry and put it in a big mug. While she waited for the kettle to boil, she peeled the remaining potatoes, washed them, chopped them, and put them in a pot. When the water was boiling, she filled the mug, then used the remaining water to boil the potatoes. She then knocked on Paul's door and handed the mug to Leah.

"Dinner should be an hour. I hope you like shepherd's pie."

"I'm a vegetarian," Leah said.

"No problem, I can make a separate dish for you using haricot and red kidney beans instead."

"Sounds great, thank you."

Sally left the teenagers to their school project and dashed downstairs to check that she had the ingredients she needed in the pantry to make the dish she had promised Leah. Thankfully, she did. Upstairs, she heard Paul laugh. It was good to hear him enjoying himself. She wasn't going to spoil his night and complain that she'd been demoted at work. At some point Sally had to tell Paul that she had started legal proceedings to keep full custody but that too could wait.

She focused on making the beans in tomato sauce with a bit of spice, onion, and garlic to make it tasty. She was aiming for southern baked beans, but without the added bacon.

There was a knock at the front door and her first thought was that it was Scott. But the knock was too gentle.

"Who is it?" Sally called through the locked house door.

A memory flash of Sobral calling out to her through his house door momentarily stabbed at her heart. The man was dead, and Sally wished that she had believed him when he said he saw a man on the front porch the night Joseph Austin was killed.

"It's Clarence."

Relieved, Sally opened the door and invited the young cop in. "Would you like a beer?"

"Thanks, but no. I'm on my way home. I thought you'd appreciate some good news for a change. The warrant came through. We have access to Fiona's Bank of Detroit account and it's blown the case wide open."

"What did you find?" she said.

"Regular payments from several individuals. One man stands out. He's deposited large sums since 2005."

"Who?"

"Calls himself Wilbur Smith."

Sally laughed. "You mean like the adventure thriller writer?"

"Yup. I guess someone doesn't want to be identified."

"I'd say so. Tell me more."

"Since 2005 Wilbur Smith has deposited monthly payments into this account. I've done a quick calculation and this one guy has given Fiona Austin a whopping $1,320,000."

"Wow! And the others?"

"Nine other people have made regular payments or lump sums. It has to be blackmail money, right?" Clarence said.

Sally massaged her right temple. "It could be. Or maybe Fiona ran a business that she doesn't want us to know about. Either way, Fiona claimed she had nothing to do with the finances and left it all to Joseph. This proves that's a lie. I can't believe I fell for her innocent old lady act." Sally paused while she thought about the best way to use this new information. "We have to locate these people as soon as possible."

"Two of them have passed away. And one in particular was easy to locate. Silvia Tofano deposited $20,000 and she lives in Peakhurst."

"Has she been brought in for questioning?"

"Lin said in the morning. If they are being blackmailed, they have motive for murder, right?"

"It's possible. I wonder why he killed Joseph first, instead of Fiona. It was her bank account, after all."

"Maybe Joseph was the victim's contact. He made them pay," Clarence suggested.

"That makes sense. Thanks for keeping me in the loop."

"I must run. See you tomorrow," Clarence said.

She watched him drive away.

"Well, Fiona, you really aren't what you seem," Sally said to herself, then she turned her attention back to making dinner.

FIFTY-FIVE

The phone call from Harper came at 8:48 p.m. as Sally was stacking the dishwasher. Harper was hysterical and it took several attempts to get her to calm down enough to tell her what was wrong.

"He's gone crazy. Like, psycho crazy. He pinned me against the wall. Screamed in my face. Kept asking who I told." Harper started to bawl.

"About what?"

"Someone broke into his lockup. Took a box. He kept going on about a box."

Did Foster go ahead and locate the missing evidence box even though she told him not to because the price he demanded in return was too high? "What was in the box?"

"Evidence." Harper sniffed between sobs. "He thinks you took it and blames me. He didn't even tell me about it at the time. I'm scared, Sally."

Her first thought was that she must keep Paul safe, should Scott try to get into her house. Her second thought was the danger that Harper and Eli were in.

"Is Scott on his way here?"

"I haven't a clue. He's working tonight, but that won't stop him driving by your place. I had to warn you."

"Thanks for the warning. Did he hurt you?"

"Some bruises. Sally, I can't stay here. I'm leaving tonight. I'm afraid he'll kill me."

Sally's mind was racing. To get Harper to safety would mean Sally driving her and Eli to Eacham. But what about Paul, Leah, and the puppy? There was no way she'd leave them alone in the house to face Scott battering the door down.

"Is Scott at work?"

"Yes, until ten."

"Pack a small bag. Wait for me. I'll take you and Eli to your aunt Barbara's, but first I have to get my son to safety. Give me an hour. Where do you live?"

Harper gave Sally the address.

Sally said, "I'll message you when I'm outside your building."

"What do I do if he comes back?"

"Hide the bag under the bed. And don't tell anyone where you're going. One hour, okay?"

"Okay."

Sally then called the police evidence storage facility and asked the officer on duty to check on a specific box. She gave him the details. Five minutes passed, then the officer confirmed the box was on the shelf. "That's strange. There's a note here that it was missing," the officer said.

Next, she called Margie who was happy to have Paul, Leah, and the pup for the night. She explained that Paul and Leah were working on a school project. Sally warned her friend that Scott was on the warpath and potentially dangerous.

"If he turns up," Sally said, "call the police."

"Keep safe, my friend. I'm proud of you," Margie said.

Sally then put the half-made dinner in containers and put them in the refrigerator. Then she spoke to Paul and Leah.

"Guys, I have an emergency to deal with and have to go out. It could take all night. I've asked my friend Margie to have you stay. You too, Leah, if you like. I know you want to work on the project together."

"I'll have to check with Mom." Leah left the room to make the call.

While she was gone, Sally whispered to Paul that Scott was on the warpath and might turn up at the house.

"Please keep this to yourself. I'm taking Harper someplace safe. She's afraid Scott will hurt her."

"When did you get to know Harper?" Paul asked.

"Long story and not enough time. I'll explain in the morning."

"If Dad catches you, he'll go ballistic. Maybe I should go with you?"

"I'll be careful, I promise."

———————

Sally made sure that she had a full tank. When she pulled up on the street where Harper lived, she sent a text message. Harper appeared with a small duffel bag lying on the seat of the stroller and Eli, asleep in a sling toddler carrier.

"Get in, quick," Sally said, getting out and putting the stroller and the bag in the trunk.

Harper got in the back and laid Eli on the seat where he continued to sleep. Sally set off and once they were on the freeway she felt a lot better. She caught glimpses in the rearview mirror of Harper, who regularly turned to look behind her. "You're certain Scott won't think you've gone to Barbara's place?"

"He's never been there. Doesn't know the address."

"Does she know you're coming?"

"No, you said not to call her."

"Good. It's okay to give her a call now that we're on our way. Make sure she knows not to tell anyone, okay?"

"Okay." Harper did as she was asked and stipulated that Barbara not tell anyone, including Harper's parents. "She says she won't tell a soul." Sally's mouth was dry and she wished she'd remembered to bring a water bottle, but she wasn't going to stop until they were at Barbara's house. "What's your aunt's surname?"

"MacKenzie."

In the rearview mirror, Sally noticed Harper turn her head to stare at the bright headlights of the cars behind them.

"No one is following us," Sally said, "I've checked."

"You don't understand. He always finds me. I was at a café with a moms' group the other day and he found me and I'd kept it secret."

Sally swerved to the side of the freeway and stopped. "Maybe he has a tracker on you? Is there something you always wear, always have with you?"

"This coat?"

"Take off your coat and pass it to me."

It was a long coat and Harper had to wriggle free of the fabric. Sally felt along the collar and cuffs and the hem. She was searching for a bugging device and found nothing. "The coat's good. I'm going to check the stroller."

Cars sped past as she made her way to the back of the car. The treelined freeway was eerie at night and stopping on the hard shoulder was dangerous. She popped the trunk and using her phone's flashlight, she searched the stroller's surfaces. She found a bugging device underneath the seat. Sally ripped it away and stamped on it until it was totally shattered, then she sat back in the car and drove off.

"He bugged the stroller. I hope he hasn't been paying attention to it."

"You think he'll guess where we're going?"

"We're only just outside of Franklin. We could be going anywhere north. Let's stay positive, okay?" Sally said.

She drove in silence for a while, but she had a burning question that had to be asked.

"Harper, would you be willing to testify in court about the way Scott abuses you?"

"I couldn't face him in court. I just want to get away from him. I'll change my name or something. Move out of state."

"You could be running for the rest of your life. The abuse you've suffered is enough to send him to jail."

"It isn't enough. But I have a video that could."

Sally stared at Harper in her rearview mirror. "What video?"

"At first he was tender and kind. I know now that was an act. It started when we'd been out at a bar and I didn't feel so good and I wanted to go to sleep when we got to his place. But he had sex with me anyway. I ignored it the first time, then it happened again. It was like he liked it best when I said no. I tried to end it, but he wouldn't listen. It was like I had no choice. I didn't know what to do. He was a cop, so who would believe me? So I hid my phone in my bedroom. My parents were out. That night, I told him I didn't want sex, and he raped me. It's all on the video."

"Did you take the video to a lawyer or the police?"

"I was going to, but then I found out I was pregnant. I was trapped. My parents blamed me. They insisted Scott marry me. I didn't want any of it, but I had a baby on the way and my parents wouldn't have me in the house. They called me a slut and said I brought shame on them."

Nice parents, Sally thought. *The poor girl had no one to turn to.*

"Do you still have the video?"

"Yeah. It's in my purse."

"Good. When we get to Barbara's house, I'm going to copy

it, then I'm going to take it to a lawyer and ask them if it's enough to convict Scott. You okay with that?"

"I guess. But all I care about is being free. I can't live my life in Scott's shadow."

"Me neither," Sally said.

FIFTY-SIX

September 14, 2016

Wednesday morning, Sally stepped out of the FPD elevator as her phone rang. It was Harper's Auntie Barbara. She wanted Sally to know that Harper and Eli were doing well.

"Scott will be searching for them," Sally warned her. "Be very careful. He can be charming when he wants to be, so don't be fooled by him. Does her mom know that she's with you?"

"Harper asked me not to tell her, so I won't. Even though I'm tempted to give her a piece of my mind. The stupid woman has a soft spot for Scott. She always was a poor judge of character."

"Stay safe."

Sally rolled her shoulders, releasing some of the tension she'd been carrying around since she drove Harper and Eli to Eacham. Scott would move heaven and earth to locate them and if he ever did, she feared for Harper's life. Just then, Sally realized that in her hurry to return home last night, she'd forgotten to make a copy of Harper's incriminating video. She immediately called Barbara and asked her to email Sally the video and she gave Barbara her work email.

She then found Lin and Clarence in the incident room.

"Hey, Sally," Lin said happily. "Good to have you back. Look, for what it's worth, I think you and Clarence have done a great job on this case. You eliminated Troy Vincent as a suspect for the murders, you found a new suspect in Niall Pickerd, you also discovered that Fiona's been receiving large payments into a secret bank account and this money could possibly be a motive for murder."

"Thanks, Esme." Sally glowed with pride.

"Sally, I have some more good news. Fiona's evidence box has turned up and it's on your desk. I'd like you to go through it."

Sally nodded.

Lin said, "I spoke to my contact in the FBI about identifying Wilbur Smith. This person was clever enough to move his deposits through numerous offshore accounts. They've warned us that tracking the source may take months."

"We can't wait that long," said Sally. "He's potentially already murdered three people. It would save us all a lot of time if Fiona told us who Wilbur Smith really is. But we've been asked to stay away from her."

"Yeah, well, I'm in charge now," Lin said. "Sally, you come with me. We're paying Fiona a visit. Clarence, you go see Tofano. I want to know why she is paying money to Fiona. And don't accept any bullshit, okay?"

"Okay," said Clarence.

"I don't think I can go with you," Sally said. "La Cava was clear that she didn't want me interviewing Fiona."

"Fiona has been lying to us. I have a good mind to charge her with obstructing a homicide investigation. Maybe the threat of that will get her talking."

"I'd prefer not to threaten her, unless we have to," said Sally. "Can we use that as a last resort?"

"You're too nice, Sally."

The first thing Sally looked at in the evidence box was Fiona's phone, which had just enough power to switch on. Sally checked the last call Fiona received. It was from Robin Kerns at 11:37 p.m. on July 26. She looked up. "I'd also like to ask Fiona why Robin Kerns called her, most probably minutes before Joseph was murdered."

Sally knocked on the hospital room door, then both she and Lin entered. Fiona lay curled up on her side, her eyes closed. She appeared to be sleeping. The only chair in the room was already positioned next to the bed as if another visitor had just left. Given Fiona was only allowed to see the police or her lawyer, Sally guessed that La Cava had recently been there. Lin indicated that Sally should take the chair. Lin stood near the door.

In Sally's hand was a big bunch of cellophane-wrapped pink flowers, which needed a vase. When she was seated, she rested the bouquet across her lap. The cellophane made a crinkling sound and Fiona opened her eyes.

"I didn't mean to wake you," Sally said soothingly.

Fiona's rheumy blue eyes blinked rapidly at the pink lilies and roses in the bouquet. Then she looked up at Sally. "Oh, it's you. My lawyer said I shouldn't see you."

"I wanted to give you these. I hope you like them," Sally said.

"They're lovely." Fiona reached out an arthritic hand for the bed's control button, which hung over the bed's edge.

Sally handed it to her. "Do you want to sit up?"

Fiona rolled onto her back. "I can do it. I have to. When I go home, I'll have to do all manner of things I didn't need to do before... before Joseph was..."

Whatever Fiona was or wasn't guilty of, there was no doubt that she was fragile and that managing such a large house on her own just wasn't going to work. She would need help if she was going to continue living there. Fiona pressed a button, and the top part of the bed began to lift. She kept her finger on the button until she sat comfortably upright. Sally got up and positioned a pillow behind her shoulders.

"Thank you, dear. And who's this?" Fiona said, smiling sweetly at Lin.

This time Sally wasn't falling for the sweet and easy-going old lady act.

"This is Detective Esme Lin. She's now working with us."

"My! Aren't you pretty," Fiona said, smiling at Lin. "And I love your biker boots. Do you ride a motorcycle?"

"Hello, Fiona," Lin said. "I do have a motorcycle. How are you progressing?"

"Going home on Friday. I'm not looking forward to it. Dallas has organized a cleaner to... you know. But it won't be the same without my darling Joseph."

"Perhaps you could stay someplace else?" Sally suggested, "A friend's house maybe? What about Robin Kerns?"

"Oh, I don't want to trouble him." Fiona brushed a hand across the sheet as if flicking crumbs away. "He's got more than enough on his plate. Betty has Alzheimer's. She doesn't recognize him when he visits her, you know. It's so sad."

"I'm sure he won't mind you staying at his place for a while. Shall I ask him?" said Sally.

"No!"

Sally had never heard Fiona speak sharply before.

"I mean, thank you, but no. I think I'll advertise for a lodger, someone young and energetic who can help me around the house. Will a police officer watch my house?"

"Until the killer is caught, yes," said Lin. "We'll keep you safe, Fiona."

Sally said, "I'd like to clear the air. I'm sorry if you felt harassed by me. It wasn't my intention. I was simply trying to find the man who attacked you and killed Joseph."

"Oh, dear, I think that was my fault. I'm not sure exactly what I said but I was quite agitated after you left and Lisa arrived soon after and she asked me what was wrong. I never meant you to get into trouble."

Fiona was a good liar. "I met Robin Kerns yesterday."

Sally watched Fiona's reaction. Fiona's eyelids fluttered.

"Dear Robin! How is he? He sent me such a lovely get-well card."

"He's good. Asked after you. He told me all about the photo of the four of you that we found next to you."

Fiona's pupils dilated. "He did?" Her voice faltered.

"Betty was pregnant with their first child. You were celebrating the announcement."

Fiona exhaled loudly, as if relieved. "Oh, yes. So how is the investigation going, Detective?"

That was a fast change of topic. Fiona didn't want to talk about that photograph. Sally decided to let it pass for now.

"Making progress." Sally kept her answer vague. "There is one query I think you can help me with, if you don't mind me asking?"

"I'll do my best. Everything's very fuzzy after the blow to my head."

"You received a phone call from Robin at eleven thirty-seven p.m. on the night Joseph was killed. What was it about?"

More fluttering eyelids. "I don't remember."

"Robin called your cell."

"Oh, that thing." She waved a hand dismissively. "I hardly use it. I much prefer the landline."

"Your cell phone was found in the kitchen." Sally had

checked the crime scene photos. "The call was a minute long. Why did Robin call you so late at night?"

Fiona looked down and shook her head. "I wish I could help, but I can't remember. Perhaps Joseph took the call?"

"He was in his study. Please, Fiona, try to remember," Sally persevered.

"I'm sorry. I don't know."

"Oh, well. Maybe it'll come to you." Sally noticed more get-well cards lining the window ledge and bunches of flowers in vases. "Look at all the lovely cards!"

"Aren't they wonderful?" Fiona said. "It's such a comfort to have such caring friends." Sally picked up the card with the puppy with a cone around his neck. Sally showed it to Fiona. "Who is Niall?"

"I don't know," Fiona replied. "A neighbor, perhaps. What a sweet card!"

There was a knock on the door and a woman entered, offering Fiona coffee or tea. Fiona asked for tea with one sugar. Sally waited patiently until the woman was gone. "Fiona, the last time I was here I asked you about a bank account in your name."

"Yes, yes, and I told you I know nothing about it." Fiona sipped her tea.

Lin chipped in, "Fiona, the account has your signature. You therefore set it up, so please stop pretending you know nothing about it."

"Well!" Fiona exclaimed. "There's no need to be rude. I'm old. I forget things."

"Fiona, this account received payments from several people," Sally said. "Someone calling themselves Wilbur Smith has paid $1.3 million into your Bank of Detroit account. Why would he pay you so much money?"

Fiona put down her teacup. "Sally, please stop this. You're

putting me off my tea and my lawyer has been very clear that I shouldn't talk about the case."

"It's possible that this Wilbur Smith is the man who killed your husband and two other people," Sally said. "I need you to think hard about who this Wilbur Smith might be."

"My dear, all I know is that Joseph loved the man's books."

Getting nowhere, Sally decided to go off script. "You said you don't know who Niall is. I'm going to tell you. He was bribed by your husband to stay away from you."

"Joseph wouldn't bribe anyone."

"Before you were married, you had a child and that child was adopted."

Fiona gawped. "How do you know that?"

"I've contacted the adoption agency. He was adopted by a local family who then moved to Atlanta. Recently, Niall tried to find you. Eventually he discovered you lived in Franklin, and he moved here so he could be with you. He's fifty-two years old and his name is Niall Pickerd."

Fiona stared at Sally, the color draining from her already pallid face.

Sally took her hand. "He's safe and well, Fiona. And he really wants to meet you."

"Dear lord! The shame. He must hate me."

"Not at all. He's excited about meeting you."

"Truly?"

"He's tried several times to meet you, but Joseph stopped him."

"No, Joseph would never... He knew how I felt about losing my only child... So many times I wanted to reach out and find him."

"I'm sorry to tell you that Joseph paid Niall to go away."

Fiona's arthritic fingers covered her mouth. A sob escaped her. "He bribed my son to stay away from me? No, I don't believe it."

"Niall wishes he hadn't taken the money. He wants to give it back. He wants to meet his birth mother."

Fiona reached out and squeezed Sally's hand. "I must see him. Please!"

Sally looked at Lin for approval. Lin nodded. "If the doctor says it's okay, I can arrange it," Sally said.

"Oh, thank you. Do you have a picture of him?"

Sally showed Fiona the photo of Pickerd she had in her phone.

"Oh, he looks like a big strong boy. My son! I can hardly believe it!"

"Fiona, he's a suspect in Joseph's murder, which is why he will be accompanied by two police officers."

"No, no, that can't be so. My son wouldn't kill."

"Joseph isn't the father, is he?"

"I... No, he isn't."

"Niall has no alibi for the time the intruder was in your house, and he has motive to kill Joseph."

"I tell you, he didn't do it."

"How do you know?"

Sally held her breath. Would Fiona reveal what she really knew about the night of the murder?

Fiona's lips parted. She paused. "I'll know the voice. Let me hear Niall's voice, then I can tell you if he killed my husband."

FIFTY-SEVEN

A patrol car collected Niall Pickerd from his apartment and drove him to the hospital to meet Fiona. He was a bundle of nerves.

"Do I look okay?" he asked Sally.

Pickerd was not in his customary hoodie. He wore a smart shirt and jeans.

"You look great."

Sally poked her head around the door to make sure that Fiona was as ready as she could be to meet her long-lost son, sitting up in bed in a fresh nightie. She looked as nervous as Pickerd. Sally then led Pickerd into the room, followed by the two police officers who stayed by the door.

Fiona held her arms out, "Oh, my darling boy!"

Pickerd didn't seem the type of guy to cry but as he walked toward Fiona, all pretense of self-control left him and her took his mother in his arms and sobbed. Sally looked on, her eyes teary at the heartening scene. Even the male cops with her seemed moved by the reunion. They both had smiles on their faces.

"I'm so sorry, my son. I didn't want to give you away. But my family insisted. I've never stopped thinking about you," Fiona said.

Pickerd sat on the edge of the bed. "I looked for you. Took me two years to find you. Then Joseph paid me to go away. And I'm ashamed to say that I took it. I had no money. Nothing." He dropped his head.

Fiona kissed her son's hand. "I didn't know. He kept you from me."

"They think I killed him," Pickerd said. "I swear I didn't. I so wanted to meet you, but I would never kill for it."

Fiona looked over Pickerd's shoulder at Sally. "Niall isn't the man I heard talking to Joseph. He's not a killer."

"Are you certain?" Sally asked. "You told us your hearing wasn't so good."

"Yes, I am." This was the first time that Fiona had been certain about anything.

"Did you see the killer at all?" Sally asked. Fiona had already denied it, but Sally had a hunch that she knew who the killer was.

"I... no. It's the voice. It's not Niall."

"I think Joseph's killer is someone you know, Fiona, and we're going to find him. It would just make it a whole lot easier if you told me."

"Mom? You know who hurt you?" Pickerd asked.

"You're wrong, Sally. If I knew, I'd tell you."

"I think you know more than you're telling us. If you believe that keeping quiet will keep you safe, I'm sorry to say you're wrong. The killer may think that you can identify him. That places you in grave danger."

Pickerd said, "I'll keep her safe. If she'll let me. I can camp in the yard. Watch the house."

"We'll have cops watching Fiona until the killer is caught."

"Oh, I'd love Niall to stay with me. Will you?"

"You bet. Now I've found you, nobody is going to take you from me."

As they left the hospital, Clarence called Lin and she put his call on speaker.

"Silvia Tofano won't talk and she's getting lawyered up. What do you want me to do?" Clarence said.

"Stay where you are," Lin said. "We're on our way."

Ten minutes later, they met Clarence who led them into a yoga studio, which Tofano ran with a friend and business partner, Marie Colombo, who was taking a class. Tofano was in the middle of enrolling a new client when they walked in. Tofano gave Clarence an annoyed scowl. Tofano, thirty-eight, had hair dyed auburn, tied back in a long straight ponytail, and was a great advocate for Japanese yoga. When the client had signed the paperwork and left, Tofano spoke to Clarence.

"Officer, I've already told you I won't say a thing without my lawyer present."

Lin stepped forward and showed her police ID. "I'm Detective Lin and this is Detective Fairburn. We need you to tell us why you were making regular payments to Fiona Austin."

"Shush, please." Tofano scowled, looking around furtively. "Come with me."

Tofano pulled open a swing door behind the reception counter and led the three of them into a small office.

"I'm the only one on reception this morning. We're down two people today so I'll have to keep one eye on reception." Tofano left the door ajar. "What's this about?"

"For two years you've paid money into Fiona Austin's account with the Bank of Detroit." Sally held out printouts of the most recent months and she pointed at her name. "Were you being blackmailed?"

"No comment."

"Don't play games, Mrs. Tofano. You could be charged with obstructing a homicide investigation. So please answer Sally's question."

Tofano's tough façade dropped. "Oh, god, please don't tell my husband."

"So you were being blackmailed?"

"Yes, and I know what you're thinking, but I didn't kill Joseph. I couldn't. I mean, I wouldn't." She was babbling. "Oh, god, this will ruin my life."

"Why were they blackmailing you?"

Tofano used her index finger and thumb to pinch together her eyebrows. "If he finds out, he'll leave me."

"Who?"

"My husband." Someone called out from the reception desk, and Tofano poked her head out of the office door. "Be with you in a few moments. Please take a seat." Then she shut the door and sat down again.

"Why was Joseph blackmailing you?" Sally asked again.

"Joseph? No, no. It was Fiona. She watches from the top-floor window. It's like her ivory tower. She uses binoculars. She saw me, um, with a man who isn't my husband. He was leaving my house and she took a photo of us kissing."

"Who were you having an affair with?" Sally asked for clarity.

"Travis, a guy who practices yoga here. I give private lessons as well as teach classes." She blushed. "One thing led to another."

"How did Fiona approach you?"

"She and Joseph came to my house. They were always complaining about one neighbor or another and I thought they were there to complain about our noisy kids. I invited them in, and they showed me photos of Travis coming and going from the house. They even had videos."

If Fiona was able to leave the house to visit Tofano, she most certainly wasn't agoraphobic.

"How did they manage to shoot the video of the two of you?" Sally asked.

Tofano kept her eyes down, clearly too embarrassed to look at Sally. "The bedroom is on the ground floor. One of them must have filmed us through the window."

The more she learned about Joseph and Fiona, the more she realized why plenty of people might have wanted them dead.

"They asked for money?" Sally prompted.

"Yes. I told them I'd end the affair and begged them to destroy the evidence, but they just kept saying that they'd show my husband everything if I didn't pay them one thousand dollars per month."

"Did your husband notice the money disappearing from the account?"

"No, I pay them from my business account. The money comes from the salary I pay myself, so it doesn't impact the business. My business partner knows I do it although she told me time and time again to go to the police. But I couldn't risk wrecking my marriage."

"I'd like to see the business accounts."

"Anything."

"I have to ask you where you were on the night of July twenty-sixth."

"You think... I killed him?" She shook her head energetically. "No way."

"Where were you?"

Tofano searched the diary on her phone. "We had friends to dinner at our place. They left about, oh, eleven-thirty p.m. Then we cleared up and went to bed."

"Your husband is your alibi?"

"Yes."

Sally wondered if he would continue as her alibi if he discovered the affair. "Can anyone else vouch for you?"

"Jessica, my daughter, had a nightmare. It must have been one or two in the morning. She came into our room and spent the rest of the night sleeping between us. I remember because I slept badly after that and had a shit day at work. I wasn't paying attention and twisted my ankle."

"How old is Jessica?"

"Seven. Please, Detective, don't involve my husband and kids. The affair is over."

But Sally couldn't promise that. "Is it possible that your husband knows about the affair and killed Joseph to put an end to the blackmailing?"

"No, no way. I'd know if he did. He's not a forgiving person. If he had found out, he'd want a divorce."

Tofano agreed to give her fingerprints and DNA. Clarence used a kit he had with him to take both. Tofano also agreed to hand over some of her husband's hair from his comb so that he could be eliminated without Tofano having to tell him about her infidelity.

Outside in the street, Lin asked Clarence to head for the forensics lab while Sally and Lin would visit Robin Kerns.

"Fiona was jumpy when you asked about Robin. I want to know why," Lin said.

FIFTY-EIGHT

Sally and Lin stood on Robin Kerns's red brick porch, waiting for him to open the door.

"You take the lead," Lin said. "He's met you before."

Sally swallowed a lump in her throat. If Robin was Wilbur Smith, they might be about to interview a killer.

"Try again," Lin directed, and Sally pressed the doorbell.

Again, no response. Perhaps he was with Betty at the nursing home? Sally turned to look up and down the street and spotted Robin, tall and languid, head down, and coming their way. He only noticed Sally and Lin when he was through the garden gate.

There was a moment of shock, which he quickly recovered from.

"Sally, how lovely to see you. I do hope you have good news."

She waited until he was on the porch to reply. "This is Detective Lin." Lin held up her police ID. "Can we come in? This won't take a moment."

"Sure."

Robin showed them into the hallway of marble slabs and an

elegant staircase with swirling banisters. They followed him into the living room and sat on a couch facing the suspect.

"How is Fiona?" Robin asked.

"She's recovering well."

"Can I see her?"

"Not until we find Joseph's killer. Which brings me to the reason for this chat. We've identified several people we believe Joseph and Fiona blackmailed, and I think you are one of them."

"Excuse me?"

"There is no shame in admitting that you were a victim of blackmail."

His mouth hung open. "I have no idea what you're talking about."

"We believe the blackmail began in 2005. You were a partner in one of Franklin's largest accountancy firms. Did the Austins threaten to expose something you had done? Something morally dubious or illegal perhaps? Something that might have destroyed your career?"

"I have no idea where this is coming from, but I have never been blackmailed, least of all by my dear friends."

"Are you a fan of the Wilbur Smith novels?" Lin asked.

He balked at the question. "Excuse me? What does an author have to do with Joseph's murder?"

"Please answer the question."

"Yes, I have all Wilbur Smith's novels. So what?"

"A person calling themselves Wilbur Smith has paid large sums into Fiona's private account for eleven years," Lin said. "Over one point three million dollars." Robin's eyes bulged. "Are you the man calling himself Wilbur Smith?"

Robin's face darkened. "Why on earth would you think it's me? Listen, Detective, there is nothing in my life I'm ashamed of. I haven't broken the law, except perhaps a speeding fine or two, nor has Betty."

"I'd like to speak with your wife," Lin said.

"Absolutely not, I forbid it. You'll frighten her."

"Sir, I..."

"She is mentally incapacitated and as her legal guardian I will not allow it."

Sally could understand why Robin had reacted so forcefully to Lin's suggestion, but Lin clearly didn't want to leave any stone unturned. "I'd like to take your fingerprints and DNA."

"Oh, for goodness' sake. If I let you, will you leave me alone?"

"It will help us to eliminate you."

"Yes, all right. I'll do it."

"Robin," said Sally, "it would help us believe you if you told us why you called Fiona's cell shortly before Joseph was murdered. Were you warning Fiona? Do you know who killed Joseph?"

"This is preposterous. You can have my fingerprints and DNA and that's all. If you want to ask me more questions, it will be with my attorney present."

FIFTY-NINE

It was late afternoon by the time Clarence had a warrant to access Robin Kerns's bank accounts. Robin's DNA and fingerprints were now at the lab and Sally was eager to learn if his DNA matched the fingernail found at the crime scene.

"Robin has two accounts," Clarence said. "One in this country and one in South Africa."

Sally looked up from her screen. In her mind this information reinforced Robin's connection to the author, Wilbur Smith, who was based in Cape Town.

Clarence shook his head. "It's going to take a long time to go through."

"I'll help you," Sally said. "I'll take the South African Bank."

"Apologies, guys," Lin said, racing into the room. "The shit's hit the fan on the Megan Chou case. Clarke wants me back on that team." Lin picked up her favorite mug. "Call me if you need to bounce ideas off me."

Then Lin was gone. "I guess that means Clarke is happy for the two of us to continue," Sally said.

Clarence leaned back. "I've been thinking about the

contents of the safe. What if it held blackmailing material? Incriminating photos, videos, documents, that kinda thing."

"That makes sense."

Her phone rang and she was pleased to see it was Dr. Mani calling.

"Please tell me you have good news," Sally said.

"I think I do, although it isn't conclusive," Dr. Mani replied.

"I'm putting you on speaker," Sally said. "I'm with Officer Pew."

"We have run Robin Kerns's DNA and fingerprints through our databases and something interesting came up."

Sally sat upright. "Go on."

"You remember the fingernail from the Austins' bathroom?"

"Yes."

"It is a partial match to Robin Kerns."

"Partial?" Sally asked. Her heart was racing. Could this be the break they had been hoping for?

"Yes, but before you charge around there and arrest him, I need to be clear that it is *not* an exact DNA match. It is more likely to belong to a close relative, such as a sibling or child."

Sally's mind was spinning. "Robin has two grown children. One lives in Australia so unless she was visiting at the time of the murder, I think we can rule her out. The other, a son, lives on the same street as Robin. Name of Bob Kerns."

"How old is he?" Mani asked.

"I was told he's in his thirties," Sally said.

"Remember, there were no roots to the hairs found in their bathroom, so it's challenging to get DNA results. However, the hairs are in good condition, which indicates a younger rather than an older person. I need the son's DNA and fingerprints."

"Thanks, Dr. Mani, this is the best news we've had."

They both felt it. The tingle of anticipation as Sally and Clarence walked into Franklin Radiology where Bob Kerns was the medical director. He was soon to marry Janey Wildner, the daughter of Senator Josh Wildner and from his LinkedIn and Facebook profile, it was clear he was mixing in rich and influential social circles. From his photos, Sally knew he had brown, straight hair, cut short at the sides and back, with longer hair on top. It was hard to tell his build from photos, but his bride was almost as tall as him and in group photos he was one of the shorter men. At the back of Sally's mind was the size ten boot print found at the crime scenes.

"He has to be our guy," Clarence said, taking long strides.

"Don't jump the gun. He may have an alibi. And we need to go easy on him."

"Because he's marrying a senator's daughter?" Clarence asked.

"No, because this is the first time we have questioned him and all we have is a partial DNA match. Robin has three siblings still alive and we haven't spoken to them yet."

At the reception desk Sally showed her police ID and asked to speak to him. The receptionist said that he was with a patient and they would need to wait.

"Could someone please notify him that we're here and need to see him urgently?"

"I suppose I could do it." She leaned over to her colleague, told the male receptionist that she would be back in a minute, and used a security pass to go through a frosted glass door.

Sally and Clarence stood aside and waited. When the receptionist returned she said that Bob could see them in ten minutes, and did they want tea or coffee. Sally declined the drinks, as did Clarence, and they both took seats near the frosted door.

"I wonder if he's calling his lawyer," Sally whispered into Clarence's ear.

"He'd only call a lawyer if he had something to hide, right?"

"Right."

After the medical center's wall clock had circled the face seven times, a short, slim man in a button-up shirt, which he wore open at the neck, shook both their hands and showed them to the rear of the medical center.

"Are Mom and Dad okay?" he asked as soon as they were through the frosted door.

"We're not here about your parents, Mr. Kerns. We're investigating the murder of Joseph Austin."

He nodded. "Ah, Dad's friend. Of course, come with me."

They followed him past a changing area with cubicles fronted by curtains and then six doors with lights above to alert people that the room was being used.

"How long have you been a radiologist?" Sally asked.

"Started as soon as I graduated. Must be eleven years now."

He had a small peak of hair above his brow that was gelled upward, which gave him a boyish look, but the Longines watch on his right wrist said that he was a man at the height of his career. Sally glanced at his shoes—polished tassel moccasin loafers that looked expensive. She wondered what size they were.

He showed them into an office. It wasn't extensive or expensively furnished but it was neat and had a view of the park. He asked them to take a seat and walked around the back of his desk, on which was a small, framed photo of him and his fiancée, Janey. "I'm not sure how I can be of any help. I was at home with my girlfriend that night."

Sally had the feeling his alibi was prepared. Perhaps his father had warned his son about them. Perhaps a lawyer had advised him to present his alibi upfront so as to take the wind out of their sails. From the corner of her eye, she caught Clarence's shoulders sagging with disappointment.

"You may have seen more than you think," Sally said. She

waited for him to sit. He rested one hand on the desk before him, the other on the arm of his chair. She tried to imagine his fingers splayed and the hand pressed against a tiled wall. "We're taking a fresh look at the case and reinterviewing possible witnesses and suspects."

"Which one am I?" he said with a chuckle, presumably expecting her to say that of course he was a possible witness.

"That depends on many things, not least, what you saw on the night of the murder."

"I thought it was a burglary and Joseph accosted the intruder?"

"That's what the media has been saying, but it's clear that Joseph was the target, as was the contents of the safe." She watched his boyish face. The smile was still there but the edges dropped for a second or two, then it was back. "I don't believe you were interviewed at the time?"

"Why would I be?"

"No time like the present," Sally said. "You seem very sure that you were at home the night of the murder?"

"That's because I am sure. Dad called me the morning Joseph's body was found. He was in a terrible state. He told me that Joseph was dead, and Fiona was in a critical condition. It's not something you forget easily."

"How well did you know Fiona and Joseph Austin?"

"They're like an aunt and uncle. Always been a part of my life. I was horrified when I heard what happened, but I was more concerned about Dad. They've been best friends for decades."

"And your mom? Did she regard them as friends?"

"Yes, she adored them. We haven't told her about Joseph's passing. It will break her heart. Of course, she'll forget about it—that's what Alzheimer's does—but we talked about it and decided it was best not to tell her."

"I understand," Sally said. "When did you last see Joseph?"

"Oh, must be months. I've been busy with work and organizing my wedding."

"And Fiona? When did you last see her?"

"The same. I can't remember exactly."

"When was the last time you were in their house?"

Bob closed his eyes for a few seconds as if trying to remember. "Must be Fiona's birthday. May tenth."

Clarence made notes.

"Tell me about your movements on the night of July twenty-sixth," Sally said.

"Janey and I went to dinner at a new Italian restaurant, Scopri. Just opened, fabulous food. We got to my place about ten-thirty p.m. Janey stayed the night and left the following morning." He looked smug, like he was convinced that he was untouchable.

"Your address is twenty-eight Chestnut Close?"

"Yes."

"Were you and Janey at your house all night?"

"Yes, of course."

"Neither of you left before morning?"

"No, as I said, we were asleep in bed all night." Irritation had drifted into his tone. "Janey left for work about eight a.m."

"Did you hear or see anything unusual that night?"

"No. Look, I don't mean to be rude, but I was nowhere near Willow Way, so I couldn't have seen anything, now could I? And if you'll excuse me, I have patients waiting to see me."

"I haven't quite finished, Mr. Kerns. Are you aware that Joseph blackmailed a number of people over many years?"

"Dad told me you said that, but, like him, I find it hard to believe."

As Sally had expected, Robin had told his son about her questioning him. "Are you aware of your father or mother being blackmailed?"

He snorted derisively. "That's ridiculous! Mom and Dad

are good people. There would be nothing to blackmail. And, besides, Joseph just wouldn't do it."

"Does the name Wilbur Smith mean anything to you?"

"Dad told me you think some guy using Wilbur Smith's name paid Joseph blackmail money. The whole thing is ludicrous. You've seized Dad's bank records, I hear. You'll see that Dad isn't guilty of a damn thing."

"What size shoes do you wear?"

"Nine. Why?"

Damn! Sally thought but then immediately considered that Bob could have worn larger boots to throw them off the scent.

"The simplest way to rule you out of the investigation is to do a DNA test and take your fingerprints."

"Excuse me? Why?"

"Because a fingernail was found in the victims' bathroom, which is a partial DNA match to your father."

"Hold on a second! You're not serious. You think I did it?" He laughed, a mocking laugh that didn't quite ring true. "Now I've heard it all."

"Will you come to the station with us now? The sooner we clear you the better."

Bob stood slowly. "This conversation is over. I'm not saying another word without a lawyer." He walked to the door and opened it. "I'd think long and hard about pursuing this, Detective. My fiancée is Senator Josh Wildner's daughter. I don't think the senator will be happy to find his daughter dragged into a murder investigation."

SIXTY

"We need a look at Bob's bank accounts," Sally said. She and Clarence were back in their incident room. "He was too smug, and the threat at the end... Why say that?" Sally said.

"To scare us away." Clarence thought for a moment. "There's something not right about him, like he'd rehearsed what he was going to say."

"I thought that too. We should talk to Janey, the fiancée."

"That won't be easy."

"I'll talk to Clarke. The last thing I want is for Senator Wildner to come down on us like a ton of bricks."

Sally left the room and found Clarke had his door shut and was on the phone. He gestured for her to wait and so she hung around outside. Through the glass partition, she heard rumbles of a conversation that had Clarke replying tersely. When he opened his door, he wore a deep frown.

"I've just had Senator Wildner's chief-of-staff on the phone."

Bob's called in the big guns already.

Sally followed Clarke into his office and shut the door. Clarke continued, "He wanted to impress on me the importance of keeping his daughter out of the murder investigation. The election's in a few months and this could rock the boat for him."

"That could be a problem, sir, given that she is our prime suspect's alibi."

"Prime suspect? Tell me why you think it's him."

Sally told him about the fingernail found at the crime scene, which was a partial DNA match to Robin Kerns. "Dr. Mani explained that the partial match had to be from a close relative such as his kids or siblings. In addition, Bob knows the victims, which explains why Joseph let him into his home so late at night. When I asked for a DNA sample, Bob became defensive and refused. Given that his alibi is the senator's daughter, we have to speak to her. And I want to go through Bob's bank accounts. He may be our Wilbur Smith, the person who was blackmailed by Joseph for eleven years. He therefore has motive. Roisin and Sobral were probably killed because they were witnesses."

"Do you have anything concrete on Bob Kerns, apart from a partial DNA match?"

"Not yet. If we get a search warrant we can also search the house for size ten boots. His feet are a size nine but with an extra layer of socks it would be easy for him to wear size ten."

"Have you definitely ruled out Robin as a suspect?" Clarke asked.

"Clarence is working through Robin's bank statements, but, so far, there's nothing linking Robin to Fiona's Detroit account."

"What was your feel of the man? Bob, I mean."

"Cocky. Mixes in all the right circles. Wears an expensive watch and shoes. A top-of-the-range Mercedes in the parking lot at the front of the radiology center. I'd say he could afford to pay such a large sum of money to his blackmailer. He's marrying a senator's daughter. That's a big deal. Any scandal about his past life could ruin his life, in particular his marriage into such a high-profile family."

"And he lives, what, five minutes' walk from the victims' house?" Clarke asked.

"Five or ten at most."

"Your problem is opportunity. If Janey says he was with her all night, then we have nothing." Clarke rolled his lips together, thinking. "Our other problem is that Senator Wildner doesn't want it known that his daughter is sleeping with her fiancé before their wedding day. They are a high-profile Catholic family."

"Oh, perfect!" Sally groaned. "So where to from here?"

"I'll set up a meeting with Janey and I'll lead the interview. She'll be lawyered up, no doubt, and will have been coached. I want you to observe her and ask questions that get under her skin."

"Yes, boss." Sally was relieved that Clarke would take the lead. The last thing she wanted to do was offend a senator's daughter.

"In the meantime, dig into Bob's past. Why did the blackmail start in 2005? He must have done something really bad to accept his blackmailer's demand for money."

"Will do."

"And keep searching for proof that Bob left his house that night. A neighbor driving home late?"

With Bob Kerns refusing to cooperate, how was Sally going to do that?

SIXTY-ONE

It came to her as she stared at the depleted list of suspects on the whiteboard. Her eyes danced from Robin Kerns who lived at 22 Chestnut Close, to his son Bob, at number 28, and then to witnesses Felicia and Jonathan Suri, at number 25.

She pulled up Google Maps on her computer and opted for the street view, using the Suri's house as the base. Then she used the arrows on Google Maps to turn 180 degrees around so that she was able to see the view opposite. It appeared that the Suri's home was not directly opposite Bob Kerns's home. It was just a little to the left, but it gave Sally an idea. She called Felicia.

"You have security cameras at your house, right?" Sally asked.

"Yes, why?"

"Do any of them point across the street?"

"No, they're positioned close to the house. Front door, back door, lower floor windows. What's this about?"

"I was hoping you might have footage of the street on the night of July twenty-sixth."

"I don't understand. The murders were on Willow Way."

"We are exploring the possibility the suspect walked down your street." Sally rubbed her forehead, disappointed that her idea hadn't worked out. "Never mind. Thanks for your assistance."

"Wait! There's our doorbell video. The camera points toward the street. It's wide angle."

"Does it have nighttime recording?"

"Yes, in black and white but it's usually quite clear."

"Do you have the footage from that night?"

"Should have. They stay in our account for one hundred and eighty days. It's normally sixty days but we extended it, just in case. Jonathan is a stickler for data. He won't delete anything, not unless I nag him."

A rush of adrenaline surged through Sally's body. "I need to see the footage urgently. Can you email it to me or is it too large a file?"

"I'd rather you view it here. I don't trust the internet."

"I'll be with you in thirty minutes."

Sally punched the air when the call was finished. Clarence was on the phone to the university where Bob completed his degree in radiology. Sally had given him the job of investigating Bob Kerns's past, in particular what happened in 2005 that might have led to him being blackmailed. Sally waited until Clarence finished the call.

"I think we just caught a break," she said. "Felicia Suri has doorbell video footage of the night of July twenty-sixth. It could show Bob Kerns leaving his house. I'm going there now. Anything on Bob yet?"

"Not yet. He liked to party. But that's what college kids do, right?"

"I guess." Sally checked that her gun was in her holster, put on her jacket, and pocketed her badge. "Call me if you find anything."

Felicia set Sally up in a paneled office in front of a monitor to view the footage from the night of the murder. She offered Sally a drink and Sally gratefully accepted coffee, then Felicia hovered near Sally.

"I should come clean about something."

"Go ahead," Sally said.

"I lied when I said my husband was here all night."

"Where was he?"

"I'm not sure. I mean, he was probably with his mistress, but I never ask about her and Jonathan tells me nothing."

"Did he ask you to say that he was with you the night of July twenty-sixth?" Felicia nodded. Sally continued, "I guess the doorbell camera will show him coming and going."

"Yes, but he has no reason to kill Joseph."

"Thanks for telling me. I'll organize an officer to interview your husband."

"I'll leave you to it," Felicia said.

When she was gone, Sally contacted Clarence and asked him to visit Jonathan Suri.

Then Sally started going through the doorbell footage, beginning at 6 p.m. on July 26. It was possible that the killer left home early to prepare for the assault. The footage was of better quality than she'd expected but every time a vehicle's headlights passed the Suri's home, there was a burst of white light that blurred out everything else. There was no direct view of Robin's home, but Bob's house was partially visible. Sally wasn't able to see Bob's front door, but she hoped that if he left his house in the night, he'd be caught on camera when he reached the street. She could, however, see a car in the drive.

Sally's eyesight was good but very soon she found herself moving closer to the screen. She quickly discovered that it wasn't possible to identify the vehicle's license plate but it looked like Bob's Mercedes. As she'd expected, after 11 p.m. there wasn't a lot of movement in the quiet suburban street, just a group of teenagers and a few cars passing by.

Then someone walked into the range of the doorbell camera at 11:44 p.m. The person left Bob Kerns's driveway and walked quickly along the street. A rush of adrenaline surged through her. She paused the footage. Maybe a man in pants and a hoodie over his head. What was on his back? A backpack? It was flat, so it didn't carry much. She let the video run. The person then walked out of the camera's sight.

She let the footage run on, stopping every now and again, but only one other person and a cat triggered the camera. Then at 12:53 a.m. a person appeared, heading in the opposite direction. Was he or she a different person? Same walk, different clothes. The hoodie was gone. The backpack was bulging. Did it hold his bloody clothes and towel? The problem was that she couldn't be sure who it was. Then she yelped with elation. The person turned into Bob's drive and walked past the Mercedes and disappeared into the darkness down one side of the house.

She couldn't prove definitively this was Bob Kerns, but it was enough to get a search warrant.

She found Felicia in the kitchen arranging flowers. "Felicia, I'm calling in our tech guys. They will take a copy of this and try to enhance the footage. I don't want you to touch this. It's now evidence in a murder inquiry. Do you understand?"

Felicia sounded flustered. "Yes, I suppose. I must tell Jonathan. He won't like it."

"By all means, call him. I'll stay here until the tech people arrive."

Once the tech team were organized, Sally called Clarke. "I may have the proof we need."

SIXTY-TWO

September 15, 2016

Janey Wildner's attorney, Karl Cornell, made Clarke and Sally wait until 8 a.m. the following morning for their meeting. This worked out well for them because the tech team came back with clearer footage of the person leaving and then returning to Bob Kerns's home on the night of Joseph's murder. They now knew the suspect wore a Champion sweatshirt on the return trip, the word emblazoned on its front.

The apartment's concierge phoned Janey to let her know that they had visitors, then he sent Clarke and Sally to level eighteen.

"You look nervous," Clarke said to Sally. She couldn't keep her hands still.

"I am nervous."

"You're a detective," Clarke said. "You're doing your job. Don't be intimidated."

Sally nodded, but she felt nauseated.

When the elevator opened at the penthouse, where Cornell greeted them, Sally did her best to appear confident, although from the dismissive glance she received from Cornell, she was sure that he sensed her trepidation, which only increased when she saw the apartment was the whole floor. The Wildners sure had bags of money and with it came power.

The attorney—white hair, slick suit, slimy smile—and Janey Wildner sat in chairs. The detectives were given the couch to sit on, which had them, no doubt intentionally, seated at a lower level than Cornell and Janey.

Clarke had warned Sally before they entered the building that Cornell had worked for the senator for over thirty years and he was very loyal to the family.

Janey didn't get up to greet them, her slender legs resting together at the ankles and to one side, in the way finishing schools teach young ladies. She nodded as they introduced themselves.

"Janey is more than happy to assist the police, but she would like me to stress that she knows nothing about what happened to Joseph and Fiona Austin on July twenty-sixth." Cornell gave them a glinting smile.

"Thank you for your cooperation, Ms. Wildner," Clarke said, directing his attention to Bob's alibi. "Can you take us through your movements on July twenty-sixth this year, starting from when you left work?" Janey worked in PR.

Janey was a blonde-haired, blue-eyed, pretty young woman, who would always look amazing, even without her perfectly applied make-up. She glanced at the attorney, clearly seeking his permission to speak, and when he nodded, she cleared her throat.

"I left the office at six-thirty p.m. and took a cab to The Everleigh where I met Bob. We had a cocktail each, then walked to Scopri for dinner at seven-thirty p.m. We caught a cab to Bob's house at nine-thirty p.m. We talked, then went to bed at about ten-thirty p.m." She leaned back in the armchair, a look of relief on her face.

Neat and rehearsed, Sally thought.

"Which cab service did you use to go to Bob's house?" Clarke asked.

"Silver Service."

"What time did you leave Bob's house the next morning?" Clarke asked.

"I keep some clothes in his closet so I can stay over. I must have left about eight a.m. Bob called me a cab."

Cornell intervened, "The cab company was once again Silver Service. Bob has an account. You can check."

"We will," Clarke said. "Did Bob leave his home at any time during the night?"

"Why do you ask?" Janey blushed with anger. "He wouldn't hurt anyone."

Cornell said, "Janey has already answered your question, Detective. Please move onto your next question."

Janey hadn't actually answered the question, Sally thought.

"Ms. Wildner, to eliminate Bob from our inquiries we have to question you about his whereabouts. So, did Bob leave the house at any point between the time you arrived at his house on the twenty-sixth and when you left on the twenty-seventh?"

"No. He was in bed with me all night."

Cornell again stuck his oar in. "This is not a fact Janey or her parents wish to be made public. Can I count on your discretion?"

"I will be discreet but if we charge Bob, the details will come out."

Janey looked at Cornell, horrified. "They can't do that, Karl."

Cornell smiled reassuringly at Janey. "It won't come to that. He's innocent."

Clarke continued, "Ms. Wildner, do you take sleeping pills?"

"Yes, why?"

"Is it possible you failed to notice Bob leave the bedroom in the night because of the sleeping pill you took?"

"I must object," Cornell said. "Janey, don't answer."

Janey gripped her lips into a line, like a child holding in a lie.

"Which brand of sleeping pill do you use?"

Cornell nodded at Janey. "Ambien," she answered. "It's just for the short term. The wedding is stressing me out. There's so much to organize."

Sally's doctor had suggested she might take this drug after Zelda had died. It was a prescription-only sedative drug that helped people go to sleep and stay asleep, but it could be addictive.

"That can send you into a deep sleep," Sally said, speaking up for the first time. "You might not have heard your fiancé leave."

Janey shook her head. "I would have heard."

"Ms. Wildner," Clarke said. "Through DNA evidence we know that Joseph Austin's killer is a close relative of Robin Kerns." Her blue eyes widened. "We also know that Joseph was blackmailing several people including someone who calls himself Wilbur Smith and who paid Joseph $1.3 million over the course of eleven years. Do you know if Bob has ever been called Wilbur Smith or likened to him?"

Janey shook her head, but a red rash had appeared on her neck.

"I was not made aware of this evidence," Cornell said. "Janey won't answer questions relating to it."

"Did you leave Bob's house at any time during the night of July twenty-sixth?" Clarke asked.

"That's enough," Cornell said. "Are you seriously suggesting that my client killed Joseph Austin?"

"Ms. Wildner, we have video evidence of a person leaving twenty-eight Chestnut Close at eleven forty-four p.m. and returning at twelve fifty-three a.m. It was either you or Bob. So who was it?"

Janey stared with pleading eyes at the lawyer, the rash on her neck deepening with her growing agitation.

Cornell said, "That proves nothing, Detective. You obviously can't identify this person. If you could, you'd have arrested them. You're grasping at straws and upsetting my client. This interview is over."

Clarke was bluffing. Janey was too petite to be the person captured on video. Sally suspected her distress was not about her possible guilt. It was about the doubts creeping in about her fiancé.

"Janey," Sally said. "This must be very difficult for you but, for your sake, you should know who it is you are marrying. I made the mistake of ignoring my intuition about my ex-husband. Don't make the same mistake I did. If you think of anything unusual about your fiancé's behavior, just call me. Please." Sally handed Janey a card with her contact details.

Cornell showed them to the door. As Sally and Clarke took the elevator down to the foyer, Clarke said, "She's lying."

"I agree."

"Has Janey ever met Officer Pew?"

"No."

"Have him tail her. I won't be surprised if she has it out with Bob next. Sally, you get the search warrant."

SIXTY-THREE

Clarke clutched the warrant in his right hand as he led his team up the winding path of Bob Kerns's home. Sally was a step or two behind him, and she was followed by Clarence and Detective Lin, as well as four uniformed officers.

"Janey's with him," Clarence said, who had been tailing her.

Sally had already checked out the two cars in the driveway: Bob's Mercedes and a convertible Mazda sports car.

"Stay close to Janey, Sally," Clarke directed. "We don't know how Kerns will react."

"Will do."

A harsh wind blew diagonally across the front yard, ripping leaves off trees and hurling them at the officers. It was 1:49 p.m. and storm clouds, high and menacing, were rolling in from the north.

It had been touch-and-go on the search warrant. Bob's attorney, Cornell, had tried to sway the judge to refuse the application, but, fortunately, the judge had fallen out with Janey's father, Senator Wildner, when he tried to scupper the judge's appointment three years ago. There had been a satisfied look on the judge's face when he signed off on the warrant.

"Cornell will have alerted Kerns," Clarke had said before they left the office.

When a separate team of detectives had arrived at the radiology clinic, which was also to be searched, they were informed that Bob had left the clinic in a hurry.

Clarke lifted his hand to ring Bob's doorbell. Raised voices carried through the paneled beech door and Clarke paused and listened.

"Promise me you didn't do it!" Janey yelled.

Sally and Clarke exchanged knowing glances. If Bob and Janey had been asleep together all night as they claimed, how could Janey doubt his innocence?

"Janey!" Bob's voice carried through the door. "I didn't do it!"

"You lied!"

"For god's sake, keep your voice down. They'll be here any minute."

Clarke took that as his cue. He pressed his finger on the doorbell and shouted, "Police!"

"Oh, my god!" Janey yelped. "I can't be here."

"I need you," Bob pleaded. "Please, Janey."

Clarke ordered two cops to go around the back. "Nobody leaves," he directed.

The cops ran down the steps and along the side of the house.

"Mr. Kerns! Open the door. We have a warrant to search your premises."

The door flew open, and a flushed and angry Bob Kerns stood there. "Do you have to be so heavy-handed?" He looked past Clarke and his team, across the street. "Come in. Quickly!" He waved them in and slammed the door. "This is embarrassing enough."

Beckoning them into the hall, he shut the door, then held out his hand. "Show me the warrant."

Clarke passed it to him, but he didn't wait for Bob's approval.

"Where's your study, sir?"

Bob looked up from the warrant. "What do you want in there?"

"Sir, just point us in the right direction. Lin will accompany you."

"It's through there." Bob pointed at the third door on the right.

Clarke directed the two remaining officers, "Start at the top of the house and work down."

The officers climbed the stairs, ignoring Bob's complaints. They had all been briefed to search for computers, phones, security footage, any evidence that proved Bob was being blackmailed, and the murder weapon—a hammer—a Champion hoodie, jeans or pants spattered with blood, size ten work boots with soil and blood on them.

Clarke held out a transparent evidence bag. "Hand over your phone."

"I need it for work."

"It will be returned to you when we're done."

Bob scowled, but he pulled the phone from his back pocket and dropped it in the evidence bag. Clarke sealed it and handed it to Lin who was in charge of the evidence collection.

"This is unbelievable," Bob said, slapping the paper warrant.

If he were the murderer, Sally expected him to be more afraid. Presently he appeared more annoyed than anything. Had Sally made a mistake about him?

"Do you have any other properties, lockups, garages, or use of a storage facility?" Clarke asked.

"No."

"Show Lin your study, sir," Clarke ordered.

For a moment it looked as if Bob might refuse again, but he

must have thought better of it. He led them down the marble hall to an oak-paneled study. There were a couple of Chippendale armchairs near the fireplace.

"Take a seat." Clarke nodded at the chairs. "Where is Janey?"

"Here somewhere." Bob sat sulkily.

"Sally, find Janey."

Sally nodded and headed for the voluminous hall. She knew what to do. Her job was to find Janey and encourage her to talk. Where might she be? She had sounded distressed. In a panic. Did she need time to calm down? Sally headed for what she guessed was the powder room. She tried the door handle. It was locked.

"Janey? It's Detective Fairburn. Are you in there?"

A couple of seconds passed, long enough for Sally to wonder if Janey had escaped via the window.

"Give me a minute," Janey called through the door.

"Open the door."

Sally heard the sound of running water. Janey unlocked the door. The woman's hairline was damp, and her make-up smudged. The basin mirror was covered in splashes.

Janey edged out of the powder room. "I'm so sorry. I have to go. Daddy doesn't want me caught up in this."

"I'm sure he doesn't. He's just trying to protect you as I would too if you were my daughter," Sally said. "But I want to have a chat before you go."

Janey hunched her shoulders and hung her head. "I can't deal with all this. I'm already stressed with the wedding. And now you people turn up here." She sniffled back tears.

"Shall we sit? Take me to the kitchen."

Janey hesitated then led the way to a minimalist kitchen in dark gray marble and smooth cabinet surfaces with no kitchen appliances on the countertops. She sat on a startling yellow plastic chair, one of four—the only color in the room.

"Your loyalty to your fiancé is commendable, but you have to start thinking about yourself. Janey, we know Bob left the house that night."

A tear bulged in the corner of her eye and dropped down her cheek. "I can't believe this is happening," Janey wailed.

"Just tell me the truth," Sally said.

"He's not a killer. I know him. He's a sweet, kind man."

"Then he has nothing to fear. But if you lie for him, that reflects badly on you."

Janey left the chair and opened a drawer, took out a box of tissues, and then blew her nose. "He went for a walk, that's all. He knew it would make him a suspect, so he asked me to be his alibi."

"What time did he leave the house?"

"I'm not sure. I had taken a sleeping pill. I was groggy. He told me to go back to sleep. Said he was restless and needed to get some fresh air."

"How long was he gone?" Sally asked.

Janey sniffed back another tear. "This is ruining everything." She shook her head, frowning. "I shouldn't say any more. Karl told me not to speak to you."

"You've done the right thing. Just tell me what time he returned to the bedroom."

"I don't know. He was there when my alarm went off at six-thirty a.m."

"Tell me, does Bob have a favorite hoodie?"

"He's got plenty."

"What brands does he like?"

"There are so many."

Janey blew her nose again.

"Come with me to the bedroom." Sally wanted to ask Janey if Bob had a Champion sweatshirt and where he kept it.

"I want to go home."

"Please. Just this one thing and then you can go."

Janey meekly followed Sally toward the grand staircase but in so doing they passed the entrance to the study and Bob caught sight of them.

"Janey!" Bob left his chair before Clarke could ask him to stay put, and he took Janey in a hug.

"Oh, my darling, are you okay?" he said.

"Mr. Kerns, please sit down," Clarke called out.

"We're going upstairs," Sally told Clarke.

"No," Bob said, "She stays with me. I don't want you intimidating her."

It's more likely that you don't want her implicating you, Sally thought.

"Ms. Wildner, please go with Detective Fairburn," Clarke directed.

"You have no right to make Janey do anything. She stays here."

Janey's silent tears became a loud bawl. Sally felt for her. She was being torn in two directions.

"Okay, Janey stays with you for now," Clarke said, trying to defuse the rising tension. "Can you please both take a seat?" Bob steered Janey into the study and helped her sit on an armchair. He took the other one. "Mr. Kerns, where is the safe?" Clarke asked.

"Behind that painting." It was a modern work with a stark white background, the only color was orange and there were black tubes painted on the canvas. "It won't open without a retinal scan."

Fancy safe, Sally thought. *If Joseph's blackmail material is in there, this whole case can be put to bed.*

"Please open it, sir," Clarke said.

Bob stepped up to the painting, took it off the wall, tapped in a code, then placed his right eye in front of a retinal scanner. The safe door clicked open.

"Please step away, sir," Clarke ordered.

Bob sat down again, looking far too relaxed. Clarke asked Lin for an evidence bag. He took out wads of cash and a passport and dropped them in the evidence bag.

"Where have you hidden the contents of Joseph Austin's safe?"

"For the last time, I didn't break into Joseph's house!" Bob replied.

"Where are the bloodstained clothes you wore the night you used a hammer to beat Joseph Austin to death?"

Janey squealed. "Stop! This is too awful."

"I didn't kill Joseph, or Roisin, or Salvador."

"Sir," Sally said, "Can I have a word?" Clarke should know that Bob no longer had an alibi.

Janey turned to her fiancé. "I can't do this, Bob. I can't lie for you."

Bob kneeled in front of her. "You're upset. You don't know what you're saying. I'll take you home."

"Mr. Kerns," Clarke said, "please step away from Ms. Wildner."

"I'm taking her home. Come on, Janey, we're leaving."

Janey shook her head. "Leave me alone."

Sally spoke, "Janey, you told me that Bob did leave the house the night of the murder."

Bob jerked away from her, as if he had received an electric shock. "Why would you say that?"

"Because it's true!" Janey shouted.

Bob took a step back, his hand in his hair giving him a crazed look. "No, it's not! What are you doing?"

The friction between Janey and Bob was palpable. Sally's pulse was racing, and adrenaline flooded her body.

"You went for a walk, or that's what you told me," Janey said between sobs.

Bob hauled her up from her chair. Both Clarke and Sally lunged forward to intervene, but they had miscalculated the danger Janey was in, and the distance between them and Janey was too far. From seemingly nowhere, he produced a pistol and, grasping Janey tight, he held the gun to her head.

"Get out of my house!" he shouted. "All of you. Or I kill her."

SIXTY-FOUR

Clarke, Lin, and Sally crouched behind their Suburban, using the vehicle as a barrier between them and Bob Kerns who was inside the house with Janey Wildner as his hostage. As Bob had demanded, all the police officers had left the house and Clarke was on the phone to the communications room about the developing hostage situation. He used the driver's door as a shield while he spoke to the communications officer.

"And remember, this isn't any old hostage. Janey is a senator's daughter. We have to get her out of there alive or we'll all lose our jobs."

Despite the cold wind that ruffled his hair through the open window, Clarke was perspiring. He rubbed away a bead of sweat above his lip.

"We've secured the perimeter as best we can. We need backup ASAP and a hostage negotiator. If he's available, I want Del Hicks. And a SWAT team. And a police chopper to give us eyes in the sky. Oh and send someone to handle the senator," Clarke said, ending the call. "I don't want him here."

Sally had her pistol resting on the level part of the doorframe where glass would have been if the window wasn't completely down. Detective Lin was communicating with the police officers already on the scene via a two-way radio.

"Team one, are you in position?" Lin asked, her tone calm and authoritative.

Lin wanted two officers at the back of the house, two in the side yard, which left the three of them at the front.

"This'll turn into a media frenzy," Clarke said, exhaling heavily. "Once the TV news chopper arrives, there's no way we can control what Bob does and doesn't know. He just has to switch on the TV, and he'll be able to see what we see."

And word would get out. All it took was a neighbor posting on social media about police officers surrounding a house that belonged to the fiancé of a senator's daughter and before they knew it, TV vans and helicopters would descend on the place.

The adrenaline coursing through Sally's body had her in fight-or-flight mode and her thinking was as clear and crisp as fresh ice. Bob Kerns was their killer. His actions confirmed it. That wasn't their problem now, although it proved that Bob was capable of murder.

Their problem was ensuring that Janey Wildner left that house alive. The best outcome would be that Bob was talked down and gave himself and Janey up unharmed. Sally knew that if it looked like Janey might be killed, a SWAT shooter would receive the order to kill Bob. If that wasn't possible, the SWAT team would enter the house, possibly using tear gas to confuse Bob, and they would kill him to save the hostage. Sally didn't want it to get to that stage. There had to be a way to persuade Bob to give himself up. But how?

Clarke took a call, listened, nodded, and ended it.

"The hostage negotiation team and the SWAT team will be here in fifteen."

Before he'd finished the sentence, the wail of two police cars could be heard above the whoosh of the wind, which was fierce enough to snap twigs off branches and blow paper and empty cans down the street. The first patrol car sped toward them, closely followed by the second.

"Lin, seal off the street. Sally, you're the best shooter here right now. You stay put and keep your pistol on the house. Okay?"

"Yes, boss."

Sally doubted that she was the best shot there. But given that this was her first hostage situation, she was happy to have one simple task. It worried her that she hadn't caught a glimpse of the young woman at all since they left the house.

Sally cursed herself for not thinking to question whether Bob had a gun in the house or that he might panic and threaten to use it. She had read him wrong. He had appeared to be the type to bluff his way out of the mess he was in, to let his wily lawyer do what it took to keep him out of jail. But no. Bob Kerns had panicked, and Sally wished she had seen the signs before it had gotten to a hostage situation.

Again, Clarke's phone rang. He answered and didn't sound happy. "No, we don't want the senator here. For chrissake! It'll turn into a circus. Tell his aide that it isn't safe." A pause while Clarke listened. "No, I won't allow him to negotiate with Bob."

Sally was getting distracted by Clarke's conversations. She tried to clear her mind and tighten her concentration. Until the SWAT team arrived and set up position, she must stay focused on containing Bob. But her mind wandered to her son, hanging out with Olivia at the bookstore until Sally could pick him up. She'd spoken briefly to Olivia earlier, explained there was an emergency she had to attend, and Olivia had offered to have Paul and Jax with her for the night. She imagined Paul working his way through Olivia's cakes and playing with his puppy. He would be fine until there was news coverage of the hostage situation, but then it wouldn't take long for him to realize that his mom was at the scene. Then he would fret.

Sally wanted to warn him and tell him not to worry, that the SWAT team would be in the firing line. But she couldn't disobey Clarke's order and make a call right now because that meant taking her eye off the house and, in that moment, Bob might act and she wouldn't be ready to respond. Clarke finished the call.

Lin jogged back to the Suburban. "Securing the road now, sir," Lin reported. Another police car arrived in a blitz of noise and flashing lights. "You want me to start evacuating the neighbors?"

"Yes, and the houses at the back too," Clarke said. "You can say it's a hostage situation but for god's sake don't tell them anything more. No mention of Janey Wildner, got it?" Lin must have looked skeptical. The media knew Bob Kerns was engaged to Janey and Janey's employer had already told a reporter that Janey went to see her fiancé earlier.

"I know," Clarke said, "just do your best."

Lin jogged away to round up cops to talk to the neighbors, and Clarke phoned his communications contact back at the base. Sally couldn't see much inside the house. The front door was solid wood and the drapes and blinds on the entry level had been closed. Sally had a brief glimpse of Bob at a first-floor window, no more than half his face and an arm. In the blink of an eye the drapes were drawn.

"Sir, he's closing drapes and blinds in bedroom one."

Clarke, Sally, and Lin had looked at the house layout, using a plan on the real estate website that advertised the place for sale two years ago. The SWAT team would bring with them a hard copy and an up-to-date map of the house layout, should the real estate diagram be incorrect. Clarke jerked his chin up in acknowledgment of her comment and then carried on talking into the phone. Sally kept her pistol resting on the doorframe as she slid her phone from her jacket pocket to text Paul.

Am at hostage situation. Could be here a while but I'm safe so don't worry. Love you.

She wanted to say more, but in the few seconds it had taken to send her son that message, Bob had managed to draw another pair of drapes and was now in bedroom three. She blinked away some dust in one eye and focused back on the hostage taker's house. There was now so much adrenaline in her system that she was developing a headache. She cricked her neck to loosen the tension a bit.

Sally heard shouting and looked to her right. Robin Kerns, Bob's father, was arguing with a cop.

"Let me through!" Robin yelled.

Between Robin and Sally was a long stretch of road and yellow and black tape. Robin lived three houses away. He must have seen the commotion in the street.

"Sir?" she said to Clarke. "Bob's father is here." She nodded in Robin's direction.

"I'll deal with him," Clarke said.

Clarke stood and, keeping his head down, ran to where Robin was demanding to know what was going on.

Sally didn't envy Clarke for having to tell him the situation and she felt sympathy for Robin who was about to learn that his son was most likely a murderer.

Her mind wandered to Janey and how terrified she must be right now. It was likely that she would be pleading for Bob to stop the madness and to let her go. She must know by now that he killed Joseph, Roisin, and Salvador, and attempted to murder Fiona. The poor woman would realize that she had been about to marry a monster.

How did Joseph manage to extract so much money over such a long period of time from him? What was Bob's secret? After eleven years of blackmail, did Bob finally snap on the night of the murder? Sally tried to imagine how much such a terrible secret would weigh on the man. Bob must have been terrified that Joseph would reveal to Janey that very secret. The timing of Joseph's murder had to be related to his impending wedding. Did Joseph push for more money than the regular amount, threatening to destroy Bob's future life with Janey and ruin his career as medical director?

What was unfurling now was Bob's worst nightmare.

Soon the whole world would want to know why he held his fiancée hostage. All too soon, Bob would be named a killer. But what attention would be paid to why Bob did what he did? Sally had to know what kind of hold Joseph and Fiona still had over him. And there was only one person who could tell her.

Two black SUVs barreled down the street and skidded to a halt, followed by an unmarked white car from which exited the hostage negotiator. Del Hicks was a legend at the FPD. Only a few months back, he'd successfully managed to defuse an armed robbery at which seventeen people were held hostage and the only fatality was one of the two hostage takers.

The SWAT team spilled from the second SUV dressed in black bulletproof vests and black helmets with cameras mounted on top. They had with them a whole gamut of weapons: submachine guns and assault rifles and sniper rifles, as well as smoke and stun grenades. At the sight of so much gunpower, a lump formed in Sally's throat, and she tried and failed to swallow it. If Bob didn't hand over Janey soon, it was likely that he wouldn't come out of this alive.

Sally didn't want more blood to be shed. Preventing that from happening was now down to the hostage negotiator who would start off by trying to end the situation peacefully. A plan began to formulate in her head. There might be another way to resolve the hostage situation with no lives lost.

Clarke had joined the SWAT leader and Hicks beyond the cordoned-off zone. They had a large map on the hood of the first SUV. She guessed they were discussing exactly where the SWAT team should be positioned. When the SWAT leader moved away to brief his team, Clarke brought Hicks into the cordoned zone and they both crouched next to Sally.

"Sally, I understand you are best positioned to help me understand how Bob thinks."

"Sir, can I take my eye off the house?" Sally asked Clarke.

"Yes, we have enough cops covering the front now."

Sally holstered her Glock and moved the fingers of her gun hand, which had grown stiff.

"Tell me about Bob Kerns," Hicks said.

She gave Hicks a brief update on Bob's background, career, impending marriage to Janey Wildner, his father Robin, and his mother with Alzheimer's in a nursing home. "Right now, he's desperate and angry and his only way to control the situation is with a gun."

"My first conversation with him will be about rapport. Creating a connection. I'll aim to get proof of life for Janey Wildner and to persuade him to free her. In your opinion, does he love Janey?"

"I think so."

"Would he kill her?" Hicks asked.

"I honestly don't know."

"Do you think Bob would listen to his father?" Hicks asked.

"They're very close," Sally said. "He might be able to talk him down, but it depends on how Robin reacts. Will he be angry with his son? Or compassionate?"

"Tell me about the blackmailing," Hicks said.

"Since Bob was twenty-three, he's been blackmailed by Joseph Austin. Eleven years later, Bob's paid over a million dollars. I suspect that when Joseph knew Bob was marrying into such a high-profile family, Joseph demanded more money. Again, I don't know if this is correct, but I think he went to see Joseph that night to beg Joseph to stop the blackmail and Joseph refused. I suspect that Bob snapped and killed his blackmailer."

"Bob will feel isolated right now," said Hicks. "He likely feels ashamed at disappointing his father. I'll only consider using Robin if I feel confident that he can remain calm and do as we tell him."

Sally looked across the street to where Robin was arguing loudly with the cop. Robin attempted to barge past the officer, who grabbed him and led him away. He certainly didn't look calm.

Hicks continued, "Has Bob Kerns made any demands since you left the house?"

Clarke answered. "Yes. He wants a jet to take him to Cuba. And he wants Fiona Austin to apologize publicly for black-mailing him."

"Who did he make these demands to?" Hicks asked.

"Me," Sally said. "He knew my cell number."

"What was your response?"

"I'd need time to discuss it with my superiors. He gave me thirty minutes." She looked at her watch. "Time's up in five minutes."

Hicks asked, "Has Fiona confessed to the blackmailing?"

"Not yet. But she might be persuaded to apologize on behalf of Joseph."

Clarke said, "Bob murdered three people and attempted to murder Fiona. She's not going to apologize nor should she."

"I don't think Fiona is exactly innocent, sir," Sally said. "But she's old and perhaps she'll be willing to right her mistakes."

How they proceeded was up to Hicks. Hicks stared at the house for a long moment before he gave directions to Clarke and Sally.

"I'll make a call to Bob. I'll tell him we need more time. Detective Clarke, establish if Robin is the right person to talk Bob down. Sally, head over to the hospital. Work on Fiona. Find out if she's willing to apologize on behalf of Joseph or admit to her crimes. Either way, I need you to prepare Fiona to help me end this hostage situation."

SIXTY-FIVE

Sally jogged through the hospital's main entrance acutely aware that every second counted. Any moment Bob might shoot and kill Janey and himself. She wanted to do everything possible to stop that from happening. She called Paul, knowing that once she was with Fiona, she would have to give the hostage situation her undivided attention.

"Hey, Mom. Are you okay? It's on the news."

"Yes, I'm good. Are you okay?"

"Yeah, we are following the live news. All the SWAT guys. Cops everywhere." He sounded pumped. "Is it true he has a senator's daughter in there?"

So the media knew. Chestnut Close would be full of news vans by now. "Yes, I'm afraid so. Love you. I'll call you when I can, okay?"

Relieved that her son was looked after, Sally drove to the gym where Niall Pickerd taught boxing. She'd called him on the way and asked him to accompany her to the hospital to which he readily agreed. She found Pickerd was waiting outside the gym, a gym bag slung over one shoulder. He jumped into the passenger seat, dropping his bag on the floor.

She sped off before he even had his seat belt secured.

"You really believe Fiona blackmailed that guy?" Pickerd asked.

Sally didn't blame him for wishing it wasn't true. He had only just met his biological mother and now he had to contend with the idea that she might be a blackmailer. Or at the very least, that Joseph drove a man to murder and hostage taking.

"I don't know for sure, but all the blackmail money went into her account. She says she didn't know about it, but I think we'll find that she did." She glanced at him and could tell he was struggling to come to terms with the idea that such a sweet old woman could be a criminal. "Look, Niall, there's a hostage situation. A young woman could die. If Fiona tells me the truth and is prepared to apologize to Bob, it might be enough to diffuse the situation. We want Bob to give himself up."

"You want a frail old woman to talk to a lunatic with a gun?" Pickerd said.

"She won't be put in danger. She'll be on a phone, out of firing range, that is, if she is willing to do it. That's why I need your help."

"You want me to ask her? If she admits to it, she'll go to jail. I don't want that."

"Depends on what she admits to. And she's almost seventy. Maybe she'll escape a custodial sentence."

Pickerd cursed under his breath. "I never get a break. I finally find my mom and now she could go to jail."

"But you'll help me? He has an innocent hostage. They may both die if we don't do something."

"Yeah, I'll help. You helped me connect with her when everyone else stood in my way. I owe you for that." Pickerd stared out of the window for the rest of the trip.

At the hospital, they found Officer Deidre Kelly outside Fiona's door. As soon as she saw Sally heading down the corridor, she stood expectantly.

"Is it true? He's threatening to kill a senator's daughter?" Deidre asked.

"Yes."

"Holy mother! That's not going to end well." Deidre shook her head.

"I need to hurry. Niall is coming in with me." She glanced at her companion. "If Fiona's lawyer turns up, find any excuse to prevent her from interrupting us, okay?"

"Leave it to me."

When they entered the room, Fiona was sitting up in bed reading a large-print paperback book. She saw Sally first, then Pickerd. At the sight of her son, her eyes lit up.

"Niall, I'm so happy to see you," she said, placing a book-mark into the book and closing the cover.

"Hey, Mom!" Pickerd said, taking his frail mother in a gentle embrace.

Despite the drama going on, Sally was moved by the tender-ness of the wiry boxer. He then perched on the edge of her bed. Sally stood near the nightstand so she could observe both of their faces. He flicked a questioning look at Sally and Sally gave a quick nod.

"Mom, you know Bob Kerns, right?"

"Such a lovely man. And so clever. He has his own radi-ology center, you know."

"Well, he's taken his fiancée hostage."

"I think you must be muddled, my darling boy. He loves Janey." Fiona took one of his rough hands in her bony one and patted it. "Let's not talk about nasty things. Tell me about your day."

"I'm sorry, Mom, but I gotta talk about it. He's threatening to kill her and it's because he doesn't want to go to jail."

Fiona's rheumy blue eyes widened. Releasing her son's hand, she said, "Oh, my! What will Robin say? He'll be so worried. Should I call him, do you think?"

It would have been all too easy for Sally to buy into the innocence of Fiona's remark. But Sally knew there was more to this old woman than met the eye. She could tell that Pickerd was struggling to broach the reason they were both there.

Sally asked, stepping forward, "Fiona. We know that Bob killed your husband and attacked you because you were blackmailing him."

Fiona fiddled with her thin gray hair, which she had in a loose bun. She took a bobby pin from the back, tucked a few stray strands into the bun at the back, then put the bobby pin back in position. "Don't be silly, dear. Joseph wouldn't do such a thing and Bob's too nice to hurt anyone."

"Nice people can become killers if they are put under enough pressure and Joseph did just that, and I think you know this already. It was your bank account that received Bob's payments."

Fiona raised her almost hairless brows in shock and looked from Sally to Pickerd. "But we didn't do anything of the kind. That's such a ridiculous thing to say."

"Is it?" Sally asked. "Silvia Tofano has made a statement that you, not Joseph, photographed her having an affair and that you initiated the blackmail."

Fiona raised a hand to her heart. "How could little old me do that? I hardly ever leave the house. I'm agoraphobic. It's been diagnosed."

Sally ignored the lie.

"Fiona, please. Robin's son could die. He needs you to admit that you and your husband blackmailed him. He's had a breakdown because of what you did. And you have to step up and take responsibility for that."

"Nonsense. Niall." She looked at her son pleadingly. "I want her to leave me alone. Would you be a darling and ask her to leave?"

The boxer seemed to grapple with conflicting emotions. He

gently squeezed his mom's hand, then shook his head. "I can't do that, Mom. I know you have a good heart and you won't want Bob or Janey to die. It's only right that you tell Sally what really happened."

Fiona pulled her hand free. Her expression hardened. "I have nothing to say."

"Okay, forget your part in it," Sally said. "Let's say it was Joseph who was the blackmailer. What did Bob do in 2005 that justified the blackmail?"

Fiona began to pick at the cotton sheet with a fingernail.

The seconds that ticked by felt like minutes as Sally waited for Fiona to speak.

"Bob was twenty-three and driving home from a party. He'd had far too much to drink, or so Joseph told me. At the time we owned a Jack Russell called Topaz and Joseph walked him before we went to bed so the little rascal wouldn't disturb us in the night. Joseph saw Bob take a corner too fast. He hit a cyclist. The cyclist was dead, his neck broken. Bob was in a terrible state. He didn't know what to do. He wanted to go to the police."

Fiona paused, her voice scratchy. She asked Pickerd to hand her some water and he passed her a cup. She took some sips.

Fiona continued, "Joseph wasn't a bad man. He was just ambitious. His intention was to help Bob, the idea of blackmail came later." She stopped speaking. "Please don't look at me like that."

Pickerd's frown relaxed a little. "I get it, Mom. The road to hell is paved with good intentions. Please, keep going."

"There were no other witnesses, but the bumper and the hood on Bob's car were damaged, the headlight broken. At the time, Joseph had inherited his father's farm. Well, it wasn't a working farm anymore, just a fallen-down house and a barn. The land was next to a carpet manufacturing company that pumped chemicals into the river. The cows died and the soil was toxic. Nobody wanted to buy the land. So Joseph was stuck with it. Anyway, he drove Bob's car to the farm and hid it in the barn. He told Bob to walk the rest of the way home and report his car stolen in the morning."

"And the cyclist?" Pickerd asked.

"He was dead. There was nothing they could do."

"They left him in the road?" Pickerd sounded shocked.

"Don't judge him, Niall. He was trying to help a young man who had made a terrible mistake."

"When did the blackmail begin?" Sally asked.

"Some months later, I believe. The insurance company covered the cost of the 'stolen' car. Joseph happened to mention it over breakfast. It was twenty-five thousand dollars and I suggested that Bob should give that money to us, given that Joseph took a huge risk to save that boy's ass."

"That's how the blackmail began?" Sally asked.

"I guess so. I swear I didn't know about the bank account. Joseph must have set it up. He never told me about it."

Sally knew that was a lie. Only Fiona could have set up an account in her name, but now was not the time to argue.

"And Silvia Tofano? She said that you asked her for money to keep quiet about her affair."

"I might have mentioned that a small token of her gratitude would be appreciated. But I left all financial matters to Joseph. If he asked her for regular payments, I didn't know."

Very probably another lie. "Fiona, thank you for your candor. Is Bob Kerns the Wilbur Smith who paid one point three million dollars into your account?"

"He must be. Father and son loved that author's novels. But I can't say for sure." Fiona paused. "I don't understand any of this. Joseph was a good man."

"Fiona, this is a life-and-death situation. Bob is holed up in his house threatening a senator's daughter with a gun. There's a

SWAT team ready to storm the house and you know what that means, right?"

Fiona's yes was little more than a whisper. Perhaps the ramifications of their ruthless blackmailing spree were finally hitting home.

"You love Bob, don't you?" Sally asked.

"Yes."

"Bob is refusing to set Janey free or give himself up. He needs you to share the responsibility for the situation he's now in. Joseph's blackmailing has driven him to murder and now an innocent woman's life hangs in the balance."

Fiona stiffened. "I told you, I had nothing to do with it."

"Joseph isn't here to apologize. You need to do it for him."

"Bob killed my husband, why should I apologize to him?" she said angrily.

"But he wasn't evil once, was he? He was just a young man who'd had too much to drink and mistakenly killed a cyclist. Do you seriously think this chain of events would have happened if Joseph hadn't intervened? Bob wanted to call the police and admit to the accident, but Joseph stopped him and, in so doing, changed the course of Bob's life. Please Fiona, speak to Bob and tell him that on behalf of Joseph you are sorry."

Fiona's voice was tremulous. "The shame of it. I can't."

"You could save two lives. Bob deserves a second chance, don't you think?"

Pickerd stepped forward. "Mom, please make it right."

Fiona's eyes fluttered. "What will happen to me?"

"If it transpires that you were ignorant of your husband's blackmailing, then nothing is going to happen to you."

Sally could imagine Fiona's mind working fast, trying to come to a decision.

Sally waited. Held her breath. Fiona looked into the eyes of her son.

"You think I should do it?" Fiona asked him.

He held her hand. "You've gotta set it right."

A pause. Sally could feel her heart thumping.

"I'll do it," Fiona said. "From my bed."

"Thank you. We'll set you up with a special phone line."

Sally could have kissed Fiona. Elated, she ducked out of the room, gave Deidre a big smile, and called Clarke with the news.

"I'll send a tech team to you," Clarke said. "We'll keep Fiona on standby."

"And Robin?"

"He's a no-go. We can't trust him to stay on script."

"Too angry?" Sally asked.

"Seething."

"With the Austins?"

"With his son."

Sally's heart sank.

SIXTY-SIX

The police tech team were setting Fiona up to speak to Bob through a headset. Fiona nervously fiddled with the mouth-piece, then removed the headset, dropping it on her hospital bed.

"I can't use this thing."

"Can she use a phone on speaker instead?" Pickerd suggested.

"No, it must be the headsets. They enable Bob, Fiona, and Hicks to talk, and for me and Sally to listen in," the tech guy replied.

"Try it again, Mom," Pickerd encouraged. He carefully placed the headset on Fiona's head.

Sally's shoulders ached with tension. She glanced at the time on her phone: 4:08 p.m. Sally's phone rang. It was Hicks. "Is Fiona ready?"

"She's nervous but I think she is," Sally said.

"Bob's still demanding the jet and the apology. We can give him the apology but you and I both know, he's not leaving the house until he hands over Janey, alive and well. I'd normally advise that we wait it out. Make the guy sweat. But powerful people are demanding action. They want Janey rescued right away."

"You mean the senator?"

"Yep, and the police chief and the mayor." He sighed. "SWAT are ready to storm the house."

Sally cringed at the thought. "If the SWAT team goes in, there's a high risk they not only kill Bob but also Janey, right?"

"That's why I'm loath to give SWAT the go-ahead. Bob's behavior is getting more erratic with every call. He's screaming down the phone. He's no longer capable of rational thought and that's very dangerous."

"Before SWAT goes in, have Fiona speak to him," Sally said. "We've rehearsed what she's going to say."

"Can you guarantee Fiona will stay on script? One wrong word could trigger Janey's death."

"I think Fiona can do this. Give her a chance. If she goes off script, we pull the plug."

Was Fiona ready, though? Pickerd was hugging her, doing his best to settle her down. Did Fiona have the strength and moral fiber to follow through on her promise?

Silence on the other end of the line. "Okay," Hicks said, finally. "Your headset is different. I can also speak directly with you without Fiona or Bob hearing me. Bob mustn't know you are guiding Fiona. You understand?"

"I understand. And I'll ensure she's wearing her reading glasses."

In the room with Fiona were Sally, Pickerd who sat on the bed and held her hand, the tech guy from the hostage negotiation team, and Officer Deidre Kelly, who stood by the door. Outside that same door was another cop, whose sole job was to ensure nobody entered the room.

Fiona's voice was reedy. "Sally?"

"I'm right here, Fiona. You'll be great." Sally's earpiece was fitted, and Hicks was in the middle of briefing her through it.

"We'll patch Fiona through to Bob in one minute," Hicks said. "You'll both hear a countdown."

Sally had paper and pen ready, and she positioned herself at the end of Fiona's bed so that Fiona could see her at all times. "Are you ready, Fiona?"

"I'm not sure. I suppose so."

"This is all about him surrendering and releasing Janey, okay?" Sally said.

"Oh, my, the pressure. I hope I don't mess it up," Fiona said.

"You won't. Just be your normal, warm self, okay?"

The tech guy counted down the seconds. "Five, four, three, two, one."

Hicks's voice boomed through Sally's headphone. "Bob, I have someone who would like to speak to you. Fiona Austin. She wants to say how sorry she is for what Joseph put you through. Can I put her on?"

"I want everyone to hear her confession," Bob hissed. "I'm live streaming on YouTube."

Sally stared at the tech guy who nodded. "He's live streaming."

"Bob, this is between you and Fiona. Switch off the live feed and let Fiona speak to you."

"No!" Bob shrieked. "I've lost everything because of her and Joseph. I want her to suffer the humiliation of telling the world what she did!"

He's ruining his last chance to come out of this alive, Sally thought.

Fiona shook her head. "I can't do this," she mouthed at Sally.

Sally used hand gestures to try to silently calm her.

Hicks said, "Bob, we're doing our best to give you what you

want. Why don't you cut her some slack and switch off the live feed? The media will find out soon enough."

"You're trying to distract me. Don't think I haven't seen the sniper on the roof, and the SWAT guys positioned around my house."

"You have my word that the SWAT team won't move while you're speaking with Fiona, unless you pose a threat to Janey's life."

"If they move an inch, I kill Janey. And Fiona's confession goes live! I dictate the terms. Not you!" Bob yelled.

"Understood. Give me a minute and I'll call you back."

The line linking Hicks, Fiona, and Bob was cut. Sally could still hear Hicks through her headset.

"Will Fiona do it live?" Hicks asked Sally.

"Let me find out."

Sally drew closer to Fiona who shook her head. "I won't do it."

Sally said, "Fiona, ignore the live feed. It doesn't matter. Hicks is right, news of your conversation with Bob will come out anyway, but this is about you apologizing for Joseph. It's an honorable thing to do. And a brave thing. Please, Fiona. You can save Janey's life and Bob's too, if he gives himself up."

Pickerd gently squeezed his mother's hand. "Mom, please. Do it for me."

Fiona's hard expression softened. "Oh, all right."

Sally then confirmed with Hicks that Fiona would go ahead.

"Good," said Hicks.

There was brief silence on the hostage negotiation line, then Hicks said, "Bob, Fiona, your line is open."

"Bobby, is that you?" Fiona said.

"How could you do it?" Bob said. "You've destroyed my life. I wish I had died the night of the accident."

"Darling boy, please don't say such things."

"You blackmailed me! Everything that's happened is because of you!"

"It was Joseph," Fiona bleated. "I swear. I didn't know. It was..." *Say it*, Sally thought. "It was wrong. Joseph was wrong to do it. I'm so very sorry it's led to this."

Sally wanted to punch the air. Then she realized that Bob hadn't said anything. There was a gulp and then what sounded like a sob.

"He told me he'd help me," Bob said. "I wanted to tell the police. But your husband told me he'd make it right. He'd hide the car and he'd make it all go away. It was a trap. For eleven years Joseph blackmailed me and kept threatening to reveal what I had done. He wouldn't let me go. I begged him. I told him how much I loved Janey and I had to be free of this terrible burden. You know what your husband did? He laughed."

"Oh, Bobby, I'm so sorry. He was ruthless in the pursuit of money. I didn't know, Bobby. I promise. I wish I could make it up to you."

"It's too late. I have no way out." He wept down the phone.

Sally scribbled a message in block capital letters and held it up for Fiona to read.

LET JANEY GO

"I know how much you love Janey. Please let her go," Fiona said.

"They'll kill me if I do," Bob said.

"Let her leave, Bobby, then throw out your gun. If you do that, I'll beg the jury to be lenient on you. Joseph did wrong and I want to do what I can to put it right."

All they heard was Bob sobbing. "Tell them Janey is coming out. You'll tell them?"

"Yes," Fiona said. "I'll tell them."

"And tell Dad I love him." Bob's line went dead.

But Sally could still hear Hicks.

"Good work, Fiona. You were great," Sally said.

Through her headset, she heard Hicks ordering the SWAT team not to fire because Janey was coming out.

Sally was worried. It sounded like Bob's last words were a farewell.

"I can see Janey," Hicks said into Sally's earpiece. "She's walking down the front steps."

A single gunshot. A woman's scream.

"What's happening?" Sally asked.

"Janey's okay. The shot came from the house. We're going in."

Sally's knees threatened to give way and she had to grip the bedrail. She had a terrible feeling that Bob had taken his life.

"Is Janey all right?" Fiona asked.

Hicks replied, "She's safe."

From behind Sally, a loud gunshot. Fiona clutched her chest. Sally swiveled to face the shooter and drew her Glock. But Deidre was a few seconds ahead. The cop fired and Robin Kerns collapsed to the ground. He was dead by the time he hit the floor. Sally turned back to Fiona. Pickerd held her in his arms.

"Mom, stay with me!" Pickerd begged.

But Fiona's eyes glazed over, and she took her last breath.

SIXTY-SEVEN

The adrenaline rush from the hostage situation had Sally feeling lightheaded and unsteady on her feet. Bob Kerns was pronounced dead by the SWAT team leader. At the hospital, doctors confirmed that Robin Kerns and Fiona Austin were also dead.

Pickerd refused to leave his dead mother's side.

"I'm so sorry, Niall. We had no idea that Robin would do that."

Pickerd didn't look up. He kissed Fiona's hand, then rested his forehead on it and wept.

Clarke talked through Sally's headset. "Janey's alive and well, Sally. You did good."

"But three people are dead."

"And an officer is wounded." Clarke meant the cop who had been at the hospital door and Robin had knocked on the head with his gun. "But we saved Janey. The body count could have been higher."

She bent forward and covered her face with her hands. "What possessed Robin to murder Fiona?"

"Guilt?" Clarke suggested. "Perhaps he felt that he could

have prevented his son from murdering Joseph. You remember the call to Fiona's cell phone shortly before Joseph's murder?"

"I do."

"When Robin first arrived at the hostage scene, he told me the situation was his fault. He said he should have listened to his son when Bob told him about the blackmail, which he did on the evening of July twenty-sixth. Robin refused to believe the story. He had immediately phoned Fiona. She denied it. That was the trigger for Bob, who must have felt betrayed by his father too. Bob then went around to the Austins' house where he killed Joseph and very nearly killed Fiona too."

"The whole thing is so tragic," Sally said.

"You okay?" Clarke asked.

"I will be." She stared across the room at Pickerd, who clung to Fiona's lifeless hand. "I'm not so sure about Niall. He found and lost his mom in the space of a week."

"Ask Deidre to drive him home. You've done enough. Write up a report, then take yourself home."

"Will do, boss."

Sally spoke to Deidre. "How are you holding up?"

"Okay. I think. I'm okay to drive if that's what you mean?"

"Your fast response saved our lives. Who knows who else he might have shot?"

Deidre smiled her thanks then gently steered Pickerd out of the room.

Sally's phone rang. When she saw the number, she wandered along the ward corridor so she couldn't be overheard.

"Barbara?" Sally said.

"He's taken her!" Barbara screeched. "And Eli!"

"What? Scott found them?"

"I didn't tell anyone, I swear."

Sally's mouth felt suddenly dry and her tongue thick. "Where did he take them?"

"I don't know. Sheriff Golan is searching for her."

"Our problem is that Scott is police."

"Golan isn't a fan of city cops telling him what to do. And he's a good man. He's done a lot here to stop domestic violence. I told him Scott kept Harper prisoner and starved her, and he was mighty riled up. There's an all-points bulletin out for Scott."

"How long ago were they taken?"

"Maybe twenty minutes."

He could be anywhere by now, Sally thought.

Scott would be at breaking point. He'd failed to intimidate and control her and Paul. And his child bride and their son had run away, yet again. He'd been thwarted in trying to discredit her ability as a detective. This made Scott extremely dangerous.

"Did he have a gun?"

"I didn't see one. I was too busy trying to stop him from taking her."

"I'm on my way," Sally said.

Sally didn't give Clarke the details, but he probably guessed her need for a high-speed vehicle was due to Scott. He agreed she could take an unmarked police car for her "emergency." It was more powerful than her little car and it was equipped with lights and a siren. She broke the speed limit all the way to Eacham, using the lights and siren to clear a path whenever she needed it. Every second counted.

On the way there she contacted Eacham's sheriff, Taylor Golan.

"If I was a betting man," Golan said, "I'd say he's skipped town and headed for the border."

"He drives a black Jeep Wrangler," Sally said.

"That's not what he's driving now. Must have changed vehicles to something less easy to spot. Babs said it was a white SUV. That's all she could give us."

That's not much to go on, Sally thought, thanking the sheriff. "I'll be there in ten."

It was a little after 6 p.m. when Sally entered Eacham via a valley road, passing a checkpoint staffed with deputies who were stopping and questioning drivers leaving town. Sally slowed and scanned the queue of vehicles heading the other way, searching for a white SUV. Seeing none, she accelerated away. She was convinced Scott would have left town as fast as possible and therefore the checkpoints were set up too late. The question was: where would Scott go?

Eacham was on a wide, flat, and dusty plain and consisted mainly of low-rise, boxy buildings in red brick. Beige dust had coated the town, which was dwarfed by the terraced and barren mountainside that towered over it, where open-cast mining had left the earth a strange yellowish-green and completely devoid of trees. Sally drove past signs to the Eacham Bowl, which she had heard about from news coverage: an abandoned open-pit copper mine, a mile long and half-a-mile wide, now full of toxic, yellowish-brown water.

The watery pit, nestled in terraced hills high above the northern end of the town, dominated the view. Tall black metal structures dotted the hills to her left and right. She guessed the structures were gallows frames, left over from the time when the mines were deep and the miners risked their lives to go underground. All the mines had since been shut and the townsfolk had suffered financial hardships when the main employer left the area.

Sally glanced at her navigation system. She was two minutes' drive from Barbara's house. Taking a left, then a right, a few blocks later Sally stopped the car outside a small bungalow with wood siding in faded cream and an asphalt shingle roof. Behind the chain-link fence was a blue

Chevrolet Cruze, about the only thing that was bright on the whole property. Barbara must have heard the car's engine because she opened the screen door and beckoned Sally to come in.

Sally had only just closed the screen door, when Barbara said, "I'm out of my mind with worry. Nobody's seen them."

The house smelled of cigarette smoke and on a coffee table an ashtray was overflowing with cigarette butts.

"Can we sit for a moment?" Sally eyed a brown, faded faux-velvet armchair and matching couch.

"Where are my manners—would you like something to drink?"

"I'm good, thank you." Sally sat. Barbara rubbed her lower back and winced when she took her seat. "Are you okay?"

"Scott shoved me into the wall. Hurt my back."

Scott was using violence openly, which meant he no longer cared about maintaining his nice-guy façade. That was a bad sign. He was a man with nothing to lose.

"You should see a doctor."

"Never mind that. It's that poor girl I'm worried about."

"Which direction did Scott go?" Sally asked.

"South." The way Sally had come.

"Did he give any indication of where he was going?"

"No," Barbara wailed. She made a small fist and pressed it against her mouth. "I think he's going to kill her. He said she'd pushed him too far."

"Did he mention Chicago or any place?"

"Nothing like that."

Sally had a sinking feeling. Was Scott capable of murder? He'd punched Paul. He'd threatened her with violence and used violence on Harper. Harper had humiliated and defied him and he would punish her. Yes, she thought, he might kill her, then move to another state and find another victim to look after Eli for him.

"He has friends in Franklin. Maybe he's taken her there," Sally said, trying to comfort Barbara.

But Sally didn't think that likely. Not even Walter and Bettina Jackson would help Scott keep his clearly distressed wife a prisoner. They would be aiding Scott in an abduction and Walt only had a few years to retirement. He wouldn't blow his chance of a police pension, not even for his best buddy.

"Tell me about the Eacham Bowl," Sally said.

All Sally could see of Barbara's face was her eyes widening because Barbara's clenched fist was pressed to her lips. "Oh, god! You think he'd take her there?"

"Is it as dangerous as people say?"

"Worse. You can't swim or fish there. Full of chemicals like sulfuric acid. It's deadly. A flock of three hundred and forty migrating geese landed there last year and every one of them died. They cut the geese open and found burns and festering sores in the birds' throats and intestines. And it looks like the chemicals are leaching into our groundwater. It's poisoning us and we need the governor to do something."

Would he go there? Sally wondered to herself. *He would if he wanted to dispose of a body.*

"The roads in and out of there are passable, right?"

"Yes."

"Is there shelter there? Buildings with power and water?"

"There are huts full of old machinery. No power or water as far as I know. Not anymore."

Would Scott hide there for a few days until the deputies dismantled the roadblocks? But how could he hide with a crying toddler? Did he even have food with him?

"Could he cross the mountain by road?"

"Yes. Sheriff Golan has deputies up there." Barbara stared despairingly out of the window. "It'll be dark in an hour, then only a fool would go near the pit. The terraces are old. They crumble, create landslides. The ground is slippery near the toxic water. A few years back Joe Williams's son died there. He and his mates were messing around, he slipped and fell. He broke his neck."

Sally stood up. "I'm going to take a look."

"I'll come with you."

"You're hurt and, no offense, you'll slow me down. Did Scott take Harper's belongings with him?"

"Yes." Barbara hung her head. "I didn't send you the video of... you know, the rape. I forgot. I'm so sorry."

That meant that the only copy of the incriminating video was with Scott. Perhaps he didn't realize... Sally could only hope.

SIXTY-EIGHT

EACHAM

The hairpin bends became tighter and tighter, the higher Sally drove. She was on one of the many roads that ran around the Eacham Bowl, which had been used to transport mining equipment and the raw metals back and forth. These roads were unpaved, and the dust flew into the air, coating her windshield. Even with her windshield wipers on, visibility was poor and she was forced to drive slowly. Sally stopped to talk briefly to the deputies who had set up a blockade on Altitude Street, the main road linking the town to the Eacham Bowl. They knew about Sally and were happy to share information. No sightings of Scott on this road or at the three lookouts around the pit. They warned her to take care and gave her a number to call if she needed backup. Sally drove on. "Where are you?" she mumbled.

What if she was wasting time searching in the wrong place?

Fifty feet below, the toxic water glistened an unnatural yellow in the setting sun. Her tires rumbled over the rocky and sandy road. She didn't want to alert Scott to her arrival, so she kept her headlights off. When the sun went down, she'd have to turn back and check in with the sheriff's office in town.

A power pole stood at the edge of the narrow, gravel road, lines stretching up to other poles farther up the terraces. Why was power needed inside an open-cast mine? Was she near a site manager's office or one of the huts Barbara talked about? She slowed the car, unsure how to get closer to the pit. Her GPS navigation unit didn't cover the dirt roads around the pit, so she was driving blind. The road she was on took her lower and lower.

The sky had turned milky with a hint of pink and the sun was dropping closer and closer to the mountaintop. She guessed she might have twenty minutes before she needed headlights. At what appeared to be a parking lot, there was a white vehicle parked near a rockface. She approached cautiously. The car was an SUV. It had to be Scott's getaway car. Who else would be crazy enough to drive into such a hazardous place as the sun was setting?

She ground to a halt and killed the engine, giving herself enough distance to do an emergency U-turn if it was necessary. Adrenaline shot through her. What if Scott was in the car, waiting until she approached? She was alone. Well, not totally alone: she had her Glock on her hip and it was fully loaded. She called Sheriff Golan.

"I have eyes on a white SUV in a parking lot." She gave Golan the license plate details.

"Wait up," he said.

Golan then barked an order to a deputy regarding searching the state's database. While she waited to know the car owner's name, Sally looked around her. Where was she exactly? No signs to help her. The tunnel was unexpected, its dark, arched interior blending with the rockface.

"Okay," Golan said. "It was stolen earlier today from Franklin."

"It's Scott. Has to be."

"Don't approach him, Sally. You don't know the lay of the

land. The slopes are slippery and the water in the pit will kill you. Leave it to my deputies. They're on their way. Keep your phone on so we can locate you."

"I see a tunnel."

"A pedestrian tunnel?"

She squinted. The tunnel wasn't wide enough to drive through. "Yes."

"Okay, I know where you are. Sit tight."

The dust had settled around her. The car engine ticked as it cooled, but otherwise the place was eerily quiet. No bird song. No trees rustling. Just the occasional rumbling noise of stones rolling down the mountain. She looked at her watch; how long before the deputies reached her? Ten minutes, maybe? It would be pitch black by then and their headlights would inevitably alert Scott to their arrival. She toyed with the idea of ignoring the sheriff's advice. She had her gun and a flashlight. She could start the search for Harper and Eli before it was too late.

The scream shattered the quiet. Sally's heart leaped.

A woman. Surely it was Harper. She was in distress. Sally was a cop. She couldn't ignore it.

Sally called Sheriff Golan again.

"I hear screams. I'm going in. I'm armed. Tell your deputies to hurry."

She cut short their call before the sheriff could object. Pocketing her phone, she checked her gun's magazine, tested the flashlight, and left the car. The air was dry and had the mineral smell of rocks lying in hot sun. Holding the gun out in front, with the flashlight pointing ahead, Sally approached the car slowly, even though the scream had come from farther down the slope. If Scott had dragged his young wife down to the water's edge, then where was little Eli? In the car?

The beam of light bounced off the rear window. She came close to the left side of the car and pointed her flashlight at the back window. Her heart almost missed a beat when she saw Eli there, strapped into a child seat. He was asleep, his head on his chest. She exhaled heavily with relief and then a horrifying thought sent a shot of panic through her.

Scott wouldn't... would he? Not his son?

Quickly checking that the rest of the car was empty, she opened the door nearest to Eli. She had to know if he was alive. Her hand drew closer to his neck to feel for a pulse, then the boy's foot twitched. Eyes still closed, he wriggled in his seat and then was still. Eli was okay. For now. Sally unclipped the child seat from the car and carefully lifted the sleeping child and the seat.

Please don't cry, Sally thought.

He and the seat were heavy and cumbersome, but she managed to open her car's rear door and place the child seat in the back of her vehicle, clipping it into position. It wasn't perfect, but it would do.

Now to find Harper.

She closed the door, grimacing as the door clicked, which, thankfully, didn't disturb the sleeping boy.

She called Golan. "Found Eli Fairburn. He's strapped into a child seat in my Ford Interceptor. Call an ambulance. He may have been drugged."

"And Harper?"

"I'm taking the tunnel. I think she's down near the water."

"My team are five minutes away."

"Sorry, Sheriff, but that's five minutes too long."

SIXTY-NINE

The thirty feet of tunnel was arched, narrow, and made of roughly hewn stone blocks. At the far end, she caught a glimpse of a mauve sky. Using her flashlight to inspect the length of the tunnel, she took her first nervous step into the enclosed space that left her no place to hide if Scott was waiting on the other side.

Her footsteps, even her breathing, sounded too loud. Her eyes were on the exit, her gun raised and ready to fire. She counted each step she took to help her control her fear.

Shortly before the tunnel's exit, she killed the flashlight and gave herself a moment to allow her eyes to adjust. Then she crept out and found herself at the start of a winding gravel trail, no wider than her shoulders. Her eyes followed it to the bottom of the steep track and near the water's edge Sally saw movement: the silhouettes of two people. Then they were gone.

She dared not run, unsure of the path's solidity. One tumble and she could fall down the steep slope and into the vile water. There was still just enough light to see where she was stepping without the flashlight, but she had to hurry.

"No! Please!" screamed Harper.

Sally's head snapped around in the direction from which the scream came. She couldn't see them, but they were down there somewhere. She broke into a jog. The trail changed direction suddenly and she almost missed it, one of her feet very nearly sliding away from beneath her. Tiny stones rolled down the slope.

"I'm sorry!" Harper pleaded.

Sally increased her pace. The rocks obstructing her view of the toxic lake were no longer in the way. There were two people a little farther down the slope. One a stocky male, dragging the other person by her hair.

Sally couldn't believe her own eyes.

Scott's brutality had her briefly frozen to the spot. Dragging Harper by her hair! How had she once loved this man, married him, and had his children? And, now, right before her eyes, Scott was dragging his new wife to her death. Recovering from the shock, Sally ran, no longer concerned he might hear her coming. All Sally could focus on was saving Harper.

Harper, despite her waif-like physique, fought back, using her fists to pummel Scott's arms.

"Let me go! Eli needs his mom," Harper pleaded. "He needs me!"

"No one needs you, you piece of trash!" Scott yelled, his voice amplified by the mountainous bowl around them.

Sally stopped ten feet from Scott, who had his back to her. He faced the water, which had a vile stink to it like rotten eggs mixed with bleach. She crouched down. He dragged Harper to the water's edge, all pebbles and white foam. Farther out, the lake was a sinister black, like tar.

"I don't want to die!" Harper sobbed, as she struggled to break his hold on her.

Harper was on her knees, sobbing. Scott stood over her, her hair clenched in his bulging fist. He forced her head to the water. He was going to drown her.

Sally saw the gun on his hip. She took a breath and aimed at the middle of Scott's back. She had a clear shot. She could so easily pull the trigger and end it. Save Harper and Eli. End her own torment and that of Paul. No longer fear Scott and what he might do to them. It would be so easy to explain why she'd shot him in the back. She would say that she had to fire, to save Harper's life. And Harper would confirm it because it was true.

A voice in her head told her that she had to issue a warning. *No*, she thought. *This has to stop*. The man about to murder Harper had driven Sally's daughter to suicide. It was time he paid.

Sally's finger flicked off the safety catch. A rush of fury was like fire in her blood. She increased the pressure on the trigger.

Scott had never submitted to anyone in his life, least of all Sally. If she shouted a warning he'd shoot her, and then Harper.

Her hand shook and her finger wouldn't move the last millimeter on the trigger.

"Let her go!" Sally shouted, her voice echoing across the murky water. "Or I'll shoot."

Scott dropped Harper's hair and turned so fast that his arm clipped his captive's shoulder, which sent her flying sideways. His other hand felt for his gun.

"Don't even try for your gun. I'll shoot," Sally said.

"Playing hero, Sally?" Scott mocked.

"Hands on your head! Harper, back away from him," Sally ordered.

Harper was curled in a ball, sobbing. But in an instant, Scott had yanked Harper's head up and he held a knife to her throat. Sally should have known better.

"Walk away, Sally, or I'll kill you too."

His audacity was breathtaking. She had a gun aimed at him and he had a knife at Harper's throat. If she fired, would the bullet kill him fast enough to stop him slitting Harper's throat?

"Drop the knife. Deputies are on their way. Don't add

murder to your rap sheet."

"You won't shoot me," Scott sneered. "You haven't got it in you. You loved me once. You obeyed me once. You're still afraid of me, aren't you?"

Could he see her arms trembling? He was right. She was afraid, but she was more afraid of failing to save Harper.

"I won't ask again. Drop the knife and walk away from Harper."

"She's trash." His callousness was unbelievable.

"You raped her!" Sally shouted.

"Is that what she called it?" Scott smirked.

"And you sexually assaulted Stacy Green."

"Are you still going on about that little slut? How's it my problem if she likes to suck cock?"

Sally's skin burned with hatred for him. "Stacy was thirteen, you filthy pedophile! And what about Zelda? Your daughter! You threatened her. You made her keep quiet about what you did, and she killed herself because of you!"

Sally was screaming. She was losing all self-control. *Kill him*, she thought. *He deserves to die.*

"You always were pathetically prudish," Scott scorned. "Back away, Sally, otherwise I'm going to slit her throat wide open."

"Drop the knife or I fire!"

Scott chuckled. "If you were going to shoot, you'd have done it by now. Walk away, Sally, or I'll come after you. You'll never feel safe. And I'll make Paul's life hell. You know I can."

There was fire in Sally's head. Her finger tightened on the trigger. The boom was like a thunderclap. So earsplitting, Sally flinched.

Scott's head exploded outward, blood and skull spraying everywhere, spatter like dark rain against the indigo sky. The impact lifted him off his feet. There was a crunch as his body slammed into the rocks behind him and then he was still.

SEVENTY

FRANKLIN

September 19, 2016

Three days later, Sally peered into a muddy hole beneath a camellia bush in the gardens of the Sunnyview Assisted and Memory Care Home. Dr. Mani, in white coveralls and mask, took photos of the sealed black plastic bag at the bottom of the hole before she removed it and carried it to a table her team had set up earlier. Tape had been used to keep the contents dry.

Lumps of mud crumbled away from the trash bag.

"This looks promising," Mani said, using a scalpel to carefully cut a line in the plastic. "There's something heavy and hard in here."

Sally moved closer so she could see the contents of the bag. Mani took out the heaviest item and laid it on the table. A hammer with a circular head. The head and handle were covered in dark brown stains.

"Dried blood." Mani pointed at the hammer's head. "Right size and shape. I'd hazard a guess this is the murder weapon used to kill Joseph Austin."

Sally shuddered. How furious must Bob Kerns have been to smash the man's skull into pieces?

Before Bob turned his pistol on himself, he had confessed to Janey Wildner about the accidental killing of a young cyclist in 2005, and also to the murders of Joseph Austin, Roisin McGettigan, and Salvador Sobral, and the attempted murder of Fiona Austin. From Janey's account of her harrowing ordeal, Bob told her how it had torn him apart to keep the hit-and-run incident a secret. This was compounded by Joseph's never-ending demands for money. On the night that Bob murdered Joseph, he took from the safe Joseph's signed eyewitness account of the cyclist's death as a result of Bob's drunk driving.

Bob believed he had also murdered Fiona and had showered afterward, then he'd smashed the study window from the inside —a mistake Sally had picked up on—and trashed the rooms downstairs to make it appear like a burglary gone wrong. He had showered to avoid the possibility that Janey might wake up and see him covered in blood when he got back.

As Sally suspected, Roisin McGettigan had seen Bob return to the scene of his crime and recognized him, which was why he killed her. Bob had returned to the crime scene, paranoid that he'd left evidence of his guilt behind. Ironically, he'd been correct—his torn-off fingernail was found behind the toilet. He then murdered Salvador Sobral, as the only person to see Bob enter the Austins' home on the night of the murder. When Sally took over the case and reinterviewed the witness, Bob freaked and decided that Sobral had to die.

Bob Kerns's father, Robin, was driven by guilt and rage to shoot Fiona. On July 26, Bob had confessed to his father about the hit-and-run all those years ago and explained that he'd been blackmailed by Joseph and Fiona ever since. Robin chose to believe Fiona over his son, and as a result Bob committed his first murder.

How much Fiona was involved in the numerous incidents

of blackmail, Sally would never know because Fiona could no longer tell her. Nor would Sally ever know why Fiona lunged for the photo of Robin and Betty Kerns as she collapsed to the bedroom floor. Sally guessed that Fiona had recognized Bob Kerns's voice when he'd confronted Joseph and had grabbed the framed picture of his parents in a desperate attempt to leave a clue as to her assailant's identity. Why Fiona had then kept her assailant's identity secret, Sally could only surmise. Did Fiona finally realize the error of her ways and understand that the eleven torturous years that they had blackmailed Bob had driven him to breaking point?

Lisa La Cava, Fiona's lawyer, denied any knowledge of the blackmailing of Bob Kerns. Sally didn't believe her. Sally suspected that La Cava had tried to remove Sally from the investigation because even though she had a right to protect attorney-client confidentiality, La Cava's silence over the black-mailing would have cast a dark shadow over the law firm. La Cava did, however, admit that Joseph had instructed her to prepare an anti-harassment protection order against Niall Pickerd to stop him from meeting his birth mother.

At least there was some good news for Niall Pickerd. Fiona's will was the mirror of Joseph's except for one important detail. The house was to go to her biological son, should he be found, and DNA tests confirmed that Pickerd was indeed her son. The nephew, Dallas Austin, inherited the money in Fiona's bank account, minus the ten thousand dollars that went to the gardener. Sally had last heard from Pickerd when he dropped in to say goodbye. Devastated at having found, and then lost, his birth mother, Pickerd had put the house on the market and was leaving Franklin for good. Without Fiona, he saw no reason to stay.

There was a clunk as the bagged hammer was placed on the forensics table and Dr. Mani carefully removed another item from the dirt-covered bag. She held up a dark gray hoodie covered in blood spatter. Sally was sure that tests would prove it belonged to Bob. There was also a towel in the bag. It must have been the one that Bob dried himself with and then he realized it was now covered in his skin cells and hair so he had buried it along with the other items. Last were rubber boots in black.

"I'm guessing size ten," Sally said.

Mani turned them over so she could look at the soles. The rivets were still caked with soil, glued there by the blood that Bob Kerns walked throughout the house. On the arch of the boot was a number ten.

"Clever," Sally said. "He wore boots that were a size too large so we wouldn't suspect him."

Mani pulled from each boot a pair of thick socks, which provided extra padding. "I think you're right."

Sally looked beyond the evidence on the table, across the lawn and flowerbeds to the glass house, where Betty Kerns sat in a cane chair and watched them, surrounded by orchids in all shades of white and pink.

"Poor lady," Sally said. Mani followed her line of sight. Sally continued, "She's lost a son *and* a husband because of Joseph's and Fiona's greed. She's all alone now."

"It's very sad, I agree. I hate to say it, but perhaps her Alzheimer's is a blessing," Mani said, then she focused back on the newly found evidence. "I'll bag this up and take it to the lab."

Sally found it difficult to tear her eyes away from Betty. Who would visit her now? Her daughter, Anna, had flown in yesterday from Australia. Perhaps Anna would move back to Franklin to be with her mother?

Sally said goodbye to Mani.

"Smile! You solved the case. Clarke should be happy."

"He is happy." But Sally couldn't be, not when she believed she had killed her ex-husband.

Ever since she'd fired the bullet that killed Scott, she had been an emotional wreck. Harper had backed up Sally's statement, praising her for her bravery and for saving Harper's and Eli's lives, but it didn't make Sally feel any better. She kept reminding herself that Harper and Eli could now start a new life. They could live without fear. Sally had handed Clarke the flash drive with the recording of Scott raping her. In it, Scott had boasted that he had taken girls younger than her, and she should stop complaining. Word of the video's contents spread throughout the police department. Scott's buddies kept their mouths shut and avoided eye contact with Sally. Walt Jackson was under investigation for his part in the assault on Stacy Green. At the very least, by turning a blind eye, he was an accessory to the crime.

Her phone rang in her pocket, which jolted her from her thoughts.

"How are you, Sally?" Dr. Lilia asked.

"I'll be okay. Thanks for asking."

"You don't sound so good. Is this about shooting Scott?" Sally didn't answer. She didn't need to. "Just remember, you saved a young woman's life, and your own."

Sally tried to smile. "Thanks, Robert."

"I'm arranging a dinner party with you and Mani, my wife and me. It will be fun."

"I'd like that."

"Good, I'll get back to you with a date."

Sally said goodbye. She had reached her car and got in.

Paul had taken his father's death better than she had. But Paul hadn't pulled the trigger. "I want to forget Dad ever existed," Paul had said. "I don't want to be like him."

"And you won't be," she'd replied.

"Why are you so down?" Paul had asked. "He can't bully us anymore."

"I loved him once. I'm finding it hard to believe that I shot him dead. I... thought I'd aimed wide, but I guess I aimed true."

"He was evil, Mom."

"Yes, he was." She had taken him into a hug. "And we don't have to look over our shoulders ever again."

At the FPD office, Sally found Clarence at his computer, completing the end-of-case paperwork. He looked up as she walked in. "Clarke was asking for you."

Her stomach somersaulted. This had to be about Scott's death.

She dropped her purse on the desk. "Is he in his office?"

"Was ten minutes ago. Um, I... um, wanted to ask what happens next. I mean, now we solved the case, what happens to me? To you?" Clarence asked.

"Do you like working as a detective?" Sally said.

"Yeah, it's what I always dreamed of doing."

"I don't know if I'll be kept on. But I'll recommend you for a role in homicide."

Clarence grinned from ear to ear.

"You deserve it," Sally said.

Sally hurried to Clarke's office and finding his door wide open and Clarke at his desk reading a file, she knocked and walked in. He told her to shut the door, which had her stomach twisting some more.

"Is this about Scott?" she asked.

He pointed at the chair and she took it.

"Yes, the report's back." He gazed at his screen. "The cartridge found at the scene of Scott Fairburn's death was a three-thirty-eight Lapua Magnum. The report confirms that the extensive damage caused to the back of Scott's head on impact was caused by a sniper rifle. The bullet that you fired from your Glock nineteen, a nine by nineteen Parabellum, was found nearby. It hit a rock and fell to the ground. Your bullet did not kill Scott."

For the past three days, Sally had felt as if she were in the middle of a tornado as it spun around her, the wind roaring. Now that wind stopped and the tornado was gone. She released her grip on her chair's arms.

"It wasn't my gun that killed him?" she asked.

"That's right. Someone else was at the scene. You okay?" Clarke asked.

"Yes... I think so. I mean, I am now."

"It wouldn't have mattered if you had shot him dead, Sally. Harper was in fear of her life and so were you. You did the right thing."

She felt lightheaded. "So, who did kill Scott?" Sally asked.

"Good question. There'll be an investigation, of course. What intrigues me is that this has all the hallmarks of a professional hit. It was almost dark. Firing a sniper rifle in poor light and hitting the middle of the forehead is one hell of a shot."

"I guess Scott had made one too many enemies." At the back of her mind, she thought about Richard Foster, who knew some very dangerous people and who hated Scott. She shoved the thought aside. *No more thinking about Foster*, she told herself. "What now, sir?"

"I'd like to offer you a permanent position with immediate effect. I have a pile of cold cases that need solving and I think you're just the person to do it."

"I don't know what to say," Sally mumbled, taken aback.

"A simple yes is good."

"On one condition. Clarence continues to work with me."

"I'm happy with that." Clarke shoved a pile of manila folders across his desk. "Take your pick."

She left his office with the files tucked under her arm and called Paul straightaway, excited to share the news.

"I didn't kill Scott. It was a sniper."

"A sniper! Who? Why?" Paul said.

"I don't know, but I feel better that it wasn't me. And I have some other news. Clarke wants me to stay on as detective. Are you okay with that?"

Paul whooped. "That's awesome. Hey, Leah," Sally heard him say to his girlfriend. "Mom's been made a full-time detective."

"Congratulations, Mrs. Fairburn!" Leah called out, followed by a *yip, yip, yip* from the puppy.

"I'll be home soon," Sally said, and smiled.

A LETTER FROM L.A. LARKIN

Dear reader,

Thank you so much for choosing to read *First Victim*. If you enjoyed it, and you'd like to keep up to date with my latest releases, just sign up at the following link. Your email address will never be shared, and you can unsubscribe at any time.

www.bookouture.com/l-a-larkin

First Victim is the third book in the Sally Fairburn crime thriller/police procedural series. In this book, Sally has the opportunity to work on a baffling homicide case as a consulting detective. If that's not pressure enough, the one person she had hoped never to see again arrives in town, determined to wreck her life. At the center of this novel is the question: how far would you go to be free of your persecutor?

I hope you loved reading *First Victim*. If you did, would you please write a review? I love reading your feedback, and it makes such a difference helping new readers to discover this series for the first time.

See you again soon, I hope!

Happy reading!

Louisa

KEEP IN TOUCH WITH L.A. LARKIN

www.lalarkin.com

 facebook.com/LALarkinAuthor
instagram.com/la_larkin_author
twitter.com/lalarkinauthor

ACKNOWLEDGMENTS

Thank you to everyone who has read this book! I love to read your comments and reviews, and I'm delighted you have taken Sally Fairburn into your heart.

Thank you to my husband, Michael; my brother, Nic; and my friends and extended family for your support. And a special thanks to the Zumba girls who have always shown such an interest in my writing. I couldn't have created the Sally Fairburn series without the input and advice from retired detective David Gaylor, my literary agent Phil Patterson, and my first reader Carolyn Tate. Thank you so much for believing in me.

Thank you to the team at Bookouture, especially to my wonderful editor, Lucy Frederick, and to Natasha Harding, Dushi Horti, Joni Wilson, Jess Readett, Kim Nash, Melissa Tran, Sinead O'Connor, Alba Poko, Peta Nightingale, Melanie Price, and Mandy Kullar, to name but a few stars who helped make this book shine and worked so hard on the publicity.

As with the previous books in this crime-thriller series, the locations and characters are entirely fictional or mentioned in a fictitious setting.

Last, I want to mention book bloggers and reviewers. Your passion for reading and writing reviews is what keeps book publishing going. I'm serious! Readers follow your recommendations and I thank you from the bottom of my heart for recommending my new Sally Fairburn series.